A DRAW OF
KINGS

Books by Patrick Carr

THE STAFF AND THE SWORD

A Cast of Stones
The Hero's Lot
A Draw of Kings

THE STAFF & THE SWORD

A DRAW OF
KINGS

PATRICK W. CARR

BETHANYHOUSE
a division of Baker Publishing Group
Minneapolis, Minnesota

Published by Bethany House Publishers
11400 Hampshire Avenue South
Bloomington, Minnesota 55438
www.bethanyhouse.com

Bethany House Publishers is a division of
Baker Publishing Group, Grand Rapids, Michigan

Printed in the United States of America

Library of Congress Cataloging-in-Publication Data
Carr, Patrick W.
    A draw of kings / Patrick W. Carr.
        pages cm. — (The staff and the sword)
    Summary: "In the stirring conclusion to THE STAFF AND THE SWORD
fantasy epic, after the king's death Illustra faces threats both inside and outside its
borders. Will the next king be revealed in time to save their world?"— Provided by
publisher.
    ISBN 978-0-7642-1045-7 (pbk.)
    I. Title.
    PS3603.A774326D83 2014
    813'.6—dc23   2013034717

Cover design by Lookout Design, Inc.

Author represented by The Steve Laube Agency

14 15 16 17 18 19 20   7 6 5 4 3 2

To my editors at Bethany House,
Dave Long and Karen Schurrer:
To say that I couldn't have done this without you
is a ridiculous oversimplification.
You made me a better writer
and, Lord willing, will continue to do so.

And to Steve Laube:
Your unswerving commitment to tell me the truth
instead of what I wanted to hear
is why I love having you as my agent.

I hope we all get to work together again.

1

A House Divided

DEEP WITHIN, ADORA CONTINUED to harbor the possibility that her uncle, King Rodran, might still live, but the pallid faces of those on the ship, especially Errol's, refuted all hope.

As always, Errol's presence drew her gaze as a lodestone drew iron, and the thought of him made her acutely aware of herself: the feel of her hair against her face, the way the fabric of her clothes caressed her skin as she moved, the warmth of her blood pulsing through her veins.

She resisted the urge to scan the deck for him. He would be at the stern, close to the rail. Seasickness, dosed at intervals by Tek's store of zingiber root, kept him at the rear of the ship, away from her bout with Rokha.

Knees flexed, Adora attempted to distribute her weight as evenly between front foot and back as skill and practice could contrive. Tucking a contrary strand of her golden blond hair behind one ear, she sighted along the wooden staves that served as her practice sword and circled her opponent, searching for an opening that didn't exist.

The wind, bitter with cold and grief, carried the tang of salt to where she stood. When she wet her lips, the taste of decay beneath the flavor of the waters of the Beron Strait filled her mouth. Errol's majority was still less than a year in his past, yet she, the only princess of Illustra, wavered between desiring his protection and wanting to safeguard him in turn. She started to laugh but held it back.

"Is something funny, Princess?" Rokha asked. Naaman Ru's raven-haired daughter stood two paces from her, a practice sword tracing lazy circles, like a snake waiting to strike. Her dark eyes, which usually blazed with hawklike intensity, were limned with smudges of grief and fatigue over the death of her father. Only the presence of Merodach, the watchman Rokha loved, managed to kindle her customary fire.

Adora moved to her right, testing her footing on the deck through her soft-soled boots. "Yes. I don't know whether to protect him or kiss him. He may be the strangest man I've ever met."

Rokha's soft chuckle misted the air. "You've led a sheltered life on your isle, Princess. The women of Basquon will tell you all men are strange—and they speak the truth—but mostly they are all strange in the same way. Errol is odd in his strangeness. He's seen more in the past year than most men could boast in a lifetime and has saved the kingdom twice under a burden that would crush most men, yet he still seems a boy in many ways."

The princess basked in the knowledge that Errol was hers before allowing a sigh to whisper from her lips. "The kingdom hardly treats him like a hero."

Rokha's dark eyes flared, making her resemble a bird of prey even more than usual. "They made him bait for Illustra's enemies." She spat across the deck. "There is steel in that man of yours that surprises even me." Rokha's full lips parted in a grin, and she chuckled deep in her throat. "And he has other skills, Princess. His lips are soft and his kisses stirring for one so young."

Adora knew this trick—it was Rokha's favorite—but even so, a spasm of jealous anger broke her concentration for an instant before she could suppress it, and in that moment Rokha struck. The clack of swords sounded in a desperate staccato before Rokha landed a blow on Adora's shoulder. Again.

Adora held up a hand, flexed the arm. "That is a cheap trick."

Mirth melted away from Ru's daughter. "In battle there is alive and there is dead. That is all, Princess."

She shook her head in denial. "And how many will know to use Errol against me that way?"

"More than you think. You haven't made your love of him a secret. That was foolish."

For a moment she bristled, but the truth of Rokha's words couldn't be denied. She'd been rash—first to follow him, then to proclaim her love in Basquon. "He needs me, Rokha. How much can one person suffer?"

Rokha nodded. "True. I thought the priest's confession had broken him."

A fist closed around Adora's heart at the memory of Martin's revelations, how they had drained the life from Errol's eyes. She had never seen anyone still breathing appear so dead, yet some inspiration or circumstance in Merakh had restored him.

He smiled readily now, but Adora did not find herself reassured by his new, easy familiarity. Raised at court, she'd learned early to read the gestures and expressions nobles, churchmen, and courtiers used to hide the secrets locked within their hearts. Errol's dimpled smile held everything she'd once desired from him— warmth, affection, and love—but behind the deep cerulean of his eyes lurked a secret. She did not trust secrets, not with Errol, not after Martin stabbed her through the heart by announcing either Errol or Liam must die. She fumed, angry at her inability to pry Errol's plan from his lips.

The ship entered King's Port to the sound of Amos Tek calling for less sail. The captain maneuvered his charge past a pair of high-decked cogs manned by guards with crossbows.

Adora stumbled, her concern over Errol forgotten. Gusts of wind lifted oiled cloaks, revealing the livery of the men on those ships, men who should have been wearing the red of kingdom guards. Instead, each wore royal blue with a slash of white across the chest. Duke Weir's colors. And the ships were closing in. She searched the royal compound on the cliffs above, darted a glance over the port rail, and hurried to starboard. The harbor swarmed with ships, all manned by sailors in those same colors. King's Port was blockaded.

What had happened?

She spun, making for the broad steps that led below, intent on warning Martin and the rest. They met her halfway, Karele and Rale in the lead. Their pinched expressions told Adora they too had seen Weir's men. They stampeded past her, heading back toward Amos Tek, drawing her in their wake.

On the aft deck, Martin peppered Tek with questions. "What's the meaning of this, Captain? Those are Weir's men."

Tek rolled his shoulders, but the planes of his face, grown hard at the sight of the blockade, belied the casual gesture. "They've bottled up the harbor, right enough."

Martin rubbed a beefy hand across his jowls. "A precaution?"

Tek shook his head. "I doubt it, by the sea, I do. There are other ships entering the harbor without attracting this attention."

Errol came forward from his spot on the rail. He brushed his fingers across Adora's cheek in passing, and the sensation brought warmth and chills to her skin.

"They know who we are," he said. "By now the conclave and the Judica realize we've survived the trip to Merakh."

Luis nodded his agreement. Martin turned to face Karele, head of the solis, one of those who claimed to hear Aurae, the spirit of Deas. "How were they able see us?"

If the presence of Weir's ships bothered Karele, the little man gave no sign. His large brown eyes remained calm, and no hint of alarm showed on his sharp features. "For some reason, Aurae has allowed us to be discovered."

"Why?" The question crackled in the air before Adora fully realized she'd asked it. A thread of panic wormed its way into her heart. The Weir family wanted her. As the only surviving member of the royal family, Adora's hand would bestow legitimacy on the next king, and Weir meant to claim the throne.

Karele gave a brief shake of his head, the breeze ruffling his dark hair. "I'm sorry, Your Highness. I don't know."

"Then I suggest we get everyone below," Cruk said. His voice sounded like gravel being broken to dust. "If Weir is searching for us, let's make sure he doesn't find what he's looking for."

Luis demurred. "There's no need. As Errol has said, the duke knows we're here. If we are visible to those readers loyal to Weir, they've seen us coming for the last two weeks."

Cruk's hand moved to his sword. "I was afraid you'd say that." He squeezed his eyes shut. "You'd think with war on our doorstep we'd be wise enough not to fight each other." His heavy face wore a deep scowl, and his right hand clenched the pommel of the sword at his waist.

Martin waved a hand, and a measure of the tension in Cruk's stance eased.

"Let us see what the good duke's intentions may be," Martin said. His gesture took in the ships that surrounded them, and his face became somber. "Conflict will only serve his ends. We must reach the Judica."

Hemmed in, Tek ordered more sail furled to keep the wind from driving them into their escort. The ship on their starboard side, bristling with blue-coated soldiers armed with crossbows, glided closer. A tall man, his hair and beard dark with oil, hailed them. "You do not fly the colors of Illustra. Drop anchor, in the name of the regent." A cloaked and hooded figure stood behind him, leaning forward as if whispering directions.

Martin stepped to the rail, his face clouded. "Regent? What man styles himself regent at Erinon?"

The man in blue flushed, but his eyes narrowed at the tone of authority in Martin's voice. "Duke Weir rules until a king is chosen."

"And by what right does the duke assume regency?" Martin

asked. As he spoke, he opened his cloak to reveal his seal of office, proclaiming himself a benefice of the church.

The man bowed. "I crave your pardon, Excellency. The Judica installed Duke Weir as regent upon King Rodran's death."

Martin's lips formed what would have been a smile had his eyes not remained so very cold. "Ah, I have been away from the Judica on church business. I pray you, Captain, please give the order to allow us to proceed. I have news that must be delivered to the Judica as soon as possible."

The hooded figure behind the captain stepped around to address Martin. "Of that, I have no doubt, but I think it best if the captain and his men escort you personally to the isle."

The muted afternoon light did not penetrate the hood, but the voice held a self-satisfied tone. Adora suppressed a chill. Her status and authority had been altered by Rodran's death. In hundreds of years no princess had ever outlived the succession of Magis's line. Until now.

She drew herself up and approached the rail, in hopes the habit of obedience to the royal family would allow her to countermand the stranger's order. "Do you know who I am, Captain?" She paused for the captain's nod and reply—"Yes, Princess"—before continuing. "I thank you for your offer of passage, but I assure you we are capable of delivering ourselves to the isle and the Judica."

Amused laughter erupted from the hood of the captain's advisor, and freckled hands rose to doff the covering. "But you won't be going to the Judica, Princess—at least not yet." A shock of red hair above a cold blue-eyed stare stabbed shards of ice into her heart. "Your business is with the regent. The captain has been commanded to deliver you to the duke, and to him you will go."

Benefice Dane gave Martin a mocking bow. "I don't think you'll be surprised to learn you've been stripped of your orders and authority, *Pater*." He stressed the last word with laughter.

His gaze lingered a moment on Martin before moving to search the rest of the party. "Ah, there you are, Earl Stone, hiding behind the legitimacy of others as usual. I must say I was surprised to find you'd survived your trip to Merakh." Rabid hunger showed in Dane's face, and he leaned toward Errol with an expression of longing. "I think the Judica will give you to me now. Once we've proven my charge against you, you will die."

Burly men with grappling hooks and rope hauled the boats together, straining until the hollow thump of their hulls struck a funeral sound, as though Rodran had died all over again. Adora crossed into the custody of Weir's men along with Errol, Martin, and Luis.

Benefice Dane laughed at the sight of Rale, Merodach, and the rest of their party lining the rail on Tek's ship, their eyes filled with violence. He turned to the captain, who tugged his beard with short, nervous jerks. "Pass the order to the other ships: keep these men on their ship and in the harbor until you hear from us."

As guards escorted the men to quarters below, Errol threw Adora a smile that was surely meant to be encouraging but only succeeded in emphasizing her vulnerability. She tried to go with them, but Dane's arm blocked her way, his smile lazy and indulgent. "Not you, Princess. You'll dine with me."

Adora straightened. She'd never been tall, but Rodran had taught her how to dominate a room despite her average stature.

The benefice fluttered a hand at her indignation. "Please spare me your royal displeasure. Duke Weir rules now, and soon the Judica and conclave will confirm him as king."

Adora laughed, filling her expression with scorn and derision. "You think the cast will fall to Duke Weir? Any number of men could be chosen."

Dane gave her a smile one might bestow on a dim-witted child. "I'm surprised to find you so naïve, Princess. Duke Weir is the most powerful man in the kingdom. There is no alternative."

Adora bit the inside of her cheek. "The cast will have to be confirmed. The Judica knows Earl Stone is alive."

Benefice Dane stepped forward, his eyes ravenous. She flinched as he brushed her cheek in a gesture that was a caricature of Errol's caress. "Earl Stone will be executed for usurping the Judica's authority. His trial is a mere formality. He will have the chance to make himself useful to the duke beforehand, however, as a way to offer penance."

She backed away until the rail stopped her.

Dane followed. His warm breath moved across her face, heavy with the scent of wine and cloves. "Don't fret, Princess. Unlike the omne, you will find your station is secure."

Blood dropped so quickly to her stomach the ship reeled and black spots danced in her vision. "What do you mean?"

Dane favored her with a tight-lipped smile, basking in her discomfort. "You will be queen, Princess." The benefice's smile grew, baring his teeth. "Oh yes, Duke Weir knows his only son lies dead in Merakh. You have much to thank me for. Originally, he blamed you almost as much as that puffed-up little peasant boy you've favored. He was going to have you both killed, but I persuaded him that your position and"—he leered—"other attributes were too valuable to waste. Duke Weir will make you the mother of the next dynasty."

She backed away. His threats couldn't be true. The archbenefice and primus would never allow it. "The duke already has a wife."

A look of profound regret twisted the benefice's features into a facade of sorrow. "I'm afraid the duchess has suffered an unfortunate accident. She fell down a flight of stairs. Oddly enough, it happened shortly after the duke learned his son had died and you were returning."

Horror threatened to overwhelm her. She clenched her hands into fists. They trembled anyway. "You're insane."

"Possibly." Dane shrugged, his smile remaining intact. "I don't think you'll find Duke Weir to be a particularly gentle lover. It seems that despite my best efforts, he still considers you at least partially responsible for his son's death. But be of good cheer, Princess. At least your fate will be better than your paramour's. Once the Judica has convicted Errol Stone of tampering with the succession, the duke plans something truly imaginative and lingering for him."

When the ship glided into dock, Adora spied more of Duke Weir's men lining the piers. The sight of the blue-clad men affronted her as if the change in attire had been designed to expunge the memory of her uncle.

When the guards brought Errol and the others from below-decks, she edged close to Martin as they crossed over from the ship to dry land. "How many men does Weir have?"

The ex-benefice shrugged, but lines of worry creased his bluff face. "By all accounts, the duke has nearly fifty thousand under arms."

Adora tried to school her features, but shock pounded through her chest like a second heartbeat. The garrisons of the kingdom totaled one hundred thousand, but few of those men could be pulled back to the Green Isle. The troops were needed to safeguard the provinces bordering Merakh and the steppes. Weir could exert total authority over the island with half the men under his command.

She looked up to see Martin watching her. "I see you've grasped the problem, Your Highness. The duke may not be Deas's choice for king, but he may end up being the Judica's. The idea of martyrdom is stirring in the tales and histories, but few men have the constitution for it in the present."

"We are undone, Martin," she whispered. Desperation constricted her throat.

"Not yet, Highness," the priest said. "Deas has surprised me too much of late for me to surrender to hopelessness. And do not forget Errol."

At the mention of him, her heart skipped. She turned to spy him some ten paces back under heavy guard.

Martin nodded. "The hand of Deas is on him. Would that I had known it sooner."

They ascended the long winding incline toward the imperial compound. Absence and circumstance made the familiar lines of the palace strange, as if the next turn might place her in a location she wouldn't recognize.

Once in the palace, the guards escorted them toward the king's—she corrected herself, the regent's—private audience chamber, where they separated them—most leading Errol, Martin, and Luis away while the rest hemmed her in.

Massive doors swung open. The echo of her footsteps warned Adora before she lifted her head to survey the nearly empty hall. Long stone benches to each side were devoid of the usual crowd of courtiers and functionaries, but at the far end, Weir filled the chair on the dais, flanked by eight blue-garbed soldiers. A jolt shot through her chest. Where were the watchmen? Granted, Weir was not king, but as regent he should have been guarded by the king's elite.

Adora noted the closed ranks of the soldiers and shook her head in disgust. Her uncle had never used more than four watchmen at a time. Perhaps it was a sign of Weir's vanity or insecurity. Either way, she chose to view it as weakness. She would not let him see her tremble.

Duke Weir, regent of all Illustra, beckoned her forward.

2

A CAST IN THE DARK

A HARD KNOT OF RESOLVE formed in Errol's midsection as the guards led him away from Adora. Benefice Dane remained with the princess, and the soldiers didn't appear to be in the mood to provide information. Martin and Luis walked ahead of him, their feet barely clearing the ground before shuffling forward.

Errol coughed to clear his throat. "Where do you think they're taking us?"

The butt of a spear in his back propelled him onto the granite floor. Errol rolled with the fall, came to his feet facing his antagonist.

A hint of a smile played around the guard's mouth, suggesting a desire to strike again. "No talking."

Errol rolled his shoulders, his hands grasping for a staff he didn't have.

They left the palace compound and walked across the broad expanse toward the watch barracks. Errol craned his neck to peer at the openings and windows as if he'd never been to the isle before, but despite his efforts, no trace of men in black could be seen. Not one watchman transited the grounds on the kingdom's business. When they passed through the large archway leading to the practice grounds of the watch, the clash of swords came, and a knot of tension between his shoulder blades eased. The watch remained.

A cold gust deepened his shock as they entered the courtyard and he saw men in Weir's livery facing each other with naked steel. A broad-shouldered man at the far end towered over them, his smile cruel. Here and there among the ranks, splotches of red discolored the blue uniforms.

Errol hadn't realized he'd stopped walking until a guard prodded him forward. They passed through the yard to the sound of strike and riposte, then moved into the quarters of the watch. The halls teemed with men whose faces were unknown to him. Of Liam, Captain Reynald, and the rest of his friends, there was no sign.

At a signal from the leader of their escort, the men around Errol separated him from Martin and Luis. A net of swords surrounded him, leaving him no choice but to watch Martin and Luis disappear into the confines of the barracks.

In moments Errol and his guards entered the sprawling complex that headquartered the church. By habit, he made the turn toward the broad granite stairs that led down toward the halls and offices of the conclave, but instead the guards directed him toward the cathedral proper, where the Judica met to decide the fate of the kingdom.

Were they going to try him immediately?

But they turned aside, and the hallways and staircases grew smaller until they entered a long corridor populated with plain wooden doors: the postulates' wing. Hundreds of men, young or old, who wished to take orders could have been housed there, but the sound of their footsteps and the stale smell of the air told him the rooms were empty.

The guards shoved Errol into an empty cell close to the middle of the hallway, then locked the heavy door. He grimaced. His cell contained even fewer comforts than the quarters on Tek's ship. Against one wall lay a cot with a hard pallet and a small blanket. Opposite that was a small desk and chair with a candle. He struck flint to light the candle, watching as the flame grew in the dead air, tapering to a point a handsbreadth above the wick.

He settled himself to wait.

Martin followed Luis down a broad granite stairwell through air chilled by the assault of winter cold enough to raise gooseflesh on his skin. They passed a guard station, a cavernous room populated by heavily cloaked men who diced at rough oak tables or sharpened weapons. A few of the guards paused to spare them a glance. One gave a raucous laugh. "About time to let the headsman thin out the populace a bit."

They marched down a long hallway lined with doors showing barred portholes and narrow slits for food and water. Through the bars Martin caught glimpses of black-robed watchmen. Farther on he stumbled at the sight of a benefice behind one of those stout doors, still wearing the deep red of his ceremonial robes, and later, a flash of a blue reader's cloak in a cell completed his grief.

They turned a corner, and the parade of colors continued. The guard hadn't jested; every cell they passed held an unwilling occupant.

Around another corner, light from the last torch faded, forcing them to continue into deepening gloom. The echo of bootheels against the floor seemed louder, and it became difficult to see. Rough hands propelled him with Luis through an open door into a cell. The door closed with an echoing boom, bringing darkness so thick it repudiated any memory of light. The smell of must and ancient decay filled Martin's nose.

"Unexpected," Luis said. His voice sounded hollow in the confines of their prison.

Martin grunted in the darkness, the tenor strange to his own ears. "Captivity hasn't lessened your gift for understatement, my friend. I am a fool. I should have at least suspected Weir would attempt to usurp the throne upon Rodran's death."

They shuffled toward the hint of light that came through the small barred grill in their prison door. Martin slid down the rough-cut granite wall to seat himself, trying not to think about what might be on the floor. Cold stone sucked the heat from his back through the thick wool of his cloak. His thoughts roiled like a boiling pot. "Why didn't Aurae warn us?"

A chuckle that failed to disturb the air in their cell preceded Luis's reply. "I remember being impatient with Karele's refrain about how the solis served Aurae and not the other way around. Now I begin to understand his meaning." Mist from his sigh ghosted across Martin's vision.

"I am too new to this, old friend. In the last six months the primacy of lots and the unassailability of centuries-old doctrine of the church have both been overthrown. I find myself without what we believed to be the foundations of our faith."

Martin grunted as he tested the strength of the door. "Weir is foolish in the extreme to squander the kingdom's power in a fight for the throne. The Merakhi and Morgols will come flooding across our borders as soon as winter breaks."

"If he is foolish and we are his prisoners, what does that make us?" Luis asked. His wry tone blunted the sting of his words.

"Dangerous," Martin said. "If they bring us before the Judica, the truth of what we saw in Merakh would be enough to send Weir to the headsman."

Silence greeted him for a moment before Luis spoke. "They will not bring us before the Judica, my friend. They dare not. Weir fears discovery. They will keep us here until they are sure of their power, and then they will kill us."

Luis's dour pronouncement stood at odds with the note of abstraction in his voice. Something besides the likely outcome of their fate wandered through his friend's thoughts. Now that Sarin Valon was dead, Luis Montari possessed the second finest mind in the conclave, behind Primus Sten.

"Something more troubles you."

As his eyes adjusted to the dim light from the door grate, Martin thought he saw his friend shake his head in the gloom.

Luis sighed. "I forget sometimes how well you know me. It is the same question that has bothered me for months, and I am no closer to finding an answer. Why did the cast to reveal our future king fail? Despite my protests to the contrary, the preliminary cast in wood should have foretold the draw in stone." He flung his hands up in surrender. "Yet the query in wood appears to have succeeded while a cast of stones, which should have been incontestable, failed. If the account of this time is ever written, Martin, I will be recorded as the reader who failed in the most important task in the history of the conclave."

The depth of Luis's self-doubt echoed his own, but he had few words to offer, for the lore and training of the conclave lay outside his expertise. Martin sighed. "You were born for your craft. No reader outside of Enoch Sten possesses greater skill at discerning the question. What did you ask?"

"It was always the same. Who will be king? I held the thought of the soteregia in my head for years."

Martin nodded. In all the writings of the church and the conclave, the king was referred to as *soteregia*, the title Magis earned for himself by taking the crown and becoming Illustra's savior through his death.

Since he could not comprehend the workings of the cast, Martin offered no succor for Luis's failure, turning his efforts instead to diverting him. "If you could cast now, what question would you ask?"

His friend's eyes might have twinkled in the dim light as he reached into the pockets of his cloak and withdrew a pair of wooden cubes.

Surprise and suspicion warred within Martin. "They left you with blanks? Are they so foolish?"

Luis shrugged. "They're soldiers . . . not churchmen. They considered the blade the bigger threat." He paused. "What is it we most desire to know?" Luis rose to peer through the small barred window of their cell. Martin had done so earlier. Little could be seen. A man could conceal himself in the hall just outside without their knowledge. "Does he still live?" Luis whispered.

He nodded. Names were unnecessary. The two men who mattered most to the kingdom's survival were Errol and Liam, the lots Luis pulled times without number for his cast for king, and they knew Errol was imprisoned.

But did Liam still live? A whisper in his mind told him he would have known if Liam had died, but doubt warred against the thought. He stared through the dusk of their cell at the blocks in Luis's hands. "You can't cast without a knife."

"I can . . ."

A noise like the scrape of cloth against stone froze him, and he held his hand out for silence. He rose to press his ear against the barred opening of their door, counting fifty beats of his heart before putting his mouth next to Luis's ear.

"There may be guards in the hall," he breathed. "Keep your voice low, but tell me."

Luis nodded assent and pointed with his free hand toward the walls of their prison. "The roughness of the stone and mortar will suffice to grind the lots to shape."

Martin stared. "Deas have mercy. How long will that take?"

His friend shrugged in the darkness. "Hours, but it has been done before."

Luis's suggestion daunted him. A reader held the question and its possible answer within his mind for the duration he crafted a lot, usually taking only ten to twenty minutes for a single sphere—after which, the reader could stop to clear his mind of distractions before repeating the process with the same question and another answer. Readers trained for years to extend their ability to produce lots with shorter breaks, but this . . . ? "Do you know what you're suggesting? You will have to hold the question and answer for hours."

Luis stiffened as if he could redeem his inadequacy. "I failed before. If I must, I will hold the question for days."

If the secondus had any say in it, they would know if Liam was safe. Only Deas's will could block the truth. He squeezed Luis's shoulder. "I'll keep watch at the door."

A pause in the air, as if the entire prison held its breath, settled over their cell as Luis stilled. Then he took a cube of wood no wider than half the length of his hand and scraped it against a seam of mortar.

The scratch fractured the silence, and Martin winced. A second later he chided himself. This far from the guardroom, only screams would alert Weir's men.

Endeavoring to treat the armed men at her side not as guards, but as her escort, Adora moved forward, her back tense, to face Weir. He smiled. With wide-spaced brown eyes and a cleft chin, the most powerful man in Illustra would have been considered handsome by some, perhaps even herself at one time, but perpetual arrogance had twisted his features. She doubted whether the duke could gaze upon anyone or anything without the look of condescension he now wore.

His hair, cropped just above his eyebrows, held most of the light brown of its youth. She amended her assessment. Some women would consider him attractive still, but she fought to keep from clenching her fists in disgust under the baleful gaze of his regard.

"Welcome home, Princess." Weir didn't bother to stand or even offer a bow from his seat.

At the bottom of the dais, Adora was forced to look up to meet Weir's eyes. "Your hospitality fails to warm me."

His mouth compressed at the absence of his title, and he nodded to the guard on her left. Her head whipped to the side, and her cheek burned from the impact, but days of sparring with Rokha had inured her to such small hurts. Her eyes remained dry, but she allowed her hatred to blaze in them.

The duke's gaze widened a fraction at her silence, but he settled himself deeper into his seat. "You will remember to address me as *Your Grace*, Princess."

Laughter bubbled from her before she could prevent it. "And when did I become your inferior, that I should address you so, *my lord*?"

Weir glowered at the insult and flicked a finger. The guard on her right struck her other cheek. Adora straightened from the blow, fixed her smile on her face. Did he think to break her with such treatment? She savored the surprised look on the face of her guards.

"You became my inferior in name when your uncle did Illustra the favor of dying." The duke's eyes flared with anger. "You became my inferior in truth when my son died at the hands of your peasant."

Adora tossed her head. "Your son died a victim of his own pride and arrogance in the hall of the ilhotep. That *peasant*, as you call him, saved the kingdom while your son preened through the palace like a peacock in love with his reflection." She let the scorn she felt twist her face into an expression of contempt. "Do you intend to kill me, Weir?"

Weir's mouth compressed into a line, and she took the blow across her temple. Spots swam in her vision.

Blood rushed into Weir's face. "What makes you think I would find you deserving of such favor? You owe a debt to my house, Princess. Since I currently have no heir, you will spend your days repaying that debt, with interest. After I deem it paid, we shall see what kind of end can be devised for you."

"I think you should make for your province now, Your Grace." She added the title not out of fear, but from a simple desire to finish speaking. "The hand of Deas is on Earl Stone. You will find yourself outflanked by circumstances beyond your ability to predict or understand."

The strike across her cheek took her by surprise, and she stumbled.

"Let that be a lesson, Princess," Weir said. "Every breath you take from this point is mine to give. Every moment you have without pain or punishment for the death of my son is by my whim." Weir nodded to the guards. "Escort the princess to her quarters. I want a pair of soldiers outside her room at all times." He waved a hand in dismissal, then signaled the guards to a halt. "Before you leave, Princess, there is a piece of information you could provide that might make your stay here in the palace more pleasant."

Weir's posture betrayed no hint of tension; if anything, his relaxed pose suggested his change of conversation carried mere idle curiosity, but the gleam in his eyes told her a different tale. They had at last come to the point of his questioning and threats.

She gave the briefest incline of her head. "What might that be . . . Your Grace?"

A smirk creased his face, and his gaze became avid. "Rumor has it that your uncle made use of a nuntius just before he died." He shrugged, no doubt in an attempt to appear casual, but his shoulders jerked as if he wrestled. "Yet there is no record of a nuntius sent to him in the logs of their office. Doubtless you would wish to hear your uncle's dying words and there may be some knowledge he would wish passed on to me, his successor. Who was his messenger?"

She did not need to feign surprise. News of a nuntius taking her uncle's dying words stunned her, and the room wavered in and out of focus. She shook her head, both to clear her vision and to respond. "My uncle did not trust the nuntia. He seldom used them. He would certainly not give his dying words to one of the crows."

Weir's mouth tightened. After a moment he forced it to relax. "Perhaps you will recall the name of the king's nuntius later, after encouragement." He waved his hand at last in dismissal. "We'll talk anon, Princess. I have a kingdom to run and a coronation to prepare. Oh, I've taken the liberty of assigning my daughter, the lady Sevra, to be your chief lady-in-waiting. I'm sure you remember her. She'll be your constant companion."

Adora walked between the guards to her quarters, her feet finding the way without direction. She could hardly forget Lady Sevra. In the duke's daughter all the haughtiness and arrogance of Weir and his son had been distilled to purity without the slightest hint of compassion or mercy.

They entered the portion of the palace containing the royal family's personal quarters. Adora grieved the absence of any familiar faces among the staff who walked the halls. She sighed. Weir's suspicious nature would allow for no less than a complete purge. She ascended a broad spiral staircase to the upper floors, then moved down a hallway wide enough to hold ten men abreast to the large double doors of her private quarters. One of the guards stepped forward and opened the door for her, the first sign of deference she'd seen, admitting her to her own waiting room.

Sevra stood waiting. The duke's daughter, gangly and fierce, gazed at her with a pair of ladies she could not recall seeing around the palace before. Doubtless Weir had imported them from his provincial stronghold.

The duke's daughter smiled, and for a moment Adora felt again the chill wind from the Beron Strait. With a flick of her wrist, Sevra signaled her ladies, who came forward. Too late, Adora noticed the riding crop in Sevra's hand and surmised her intention. Hands strong enough to belong to milkmaids clamped her arms.

Adora allowed the scorn she felt to narrow her glance, used her anger to stifle the quiver that threatened to rob her voice of its strength. "Have a care, lady. My memory is long, and your father is not yet king."

Sevra hesitated but then straightened, as if ashamed of her momentary weakness. "My brother is dead because you chose to consort with that peasant." She ran the tip of her crop along Adora's jawline, the leather smooth and cold to the touch. "You are nothing but a strumpet, a gutter woman, with your base desires that you misname love." She smiled, and her voice dipped to a purr. "Father has given your discipline into my hands. I will train you as I would a reluctant brood mare." She nodded to the women, who forced Adora around.

Sevra's hand yanked Adora's cloak from her shoulders, the fabric scraping across her neck. Then the duke's daughter ripped her shirt, exposing her back.

Sevra's mouth rested against Adora's ear. "Such beautiful skin, strumpet. It's a shame, really, that Father has forbidden me to mark you until you've given him an heir, but that won't save you. You're about to discover how much pain I can inflict without leaving a scar."

The crop whistled before it fell across her back to lace her skin with fire. She jerked and for a moment managed to pull one arm free. She doubled her fist and punched the nearest lady in the nose before a blow like a hammer to her stomach doubled her over.

Sevra's lash fell again, and Adora's arm was caught once more. "Be still, little princess." Her voice cracked like a whip. "Learn to accept your penance with such royal reserve as you can muster, and perhaps I will shorten your punishment."

Adora knew Sevra spoke the simple truth. Yet she realized with a clarity that squeezed her insides with fright that she must fight. There would be no going back if she surrendered. One act of concession would surely lead her to ever greater acts of submission until Sevra owned her. She did not have to win. Indeed, she could not. The two women who held her arms were each stronger than she, and even if she managed to break free, one cry of alarm would bring the guards stationed outside the door.

Adora lifted her leg and kicked the other lady in the stomach. Once again she was free. She jumped and twisted, taking the blow intended for her gut on the thigh. As she descended she head-butted the woman on the nose. Blood spurted across her face.

Before the first woman could catch her, Adora launched herself at Sevra. The duke's daughter gaped as if the princess had turned into something unrecognizable, and she shrank away, eyes wide. Adora managed to land a blow between Sevra's eyes that dropped the fiend to her knees.

Then the women were upon her, their weight bearing her to the floor, their fists pounding into her until the blows forced her to curl into a ball. The pointed toe of a lady's boot joined in after a moment, and Adora covered her head and chest.

"Courtesan! Strumpet! How dare you strike your better!" Sevra punctuated her screams with kicks to her legs and arms. The door creaked and for a moment the blows stopped. "Get out of here! The affairs of the duke are not your business."

Then the beating began again. A kick landed between her hands and the room went black.

Less than an hour after Errol entered the postulate's cell, the door opened to admit Benefice Dane, his blue eyes glittering with malice, his grin splitting the face under the crop of red hair, showing full white teeth. "I see you are surprised to see me, boy."

Dane gave Errol an indulgent smile. "There are pressing duties that require our attention." He gave a theatrical shrug. "Alas, the business of the church compels us to ever greater efforts on her behalf."

Errol didn't rise, but despair bubbled behind the mask he made of his face. No trace of reason or pity marked the benefice's demeanor. Only the fact Duke Weir hoped to use Errol in some way kept him alive.

Dane crooked a finger at the door, where two hooded figures waited. They entered, knives drawn.

"I find myself in your debt, Earl Stone," Dane said. "Your return to Erinon has bolstered my argument before the duke that every remaining member of the Judica and the conclave should be tested for their loyalty."

Errol forced himself to speak past his revulsion. "It is unlawful for the church to cast against its own."

Dane's smile grew. "It was unlawful, true, but it seems that Duke Weir's ascension has provided those who remain in the

Judica the motivation required to change the law." He neared until Errol could smell the sour wine on his breath. "Once those remaining in the Judica and conclave have passed their test, we will turn our attention to hunting down the pretender."

Pretender? Someone else had laid claim to the throne? "Who is it the duke fears so much?"

Dane shrugged away the question. "We have not yet discovered his identity, but when the purity of the conclave is established we will find him, along with those of the watch who think to support him, and root them out of their hiding places."

Errol coughed to hide his surprise. Dane didn't know the results of Luis's cast. More, Liam must have survived Weir's coup.

With a snap of his fingers, the benefice signaled the men in hoods, who disappeared into the hallway and then returned, each carrying a large crate of pine blanks. Errol sighed. Dane meant to cull the Judica and the conclave without delay, but it would take days to cast so many lots.

The benefice pulled several sheets of parchment from his robes and showed the first one to the hooded men, who nodded and began carving, their hands moving with the fluid motions of those who'd exercised their art for years. Desperation welled in Errol. If Weir and Dane felt compelled to test everyone, there must be some remnant still loyal to Illustra, men willing to risk their lives to save the kingdom from Weir.

Errol could not allow the cast to proceed. That they used him at all meant that even these two readers were not completely trusted. Could he turn the duke's distrust to his advantage? Possibly. If he refused to verify the cast, Dane would be less than sure of the results and only a fool killed his allies.

He looked up to see the benefice eying him with amusement. "We hold the princess. Failure to cooperate would prove . . . unpleasant."

Inside he raged. Dane held his aid captive. Once the Judica and conclave were tested, the duke would force him to confirm the read for Liam's location. There had to be something he could do. Adora would never forgive him if he sacrificed the kingdom to save her.

If he sacrificed her to save Illustra, he would never forgive himself.

If only Karele were there. The head of the solis had shown himself superior to the conclave. That thought brought Errol up short. It hadn't been Karele. The former Morgol captive had said so himself. It had been Aurae working through him.

Which only made sense. The book of Magis said Aurae, the spirit of Deas, was knowable. And Errol believed it. Could someone besides the head of the solis call upon Aurae?

The readers had almost completed their lots. Errol floundered. How did one call upon Aurae? Karele had never explained.

In the vault of his mind, he blindly cried out to Deas, Eleison, and Aurae.

Nothing happened. Only a puff of wind swirled through the crack under the door, lifting a bit of sawdust from the floor. The readers continued to sand the first pair of lots they would use to test some reader's loyalty, while Dane wore his triumph like a jackal over his kill.

The lots went into the drawing bags. *Oh, Deas.* He hoped Adora would forgive him. The men drew, tallied their results before passing the lots in turn to Errol. He turned them in the light of the lantern. "This one says *Traitor.*" He gave the lot back to the reader who cast it, then read the other one. "This one says *Loyal.*"

Dane's brows, red like his hair, furrowed over his aristocratic nose, but the smile of triumph remained. The readers drew again. Errol looked at the writing. It seemed unfamiliar. His time in the conclave had been short, but he'd thought he'd seen an example of every reader's script. These readers were unknown to him. "Loyal. Traitor."

Dane shrugged, but his smile slipped.

The third draw swapped the results again. Traitor. Loyal. When the fourth draw changed the results once more, Dane confronted the readers.

"What is the meaning of this?"

The reader on the left spoke, his voice dusty, unfamiliar. "I don't know, Benefice. But he tells the truth, we are reading the same."

Errol stood. "You're not from the conclave."

Dane pointed at him. "Is he doing this?"

The reader shook his head. "An omne does not have the power to confound the draw."

Errol couldn't help but smile. "Maybe the duke's readers lack the proper training to cast, Benefice Dane. Of course the use of unlawful readers would explain the duke's vast wealth. Perhaps if he petitions the rightful king, he'll be granted some measure of mercy."

Dane confronted him with a snarl. "Are you doing this?"

Errol allowed all of his joy to show in his smile. "No."

The benefice snapped his fingers at the two readers. Ten minutes later, their lots confirmed what Errol had spoken. Led by Dane, they left.

Errol's heart exulted in his triumph—and somehow in the victory of Deas.

Hours passed. Martin kept his ear to the door while Luis, head bowed and eyes unseeing, turned and scraped without ceasing. Martin's sense of time became confused. Finally, Luis's hand on his shoulder startled him, though his eyes were still open.

"The first one is done."

Creases lined Luis's face, and sweat beaded on the dome of his bald head despite the chill, and his eyes appeared even deeper set.

"Is it so difficult, then?" Martin asked.

He nodded. "The concentration required is no more than for an ordinary cast but must be held without interruption. I can assure you, stone-ground lots will never come into favor in the conclave. My shoulders ache."

Martin sighed. They were so close, but the effort would be wasted if fatigue ruined the cast. "Rest, my friend. We appear to have all the time you will need."

Luis nodded and slumped down the wall to sit with his head on his arms. Soft snores echoed in the cell moments later. Martin slid down next to him and pulled Luis toward him so his friend would not fall in his slumber.

The sound of footsteps woke him, and he jerked. Luis came awake, rubbing his shoulders and wincing. A sneeze and a clank of metal just outside their cell brought him to his feet, his hands groping the air. In the gloom a tin plate came through, filled with water. There was no food.

Martin pushed his face against the small barred window. "Guard, what time is it?"

Rough laughter answered him. "Morning or evening," the guard said. "What does time matter to you?"

"I wish to know whether to offer the prayers for lauds or vespers."

"Ha. You and all those other churchmen caught in your own web. Do you think your prayers will make it to Deas from here?"

"Deas is everywhere," Martin said without anger. "If you tell me the time of day, I will pray for you."

Silence greeted his request for a moment.

"It is evening. Say your vespers."

The footsteps moved away.

He turned his attention to the water. It held the same musty smell as the air in their prison, but other than that it seemed safe enough. He took a sip, then drank half.

"Here."

Luis drained the tin, and when the guard's footsteps receded from their hearing, Luis took the other blank and began grinding.

Hours slipped by, measured by the increments in which Luis ground a cube into a sphere. When, wan and lined by the effort, he held it up to the light, Martin rejoiced. "Circumstances have taught me to doubt everything now, my friend. Draw and let Deas's truth be known."

Luis dropped the lots into his oversized cloak pocket with a soft clack, shook the garment, and drew. He rotated the wood against the faint light, squinting with the effort. Then he nodded. Eleven more times he drew before his smile blazed like a torch in their cell.

"He lives."

For a brief instant, Martin's heart leapt. Illustra could still be saved if they could somehow free Errol. If they could determine whether he or Liam should be king. His joy faded as he tallied up all the *ifs*.

Boots thundered in the hallway, coming for them. "Quickly, hide the lots."

The door flew open and guards entered, steel drawn. Lantern light filled their cell, and Martin shielded his eyes against the glare, but not before he saw a hole in the back wall and furtive movement beyond it. They'd been heard.

"Search them."

Martin knew that voice. He'd spent decades despising the self-indulgence of its owner. He lowered his hands and squinted against the light. "Benefice Weir."

Duke Weir's brother didn't bother to reply. Two guards ran hands up and down his clothing, searching. Another pair copied their movements with Luis. When they got to his cloak, one of the guards thrust his hand in and pulled out the lots. The smile Benefice Weir bestowed on Luis reduced his eyes to slits. "Thank you, reader. Your information is timely."

Martin kept his face neutral as he faced the benefice. "And what information would that be?" He didn't trouble himself to add Weir's title.

The benefice's eye twitched. "Lowborn priests are tiresome, always forgetting your manners. I refer to the identity of the pretender who thinks to challenge my brother for the throne."

Martin laughed while his mind raced across his conversation with Luis. Had they mentioned names? "Interesting supposition. I don't seem to recall knowing any pretenders—outside of the obvious one, of course."

Weir laughed in return. "You were always so impressed with

your own cleverness, Arwitten." He turned to the guards. "Fetch him. Let the former benefice hear his words."

The guards left and returned a moment later with a man between them, thin, with a receding hairline and a hooked nose, his cloak emblazoned with the red-stitched scroll of a church messenger.

Martin's insides clenched. A church messenger would be able to recite every word uttered within their hearing. *Oh, Deas.* Had they mentioned names?

Weir addressed him. "Nuntius, discharge all you've heard."

Inside his chest, Martin's heart hammered against the restraint of his ribs. If Weir discovered Liam's identity, the boy would be hunted with all the resources at the duke's disposal. Casts might be diverted by Aurae's power, but if Liam remained in the city, enough money would buy his location.

The nuntius, his eyes devoid of thought, spoke in a low monotone, extended gaps revealing those times Martin and Luis had whispered or been out of earshot. His guts knotted as the messenger replayed the conversation about the cast. The nuntius imparted the last of the conversation and stilled. The knot in Martin's chest slipped away, and he took a deep breath. Liam was safe. When the messenger's eyes returned to awareness, Weir gaped. "Where's the rest?"

The nuntius shook his head. "That is the conversation in its entirety, Your Excellency."

Weir's mouth worked as he tried to find words. "That can't be all, blast you. The name, Nuntius, I need the name."

The messenger's eyes grew round and he stammered. "I . . . I'm sorry, Your Excellency. If I repeated no name, it's because they didn't use one."

Weir flicked a finger, and one of the guards slammed the nuntius against the wall so hard his eyes went out of focus. "I am displeased. You were to listen until they mentioned the name of the pretender and then summon us."

The church messenger tried to prostrate himself. "I did what you asked, Excellency. I can only recite their conversation, not control it. Please, forgive me."

Weir glowered. "Of course I forgive you. I must. I am a benefice in the church, after all, but forgiveness without penance is useless. Guards, find him a cell."

The nuntius's eyes bulged. "For how long?"

Weir shrugged. "Forever."

The benefice turned his attention to Luis. "What was the outcome of the cast, reader?"

Luis shook his head. "The archbenefice, the primus, or the Judica has the authority to compel the answer from me. A single benefice does not."

Blood turned Weir's face crimson. "In this place I am Deas. Do you hear me?"

Martin kept his voice level with an effort. If he responded to Weir's anger in kind, he and Luis might well end up on the rack. "Only a joint decree from the king and the archbenefice may put a reader or priest to the question, Excellency. It has not been done since Magnus's time."

"Times change," Weir snarled and turned to Luis. "If you will not disclose the cast, reader, there is someone who will. The omne is also our guest, as is the princess."

Luis smiled. "He can only read the lots, Excellency. He cannot tell you the question that was cast."

Weir laughed. "Weakly played, reader. The peasant has been in your confidence since the beginning, and he loves the princess. If you will not reveal the name, perhaps he can."

3

Taken

COLD WOKE ADORA to a room bereft of light or warmth. Sevra and her ladies had withdrawn. The polished stone of the floor pressed against skin laced with welts and bruises. She pushed herself up, gasping with pain as tortured muscles trembled and protested against the movement. Limping to the fireplace, she struck steel and flint into the tinder until a blaze started. For long moments she measured by shuddering breaths, she nurtured her flesh with the feeble warmth.

She turned at last to retrieve her shirt and found it discarded to one side of the couch, the fabric shredded, useless. She huddled into the rough wool of her cloak. The wood in the fireplace caught at last, providing light enough to see by and Adora considered her situation.

Sevra's beatings would eventually wear away her resistance, and the duke's daughter meant to make quick work of any defiance Adora mustered. Errol and the rest of her companions were in no position to help her. She had to escape on her own.

Logic only tempted her toward despair. She moved to her bedroom, lighting candles as she went. Everything remained as she had left it. She moved to a broad wardrobe on the wall opposite the balcony and searched for warm clothes.

Silks and satins spilled across her hands like water, but most of the dresses she'd delighted in before traveling to the sand kingdom seemed frilly and superfluous to her now. As she moved them aside, her gaze fell on a pile of plain, sturdy clothes in muted shades of brown and gray. She fingered the breeches and tunic she'd used to disguise herself for her visits to the healer, Norv.

A foolhardy idea formed in her mind, but she grasped it with the desperation of a drowning woman. She lifted the pile, her heart drumming against her ribs.

It was still there. Adora raised the heavy key to the garden gate as if it were holy.

Replacing it, she moved to the balcony and surveyed the torch-lit courtyard. Her plan would require preparation, but if she could forego the sleep she so desperately needed, she might be able to make the attempt the following night.

The air blew off the great sea to the west of Erinon, but rather than chilling her, it invigorated her and filled her with hope. She looked across the broad courtyard waiting for the telltale movements in the darkness that would tell her how many men patrolled the grounds. *There.* A shift in the shadows betrayed the presence of a guard.

After a few minutes, the cold forced her back into her bedroom to fetch a blanket off the bed, but she quickly settled herself into a corner of the balcony to watch. Her eyes grew accustomed to the dark, and she sought to memorize the movements of the guards. By the time the moon set some four hours after midnight, she felt confident in her ability to evade Weir's men. With reluctance, she retreated back into her room. If fatigue caught her unaware and Sevra found her on the balcony, the duke's daughter might suspect she planned to escape.

She climbed into bed still dressed. Sleep claimed her almost before she laid her head on the pillow. Her last thought was of

Errol. Unconsciousness overtook her in the midst of a prayer to Deas on his behalf.

A stinging slap across her face brought her awake. She rolled, ready to fight, but the sight of Sevra's ladies at the foot of her bed armed with cudgels stopped her. Laughter rasped in her ears.

"That's good, strumpet. If you step out of line—and I'm sure you will—you'll find the penalty to be quite severe."

Adora noted that none of the women seemed in a hurry to approach her. She chose to take that as a sign of caution and savored the thought she'd won that much. Seating herself as if entertaining friends, she skewered Sevra with as much disdain as she could muster. "What do you want, Lady Sevra? Your father wishes to cement his power in the kingdom, but until he's proclaimed king, it appears he has no need of me."

Sevra laughed. "I've told you, strumpet. I am to train you to be a dutiful queen. Come. I will show you the price of disobedience." Sevra turned on one heel and left the bedroom. For a moment the temptation to ignore the command raged hot in her chest, but curiosity won out. She rose and followed. Outside her suite of rooms, the two guards fell in line to accompany her, one in front and the other behind.

The sight of the lead guard's sword on his left hip made her fingers twitch with need. She would require a weapon. They proceeded down the long marble staircase into the main hall of the palace with its gilded bannister and heavy chandeliers. The furnishings, which should have been as familiar as her own reflection, struck her as though she were unaccustomed to them.

They left the light of the palace to venture into the leaden gray of Erinon in winter. The blue of the guards' uniforms, vibrant under bright torchlight, faded to slate. They passed through the broad archways that led to the courtyard used by the watch. The absence of the black-garbed men struck Adora as an immense corruption, a disease that raged within the compound.

"Your father will doom us all."

One of Sevra's women approached Adora, her cudgel held

high, ready to strike, but Sevra held up a hand, restraining her. "And how would a cloistered princess know such a thing?"

Despite the cold, Adora threw her shoulders back. "The Merakhi and the Morgols mobilized their countries in preparation for King Rodran's death. Your father squanders the kingdom's strength on his bid for the throne." Adora could not help but shake her head at the brazen stupidity. "Without an omne to confirm his ascension, competing factions will divide Illustra at a time when every man is needed to fight the threats from the south and east."

Sevra laughed and favored Adora with a gaze that traveled slowly from head to foot. "You are ignorant, Princess. If not for your bloodline, you would doubtlessly have had to find work in some menial trade." She turned to continue toward the far end of the yard, where two guards and a cloaked and hooded figure waited. "There will be no war. Father has already struck an agreement with the Merakhi."

Adora's laughed cracked in the cold air. "Then your father is a fool. The Merakhi are led by a man possessed by a malus. Belaaz will not settle for rule. He longs for destruction."

Sevra nodded to one of the women, who thrust her cudgel into Adora's midsection. She doubled over, retching, gasping for breath.

"When you mention my father, Princess, you must speak with respect as befits a queen of her king. Come."

They drew closer to a hooded figure, his hands tied behind his back. The hood concealed his identity, but his height was just slightly less than average.

Errol.

No. Please, Deas, no.

Sevra smiled, her eyes glinting, lit by avid cruelty. She flicked her wrist, and one of the guards reached up to yank the hood off. Adora found herself facing Oliver Turing, Rodran's flamboyant chamberlain. Bruises marked his face like splotches of plague, and one eye was swollen shut, but his insouciant smile remained despite a pair of broken teeth.

Adora's relief flooded through her, taking her to her knees. Guilt at feeling it brought the tears that Sevra's beatings could not.

"Your father's chamberlain refuses to tell me the name of his nuntius," Sevra said. Her voice rasped with frustration. "There is information that I require. I am merciful, strumpet. I am giving you a chance to provide it."

Above her, she heard Turing sigh. "The Merakhi sun favors you, Princess. The freckles give you a fresh, girlish air, but you shouldn't cry. Your eyes and nose turn red. It completely ruins the look."

"I want the name!" Sevra screeched.

Turing looked heavenward and sighed. "I told you already, his identity is hidden. I'm no more able to identify him than be him."

Adora laughed and raised her head to meet Oliver's gaze through a fresh onslaught of tears, but the chamberlain's expression, deadly serious, bored into her, as if commanding her to understand something. Then the moment passed.

A guard struck him, and he staggered. Turing rolled his eyes and sighed theatrically. "These people have no sense of style. There's just no color that goes with facial bruises."

Sevra's mouth compressed into a line. "You have more to worry about than style, popinjay."

Turing donned a look of exaggerated horror. "You mean you're going to force me to make you presentable? I'm sorry. It just can't be done. You can't make silk from burlap, you know."

A guard clubbed Turing across the mouth with the hilt of his sword. The former chamberlain dropped to the ground spitting blood. At a nod from Sevra, the guard kicked him in the head so hard he flipped to land on his back.

Weir's daughter snapped her fingers, and two of the guards hauled Turing to his feet. She turned to Adora. "This is your first and most important lesson, Princess. Every time you contest me, every time you think to thwart my desire, one of your friends will die."

Adora shook her head. "Please, you don't have to do this. I won't fight you anymore."

Sevra's smile stretched her face into an obscene parody of childlike joy, her eyes wide. The expression chilled her. "Then tell me the name of your uncle's nuntius."

Adora gaped, desperate to surrender a name she didn't possess.

"Well then, Princess, I'm not killing him." Sevra motioned and the guard next to her drew his sword and ran Turing slowly through the chest. "You are."

The guard pulled his weapon from Turing's body, his face blank. The chamberlain collapsed, his arms and legs folding in on themselves like discarded rags. Adora fell to his side, pulled his head to her lap. Turing smiled through the blood on his lips.

"Take . . . care . . . Princess . . . Don't ruin . . . the . . . look."

Sevra laughed like a child at play as she turned back toward her quarters.

Adora's hair cascaded down, hiding Turing's face and hers. The chamberlain inhaled wetly. His eyes glazed, bringing a stab of grief, but the chamberlain forced air through his lips. "I swear the message I am to deliver is the word of Rodran son of Rodrick, king of Illustra." He stiffened, desperate to force the words of her uncle's disclosure through his lips, his hands clutching at her, their strength fading as he spoke. "*You* don't look like your father." The fingers slipped. "Find him."

Turing's head rolled to one side. The king's nuntius was dead.

4

Flex

ADORA SHOOK WITH EACH STEP she took back to her quarters, her body aching with the suppressed need to strike Sevra Weir. If she had to spend the rest of her days enduring one beating after another, she would find a way to make an answer to Oliver Turing's death, but no recompense could be made until she escaped.

She drew a trembling breath that mirrored the shaking in her hands. Sevra must not be allowed to suspect she intended to escape. The consequences of discovery chilled her more than the wind that cut across the island. The duke's daughter had killed Turing both as a punishment and as a goad. Sevra wanted her to fight back. It would give her the justification she needed to have her beaten again.

And Adora would have to allow it. Sudden compliance on her part would arouse Sevra's suspicions. Yet her response would have to be measured. If she pushed Sevra too far, the woman would have her bound or placed under constant watch. Escape would be impossible.

Dread of another beating compressed the time it took to make the trip back to her quarters. Inside the sitting room with the guards posted outside once more, Sevra regarded her with a broad, condescending smile, which did nothing to relieve the cruel severity of her features. The duke's daughter resembled a gleeful vulture, feasting on another's death. Adora waited. Nothing she did could appear premeditated. She allowed all the disdain and contempt she felt to show in her eyes.

Sevra's head rocked with laughter. "I'm surprised you haven't thanked me yet, Your Highness. After all, that could have been your peasant lover." She came forward, her head jutting forth on her neck like a stinkweed blossom on its stalk. "He'll die, Princess, and I promise you'll be there to see it. Thank me, Highness. Thank me for allowing you to see your filthy little peasant one last time."

Before Sevra could dodge, Adora leapt forward and backhanded her across the mouth. Savoring the impact of Sevra's skin against her knuckles, she clenched her fist for a return strike, but the women were on her with cudgels, pounding her into submission. Sevra's boots beat into her with the force of hammers. Adora rolled away, toward the cudgels, but the duke's daughter followed.

Adora tried to rise, but the women pressed her down while Sevra continued to kick her. Several times she missed, connecting instead with her ladies-in-waiting. Adora squirmed in their grasp, trying to spread the blows. Her plan would fail if she could not stand or lift a sword.

At last they stopped. She made no attempt to hide her tears, vowing instead to make them serve her.

Sevra backed away. "Let us see what a few days without food will do for your temperament."

When the door closed after them, Adora wanted to cry in triumph. Instead she raised herself off the floor on arms and legs mottled with new bruises and tottered to the window. Sunset would be six hours or more in coming.

Ignoring the screams from her abused muscles, she moved through her bedroom to the balcony. The sight of the drop made the world pitch, and she grabbed the stone rail in an attempt to force her vision to normalcy. Heights always appeared greater looking down. Still, the distance had to be thirty or forty feet. A jump from such an elevation would at least break her legs if it didn't kill her. Despair crashed in on waves as grim and cold as any in the Beron Strait. She needed a sword and a way down. Impossible.

Tears, hot against her skin, wet her cheeks. *No.* She pounded her fist against the stone. The attempt must be made. She returned to the bedroom and began ripping blankets into strips, testing and tying, working the cloth in an attempt to keep visions of falling from conquering her resolve. She considered it might make more sense to forego a weapon and simply sneak over the balcony under the cover of night, but when she envisioned discovery, the need for a sword consumed her.

At sunset she knotted her improvised rope to the heavy baluster, set a pack carrying her disguise on the balcony—in case she had to attempt a quick exit—and moved to the door in her sitting room that opened onto the hallway. She curled up in her cloak on the floor with her ear to the crack and listened. Church guards split the day into four watches and changed duty near sunset when vespers rang, but did Weir's men follow the same schedule? The sky outside darkened from crimson to purple to black, and still the same two voices carried on their murmured conversation. The bruises on her legs throbbed in time to the grief measured by each sluggish pulse of her blood. She closed her eyes.

Adora started awake, her heart hammering with the realization she'd fallen asleep. No. She couldn't have. The sky outside was still black, but no voices came from outside the door. Had the guard changed?

She cursed herself. How could she have fallen asleep? Breath shuddered into her lungs. The attempt must be made. She stood, shed her cloak, and ripped her clothes to reveal as much skin as she dared.

Shame heated her face, but she rebuked it. If she could stand being paraded in silk inside the ilhotep's harem, she could endure this charade. She ripped the back of her shirt. The bruises needed to show. If Weir's men retained any sense of justice or chivalry, they would help her. If not . . .

Adora shrugged away the thought of what might happen when the guards saw so much of her. She stepped to the door and threw it open. Before either man could react, she fell against the nearest, clutching at his hand. "Please. You have to help me." She allowed enough of her fear loose to make her voice tremble. "She'll kill me."

The guard smiled at her, but his gaze lingered on her torn clothing. "I'll help you, Highness." One hand wandered to a hole in her shirt, his fingers rough against her skin.

The other guard stepped in. "If the duke discovers you've had her, he'll have your head."

The first guard gave a coarse laugh. "The way the lady's been training her, the princess would say anything now, wouldn't she? Nobody will believe her." His gaze met Adora's at last, looking at her as if she were a thing to be taken.

She let her eyes grow wide. *Now.* It had to be now, before he took hold of her. With a sob she brought her knee up to the guard's groin and yanked his sword free. Instead of doubling over, the guard lunged at her. With a twitch of her wrists, she brought the point in line . . . and watched in horror as the blade slipped between his ribs like a knife falling into water.

He died before he hit the floor.

Adora danced backward, but the other guard only looked at her. The sole evidence of any concern he had lay in the increased distance between them.

"Barda never was too bright." He shrugged as if he'd just noted the weather. "I imagine most people would say he got what he deserved."

She'd killed him. A minute ago there'd been a man—a cruel, opportunistic brute of a man, but a living being. Now there was just a corpse, a hunk of meat, as Rokha would say. Blood dropped from her head into her stomach at the thought, and the taste of bile rested on the back of her tongue. If she'd been allowed to eat, she'd be throwing up.

"I wouldn't let it bother you none, Princess. There's no shortage of people, women mostly, that would thank you." He drew his sword, gestured toward the door of her apartment. "Drop the sword, Your Highness. I'll tell Sevra what happened."

Adora almost succeeded in keeping the hysterical tone from her laughter. "Do you think she'll care?" She straightened so the guard could see the evidence of Sevra's abuse, but she continued to grip the sword like a club, with the point trained on the guard's chest. "You know her. What kind of punishment will she contrive for this?"

The guard's face went cold and flat as he advanced. "That's not my place. You don't even know how to hold a sword, Your Highness."

She didn't want to kill again. This man wasn't her enemy. "Help me escape."

The guard shook his head. "No, Highness, a man who changes sides is never trusted. I'm the duke's man until he dies or I do. You can't hope to get away. The moment our swords cross, the rest of the guards will come running."

He was right. Without changing her grip, she shuffled her feet into position, as Count Rula had taught her. She would have only one chance. The guard glowered at her in frustration and stepped forward, his blade whistling to knock the sword from her hands.

Now. She dropped her left hand from her sword and pivoted to present her right side. With a flex of her wrist, she forced her blade down, out of the path of his strike. The guard's stroke met nothing but air, leaving him exposed.

Adora lunged, saw the guard's eyes widen as he realized his mistake. She saw his brows lower as he braced for the blow that would kill him. The tip took him in the chest.

Time slowed. The guard tried to counter. Adora's sword entered his side. His riposte came at her, a final attempt to rouse the guards. She pushed and twisted, striving for his heart. She wasn't going to make it. The swords were going to hit.

Adora fell into her thrust, taking the guard's stroke along her shoulder. The blade found one of the rents in her shirt, bit into her flesh. She twisted her wrist, tried to ignore his shuddering gasp as her sword found his heart.

The guard sighed. With her free hand, she grabbed his hilt. The thud of his body against the floor sounded no louder than a casual footfall.

The hall remained empty.

Her hands trembled so violently she almost dropped the swords she held. She stumbled to the sitting room and tossed the bloody weapons onto a couch. Shaking, she dragged the dead weight of the guards just inside the door and wiped the blood from the polished marble of the hallway. *Deadweight.* The thought threatened to send her into hysterics until her hand closed on the red-stained tunic of one of the men she'd killed.

Killed. She threw the door closed and shot the bolt home as sobs wracked her body. Her breath came in shuddering gasps as her fury drained away. She'd killed two of her own subjects, one of whom had committed no wrong other than to be loyal to the lord who'd employed him.

She cursed Duke Weir and his entire questionable lineage. After her weeping subsided to tremors, she extinguished the candles in her sitting room, recovered her pack of clothes from the balcony, and donned the disguise she'd worn numerous times to sneak out into the city to help Healer Norv with the sick. The practice, almost forgotten after all she'd been through in past months, stilled the trembling in her chest as she became "Dorrie" once again.

Pocketing the key, she extinguished the last of the candles in her rooms. Before she moved to the balcony, she smudged her face and hair with ash from the fireplace. She threw her makeshift rope over the balcony . . . and stopped. The sword. She'd nearly forgotten. She groped her way back to the sitting room for the weapon.

A knock at the door pulled a frightened gasp from her lungs. She'd floundered back to her balcony when the knock came again, insistent and pounding. The fabric of her knotted sheets burned her hands as she slid toward the ground. Above her, heavy impacts sounded against the wooden frame.

Her heartbeat screamed at her to run straight for the garden door. With an effort she ignored it. No one had noticed her descent. The winter cloud cover obscured the moon, and unless she drew attention to herself, she would be difficult to spot.

How long before they broke down her door?

Adora merged with the shadows and moved as quickly as she dared toward the gate. Halfway there, she stopped. A guard, walking with the bored gait of a soldier in peacetime, blocked her path, standing within feet of the thick ivy that hid the gate. She crouched beneath the boughs of a holly tree, willing him to make his turn and go back.

A retort of splintering wood sounded from the area of her apartments.

"Guards!" a man's voice yelled. "Someone has taken the princess. Search the grounds."

Adora stared. They believed someone had taken her? The guard by the gate peered into the darkness but made no move. A reckless ploy took root in her mind. She twisted the sword belt around to hide the weapon behind her back, then she broke cover and ran toward the guard.

"Over there," she gasped, pointing back the way she'd come. "They're behind those trees."

The guard followed her point and nodded. "Guards, to me," he yelled and charged away, his weapon flashing.

Men with weapons and lanterns cascaded into the courtyard as Adora squirmed behind the thick wall of ivy, trying to ignore the scratch of vines against her skin. She pulled the key from her pocket.

"Where's the princess?" The voice, uncomfortably close, belonged to the guard she'd sent away.

A detachment of guards milling beneath her balcony headed toward her. The lock wouldn't turn. No, it had to. With both hands on the key she wrenched at the mechanism. Then, with a soft groan the tumblers moved, and the door swung open. She slipped through into another mass of ivy that hid the door from the other side, pausing just long enough to lock the gate and pocket the key. Hugging the wall, she inched along behind the vines until she emerged into the open air forty paces later.

A clean wind lifted her hair. Adora loosed the restraint that had bound her movements in stealth and ran toward the city.

5

WHAT MUST NOT BE READ

ERROL'S STOMACH COMPLAINED of the lack of food, curiosity gnawing at him as well. Was depriving him a conscious act or an oversight? He hoped it to be the latter. Perhaps events had conspired to spiral out of Duke Weir's control.

His cell offered nothing in the way of diversion, so he'd slept to pass the time of his imprisonment, but now a cascade of footsteps sounded in the hall, sharp and harsh with the heavy-heeled walk of military men. The darkness receded in half-seen flickers of torchlight as the footsteps approached the door. Someone thrust a flaming brand into the cell, and Errol threw up an arm.

"Come. Duke Weir requires your presence."

Errol suppressed a snicker as half a dozen guards escorted him. What did they think one peasant without a weapon could do? Weir either believed in taking no chances or he lived in fear. Such knowledge of the duke might be important if he managed to escape. A man prone to overplanning might be surprised. A leader who lived in fear of betrayal might see enemies where none existed. Either could prove useful.

He followed the guards through levels of the church offices

that sounded and smelled of occupants and out onto the imperial grounds toward the king's palace. As they crossed the space, led by sickly yellow puddles of firelight, a gibbous moon drifted through clouds overhead. It felt late, but he couldn't be sure of the time.

At the entrance to the king's audience chamber, another half dozen guards stood around Martin and Luis. By the exit stood a benefice, robed in the rich red of his office, though such formality would not be required apart from the deliberations of the Judica. Errol recognized the twisted smile almost as quickly as the shock of red hair above it. Dane.

"I think your time in contemplation has improved your appearance, if not your odor," Dane said. His eyes glittered with joyful malice as his gaze surveyed the three of them. "Let us hope isolation has brought about that change of heart that will allow you to reveal to Duke Weir the knowledge he requires."

Martin cleared his throat and spat to one side. "You're mad, Dane. Don't you understand what Rodran's passing means? Illustra needs a king, a true king."

The benefice smirked, his lips pulling to one side beneath his broad nose. "You refer to that drivel about the barrier falling." He made a show of looking around the guard chamber. "I don't see any malus-possessed monsters here to slay us." He turned to the soldier beside him. "Do you?"

The soldier stared ahead, unblinking. "No, Excellency."

Dane simpered. "There. You see. The barrier was a myth. Just another of the outmoded beliefs the church ascribed to simply because it was old."

His mouth turned up at the corners, and he wheeled, his soft red boots whispering against the floor. "Bring them."

Soldiers surrounded them on every side. Errol squinted against the glare of unaccustomed light. When they passed through double doors large enough for eight men to walk abreast, the absence of the usual courtiers and functionaries in the king's audience chamber struck him as another loss. Rodran had endeavored to keep as much of the kingdom's business in the open as possible. But the only person of note in the chamber besides the duke himself was Benefice Weir, the duke's brother, who stood to one side of the throne.

Errol started and corrected that observation. Partly obscured by shadows, stood a pair of readers. On a table in front of them, Errol could see blanks, knives, and rubbing cloths. He peered into the gloom but couldn't discern whether the two were the same who had visited him in his cell.

Duke Weir meant to test them.

The guards led them forward before they formed ranks, the majority between the three of them and Weir. The duke looked at them as if the taste of spoiled meat lingered on his palate. Errol noted the duke's flat-eyed glare but refused to respond. The division of the guards told him the answer to his earlier question—the duke trusted no one. Errol resolved to keep his silence at whatever cost.

"You have information I require," the duke said without preamble. "Give it to me."

Martin bowed, his manner deferential but nothing more. "If you would provide me the context of this information you seek, I would be happy to provide you with an answer . . . so long as it does not contravene the authority of the church."

The duke slapped his palm against the ornately carved arm of the throne. "I think you know what information I seek, priest. Do not think the Judica will save you. Those who were loyal to that traitorous archbenefice have wisely fled."

Martin nodded. "Then who governs the Judica, Your Grace? The question of the succession, once taken up, must be answered."

The duke smiled with the look of a man about to kill a long-hated adversary. "Benefice Weir has assumed the chair."

"Ah. The deliberations must have been done in haste, Your Grace. It usually takes weeks to select a new archbenefice."

Dane moved forward to stand beside Benefice Weir. Errol

shook his head in disbelief. Other than red hair, Dane's resemblance to the duke and Benefice Weir was startling.

"I am through dissembling, priest," Weir said. "I require the name of the man you thought to put on the throne."

"I'm so very sorry, Your Grace." Martin fixed his eyes on Dane. "I think you've been misinformed. Even before I was stripped of my orders, I was only one of many in the Judica. It is not within my power alone to put anyone on the throne."

Weir fumed. Errol could hear him grinding his teeth from where he stood. The duke's dilemma became clear: though Martin and Luis had broken church law to cast for the next rightful king, Weir could not broach the subject in that way. To do so would mean acknowledging a monarch other than himself.

Errol drew a slow breath. Martin played a very dangerous game. The duke, paranoid and fearful, would not tolerate being balked. He might have them killed from sheer frustration.

Duke Weir jerked forward, his face florid. "We have traced your movements for the past six years, priest." He glanced at Luis. "And you took a reader with you. Give me the name."

Martin folded his hands across his stomach. It was smaller than it used to be. "If you would speak plainly, I would be most happy to comply."

Weir jerked out of his seat, shaking with rage. "Curse you! I want the result of your cast for king. Give me the name, or I will have it wrung from you."

Martin smiled. "Out of your own mouth you acknowledge the existence of a rightful sovereign. Alas, Your Grace, I do not know who is supposed to be the next king."

"You lie."

Martin's smile widened as he gestured toward Weir's readers. "Do I?"

At the duke's furious wave, the readers behind their table picked up their knives and began the process of casting. Duke Weir paced the floor, sword in hand, his face a storm about to break.

A DRAW OF KINGS

The readers each cast a dozen times. "He speaks the truth," the first reader said. Weir's gaze latched onto the second, who nodded.

The duke's eyes widened until the whites showed all around. Weir gestured at Benefice Dane with his sword. "What is the meaning of this? How am I to rid myself of this rival if we cannot discover his identity?"

Dane smiled, looking confident. "All transpires to your benefit, Your Grace. If the cast was made but the answer was inconclusive, then no one can gainsay your own claim to the throne once the conclave announces it. And they will choose you, Your Grace, as the only logical choice."

Dane paused to give the two readers a look that carried portents of death. "But perhaps the omne can shed some light upon this rival's identity."

Duke Weir's sword blade appeared against Errol's throat. "You are an omne. Yes?"

Errol nodded, careful to avoid contact with the edge.

"I require your services, omne." Weir waved his free hand, and his brother came forward and placed two rough pine lots in Errol's hands.

Two lots?

Errol looked to Martin and Luis for guidance. The two men held worried looks in their eyes, but nothing in their expression explained why two wooden lots carried such importance. Luis had cast for Illustra's king in stone, and when the cast had brought up his name and Liam's in equal numbers, he'd destroyed them, convinced the cast had failed. The sword slid a fraction along Errol's skin. He hoped the duke possessed more skill with a blade than his late son. An inadvertent slip could be fatal.

"You will give me your utmost attention, boy," Weir said, "and tell me what is written on these lots."

"No."

The duke pressed forward, a small motion. A trickle of warmth worked its way down to Errol's collar. He held his breath.

"Read them."

His answer was already framed on his lips, his neck tensed against the cut that would kill him, when he saw a glimmer of writing on one of the lots. He nodded. Weir removed the sword and stepped back.

With a negligent twist of his wrist, he held the lots against the light. How would Weir react? "This one says *Yes*, the other *No*."

The duke snapped his fingers and the readers cast again. Errol pressed his hand against his neck. It came away with a smear of blood, half dried. Only a scratch, so far.

The older reader spoke first. "He speaks the truth." The second nodded affirmation.

Weir screamed curses that echoed from the walls, and his eyes became vicious in the lamplight. "Princess Adora is housed two floors above us. Her safety depends on your cooperation, omne. I had planned to take her for my wife to replace the son you killed, but I can always give her to my men. I don't think she'd like that." Froth appeared at the corners of his mouth, and he stabbed the air toward Martin. "Tell me the name of the man they mean to put on the throne. Tell me what I want to know."

Errol wet his lips. If he tried to lie, to tell Weir he didn't know, the duke's readers would strip his pretense away and leave him helpless. "I didn't kill your son."

The duke's eyes widened at the diversion.

"He lies," Dane said. "This is a mere distraction. The information we have from the minister of Merakh was quite specific."

Weir glowered at Dane and his voice dropped to a murderous whisper. "My son is not a distraction. You will remember that."

Benefice Weir looked on the verge of stepping between his brother and Benefice Dane.

Martin cleared his throat. "Your readers seem to have plenty of wood left."

The duke glared at Martin's interjection, but a moment later he threw a savage nod toward the readers, and the smell of pine drifted to Errol from their table. If the two men who served Weir decided to falsify their cast, there would be no way for Errol to disprove their tale.

But if the readers lied, their own lives were in jeopardy. Weir needed them to lie, but only once—when the cast for king would be made. Other than that one instance, the duke needed un-doubted truthfulness from the conclave as much as any king.

Errol wiped his palms on his cloak as the readers drew. One of them, short, with the silver-blond hair of a Soede, jerked in surprise at the first draw, and his expression grew worried as he drew time and again. The other man, wrinkled with age spots dotting his hands, took his lower lip between his teeth.

"Well?" the duke demanded.

The readers eyed each other, hesitating. The Soede spoke first. "Any cast from wood has a possibility of error, Your Grace, but it appears that Earl Stone is telling the truth."

Martin nodded affirmation. "I was there, Your Grace. One of the Merakhi guards killed your son for a perceived insult to the ilhotep."

Dane moved to stand between Martin and the duke. "Your Grace, it hardly matters how your son died. To a man, these three are against you. The peasant boy stole the princess from your son. Had she not followed him to Merakh, your son would still be alive."

The duke nodded. "Yes. They have much to answer for."

For a moment, palpable relief flooded across Dane's features.

The door to the audience chamber opened and a soldier in blue, a captain, hustled toward the duke. He stopped just short of the guards, who stood regarding him as if he might be a threat, and went to one knee.

Weir snapped when the man did not speak. "What?"

The captain, head bared, kept his eyes on the carpet. "Your Grace, the palace guards report the princess has been taken."

Weir threw curses toward the officer, punctuating them with slashes of his sword. "Impossible. Bring me those witless dolts who allowed her escape."

The captain licked his lips. "I cannot, Your Grace. They were found inside her apartments, dead."

The duke's gaze darted around the chamber as if he suspected the marble busts and statues of conspiring against him. "He's penetrated the palace."

Martin smiled, his eyes radiant with savage joy.

Weir snapped his fingers at his readers. "Find the pretender."

His brother stepped forward, one hand reaching as if to offer comfort, but his hand shook and the gesture appeared fearful. "Might it not be best to enlist the conclave in this?"

The duke's head jerked in denial. "No. Not until I am assured there are no traitors remaining. One false reader could cost us days." He turned to the two men with their blanks spread before them. "You will work until he is found. Success brings reward. Failure . . ." He didn't bother to finish.

"What of these, Your Grace?" Dane asked, pointing toward Errol, his eyes hungry. "Would it not be best to dispose of them now that your victory is at hand?"

Again Weir shook his head. "Your zeal becomes you, Benefice Dane, but men are a resource, like oxen or horses. In time we may do without the priest and the reader, but the peasant has services to render to us." He gave a careless wave. "Put them beneath the watch."

His gaze lashed at them all. "Men loyal to me will be posted outside your door. If I fall, you will die."

Adora made her way to the poor quarter and Healer Norv's shop. The streets held fewer people than she remembered, and more guards. Many of them wore blue, and when those who didn't crossed paths with those who did, they gave way. She followed their lead, keeping her head down and her hair tucked into the dingy cloak she wore. Taverns and shops threw yellow puddles of light into the street, beckoning with promises of warmth and laughter she spurned. When strangers approached, she put her hand on the pommel of her sword. Better if everyone assumed her to be a man.

When she arrived at her destination, a low-slung building with a healer's sign of the sheaf and pestle over the entrance, she nearly sobbed with relief. The thick door rattled in its frame with each strike from her clenched fist. Norv lived above his shop; the healer never turned anyone away.

Steps sounded from within, but instead of welcoming her, the door creaked open less than a handsbreadth before it stopped. Norv's disheveled face filled the crack.

"What's your business? I don't see people after dusk."

Adora rushed forward to put her face in the dim light of Norv's lamp. "Healer, it's me."

His eyes squinted beneath grizzled brows that were whiter than she remembered. "I require a name, lad. State your illness and go away until tomorrow. I'm old."

She reached back to free her hair from the confines of her clothing. "I'm not a lad. It's me—Dorrie."

With an oath, the healer thrust open the door and yanked her inside. Swearing under his breath, he slammed it shut again and barred it. "Are you daft, Highness, running the poor quarter after dark with the duke's men busting the skull of anyone who looks at 'em crossways?"

Adora reeled, put out a hand against a nearby table to steady herself. "How long have you known who I am?"

Norv gave an exasperated sigh. "Do you think you can be a healer if you've got mush for brains, lass? I suspected the second time you came. I had Denny follow you to make certain."

She shook her head in disbelief. "You never said anything."

"Ha, and lose my best assistant? After you started working here, Rodran started to take notice of things in the poor quarter." He dipped his head, eyes closed. "I don't think Duke Weir likes them that live here. The place is worse than it ever was. I don't much care for our next king."

"He's not going to be king."

The healer grew still. "I'm supposed to turn you in to the guard for saying such a thing, Princess. The duke issued the edict himself just after your uncle died."

Adora stepped back in case she needed room. What had happened to him? "If you're too scared to stand up to the duke, then say so and I'll leave. There must be a man on this island somewhere."

Norv's face softened until she recognized him once more. He turned to address the shadows at the back of the room. "Is that enough for you? It's the princess, for Deas's sake."

Out of the blackness that shrouded the rear of Norv's shop stepped a god. Thick blond hair cascaded to shoulders broad enough to grace a blacksmith, yet he moved with the grace of one born to the saddle. When he smiled in greeting, his blue eyes caught and amplified the light of Norv's lamp until they twinkled. Then he knelt.

Liam.

But he had changed. He rose from the floor like a lion rising from rest. The innocence of the village youth had been quenched and tempered into something more, the open look once in his face gone, replaced by a gaze that bored into her, weighing, measuring. She caught herself on the verge of bowing, as if in recognition of his nobility. Instead, she bent from the waist, deeper than his station required, but no less than her heart demanded. "Captain Liam."

"Your Highness, if you'll accompany me, I'll take you to a place of greater safety." He shrugged as if in apology. "I would have said 'someplace safe,' but Weir's men have begun searching the poor quarter of late, so there is no place safe, and we dare not risk attack until reinforcements come from the mainland garrisons."

Liam clasped hands with Norv, then led Adora through the back of the shop. The alley stank of rotting food and other smells she didn't want to think about. Unexpected turns down narrow ways and back onto broad streets in decline brought them to the rear of a large inn. Raucous laughter told her the sort of establishment they'd entered. They passed through a dirty kitchen staffed by heavy men in greasy aprons to a common room lit by dirty lamplight.

Men with hard faces and harder eyes watched them pass between rough trestle tables blackened with age. Liam nodded absently to them as he passed, oblivious to the threat of violence in the way they leaned forward in their chairs or in the way they kept their hands close to weapons.

The muscles in her back clenched. Where had he brought her? Duke Weir wanted to use her as a pawn to secure his grip on the throne. Did Liam intend to as well?

His boots thumped against the boards like a drummer's call to war. He opened a door and motioned her inside.

6

A DOOR OPENS

MORE DINGY LAMPLIGHT greeted her, reflecting back from walls that had faded to various shades of dirt. A crowd of men stepped forward as Liam moved in behind, locking the door. The first, his face dominated by a nose that had been broken more than once, rushed forward. Callused hands grabbed her, pulled her forward.

"Deas alive, girl, how did you escape?"

She gasped in Rale's embrace, her ribs protesting. Before she could answer, another man with hair like snow, quiet and still as the land in winter, put a hand on Rale's shoulder. "I think she'll answer better if she can breathe," Merodach said.

Rale released her, his face flushing, and stepped back.

It was too much—the beatings, the lack of food, her flight, all conspired against her. She tottered, but Rale caught her, putting her in a chair while he muttered something to a watchman who left by a side door. A moment later Rokha entered, her eyes sharp.

She snapped her fingers. "Stand back. The air in here is close enough without everyone crowding her."

Rokha's gaze darkened as she surveyed the bruises on her face.

61

With a healer's touch she pulled Adora's arm from beneath her cloak and pushed back the sleeve. Purple bruises surrounded red spots where Sevra's boots had found their mark. Fingers probed the cut on Adora's shoulder.

"Who did this to you?"

The answer could wait. "Could I have something to eat, and maybe some ale?"

Liam disappeared out the front door, his place taken by Merodach.

Adora nodded her thanks. "Sevra, Duke Weir's daughter, felt the need to demonstrate her grief over her brother's death." She rubbed a particularly large knot on one thigh. "She has a penchant for sharp-toed boots."

Rokha gave a sharp nod, almost a jerk, and brought forth a jar of salve from the healer's kit she kept with her. Smells of lemongrass and mint battled the less savory odors in the room.

"To what end, Highness?" Rale asked.

Adora shrugged, regretted the gesture. "Duke Weir's wife is dead. He intended to force me to marry him to replace the heir he lost." She did not mention Weir's search for her uncle's nuntius or Turing's cryptic message.

Rokha shifted her chair, moved her attention to Adora's other arm.

Then she stopped and with a lunge pulled Adora's sword from its sheath and held it up for the men clustered behind her to see.

Rale touched a finger to the sticky wetness on the point. "You drew blood?"

Adora nodded.

Rokha's smile burst forth, savage, exultant. Careless of the hurts she'd tended just moments before, she threw herself forward to pull Adora into a hug as fierce and savage as Rale's had been. "Oh, my sister! I'm so proud."

When they parted, Adora saw unshed tears in Rokha's eyes.

"Did you mark or kill?" Rokha asked.

She grew light-headed with the memory. "Kill. Two of Weir's guards."

Rokha kissed her, eyes brimming. "Now you are worthy of him. Let no one say you are not."

Rokha's regard was too much. Sobs locked away behind her imperial reserve broke loose, and Adora clutched her friend as tears washed her face. When she parted, she found the men in the room, hard men who bore the price of their service on their bodies and faces, gazing at her in pride. Then she noticed the strip of black cloth around Rokha's arm.

She touched it, her fingers sliding along the sturdy weave. "Something new comes. Since when did the watch allow women?"

Rale exchanged a look with Merodach before he answered. "It's honorary at this point, but the way will be open to her if she wants to challenge."

Merodach cleared his throat, a hint of disapproval and challenge in his voice. "She will still have to defeat a majority to qualify."

Rokha's eyes flashed with her smile. "Would I have it any other way?"

Adora nodded with pride. "No, but how did you escape the duke's men in the harbor?"

"They didn't think to put a guard on board Tek's ship," Rale said. "We slipped over the rail after dark and swam to shore." A rueful grin pulled his mouth to one side under his broad nose. "It took some of us longer than others. When Solis Karele and I finally made it to the beach, Rokha and Merodach were fighting a handful of Weir's men. They held them off until we managed to wade out of the surf." He shivered. "The water almost took us." Karele nodded from where he sat at the table.

A coded knock came from the door behind. Merodach drew his sword and cracked the door for a moment before stepping back to allow Liam to reenter bearing a mug and a plate. "It's not equal to palace fare," he said. "Watchmen aren't very good cooks, but it's edible."

Realization clicked into place. "The men in the kitchen?"

Liam nodded. "And the men in the common room as well. Outside of the palace, this is the most heavily guarded location in the kingdom." He placed the food in front of her and stepped back. "If you will permit me, Highness, I will explain while you eat.

"Weir took control of the isle and the city the day after your uncle died," Liam said. "He'd been bringing his men to the island for months, but never in the open and never so many that people would notice. Before we could muster a defense, the palace compound was in his control. Those of the watch who did not escape were either killed or imprisoned, along with every benefice and reader Benefice Weir saw as a potential threat."

"Yet much was denied him," Rale said.

For some reason, this remark brought color to Liam's cheeks, as if he were embarrassed. His hand waved Rale's observation away. A knock at the far door interrupted him, and the watchman closest to it cracked it, before bowing two men into the room.

Bertrand Canon, archbenefice of the church, and Enoch Sten, first reader of the conclave, entered. Both acknowledged Liam before taking turns to embrace her. She inhaled, drinking in the smell of the two men who'd been fixtures of security her entire life. The archbenefice smelled of incense and wine while Primus Sten wore scents of wood.

She let go with regret. "If Weir controls the Judica and the conclave and most are in prison, how did you escape?"

The archbenefice spoke first. "Captain Liam brought the watchmen under his command to our quarters as soon as he heard Weir was taking the city." His eyes shone with pride. "He has the instincts of a tactician. It was almost as if he knew they were coming."

She checked the room once more. All these men were known to her. "Duke Weir has Errol, Your Excellency, and Martin and Luis as well."

Primus Sten nodded assent, his face grave. "We know."

"I've sent messengers to the mainland," Liam said. "As soon

as we get reinforcements from the nearest garrisons, we'll be able to take back the city."

"How long ago did you send word?" Adora asked.

Liam bit his lower lip. "Five days."

A stab of ice shot through her belly. Five days? The messengers would barely have had time to reach their destinations, and one man could travel far faster than a full company. For the return they would still have to cross the strait, with the duke's ships crowding the harbor until their masts resembled a forest.

And the duke had readers.

Oh, Errol.

She shook her head. "We can't wait that long. We must rescue them."

"We don't have any choice, Highness. The duke's men outnumber us three to one."

She wrung her hands as if she could pull courage from them. "Don't you understand? Duke Weir doesn't trust anyone. The only thing keeping him in check is his fear of betrayal. He's using Errol to verify lots. Once he's tested the readers in the Judica, he'll move. There won't be anything to stop him."

Liam shook his head, suddenly wary. "You'll have to trust me, Highness. They will not find us here, and Aurae can block the readers. I won't risk a fight we cannot win. They would strike us down before we could breach the compound."

Her eyes found Karele. *Oh, Deas.* He was right. If Aurae blinded the readers, they would have all the time they needed. She wrapped her arms around her shoulders and hugged herself. But what about Errol? She couldn't imagine him working for the duke willingly. He would have to be coerced.

Her hands bumped against the hard outline of the key to the garden gate. She snatched it from her cloak pocket, held it up by its string for them to see. "What if you *could* win? We can enter the palace grounds without their knowledge. There's a door in the wall hidden by ivy. It leads to a concealed gate in the palace garden."

Rale's eyes lit with possibilities, yet his voice carried caution. "The task will be getting enough men into the compound to hold it until Weir can be taken." His gaze slid from Adora to Liam.

Liam reached forward to take the key, but she tucked it away into her pocket.

He bowed from the neck in acquiescence, his face open, intent, as if listening, before nodding. A wash of tears tracked the dirt on her cheeks as Liam gave her a chaste embrace, his massive chest and shoulders dwarfing her. "We will find him, Your Highness. It's time the kingdom began to discharge its debts to Errol Stone." He listened as she explained the door's location and then turned to Rale. "Can it be done tonight?"

Rale shook his head. "Tomorrow provides a better chance of success. The night is half gone already." He shrugged. "And we'll need Captains Cruk and Reynald to assist. Their knowledge of the palace compound exceeds mine."

Primus Sten pulled a block of pine from his robe, tossed it from one wrinkled hand to the other. "And that will give me the opportunity to tell you exactly where the duke is holding them. You need not waste time searching."

Liam nodded his thanks. Disappointment at the delay etched his face, but determination as well. "Highness, one of our number will show you to rooms where you may rest."

Adora looked at the band of black cloth around Rokha's arm. Naaman Ru's daughter would never suffer to be left behind. She vowed she wouldn't be either.

The men filed out, some speaking half-muttered words of encouragement or welcome, the rest nodding, their faces showing the confusion of those whom words had failed. Rokha shouldered her bag, extended a hand to help Adora to her feet. "My room is upstairs. The bed is creaky, but it's large enough for both of us."

Tears stung her eyes again. "Thank you. I think I've had all the privacy I'll need for a while."

Ominous creaks came from the boards as they ascended the stairs, but Rokha didn't appear concerned. At the end of a long hall covered by a strip of carpet whose yellow color had dirtied to ochre, Rokha produced a key to her room. She tossed her hair and smiled.

"Ordinarily I wouldn't feel the need for locks, but some of these men are actually better with a sword than I am." She shrugged. "And some might mistake an unlocked door as encouragement."

A patchwork of furniture covered with infrequent splotches of varnish decorated the room. Beside the bed stood a washstand with a large porcelain bowl of water on it. Rokha gestured. "Take your clothes off, Your Highness. I can tell from the way you climbed the stairs, there are few areas on your body that don't bear some type of injury."

Adora talked as she disrobed to ease her embarrassment. "It's not just me, is it? Liam, I mean. Even the archbenefice and the primus talk to him as if he's their equal."

Rokha's familiar chuckle, deep and genuine, soothed her ears as her hands explored the injuries Sevra had left. "I respect strength, not titles, but every time I see him I have to fight the urge to look at the ground. I heard Captain Reynald say Rodran had the same effect on people early in his reign." She clicked her tongue as she opened a jar that filled the room with the tang of mint and lemongrass. "Sevra wears pointed boots?"

Adora nodded, breathing deeply through her nose. A hint of lavender pulled her eyelids lower. "She's very fond of using them."

"You should have killed her, Princess." Rokha's voice carried no hint of jesting.

The idea of killing anyone, but especially a woman, was repugnant to her, but she understood Rokha's point of view. The dark-haired woman, raised to fighting and the sword, divided the world into two simple categories: those who needed to be killed and those who didn't. If someone fell into the first category, their gender wouldn't matter. Adora wished she could see things in such terms, but it was easier to give the simple answer. "I didn't get the chance."

She squirmed around enough to look Rokha in the eye. "My

uncle is dead, and I've grown up surrounded by people who saw me as his daughter first and only. Outside of Errol, no one calls me by my name. I'd like it if you would."

Rokha's full lips pursed in a smile. Her eyes carried equal parts amusement and defiance. "Is that a royal command, Your Highness?"

She shook her head. "Just a request. If I could make friends by fiat, I wouldn't be covered with bruises."

"Very well, Adora, but I will still call you Princess when you're being foolish."

The consequences of revealing her love for Errol had been beaten into her hide. At the least she'd learned to think before she acted. "I don't think you'll have much need."

Rokha's mouth broadened into a smile. "You're probably right . . . Princess."

Adora laughed into her pillow until tears wet the rough cloth. "How can I persuade Liam to allow me along on the raid?"

The hands on her back stilled. When she spoke, her voice carried none of its usual banter. "From what little I have seen of him, he carries a respect for position. If you order him to allow you along, I think he will try every tactic he can think of to talk you out of it, but he won't force you to stay behind. If that doesn't work, don't give him the key."

She continued to work salve into Adora's bruises and welts. A cut on her back she couldn't recall getting required stitches, along with the one on her shoulder. Rokha was still ministering to her when she fell asleep. She woke once, startled awake by a memory in her sleep, but Rokha slept beside her, fully clothed as if ready to fight. She drifted once more.

She rose from an empty bed with the first light to find the inn nearly deserted. The press of men had vanished, and for a moment she feared Liam had left her behind. A lone watchman with hands the size of small hams tended the kitchen, slicing bread and cheese. She didn't know his name.

"Captain Liam charged me with making sure you were fed,

Your Highness. My name is Bale." He put some food on a plate, slid it across the high table to her.

She lifted a wedge of cheese from the tray. "Where is Liam now?"

The watchman smiled, showing a pair of front teeth that had been broken off halfway up. "He is making his plans for the attack tonight." Bale's face grew serious. "You can trust him, Highness. Captain Liam doesn't leave anything to chance. I'm to take you to him the fourth hour after sunset."

"What do I do until then?"

Bale smirked and offered her the bread.

That evening, as dark shrouded the poor quarter, he led her out into the streets.

7

WAR WITHIN

INSIDE THEIR DANK CELL, Errol fought against a weight of despair as dark and heavy as their blackened dungeon. The duke was well on his way to eliminating all organized opposition on the isle. If he succeeded, the rest of the kingdom would follow the lead established by Weir's lapdog Judica and conclave. Perhaps a thousand people awaited execution in the prison beneath the watch barracks, their deaths held in abeyance until Weir's coronation. Now he, Martin, and Luis sat among them.

Restless, Errol traced his way around the confines. Dim outlines came to him as his eyes adjusted to the perpetual darkness. He turned toward Martin's filmy presence. "Do you think they've captured everyone?"

"No." His voice sounded confident. "Eight armed men guarded Weir in an empty audience room. That hardly seems like the confidence of a man who's rounded up all his adversaries."

Errol nodded, but Martin's reasoning failed to comfort him. "Will they be able to get to us?"

A sigh and a whisper came from the other shadow. "Perhaps,"

Luis said. "Though I think the prospect depends as much on Amos Tek as it does the captains."

"Even if they do manage to make land, they will have to find us," Martin added. "But don't let our circumstances trouble you, Errol. I believe Deas has a plan for us even if we don't perceive it at the moment."

Errol gave a soft laugh. "This isn't so bad, Pater. Light and food would be nice, but I can move and I'm warm enough in my cloak. It's better than a night in the stocks, and it's almost as good as the floor of Cilla's tavern." Martin and Luis grew still. Even in the gloom Errol could tell his banter took the men by surprise.

"What was it like?" Martin asked.

The conversation had taken a turn more serious than he'd intended. He didn't contrive to hide his past, but he generally made no effort to discuss it either. Yet speaking with Rale had allowed him some healing from Warrel's death; perhaps it would suffice here as well. He took a breath. "If you're asking about the beating itself, I don't know what I can tell you. If Antil came across me while I was passed out, he would carry me to the stocks and lock me in. Not so bad when it was warm, but the cold months were hard. If I was lucky, that was as far as it went.

"If I wasn't, I woke to the lash or the rod across my back. The first few times I screamed and pleaded for him to stop and fought to pull free, but that only seemed to make him angrier. After that I tried to hold my tongue. He always let me go after he beat me, almost like he was in a hurry for me to get away."

"Deas in heaven," Martin breathed. "No wonder you hate the church."

Errol's laughter bounced from the chilled stone of their cell like a hope of light, surprising even him. "I don't, Pater, not anymore. Not since Merakh."

"You amaze me, Errol," Luis said. "Have you forgiven Antil, then?"

His mirth subsided, quenched by the suggestion. "No, but someday I might."

They threaded their way through the poor quarter, avoiding the broad pools of light where Weir's men clustered. Behind the corner of a building that bordered one of the innumerable alleyways in the district, Bale stopped and snorted softly. Four soldiers in blue stood outside a tavern, furtively watching the shadows.

"If we keep to the alleys and move quietly, they won't see us, Your Highness. Those men don't like the poor quarter—no they don't. They have no intention of looking too hard at what happens in the alleys here. They might have to investigate, and that's a good way to come down with a sudden case of dead."

The sergeant's grim humor unnerved Adora. Too many times they'd passed shadows in the alleys, still places that ate sound and emanated malice. "Are *we* safe?"

Bale's chuckle held an edge. "No one is safe in the quarter, but I was raised here before I fought my way out and into the watch. Those that hunt the streets at night are smart. They prefer easy prey."

She breathed a sigh of relief.

"But you'll want to keep your hand close to your sword just in case."

The men in blue uniforms stepped back inside the tavern, their nominal patrol of the area complete. "Let's go."

They continued to work through the maze. Several streets away, three figures in black ghosted across the charcoal outline of a cobbler's shop. Adora nodded, but her heart lay like a lump of iron in her chest. According to Bale, Liam had committed every man he could spare to this attack. If it failed, there would be no second chance. To his credit, he didn't do things by half measures, but his willingness to throw everything into the assault scared her.

As they neared their destination, they stopped more often,

avoiding the other groups of watchmen and soldiers as they converged on the ivy-covered wall that hid the palace compound. In the shadow of a broad stand of holly trees, they found Liam and the other captains, Cruk, Rale, Merodach, and Reynald, but no one else.

Panic tightened a noose around her vocal cords, made her voice harsh. "Where is everyone?"

Liam regarded her as if she had not just snapped. "We cannot gather here. Even a blind man would not fail to notice such numbers." He gestured around. "Once we have assayed the door, they will follow from their positions."

He put out his hand, and Adora pulled the key from her pocket and relinquished it with a grimace. Liam started to slip behind the thick curtain of ivy that shielded her secret door from view, but Cruk put a hand on his wrist. "A leader does not command from the front. Let Elar and me go first."

Irritation marred Liam's perfect countenance. "Should I send other men to take risks that I am unwilling to bear?"

Cruk's head bobbed. "Yes, lad, that's exactly what you should do."

Liam looked at the man the watch called Elar but Adora knew as Rale. "Do you agree with this, Captain?"

At his nod, Liam gestured at the captain's insignia on their arms. "Call forth the lieutenants, then. The kingdom cannot afford to lose its best tacticians."

Rale's chuckles floated in the air in counterpoint to Cruk's glower. "Second best, I think. Our protest has been neatly turned against us. I suggest we pull back and send an expeditionary force into the royal compound first."

Cruk's growled curses drifted back to Adora's ears as they retreated to a building across the street. Inside, dozens of watchmen stood armed and ready.

"They've been arriving by ones and twos ever since Liam committed to the attack," Rale said. He called out a pair of lieutenants, grim men whose flat, emotionless stares would have scared her if worry for Errol had not commandeered that emotion. They signaled a handful of sergeants, who in turn brought five soldiers each from the shadows. In less time than Adora would have thought possible, sixty-two men stood ready.

At a nod from Rale, Liam pulled out the key.

"Slip behind the opening in the ivy on the right," Adora said. "The entrance will be roughly forty paces to your left. When you're through the door, move back to your right. You'll be in the garden."

The lieutenant on the left nodded as if he already knew her directions. He took the key, and sixty-two men moved from the building and melted into the shadows, moving in time to the clouds that crossed in front of the moon.

Minutes ticked by as Adora strained her ears to hear the sounds that would announce the fight for Erinon had begun, but nothing came. "What are they doing?"

Rale's chuckle sounded strangely warm in the cold and dark. "The night is long, Princess. It will be some time yet before everyone is in position. If we are discovered too soon, we will be hard-pressed to take the compound. Weir must not have time to organize his defense. Even in the palace we are outnumbered."

Adora nodded. Of course. "Your reputation is well deserved, Captain."

Rale inclined his head. "Thank you, Princess, but this plan is Liam's, not mine. I would not have committed so fully to the attack."

A thread of cold pierced her. "Do you doubt?"

He shook his head, the gesture barely perceived in the gloom. "I am older, Your Highness, and old men know caution above all else. But in this, Liam is right. If we do not succeed here, there is little point in holding men in reserve. Weir will be alerted to our presence, and our trail will be easy to trace. Tonight we will win or die."

The finality of his assessment silenced her. In the darkness, men faded from her perception until only Rokha, Liam, and the captains remained. Liam gave a curt nod and led them across the street. They slipped behind the thick curtain of ivy, the sharp smell of the vines muted by the winter cold that pricked uncovered skin. She blew warm breath across her hands, then tapped the hilt of her sword.

They stepped through the narrow door into the royal garden. Though she couldn't see them in the darkness, the impression of men, many men, came to her, their bodies and cloaks absorbing light and sound. The lieutenants ghosted into visibility before Liam, their faces pale from moonlight or tension. Liam didn't risk speech but held up two fingers of one hand spread apart and pointed toward the palace.

She closed the distance to Liam until her upturned face nearly touched his. "What about Errol?"

"Primus Sten has determined he, Martin, and Luis are beneath the watch barracks, Highness. If we do not capture or kill the duke and his brother, at best we will be joining them." He turned to face the palace. "Please stay close. If we become separated, I will not be able to spare men to look for you for some time." The darkness swallowed him as he moved off, but Adora stood, wondering what to do. None of the men moved toward Errol's prison.

Rokha floated into view like a wraith, her dark skin difficult to see in the moonlight, but her eyes flashing with amusement. "I took the liberty of eavesdropping on Sten's conversation with Captain Lion there." Her eyebrows lifted. "If he cannot spare any men to search for Errol, perhaps he can spare two women?"

Adora blinked away unexpected tears. "You would do this for me? Give up your chance to fight?"

Rokha laughed her deep, mischievous chuckle and waved a hand at the darkness as she pushed back her hood. "I'm a caravan guard. I find the idea of deceiving Weir's men into thinking we are nothing more than harmless women more compelling than taking orders. Plus, I enjoy the prospect of having Earl Stone in my debt."

Sounds of fighting accompanied by deep angry screams shattered the stillness. Rokha jerked her head toward the barracks. "Come, Adora. Hide your sword beneath your cloak."

They moved at a run, as if fleeing the conflict. As they neared the barracks, men in blue streamed past with steel drawn, ignoring them. Torches flared by the dozens as Weir's men shouted for light. Surprised screams testified to their shock at the breadth of the attack. Adora followed Rokha across the yard and through an archway into the barracks. The staccato slap of their boots against the plain granite floor sounded in counterpoint to the deeper pounding of the guards' hurried footsteps.

Rokha led her to one side toward a rack of weapons. When a guard spied them and made a move in their direction with questions written across his features, Rokha twisted her face into a pretense of womanly fear. "Hurry, they're attacking the cathedral."

The questions faded from the man's lowered brows. With a shout to a handful of men behind, he sprinted off in the direction of the Judica. They were alone for the moment. Rokha continued toward the weapons that had been moved inside to protect them from the winter weather, searching.

"What are you doing?" Adora asked.

She moved to the next rack, her hand brushing across the hilts of practice swords. "I'm looking for a staff. As much as I desire to have Errol in my debt, if we have to fight our way out of the compound, I want him to be armed." With a satisfied grunt, she reached deep into the stack of weapons and pulled out a piece of ash two paces in length.

They moved deeper into the building, searching for the stairs leading to the dungeons where Weir kept his prisoners. Men in blue rushed past them as word spread of the attack, while women with disheveled hair and faces contorted by fear, some not fully dressed, poured from the officers' quarters. The press grew thicker, and cries of alarm and panic merged with the echoes of strident voices giving orders. Rokha took Adora by the hand and pulled her forward.

As abruptly as a water pitcher running dry, the logjam of bodies disappeared, and they stood at the head of a flight of stairs descending into the gut rock of the island. None of the blue-coated men took any notice of them; they all moved the other way, intent on the cries of their fellows.

Rokha released her hand. "Pull your sword around, Princess. I doubt women are allowed down there. Whatever men we meet we'll likely have to fight."

Adora stroked the worn leather of her sword's hilt, as if it could still the furious drum of her heart or erase the metallic taste at the back of her throat. "I thought you weren't going to call me that unless I did something foolish."

Rokha snorted without humor. "I think this qualifies."

"But this was your idea."

Rokha's full mouth pulled to one side in a wry grimace. "That should teach you not to go along with someone just because they tell you what you want to hear."

Adora's response to the unfairness of the other woman's argument never left her lips. Rokha chose that moment to descend into darkness. The air grew colder and more damp. When they stepped on the broad landing, a glow of light came from the guardroom below.

"Stay close," Rokha muttered as she crept down the stairs, each foot placed in front with care. Adora trailed her right hand along the wall and matched her pace. They came into the light of the guardroom, where a pair of guards with drawn swords stood facing them. When they spotted the women, confusion eased the glare each man wore, but they made no move to sheathe their weapons. Down a hallway, where Adora assumed the cells lay, a cry of agony bounced from the stone before trailing off to be followed seconds later by another.

"Did the duke send you?" the guard on the left asked. The other guard circled around to their right, toward Adora.

Rokha nodded. A brief sound of struggle came from one of the cells near the guardroom and another man's scream, lower, filled the space between the walls. "He wants the prisoners kept alive until the battle is over."

Doubt showed on the guard's face and the other guard edged nearer to Adora. He had light hair and close-set cruel eyes lit by surprise. "That's the princess."

"Don't be a fool," Rokha snapped. "The princess escaped."

The first guard shifted his attention to Adora. His scrutiny slid across her face with an almost physical touch before it landed on her hair.

"Kill them."

The guard closest to Adora rushed, darting through tables with an agility that surprised her. She drew and parried in the same motion, the clash of steel stinging her hand. He pressed, hacking at her with broad strokes. With each parry, shock numbed her arm for a split second, preventing her riposte. The next blow nearly struck the sword from her grip.

He came at her again with a vast overhand chop, forcing her back as his blade struck sparks from the floor. She jumped for the nearest table, rolling across it to place it between her and the guard. She flexed her arm, tried to force blood and feeling back into it.

He grinned at her, edged toward the table, laughing as he kicked it against her. She danced back, then dodged as he upended the barrier and sent it crashing toward her. The space between them cleared, and he came toward her, his sword forward, ready for another of those brutal chopping strokes.

She had to attack. If she didn't, he would wear her down until she couldn't hold her weapon. Worms of fear writhed in her gut as she forced her sword into line and moved forward. With an evil chuckle, the guard copied her. With a quick beat against his blade she skipped forward. As the guard brought his sword back to parry, she let her point slip beneath his and, carried by her momentum, lunged into a thrust that took him in the chest.

He died with his surprise still in his eyes.

When she turned, the other guard lay dead and Rokha was

sprinting toward the cells. Adora followed, averting her eyes after she saw Master Quinn sprawled like a broken marionette inside the first cell. A flurry of sword strokes sounded in the gloom ahead of her.

With a twisting thrust, Rokha put Weir's executioner down. A ring of keys fell from his hand, clinking like small brass bells against the floor. The smell of blood filled the prison. Rokha was covered with it. Ru's daughter flipped the keys toward her. "Find him."

Adora caught the ring with her free hand. "You're not coming?"

Rokha shook her head. "I might be able to save some of these men. Send healers down here as quickly as you can."

Adora continued down the hall calling Errol's name as she went. *Oh, Deas.* What if she had already passed him? She tried calling again, but sobs choked the sound, mocking her. Voices and hands came through the small barred windows, but none of them belonged to him.

Then she heard him, his voice warm as the promise of a midday sun breaking through clouds. The keys trembled in her hands, and she cursed their defiance. When the door opened at last, she filled his arms, crying his name as his hand stroked her hair while her tears wet his filthy clothes.

8

RUIN

H E HELD HER CLOSE, drinking in the scent of winter on her hair, savoring the longing for the Sprata it woke in him. Over her shoulder, Martin's grin held a rakish look, while Luis's contained something bittersweet, hinting at a story and perhaps yet another secret, but Errol no longer felt the need to know everything.

Adora pushed him back, scrubbing tears from her eyes. "You stink."

"I've been meaning to talk to the innkeeper about the accommodations."

Martin chuckled and pulled at the jaw muscles of his large bluff face. "It's probably too late to do that now. I think there's been a change of management. How many men did you bring with you?"

Adora shook her head, and her face grew hard, harder than Errol remembered ever seeing it. "There was only Rokha and me down here, Pater. Weir's guards started killing prisoners as soon as we arrived."

"Is it over?"

She shrugged. "It may only have just begun. We came straight here. Everyone else is at the palace."

An image of Liam in danger dropped against Errol's stomach like a stone. "I need your sword."

Adora shook her head. "There's a staff in the guardroom. Rokha grabbed it for you."

He nodded his thanks and left, expecting Adora to remain behind with Martin and Luis. Instead she followed him, her strides matching his in the narrow hallway. He thought of telling her to stay with Martin and Luis, or to head back to the city, to safety, but he knew she wouldn't listen. He removed as much of his longing for her from his voice as he could. "If you're with me, I won't be able to concentrate on fighting."

She grabbed his arm, pulling him to a stop. "We will speak of this later, Earl Stone. There are some levers you should not use."

He nodded, kept his face impassive even as he steeled himself. "I would use anything to keep you safe." He watched her expression flash from surprise to affection to annoyance before she growled in surrender.

"Go then." Kissing his cheek, she rushed back into the dungeon's bowels.

He passed Rokha, who tossed him a staff. His hands slid along the grain until it balanced in his grip. Caution slowed him despite the urgency driving him forward. In the dark, one unseen arrow or sword stroke could kill him, and he needed to live for now. Yet when he crested the stairs and entered the courtyard, only servants and women streaming away from the royal palace could be seen.

He moved against the tide until he came within sight of the palace entrance. Even at that distance it was plain fighting had ceased. Men in blue stood bunched outside, their swords bared but hanging at their sides. Few of them bore signs of fighting; they pressed forward instead, listening.

Errol circled around until he came to the entrance at the kitchens, where a knot of watchmen with bows and arrows nocked stood just inside, protected from attack but covering the yard. "Stand," one of them said. "State your business."

He lifted his staff overhead. "I'm Errol Stone. I've come for Liam."

"Approach."

Twenty paces brought him close enough to identify the speaker as Sergeant Fann, slender, dark-haired, and even better with a bow than a sword. "You know me, Fann. Let me pass."

He lowered his bow, and Errol felt a knot loosen at the base of his neck. "Aye, pass. Captain Liam is in the throne room with the others." He growled something else under his breath Errol couldn't make out.

He passed through their midst and made his way up the servants' staircase toward the grand hall. At the top of the stairs, two more men of the watch guarded the way, their swords clean, but their expressions grim. What had happened here?

The stairwell opened out onto a hallway wide enough for fifteen men to march abreast. Carnage met his gaze. The battle to take the Weir had been costly. Dozens of bodies—mostly blue-clad guards but dotted with those of black-garbed watchmen—littered the floor, and little rivulets of blood filled the space between flagstones. The survivors of each side had formed up in ranks opposite each other—tense, ready to fight.

Errol walked their length in a bizarre imitation of a commander at parade. Lieutenants of the watch nodded him past until he came to the throne room, where splashes of crimson painted the floor and furniture alike. Cruk stood to one side, using his teeth and right hand to knot a bandage around a shallow wound in his left arm. He punctuated each jerk on the cloth with a muttered curse in his graveled voice.

Duke Weir, his brother, and Benefice Dane stood at one end, Dane smiling as if the swords leveled at them by soldiers of the watch were his to command. Liam, Reynald, Merodach, and Rale stood a few paces away speaking in tones Errol couldn't hear, but their gestures radiated tension.

Rale saw him, beckoned him over.

"Good to see you alive, lad."

He nodded, unsure of what to say.

Rale must have caught his confusion. "Duke Weir bargains—so far successfully—for his life."

The reason behind Dane's triumphant smile became clear. Errol's face heated as though someone had placed a torch beneath it. He wanted nothing more at that moment than to beat Dane senseless, thrash him until that insolent grin disappeared. "If he is using the members of the Judica and the conclave as leverage, he doesn't have any. Rokha is freeing them now."

Rale nodded in approval, but nothing in his countenance changed. "Look out the windows behind the throne and tell me what you see."

Errol moved to peer through one of the large clear panes framed with stained glass. In the moonlight beyond, ships crowded the harbor, each one with a brazier as big across as a man was tall and filled with fire. Rale edged in beside him.

Errol pointed at the flaming lights. "He can't be stupid enough to fire on the palace."

Rale snorted. "No, Weir plays a more dangerous game. Unless we free him and make him king, he'll fire the ships. Illustra's best chance to defend the strait against Merakh will end up as so much charcoal at the bottom of the harbor."

Errol stared at Rale, convinced his heart had quit beating. "You're considering this?" He almost shouted.

Rale's eyebrows lowered until his eyes became slits over his broad nose. "He will not be king," he whispered. He pointed at the other captains with his chin. "We are agreed. But Merakhi longboats are no match in a fight for the high-decked cogs Weir commands. If we do not diminish their numbers in the strait, we will find ourselves spread along a front that stretches the length of the southern provinces. We'll be fighting from Basquon through Talia to Lugaria."

"He's a traitor and a murderer, Rale." He couldn't quite keep the pleading from his voice. "If we leave him alive, he'll betray us the first chance he gets."

"I agree," Cruk said from behind. "Pure foolishness to leave a viper in our midst."

Captain Reynald joined them, his face twisted as if he argued both sides within himself. "The archbenefice and the primus are on their way. They will speak for the church and the conclave. I think I would like all the captains to speak for the watch."

Cruk grunted. "You are our senior, Reynald. It's your place."

The captain sighed, then shook his head. "We're looking at a two-front war come spring. Now's not the time to stand on tradition. All the captains will speak." He turned to face Errol, his manner formal. "Earl Stone, though your captaincy is, strictly speaking, honorary, I believe your voice should be heard."

Errol sighed. "Then you'll probably want to hear from Martin and Luis as well. They're in the cells beneath the barracks."

They moved to a private audience chamber beside the throne room, exchanging the vaulted ceilings and stained glass for a windowless space with simple, comfortable chairs surrounding a wide table that could seat twenty. Errol inhaled through his nose, caught a suggestion of the musty, old-man's scent he associated with Rodran.

In the king's absence, the head of the table remained empty. Reynald sat at the third chair, leaving the first two empty as well. The rest of the captains seated themselves in no particular order after him. Errol took the chair next to Captain Indurain, a tall rangy Basqu with a hooked nose. He acknowledged Errol's presence with a nod but didn't speak.

Duke Weir and his contingent came in under guard. Weir glowered and moved to sit at the head of the table.

Reynald pointed to one side. "Remove the duke's party to the corner until Archbenefice Canon determines his status at these negotiations."

Weir's eyes widened, and he chewed his lower lip in outrage, but Dane laughed as if at a jest. They sat for the next few minutes in uncomfortable silence until Martin and Luis entered, followed by the archbenefice and the primus.

Bertrand Canon, leader of the church in Illustra, seated himself to the left of Rodran's vacant chair and scowled, his grizzled eyebrows lowering like storm clouds. His trembling finger pointed at Weir. "Can someone explain to me why he's still alive?"

"I live because I hold the fate of Illustra in my hands."

Canon's eyes became shards of ice. "You will address me as Archbenefice."

Dane cleared his throat. "Please allow me to answer your query, esteemed archbenefice." He bowed deeply, his eyes reduced to slits by a sarcastic grin. "Duke Weir has commanded that the entire fleet be put to the torch unless he is made sovereign of Illustra, as is his right, most holy one. If a message is not conveyed to the ships in his hand by daybreak, they will all burn."

Canon eyed Dane as if he were a bug that had somehow appeared in his porridge. He leaned toward Sten. "I think I prefer the duke's form of disrespect. Is this true, Reynald?"

The captain spread his hands. "We do not know, Archbenefice, but I think it likely. Duke Weir strikes me as the sort of man who would happily destroy the kingdom if he could not rule it."

Enoch Sten nodded. "Quite."

"Quite," Weir echoed, his face hard and resolute. "Magis stole the crown from my ancestor. The rule of Illustra belongs to me."

"If you believe that," Martin said, "let the conclave cast for the rightful king."

Dane pointed at Errol. "So you can have your tame omne proclaim the result you desire? Hardly."

At the edge of Errol's vision, Luis whispered to Martin, who paled and then nodded. He turned toward the archbenefice, unwilling to comment further. Canon addressed the primus, Enoch Sten. "My friend, how long would it take you to test the duke's assertion?"

Sten caught Luis's gaze. "It's a simple yes or no cast, Archbenefice. The secondus can check for one answer while I check the other. The omne can verify. Perhaps ten minutes."

Canon shook his head. "No. I mean you no disrespect, Secondus, but I can see by your appearance that you have suffered misuse at the duke's hands. I would not give outsiders the excuse of saying we acted out of a desire for vengeance."

Luis bowed from the neck. "Of course, Excellency." His hand dipped into his cloak. "I took the liberty of retrieving a few blanks on the way here. Primus?"

Sten accepted the blocks with a nod of thanks. Twenty minutes later, during which time Weir and his contingent had worn various expressions of superiority, the primus sighed and waved one hand in disgust. "The duke, on this occasion, is speaking the truth. He will destroy the ships."

"Of course," Weir said. "The throne of Illustra is mine."

"Perhaps," Enoch Sten said, "we do not require the duke's ships so much as he would like us to believe."

Weir laughed a series of barks in Sten's direction. "Stick to your little blocks of wood, old man. Even your pitiful captains have more sense. Illustra is facing a two-front war. There's no way to get enough men to the Ladoga Pass to keep the Morgols from flooding through once the snow melts. The kingdom's only hope of avoiding defeat is to sink the Merakhi ships in the Forbidden Strait. If they can't land, they can't fight."

Errol struggled to breathe. Were they seriously considering giving Weir the throne? After everything he had done?

The archbenefice leaned back in his chair and folded his hands on the small paunch of his old-man's belly as he regarded the duke. "Of course, one of the questions we must consider is what kind of kingdom we would have under the duke's rule."

Benefice Dane favored the archbenefice with an indulgent smile. "Surely you're not suggesting being conquered by the Merakhi or Morgols is preferable to rule by one of Illustra's oldest and most venerated houses?"

"No," the archbenefice said, drawing out the word. "What I am suggesting is that rule by Duke Weir would be indistinguishable from that of the Merakhi or Morgols."

He turned to address Captain Reynald as Dane sputtered. "What say you, Captain? Can we win a two-front war?"

"With your permission, Archbenefice, I would ask all of the captains to speak to this matter, including honorary captain, Earl Stone."

Across the table, Benefice Dane clapped his hands in applause. "Oh, by all means, let us hear from the peasant. Perhaps he can tell us which roots in the forest are edible."

Bertrand Canon's voice dipped, became almost a whisper, but in the unexpected silence it carried to every corner of the table. "The duke is bargaining for his life, Benefice Dane. So far he has made no request concerning yours. Do you understand?"

Duke Weir's brother spluttered his indignation. "How dare you threaten a benefice of the church?"

The archbenefice snorted. "Don't you mean your son, Benefice Weir? Be silent or I shall ask the primus to cast and see whether or not you've compounded a break of your vows with the additional crime of raising your illegitimate son to wear the red of a benefice."

He turned from their reddened faces as if they no longer existed. "Captain Elar, what say you?"

Rale glanced at Cruk, who gave a single, brief shake of his head, and said, "No one in their right mind fights a two-front war if it can be avoided. With that as our starting point we're left with only one viable option. Find a way without the duke's ships to turn the situation back into a one-front war."

Rale took a deep breath, as if consideration of such a plan daunted him. "We could scorch the earth east of the tri-cities to the Ladoga Pass and south to Talia and Basquon. Bring the people of the kingdom west and north. Force our enemies to use up their stores marching through land that will not feed them. We could meet their combined armies at a place of our choosing and fight a one-front war there."

The archbenefice and the primus stared at Rale as if he'd shouted some unutterable blasphemy. Even Duke Weir looked shocked.

"By all that's holy, do you know what you're saying?" Enoch Sten asked. "You would turn Illustra into a nation of refugees. Do you know how many people would die under such a strategy?"

Rale nodded. "I do not recommend this course of action unless we are at our utmost need. You wanted an alternative to Duke Weir's bargain. I have offered it."

Uncounted masses of people uprooted from home and livelihood would fill the cities until they burst. Starvation and plague would follow. The exodus would kill more people than the war. Errol's throat constricted around a hopeless emptiness. They would have to accept Duke Weir's help and his price.

Canon looked as if he'd been punched in the gut. "Captain Cruk, surely you have something to suggest that will mitigate Elar's dour pronouncement."

Cruk shook his head slowly. "No. His assessment is accurate so far as it goes. What he didn't say was that our ability to wage war will be severely compromised by the presence of so many refugees behind our line of battle. If we deplete the farmlands behind the front, the lack of food will defeat us. So the question becomes, who starves first, us or our enemies?" His face twisted to the side in a grimace. "Not exactly the smartest way to wage war."

The archbenefice questioned the other captains, but Indurain maintained that his expertise lay in individual combat, not strategy, and Merodach merely shook his head.

"Errol," Archbenefice Canon said, "though you have no cause to love Illustra, the church, or her nobility, I would ask you to convey your thoughts. Of all of us seated at this table you alone have borne the responsibilities of every branch of our kingdom. As a reader and the only living omne, you are part of the church. In addition, as earl, you are the only noble present that may bring an accusation against the duke. Finally, though you did not accept it, you passed the challenge to become one of the watch, and Reynald made you an honorary captain. Do you see any way Illustra may be saved?"

Across the table, Dane snorted. "Yes, let's hear the wisdom of the Earl of Peasants."

The archbenefice signaled two men of the watch. "Benefice Dane seems to have forgotten his place at this gathering. Please avail yourselves of the opportunity to remind him. I don't know that you need to be overly gentle in your instruction."

Dane goggled as the men lifted him from his chair. "You pathetic old man. You will die in your folly. You will—"

One of the guard's fists truncated the remainder of his statement, and Dane spit blood and pieces of teeth. The archbenefice and the primus regarded Errol once more. They leaned forward, waiting for him to speak. Yet when Errol met their gaze, both men cut their glance to include Liam.

The advice of the captains had been for show. Canon and Sten were certain either he or Liam was destined to be king and, like Magis, would save Illustra in death. The archbenefice and the primus were going to let Errol and Liam decide the fate of Weir and the kingdom.

He wanted to throw up.

"I don't know what to say, Your Excellency. Dane's insults hold a large measure of truth. I was a peasant for much longer than I've been a reader or an earl. And as far as being an omne, I think that was just an accident of birth, like having blue eyes. It doesn't really have much to do with me."

"Your humility becomes you, Errol," Primus Sten said. "But what do you think we should do?"

They couldn't win. Even with the duke's ships, the malus-infected Merakhi would find a way to invade Illustra, and they would ravage the kingdom until he or Liam met their leader in combat at the time appointed by Deas and died. The captains and the archbenefice were engaged in a game of pretend.

"If we make Duke Weir king, we will gain his ships, but how many men will we lose because we put a murderer on the throne? I don't know as much about strategy as Cruk or Rale—Elar, I mean—but one of the things they taught me was that men need to believe in their leaders. If our king resembles what we're fighting against, what are we fighting for?"

Errol looked around the table. Most of the men appeared as if he'd just asked them to take poison. Merodach gave a sharp nod, followed by Indurain, then Cruk and Rale.

The archbenefice sighed. "What say you, Liam?"

He rose from his chair, his blond hair falling to his shoulders like a mantle and his eyes gleaming. "I think Errol Stone's humility is the most perfect embodiment of nobility I have seen. And I would add this—how can we expect Deas's favor if we knowingly elevate a usurper?"

Archbenefice Bertrand Canon sighed, his gaze fixed on his hands folded on the table in front of him. "Dissent?"

Silence filled the room, grew heavy. No one spoke.

Canon lifted his head. "The deed must be done quickly. We must not risk his rescue and a protracted civil war."

Benefice Weir started from his chair, eyes popping. "You are dooming yourselves," the benefice whined. "You must reconsider this rashness."

"Be quiet, brother. They mean to kill us now," Duke Weir snarled. "Which one of you will swing the sword that dooms the kingdom?" He looked at Errol. "Will you do it, puppy?"

Archbenefice Canon shook his head. "You will not die at the hand of any here." He turned to Reynald. "Captain, please select one of the watch, not an officer, to dispatch the criminals." He eyed Weir with iron-willed resolve. "We'll have to display their bodies as proof. No beheadings, if you please."

9

SCOUR

MARTIN FINGERED THE THICK CASSOCK that warmed him against the predawn chill of the cathedral stones. Deas have mercy, he needed a bed. A hot bath and clean clothes had not assuaged his need for sleep, only accentuated it. Luis stood on his left, as he had twice before when they'd set out for Callowford. Errol and Karele, the small man he still thought of as the master of horses, stood on the other side. Errol seemed only slightly less nervous than Martin himself. As for Karele, the little man appeared unaffected by anything outside the shadow lands.

Bertrand Canon's door opened. Cleatis, his secretary, nodded greetings to each of them, without allowing them entrance. "His Excellency is asleep, Benefice Arwitten." His voice held a strong note of remonstration.

Martin sighed. "I'm no longer a benefice, Cleatis. Wake him."

The secretary's face puckered into a circle of disapproval, but he disappeared into the expansive interior of the archbenefice's apartments.

Canon emerged after a few short moments, his hair disheveled but his eyes alert. He shrugged. "Old men sleep lightly when they sleep at all, and I am older than most. What concern brings you to me early enough to escape the notice of the rest of humanity, my friend?"

Now that the moment was upon him, thin needles of dread danced up and down Martin's spine. He took a deep breath to summon his courage. With a bow to Canon's office he met the man's gaze and cut his eyes to the archbenefice's secretary. "I have come to make confession, Excellency."

Canon's eyes widened with surprise, but the good-natured smile didn't slip from his face. "And you have brought interesting witnesses with you, I see. I always enjoy your approach to orthodoxy, Martin. Your unique interpretation of the traditions of the church never fails to lighten the tedium of an otherwise dull proceeding."

He turned to his secretary. "Thank you, Cleatis. You may withdraw. I will send someone for you when Pater Martin and I are done."

Martin raised his hand. "A moment please, Cleatis. Would you be so kind as to ask Primus Sten to join us? I feel the need for his witness most acutely."

Canon's secretary nodded and withdrew. They waited in silence until Sten, bleary-eyed and heavily robed, joined them. The archbenefice sniffed and gave himself a shake. "All right, Martin, we're all here. What's this about?"

He turned away from Canon's gaze to pace the floor. "I pray that you grant me indulgence to confess, Excellency?"

The archbenefice's thick white eyebrows rose, and he took his lower lip between his teeth in thought. When he addressed Martin again, his voice mirrored the formality. "Very well, Pater. You have invoked the office of confession. In front of these witnesses, I grant you permission to proceed. Speak no word that is untrue and omit no detail that might serve to deceive. You are adjured by Deas, Eleison, and unknowable Aurae."

Again, the archbenefice's clear blue-eyed gaze robbed Martin of the ability to speak. His steps measured the length of Canon's audience chamber, came back again. "Well, that's the point, isn't it? For centuries we've put the acolytes at their tables with ink and parchment, copying the liturgy of the church because we didn't have Magis's book, and every sheet of lambskin or vellum sent out from the isle, even to the smallest church in the most insignificant province, says Aurae is unknowable."

He took a deep shuddering breath, felt it leave his lungs in stuttering puffs of air. "And it's all wrong, Excellency. Aurae is knowable."

Canon's lips tightened in disapproval. His hands clenched the arms of his chair as if only a supreme effort of will kept him from denouncing Martin where he stood. "Pater Martin, your confession takes a most unexpected form. Are you stating fact or belief? I'm sure I need not remind you that many have gone to the block for espousing that heresy."

Martin bowed. "It is a fact, Excellency, and the reason I have asked Primus Sten here as a witness. I did not think you would trust the demonstration of proof to the secondus or the omne, since much of my journey has been shared by them."

Canon's gaze never left Martin's face, but he lifted one hand to beckon the primus forward. "Do you have your tools of office with you, Enoch?"

The primus nodded, his wispy hair fluttering with the motion. "When Cleatis summoned me, I suspected you might desire a cast." He glanced at Martin. "Though I only brought ten blanks. If the pater's demonstration requires more, we'll have to send someone to the conclave."

Martin shook his head, his stomach roiling inside like a pot of boiling water. "I do not believe so, Primus, though His Excellency may require it."

Canon regarded him, licked his lips with a pale tongue. "I find myself unprepared for such a demonstration, Martin. I think perhaps it would be best if we continued the form of the confession. There is a tale here, and I would hear it before we engage the primus in his craft."

He moved across the room, retrieved a chair, and seated himself. At his wave, the others did likewise.

Grateful the archbenefice had asked him to do so, and hoping the telling would somehow lessen the shock, Martin related his journey. Yet when he spoke of Cruk's near-death injury and their meeting with Karele, he realized he had been mistaken. Canon's thick eyebrows began a gradual climb up his forehead and stayed there. By the time Martin mentioned his encounter with Aurae in the council of the shadow lands, his superior's eyes were wide with surprise and disbelief. Yet the biggest shock remained.

Martin brought his portion of the tale to a close at the point where Lord Weir's treachery landed them in a Merakhi prison, with the captains forced to fight in the arena until they died. He turned to the young man in the chair behind him, his narrow face still boyish and open. Still.

"Errol, would you please relate what happened to you?"

To the lad's credit, he didn't protest. He rose, so different from the boy he had been, and walked the space in front of the archbenefice as he spoke of captivity, his friendship with Hadari, the ilhotep's Ongolese guard, and his encounter with the book.

Canon lurched forward in his seat. "What?"

"I read the book, Excellency," Errol said. "The book of the history of Deas and Eleison that Magis took to battle with him."

The archbenefice sat his chair, shaking his head in denial. "No. It was lost."

Martin bowed. "Lost, Excellency, not destroyed. Please continue, Errol."

"Hadari let me read it," Errol continued. "He wanted me to. The book says Aurae is knowable but incomprehensible."

"And I believe that wording, Excellency, is the source of our centuries-old error," Martin said.

Bertrand Canon slumped in his chair, slack-jawed, his right hand making vague summoning gestures in Sten's direction. The primus came forward and bent at the waist to place his head close to the archbenefice's.

"Yes, Excellency?"

Canon's mouth worked for a moment before any words came out. "Cast for this?"

"Which part?"

His eyes searched Errol and then swept to Martin and Karele. "All of it."

Sten straightened. "Your Excellency, it will take some time if I take each person's confession as a discrete quantity. There may be a more expedient approach."

The archbenefice snorted his vexation. "Out with it, man. What is it?"

"I can cast once to see if everything said is true."

"Why would you not?"

Primus Sten sighed. "Because it is not the same as casting to see if they are telling the truth. A man can believe he is speaking the truth even while he is quite wrong. This makes him mistaken, not a liar. Casting for absolute truth is a far more stringent cast than whether one believes what he is saying. Yet, I thought I should offer it in order to confirm Martin's, um, confession."

"Confession?" Canon snorted, turning to face Martin again. "You're trying to dump hundreds of years of church tradition into the sewer, Pater. You tricked me."

Martin bowed, accepting the rebuke. "My apologies, Excellency."

"Humph. Enoch, cast to see if everything said is true, absolutely true."

Twenty minutes later, Sten pulled the first of the lots from the drawing bag. "Yes."

Canon gaped. "Yes, what?"

The primus licked his lips. "Yes, it's all true."

The archbenefice pointed a shaking finger at the pine lot. "Draw again."

"How many times, Excellency?"

Canon's finger trembled in the air as if he were counting outcomes. "Twenty."

Moments later, Sten pronounced the results. "Seventeen out of twenty draws say Pater Martin and Errol Stone have spoken the absolute truth. There can be no doubt, Excellency."

Bertrand Canon's gaze swept to Martin again, but this time it passed over and through him, unseeing. Then his voice exploded, filling the room. "By all that's holy, why didn't you grab the book? Deas in heaven, Martin, we're at war! If we reveal this to the Judica, the chaos will be twice what it was during Weir's assault, ten times."

Martin winced at the rebuke. How many times in the past weeks had he reviled himself for not returning to the Merakhi capital to attempt recovery of the book? Only Deas knew how much of the upcoming wrangling in the Judica it would have eliminated.

"I'm sorry, my friend," Canon said. "That was uncharitable. Please forgive me." He breathed deeply, appeared to take hold of himself.

"Surely the timing of this is beyond coincidental, but it is difficult for me to see anything but evil in it." He shook his head in surrender. "If we tell the Judica the book still exists, they will be unable to think of anything else. And if we tell them Aurae is knowable and the solis Karele has the means to control the cast, they will dissolve into chaos, unable to confirm the most basic decisions."

He laughed but the sound contained no humor. "Forgive me for sounding less than grateful at your news, my friend, but your tidings hold edges that might bleed the kingdom of the surety it needs." He sighed, then pointed a pale, veined finger at Karele. "I think I would like to see this confounding of lots for myself."

Nearly an hour later, after several casts had yielded contradictory results, the archbenefice shook his head in wonderment. "Had I not seen it with my own eyes, I wouldn't have believed it." He grunted. "I'm still not sure I believe it."

He paused to run his hand slowly down his face before turning to Karele. "Is it possible for any power other than Aurae's to affect the lots this way?"

Karele shook his head. "Only Deas, through Aurae, can confound the cast."

The archbenefice breathed a sigh of relief. "That's something anyway." His mouth tightened. "I want every member of the Judica and conclave tested before word of this gets out. After that," he sighed, "Deas help us, it will be chaos."

Canon pronounced the Judica proceedings finished for the day and bade Errol and the rest to accompany him back to his chambers. Once there, his mien of unshakable confidence slipped from him like a discarded robe. "That makes three today, three out of twenty, and Deas alone knows how many more tomorrow."

Martin shrugged. "Hardly unexpected, Excellency. Weir brandished extraordinary power. Many perceived him as Illustra's best hope for survival. Three is not such a great number."

"There shouldn't have been any," Canon snarled. "The church is supposed to look to Deas and the conclave for . . ."

He stopped, his anger dissipating, and flopped in a chair. "I'm going to have to readjust my thinking." He gnawed one corner of his lower lip in frustration. "We're moving too slowly, gentlemen. At this rate it will take days to confirm the Judica, and then we must do the same with the conclave."

"That at least should go more quickly, Bertrand," Primus Sten said. "Every reader we confirm can assist us in confirming the rest." He covered a delicate cough. "We could have done the same with the Judica."

Canon chopped the air. "No. I will not trust vetting the benefices to any except those in this room. Too much is at stake."

Errol massaged the muscles between the forefinger and thumb of his left hand, then switched. He hadn't carved so many lots in succession since Naaman Ru held him prisoner. He was out of practice. "Since time is so important, Excellency, why did we adjourn so early?"

The archbenefice took a deep breath, appeared to relax before he spoke. "Our presence is requested at the palace by the council of nobles. Most have managed to make it back to the isle. They've asked the Judica to attend their gathering." He turned to regard Errol. "Earl Stone, have you had the pleasure of participating in the council's deliberations?"

"Only once, Excellency, when I was first raised to the nobility. I don't remember much of the proceedings."

"Ha." The archbenefice snorted. "If you think the Judica is long-winded, you're in for an unpleasant surprise. A simple rule, my boy—the more people you have in a council, the longer it's going to last. They're usually held at night to keep the deliberations as brief as possible. With this many people involved we'll be fortunate to adjourn before dawn."

The thought of having to participate in the proceedings as a member sent an icy drip of nervousness across Errol's skin. "What do they want to talk about?"

Bertrand Canon raised his eyebrows at him in surprise. "The defense of Illustra, Earl Stone. It won't be the Judica or the watch that musters the men who will fight on the kingdom's behalf, my friend." He sighed. "That task will fall to the nobles. From the greatest duchy to the meanest lord, the nobles will be responsible for conscripting an army to face our enemies once the weather breaks."

10

COUNCILS

ERROL SIDLED NEXT TO MARTIN on the walk from the archbenefice's quarters in the cathedral to the palace compound. The events of the morning had left him mentally fatigued. He wanted to sleep or work his staff in some private corner of the watch yard, but by the looks of resignation everyone wore as they trudged to the meeting of nobles, he wouldn't soon get to do either.

"What will it be like?" he asked.

"The archbenefice may have been charitable," the priest grumbled. "Without Rodran to impose some semblance of order, the nobles are unlikely to come to any consensus on how to prosecute the war."

Errol stifled a yawn. Now that the immediate crisis of revealing the truth about Aurae and the book of Magis to the archbenefice had passed, his body clamored for rest.

"Still," Martin continued, "Duke Escarion is a man of sound judgment, and with Weir gone he becomes the most powerful of the nobles. In another time, he would have made a fine king. Make sure you give him your support."

"Me?" The Escarion name sounded familiar to him, but he couldn't place it.

Martin shook his head and exhaled. "You're an earl now. You can be forgiven for being unfamiliar with your title and its responsibilities, lad, but your holding will be expected to fulfill its quota of men, arms, and supplies. Deas help us, it will be considerable."

Nobles waited in Illustra's throne room, a hall that could accommodate thousands in elevated rows of seating on either side of a long central walkway that led to the dais and royal throne. When their party entered, a man in the red livery of a palace guard announced them, and the nobles and benefices that filled the seats on opposite sides stood. As he surveyed the scores of people in the hall, an occasional sense of familiarity or recognition told him he'd seen some of these people before, but the collection of new faces overwhelmed his memory.

An escort took the archbenefice and the primus to the dais and seated them at a large table set up one step below the empty throne. Off to the side, barely noticed, Martin took a seat with Luis and Karele. The captains of the watch were seated at the same level on the opposite side of the throne.

One of the guards moved to intercept Errol before he seated himself. A tall man, fiftyish but fit, despite the gray at his temples and the web of wrinkles at the corners of his eyes, stood at the front row, calling for his attention. "Your pardon, Earl Stone, though you have no doubt earned a place at either table as an honorary captain or the omne, I would ask you to join the council of nobles on this occasion."

Errol shook his head. "How do you know me?"

"I told you he was modest to a fault," a brown-haired young man next to the speaker said. "If I had accomplished half so much, I'd simply sit back and allow the fairest maidens of the kingdom to shower me with the admiration that was my due."

Errol's face flushed. Now he remembered. The Escarion brothers—and the older man was their father, the duke.

The other brother shook his head in chagrin. "Stop it, Derek. You're embarrassing him." Darren paused to give him a supportive smile. "Besides, he has the prettiest girl in the kingdom already."

Derek smacked his forehead as if suddenly remembering. "Of course. If I had known tripping and falling at the feet of the princess would prove to be her undoing, I would have done it long ago."

The duke's eyes narrowed. "Are you two quite finished?"

"Yes," they answered together. Darren looked abashed, but Derek's eyes twinkled.

The nobles around them looked amused or affronted by turns, but Escarion turned his attention back to Errol. "Since your holding is within my domain, Earl Stone, I would ask you to take your place at my right."

He had just passed by a red-haired woman with delicate features when the duke stopped him. "Your pardon, Earl Stone, may I present my wife, Mickala, the Duchess of Escarion."

Errol eyed the woman in front of him, a hand shorter than himself with an open, welcoming smile—and she was young. Too young. He glanced between the woman and the duke's sons.

And blushed when Duchess Mickala Escarion laughed. "I assure you, Earl Stone, they're mine. My mother, Countess Murphy, could pass for my older sister." She eyed Derek and Darren with exasperation. "As you can see, in our family's male offspring, being slow to age is more internal than external."

The door opened, and every man and woman in attendance brightened as Adora moved with a stately walk down the center of the room. She mounted the dais and put out one hand to brush the purple velvet of Rodran's empty throne with trembling fingers before seating herself in a chair directly in front of it.

"Your Highness." Escarion bowed. "Thank you for attending."

Adora inclined her head in recognition. "Your invitation surprised me somewhat, Your Grace. With the passing of my uncle, my title is little more than bunting on a flag."

Escarion shot a veiled look toward Martin before turning to the archbenefice. At a nod from Canon, he clambered down from the first tier of seats and moved to the center of the hall.

"Assembled nobles, it is time to speak plainly of Illustra's need. Any of you who have cause to doubt what I tell you will have access to a reader and, if I may volunteer his services, the omne, to confirm the truth of my words."

Though Errol held a more intimate knowledge of the threats to Illustra than most present, the heightened tension of Escarion's words carried him with the rest of the assembly. The nobles were obviously ill-used to such honesty.

"Illustra," Escarion said, "is without a king. And it seems it may be without a king for some time."

Noise exploded through the hall as men shouted their fear and anger. Snippets of imprecations voiced by red-faced men buffeted Errol where he sat. "It's a plot of the Judica . . ." "conclave has failed . . ." "should have put Weir on the throne . . ."

Escarion withstood the torrent like a boulder in a flood, waiting until the shouting ebbed. "My lords," he said at last, "let us not confirm the kingdom's worst suspicions of us. Did I not tell you I would speak plainly? Before we descend into bickering, I would ask that you hear us out." He nodded to the primus.

Enoch Sten rose, raked his hand through the white of his beard, and sighed. Silence like a blanket covered the hall, and the air took on weight. "The truth is, my assembled nobles, the conclave has already cast for the next king." He held up his hand, waited for the resurgent uproar to subside. "And the cast has failed. Worse, we do not know why. In the hour of greatest need, our craft has deserted us."

Benefice Kell rose to his feet, his mouth tight. "Archbenefice, speak plainly. The Judica gave no order to the conclave to cast for the king before Rodran died." He bit his words as if they affronted him. "And Weir's usurpation has denied the Judica and the conclave the opportunity since."

Archbenefice Canon rose to face the red-robed members of

the Judica where they sat opposite the nobles. "In this, I confess Benefices Weir and Dane were correct. I appropriated the authority of the Judica unto myself. Six years ago I authorized the search for the next king. Rodran's decline had begun, yet the Judica would not authorize the cast while he lived. I will not say I regret the action, because I do not. I only regret the cast failed."

Duke Escarion endeavored to make his voice heard above the sudden din and despair, and at a moment of quiet, one of the nobles, a heavy man with a florid face and copper-red hair, stood. "Then who will command? We are not men of war. There has been no real war for more than twenty years."

Escarion nodded to Captain Reynald. The watchman stood, his face a study in reticence. "If you will allow it, my lords, the best among the watch at strategy and tactics will command until such time as the conclave can determine the soteregia."

"And who will those masters of strategy be?" Escarion asked.

Reynald turned to the table. "Captains Cruk and Elar will lead."

Most of the nobles and no small number of the Judica looked confused. Reynald sighed. "Most honored nobles and benefices, Illustra faces the threat of a two-front war. Merakhi forces are being marshaled against us at this moment, and scouts have brought us reports of an assembling of Morgols along the western border of the kingdom."

Next to Errol, Darren went pale. Even Derek looked worried.

Another noble, a duke according to his placement on the front row, stood with the help of a cane. "I have heard tale that the plains of the horsemen are endless and the men of the river kingdom fill the desert. How are we to win?" His voice cracked. "We have no allies, no means to defeat these overwhelming numbers."

A noble close to the back row stood, his soft face etched with fear. "Should we not sue for peace?"

Escarion shook his head. "Lord Mollis, these enemies do not seek peace. The Morgols are inscrutable, as always, but the Merakhi clearly desire our destruction."

The lord moaned and sat down.

The archbenefice nodded to Martin, who stood and moved to the middle of the hall. "Nobles and benefices, it is true that we have no allies as of yet, but Deas in his mercy may have provided one to help us in this time of need." His voice dropped, and everyone in attendance leaned forward, their faces illumined by sudden, impossible hope. "For centuries the church sent its excommunicates beyond its borders, outcast without worldly goods to the shadow lands south and east of the kingdom. I am sorry to say that not all banished were guilty. No others were permitted to go there—a needless precaution since none desired it.

"Yet I tell you that, through circumstances I believe were orchestrated by Deas himself, I have journeyed through the shadow lands. Did I find huddled rejects? No. Instead I found a nation that shares our belief in Deas, a nation that understands the dire consequences of the coming war, willing to be our ally."

A duke shot to his feet, tears of relief plain on his face. "How large is this nation you speak of, priest?"

Martin shrugged. "I'm not a military man, Your Grace, but I estimated their numbers to be equal to that of our largest province."

Duke Escarion rose from his seat, his hands raised for silence. "What do they desire? A nation of outcasts has no cause to love us."

The mood, hopeful only a heartbeat before, turned wary.

"Their main concern lies in the suspicion that we will regard them as a subject province and that their men will be asked to take the brunt of war."

Benefice Kell, who only months earlier had accused Errol of consorting with herbwomen and spirits, jerked to his feet. "Should they not? They are a nation of excommunicates. If the Judica decides, as it should, that their penance is to fight for us, then that is what they will do."

Martin shook his head, his face contorted with disgust. "Benefice Kell, the people of the shadow lands are not ours to command. If you excommunicate a man and drive him from his country, you also give up any right to command him."

Archbenefice Canon banged his staff of office twice on the floor. "Well spoken, Benefice Arwitten. Tell us, what surety do they desire?"

Martin turned to address Adora. "Your Highness, the council that rules the shadow lands requested that Illustra's ruler personally guarantee their autonomy in war and peace. In short, they desire that our ruler journey to them and sign a pact."

Adora, her blond hair glinting silver in the bright light of the hall, furrowed her brows. "I am not Illustra's sovereign, good priest."

"But you are the last of Rodran's line, Your Highness, and as we have stated, the cast for a new king has failed."

"I am willing to go." Adora stood to address the hall. "Nobles and benefices, are you willing to abide by the treaty I negotiate?"

The nobles, to a man, appeared to be in favor, which made perfect sense to Errol. Martin had offered an ally unknown to them a few minutes before. But the Judica appeared split. Benefice Kerran seemed to be in favor, but suppressed fury mottled Benefice Kell's face.

Errol leaned toward Duke Escarion. "If the Judica comes out against the alliance, what will happen?"

The duke sighed. "Tough to say, Earl Stone. Alliances between nations are the purview of the king. In his absence it would seem logical to have the responsibility fall to the council of nobles, but we are unused to such authority. I expect many in the Judica view the shadow lands as a people beyond the succor of the church and unworthy of alliance."

"Can't Archbenefice Canon decide?"

The duke sighed. "He could make the attempt, lad, but his confession of casting for the new king without the Judica's approval has weakened his position. The benefices might not fully trust him."

The archbenefice rapped his staff against the floor three times. "In light of the political nature of the request and in Rodran's absence, the Judica relinquishes authority in this manner to the council of nobles. As archbenefice, I so rule."

Next to Errol, Duke Escarion grunted in surprise.

"Then you should not be archbenefice!" Kell screamed. "You have admitted to usurping the authority of the Judica, and now you would bind us to these excommunicates in contravention of Deas's will." He wheeled to speak to the rest of the Judica. "I posit we remove Bertrand Canon as archbenefice."

Canon leaned forward in his seat. "You may so posit once the Judica sits, Benefice Kell, but we are not within the halls of the Judica; we are guests at the council of nobles, and it is their will that rules here, not ours. Sit down." Kell took his seat, his motions stiff with repressed fury. Canon nodded toward the duke, who stood with a sigh and looked to the men gathered around him.

"What say you?" Escarion asked.

Every noble voted in favor of the alliance and of giving Princess Adora the authority to negotiate on Illustra's behalf. In the palpable relief that flowed through Errol and the outrage that flowed back and forth between the Judica and the council, he did not notice Martin's approach until the priest stood before him.

"We need your help, lad." His dark brown eyes were grave beneath the silver of his brows.

"What do you want me to do?"

"Canon has lost the Judica. If we don't regain them, they'll depose him at tomorrow's sitting. The kingdom can't afford that, Errol. He's one of the few things holding Illustra together." He leaned in close. "I want you to tell them about the book."

Errol nodded, though the thought of addressing the crowd turned his stomach.

Martin smiled. "Let me introduce you."

Martin moved to the center of the room and stood, implacable as granite, waiting for the din to exhaust itself. At last, an expectant silence filled the hall.

"Benefices and nobles, let me speak plainly," Martin said. This brought a snort of disbelief from more than one spectator. "Illustra will need more than an alliance with the people of the shadow lands to stem the tide that threatens us. The nomads fill the steppes, and the people of the river are as numerous as the sand. We are desperate." He paused to survey the room. "Yes, I said *desperate*, and a desperate kingdom must take desperate chances."

Martin beckoned to Errol. As they stood together in the midst of everyone's expectation, Martin leaned in. "Do not ask me how I know, lad. I'm not sure I understand it myself, but I think this can secure the archbenefice's position. Tell them."

He lacked Martin's oratorical skills, and under the scrutiny of those present, his gestures and words felt stilted and artificial. Yet everyone there fixed an unswerving gaze upon Errol as he related his time in Merakh. When he finished, no uproar of hope or disbelief filled the hall, only astonishment too deep for sound.

The benefices stood as a whole, their faces at once stricken and hopeful. Little more than a whisper, the question came. "What did it say?"

Errol darted a glance at Martin, who shook his head briefly, but his intention remained unclear. With the gaze of every churchman and noble present fastened on him like leeches in a slow-moving stream, he waited. His fingers twitched, unsure of themselves.

Kell lifted his hand, his face hard. "Surely you do not expect us to believe you have read the book unless you offer some token of the truth."

The archbenefice spoke. "Earl Stone's testimony has been verified by cast." Canon looked directly at Benefice Kell. "But for those who doubt, you have access to the conclave. Test the truth of his words for yourself."

One of Kell's blue-veined hands waved the archbenefice's offer away. "Duke Weir and his brother have taught me to question the surety of lots. I would hear Earl Stone speak so that I can determine the truth or falsehood in his words."

Errol shifted to face Benefice Kell. "A token?"

Kell nodded, his assent backed by the avid postures of the rest of the Judica.

"'The three are these,'" Errol quoted, "'Deas the creator, Eleison the son, and the spirit, Aurae, who is knowable but incomprehensible.'"

Silence so heavy its stifled breath covered the hall for the space of half a dozen heartbeats before it erupted. Errol covered his ears, but Martin hid his face in his hands.

"You lie!"

Errol heard the words echo over and again, hammering at him like the pounding of water beneath the falls of the Sprata, but Kell only stared silently. As the clamor began to subside, he tottered forward on his spindly legs—his benefice's robe hanging on him as if he'd shrunk under the weight of his responsibility—and came to stand within an arm's length, searching Errol's face.

The hall stilled, waiting.

Kell's lips quivered. "It's true, isn't it? That's what the book really said."

Errol nodded.

Tears hung in the old man's eyes, and he put his hand on Errol in a gesture of infinite longing. "Has he spoken to you?"

Errol ducked his head from the weight of Kell's regard. "I'm not sure, but he has spoken to Martin."

The priest jerked at the mention of his name.

"Truly?" Kell asked.

Martin darted a look at the archbenefice before answering. "Yes. I've heard Aurae in a voice like the wind."

A red-faced benefice stood at the back. "I will not believe it. Not until I see the book for myself." He flung his arms at the rest of the Judica. "Any man could say he has heard the voice of Aurae, and there would be none to gainsay him. How can we test the truth of his words?"

"By lot, Benefice Tomah, as we always have," Canon said.

Tomah shook his head, his dark hair and dark eyes intent. "No. I do not question the lot, but I can no longer give unquestioning authority to a conclave made of men. I ask again: Without lots how can we verify the truth of a man's claim of Aurae?"

A hum filled the hall as nobles and churchmen muttered asides, grappling with Errol's revelation and Tomah's insistent question.

Martin shook his head. "That was poorly done, Errol." He pointed over Kell's shoulder toward the Judica, where men squirmed as if they'd suddenly been stripped of their authority. "The Judica is broken. Until they can answer the question of their own authority, they'll scarcely be able to exercise it."

Kell turned his stricken face to Errol, his rheumy eyes spilling his grief. "Why didn't you bring it home?"

A puff of wind washed the heat from him and Errol turned to address the Judica. "Benefice Tomah, since you no longer trust the conclave to verify questions placed before you, what would you trust?"

The churchman's mouth worked in silence, as if he labored to articulate his desire. "The book," he blurted. He turned a tight circle, looking for support from his fellow benefices. "What other truths have the ravages of time taken from the church? Deas forgive us. We may have been the authors of the very heresy we have striven to prevent. We must have the book."

Benefice Kerran stood amid a hundred murmured conversations that filled the hall like the droning of a beehive. "Where is the book now?"

Errol sighed. "I hope Hadari lived to retrieve it, but I do not know."

"You didn't cast for it?"

A laugh that touched the edge of hysteria bubbled up from his chest. "I have not been afforded the opportunity, Benefice."

Kerran flushed and nodded. "My apologies, Earl Stone. I spoke without thinking."

Errol shrugged. "If Hadari lives and the book is in his possession, he is likely in Ongol by now."

Benefice Kerran nodded and turned to Canon. "Archbenefice, with your indulgence I would ask Primus Sten to cast for the location of the book."

The primus stood. "I would gladly honor your request, Benefice, but a cast to pinpoint the book may take some time."

"Can we not simply test to see if it lies within the domain of the Ongolese?"

Martin turned to Benefice Tomah. "Will you trust the conclave in this?"

At Tomah's nod, Sten pulled his knife and began, and bare minutes later, Sten held the lot aloft as if the assembled nobles could read the answer he held. "The book of Magis lies in Ongol."

"We must retrieve it," Tomah demanded, but more than one noble and churchman shook their head in denial.

"Benefice Tomah," Canon said, "as much as I appreciate and share your desire for surety in this time, the book is beyond our grasp. Ongol lies to the south of Merakh. Even in peace the route is closed to us."

"Then send a ship!" Tomah cried.

Canon shook his head, heavy with regret. "You know we cannot. No mariner has ever succeeded in sailing to the people of the verdant."

A draft touched Errol's face, as though the air in the hall had twisted upon itself. *Oh, Deas.* He knew what he had to do.

"No ship sent to Ongol has ever returned," Martin echoed.

Even if they did not ask him, he would volunteer. A pang of sorrow threaded through the lightness in his heart at the thought of seeing Hadari and the book again. He looked at Adora, the amazing green of her eyes a mixture of pride and grief. She knew.

He faced the archbenefice. "I will go."

"No!" Martin cut the air with one hand, his gesture a duplicate of Canon's. "You cannot."

Errol smiled. "Even if Deas commands it?"

Canon made a motion that sent Martin to Errol's side. The heavy priest took his arm, pulled him close to hear soft imprecations. "You know you cannot, Errol. You or Liam will be king. This much we know. Illustra cannot let you go on this fool's quest."

"How many times have I almost died?" Errol asked. "You keep saying Deas's hand is upon me." He lifted his hands, palms up. "If that's true he will bring me back to . . ." His voice caught, and he forced himself to continue, " . . . to do whatever he has planned." He leaned closer so only Martin could hear him. "Inquire of Aurae, Pater."

Martin held his heavy jowls tight with stubborn refusal, before his brows lifted in surprise. "Deas, have mercy."

Like a man lifting burdens, he turned to the archbenefice. "I think we should cast the question, Your Excellency. I have lived to regret my assumptions before. I would not have the kingdom suffer for them now."

"You know what they'll find," Errol said.

Martin nodded. "Yes, and I also know that most of the men in this room are not prepared for the implications of your discovery."

Twenty minutes later a dozen readers reached the same conclusion: Errol was supposed to go to Ongol.

The archbenefice stood and then lowered, and for a moment Errol thought the old man had lost his balance. But Bertrand Canon righted himself and on one knee addressed him. "Errol Stone, your sacrifices are beyond our power to repay, and I vow no compulsion will ever again be placed on you while I lead the Judica. Despite your willingness to go, and despite what the lots say, you are free to refuse this request."

The hall waited for it, every man and woman present.

"Will you bring the book home?"

He nodded. No thunder of cheers greeted him. Their hope was too deep and desperate for sound.

11

PARTINGS

THE FAMILIAR CLACK of practice swords filled the watch yard, though the sharp retort of strokes being parried came less frequently than it had prior to Weir's attempt for the throne. Adora, bundled into a heavy, fur-lined cloak, sat at one of the tables with Errol by her side. Her left arm felt the chill of Green Isle's winter, but Errol held that hand, and she would not willingly surrender his touch. She let her gaze trace the fingers that held hers, surprised by the size and strength in them. It could have been a carpenter's hand or a musician's.

"How long before you leave?" Adora bit her lip, frustrated with herself for bringing up his departure.

His hand squeezed hers before he replied. "As soon as Tek is ready." His shoulders lifted beneath the dark wool cloak. "Two days, perhaps three."

She braved the cold to touch the skin of his face with her other hand. "There is no one left to contest your suit, *maitale*." When he looked at her, uncomprehending, she grunted her vexation. "We could be married."

He swallowed. "Wouldn't the wedding for a princess take a long time to plan?"

She sighed. "I don't want a wedding for a princess; I want to be married, to you, now."

His eyes grew moist, as if she'd somehow managed to touch a wound with her words, but even before he spoke she could feel his denial in the loosening of his grip.

"I cannot."

She clenched his hand, refused to be denied. "You mean you *will* not."

His face softened, melting her anger the way a summer sun would reduce frost to water within moments. "It amounts to the same thing, Adora. If we married, if you took me to be your husband, do you think I could ever suffer to leave your side? For anything?"

He laughed, but tones of rue and loss wove threads through the sound as he looked away, and his voice softened almost to a whisper. "There is no book or destiny that could compel me from you, nothing that would make me surrender your touch. Do not ask this of me." He rose, bolting from his seat, but she caught his hand, keeping him close enough to read his face.

"I would rather have two days with you than a lifetime with another." A thousand strands of fear blanketed her. "You mean to die. If not in Ongol, then back here in Illustra."

He stilled at her words, became as quiet as an oak in winter, and his expression calmed until he might have been a statue of some long-dead churchman, utterly peaceful, inhumanly content.

"Someone has to." He smiled at her. "But it's fitting. In the end, the kingdom will be saved through sacrifice, but hasn't it always been? The life of Illustra is bound up in the small sacrifices that people make constantly for the ones they love—husband for wife, mother for daughter, brother for sister. I didn't have the eyes to see it until Merakh, but it's always been there." He shrugged. "There's not so great a difference between living your sacrifice and dying it. One's just a little more . . . final than the other."

He pulled her to her feet. "I will live if I can, and I won't pretend to be without fear, but I will do anything to keep you safe." He turned, his grip on her hand tightening. "Come. The only parts of Erinon I've really seen are in the royal compound. I would like to see the island through your eyes, the parts you love, the places where you played."

She nodded, trying to content herself with the short time they would have, but failed.

He gave her a lopsided grin. "We'll need an escort."

She shook her head. "Why?"

Errol favored her with an arch of his dark brows. "In spite of my best intentions, I don't trust myself alone with you"—his gaze turned hot—"Your Highness."

Two days later, gales of wind stabbed the isle as winter deepened its grip. Frustrated by grim stone, the gusts turned to drafts that sought openings in castles and clothes alike, the needlelike cold serving to remind Adora of her loss. Her time with Errol had raced past, and now she was leaving before he started his journey.

She'd volunteered to go to the shadow lands under the assumption Errol would accompany her, before he'd made his grand offer to recover Magis's book. But the conclave, restored to a semblance of confidence after its members had been tested, informed her that Liam and Rokha would be the ones to accompany her, along with a quarter of the watch currently in Erinon to guarantee their safety.

Desperate activity covered the isle as the kingdom's political infrastructure struggled to recover from Weir's brief reign. Members of the guard, those loyal to Rodran, had returned in the crimson of their uniforms. One of the king's quartermasters, Nob, checked the load on the horses carrying supplies to support her journey.

A border of hair, red like many native to Erinon, framed the bald dome of his head like a fringe of carpet around a bare floor, but his smile, bright and youthful, drew her gaze down to crystal blue eyes. "We're almost ready, Your Highness." His voice held a light singsong, as if his words followed a melody only he could hear. "The horses will be loaded within the hour."

She nodded. Her trip to the shadow lands would be far different than Martin's earlier journey there. Letters of authority from Archbenefice Canon and Duke Escarion rested in her pack, wrapped in waxed cloth. Once they left the isle and crossed the Beron Strait to Port City, they would break to the south and thread their way east through the provinces of Gascony, Basquon, Talia, and Lugaria. At any city or village along the way, she would have the power to commandeer whatever supplies necessity required.

The captains had told her the trip should be quick, so long as the Merakhi did what was expected. She sighed. It seemed people rarely did what was expected—in fact, they often made a point of doing the opposite.

Her mind slipped to Sevra, and her hand clenched her sword. Despite the frowns of many of the nobles and most of the ladies at court, she no longer went anywhere unarmed. Duke Weir's daughter had escaped on one of the few ships that weren't burned in Erinon's western harbor. To a man, the captains of the watch dismissed Sevra as a threat. Adora wasn't so sure.

She looked to Liam, where he sat his horse like something from legend, and past Rokha, hawklike and ill-tempered, to the stretch of ground where people milled around beyond them.

Wasn't he coming? Disappointment flashed to anger, then relief as she saw him slip through the crowd with that strange metal staff in the crook of his arm.

"I didn't know two days could pass so quickly," he said after they parted from their embrace.

She nodded, not looking at him for fear of crying. "The captains tell me it will be a close thing to make it back before spring breaks winter's grip. I've always hated the cold, but now I find myself praying for a long winter."

He should have laughed. Instead he just stood there, looking at her as if trying to memorize her face. She bit her lip against the desire to hold him again, let him gaze at her until the sweet earnestness of him overpowered her and she pulled him close. "Why does it have to be you?"

His arms, strong and sinewy from countless hours with his staff, bonded her to him. His voice was calm when he spoke, so unlike the awkward young man he'd once been. "I'm the only one Hadari knows. I doubt he would surrender the book to anyone else." He shrugged as if he didn't quite believe his words. "If we start asking why, Adora, we'll be here until summer. I'm sure Deas has his reasons. Maybe he'll even explain it someday." He laughed. "But I doubt it."

A couple of paces away, Nob coughed, scuffing the grass with his foot as he examined the ground. "We'll need to be leaving, Your Highness, if we're to make the tide."

She nodded and moved to turn away, but Errol caught her by the arm and spun her back to kiss her softly despite the fierceness of his embrace.

"I will survive this," he said.

She tried to take comfort from his parting words, but the way he'd stressed the last word only reminded her of Martin's confession and a choice of Deas she didn't want to think about.

Hours later Errol stood by the King's Port docks, facing the Western Ocean. Workers in heavy cloaks used long rakes to pull burnt flotsam from the water, their breath misting the air. The smell of charred wood and seaside detritus blended in his nose and he sneezed. The objects of his farewells remained behind him in fire-warmed rooms in the palace, cathedral, and watch barracks. He strode up the gangplank to the three-masted cog, gnawing zingiber root against the seasickness that plagued him whenever Deas or circumstance contrived to put him on a ship.

Merodach and Rale waited for him on deck, though Rale's presence surprised him still. Both had been chosen by the conclave's cast, but Rale's departure meant Illustra would prepare for war without one of its best tacticians. For the first time in anyone's memory, the Judica had nearly voted to ignore the outcome of a cast. Luis Montari had been pressed to verify the decision in persimmon wood. Two lots had taken him four hours and uncounted strokes against a whetstone to complete, but in the end the original cast had been confirmed: Rale was coming with him.

Amos Tek descended the ladder from the aft deck to greet him, the small man's face enthusiastic—an eternal boy with an unexpected plaything. "Welcome aboard the *Penance*, lad. She be a fine ship, eh?"

The ship's name seemed too appropriate. He hadn't asked about the story behind it on their previous voyage, but his curiosity was piqued now. "How did you come to choose that name, Captain?"

Tek rubbed his jaw as he stared over the rail. "In truth, I thought of naming her *Contrition*, but being on the sea makes me too happy." He nodded, confirming his own argument. "But since we be likely to die on any venture we take, *Penance* seemed a good name." He shrugged. "Plus it might give enemy ships pause. They may think I be referring to them. Ha."

"Why are we likely to die on this trip, Captain? We won't be sailing into the strait, and I'm told Merakhi longships don't venture into the Western Ocean."

Tek laughed. "And why do you think they stay in the strait, lad? They be afraid of something."

"What?"

The captain shrugged. "No kingdom man knows the whole of it, but more than once over the years, kingdom ships and pirates have tried to sail past the Devil's Teeth to traffic with the Ongolese. The spice market be worth a king's ransom to any ship's captain who could cut the Merakhi out of the trade. There's a fortune to be had there, lad, but none of those ships save mine returned."

He'd told Adora he would come back. "Why did you agree to this, Captain?"

A frown wreathed Tek's weathered face. "They cast for me, boy." He snorted. "Waste of time, that was. I'm the last captain to attempt the Teeth. Only makes sense that I be the one to try and take you through them."

Errol blew breath into his hands, trying to warm them against the winter and Tek's warning. Tek clapped him on the back. "If we make it past the Hook of Merakh, lad, you'll not have to worry about the cold. We'll be lucky if we don't roast alive."

Martin held the mug close to his face and inhaled through his nose. His long association with Luis Montari had served to introduce bergamia rind to his winter tea. The aroma calmed him; he needed calming. Illustra's next king—whether Liam or Errol—had left the island, and this time Martin would not be with either. Instead he sat entombed in his apartments chewing over events like a dog worrying a bone.

Luis chuckled. "Your face is as wrinkled as a hag's."

Martin eyed his friend over the rim of his mug, took another deep breath. "They're gone, both of them."

"We need allies."

Martin put the cup down harder than he intended. The rind wasn't working. "We need a king."

For a moment Luis looked affronted, as if this simple statement of fact had been an accusation. They sat together by the fire in Martin's apartments, the ones set aside for him as a voting member of the Judica, a benefice. In the chaos of recent events no one seemed to notice or care he occupied rooms to which he was no longer entitled.

"The boy thinks he will return from Ongol alive." Luis didn't respond, so he expounded. "He's so sure he's the one who must die for Illustra that he's equally as certain Deas will preserve him until the time is right."

"He might be right," Luis said.

"Have you become one of the Feyt, then, believing everything is preordained and inevitable? I thought that sect had been dealt with centuries ago."

The secondus of the conclave waved a hand at the jibe. "No, Martin, I merely point out that, where Errol and Liam are concerned, there may be less room to maneuver than for others. Otherwise, what exactly do we mean when we say 'the hand of Deas is on him'?"

Martin grunted. "Your logic would have made you a fine benefice."

A knock at the door precluded any reply. Luis opened it as if they still played the fiction from years past of priest and servant. Karele stood outside, cloaked against the chill. "May I come in?"

A small tightening in Martin's chest, like the barest hint of a premonition, touched him as he gestured to a third chair in front of the fire. Karele accepted the seat but declined the tea with a brisk shake of his head that heightened Martin's apprehension.

"What do you want?"

Amusement wreathed the small man's sharp features and deep-set eyes. "If it were about what I want, I wouldn't have chanced disturbing you at this hour."

The invisible hand that held Martin's guts tightened as a sense of unease grew within him, and the desire to leave his chair, his apartments, even the island, bloomed. He settled deeper into the cushion, fighting the sensation. A draft blew across the back of his neck.

Karele's smile broadened. "It won't do any good to fight it, Martin. Not really. I ignored his summons for over a year. He waited for me, and as you well know, my delay cost dearly."

The knot loosened into a sigh that left him deflated. "What are we supposed to do?"

Amusement slipped from Karele's face like a priest shedding his stole. "We are being sent by Aurae to find my Morgol father, Ablajin."

A desperate hope flared in Martin's chest. "Can we persuade the Morgols to make peace?"

Karele shrugged, his eyes sympathetic. "Aurae hasn't told me why we're to go—only that we must. Past that I can only guess."

Martin smirked. "And I'm to go with you?"

Karele nodded toward Luis. "Both of you, actually."

Luis cleared his throat. "We can't get across the mountains of the Sprata. It's winter. The passes are blocked."

Martin pictured a map of Illustra. The winter snows would have blocked every pass from Frataland down the Sprata range into the province of Sorland. Only sailing through the Forbidden Strait and then around the range of mountains that divided the two kingdoms would allow them to avoid the snow-clogged passages. He looked at Karele and said as much.

The little man shook his head. "The passes aren't the only obstacle. My father roams the Little Brothers region." He shrugged away Martin's confusion. "It's the area of the steppes due east of the Bellia province. When the Merakhi began recruiting the magic men, the theurgists, among the horse people to fight against Illustra, they came along the coast of the Eastern Ocean and began there. The theurgists and the Merakhi have a tight grip on the southern steppes. No kingdom ship will land there and survive."

Something in Karele's demeanor set Martin on guard. The only route to the steppes that could even be attempted before spring had just been ruled out. Yet the master of horses sat across from him utterly content, as if he hadn't just outlined the impossible. Karele's sense of humor had been forged on the harsh plains of the horse people. Circumstances that frightened anyone with sense only amused him.

"There's another way, isn't there."

Karele nodded.

"And I'm not going to like it, am I."

Karele shrugged. "If your temperament is similar to a Morgol's, you'll despise it."

Martin snorted. "It's not, but I think I'm going to hate it anyway."

A grin played around the edges of Karele's mouth, giving him the rakish appearance of a boy about to play a jest. "The mountains near the Little Brothers are pocked with caves, some of them quite deep. A few years after Ablajin took me as a slave, something began attacking his horses—killing and devouring some on the spot and dragging others away. We tracked it to the foothills of the Shan—what Illustrans call the Sprata."

Karele's gaze grew distant as he recounted the tale. "None of the Morgols would go more than a few feet into the cave. They are a people of the plains and the sky. Enclosed spaces terrify them. I told my master I would go for him."

Martin sat forward. "And he just let you go? Wasn't he afraid you would escape?"

Karele's mouth pulled to one side. Martin couldn't tell if he was smirking or grimacing. "No, by then, in my heart, he was my father." Karele shook himself. "The caves were immense. After a day I returned to pack provisions. Water wasn't a problem, but I needed food. I followed that labyrinth for weeks and found nothing. I got so turned around that when I finally saw light ahead I thought I'd made my way back to my master. Instead I came out on the eastern edge of Bellia."

Karele glanced at Martin and Luis. "I was free, if I wanted to be. I bought more supplies from the local village, though the innkeeper looked very hard at the Morgol silver I carried. On the way back, I took a different route and came across the remains of my master's horses. Something had eaten everything except the hooves."

"How did you know they were your master's?" Martin asked.

Karele smiled. "My master loves his horses too much to endanger the bond between his servants and his herd. You'll never find a brand on the hide of one of his prizes. Instead, he places a small mark on the hoof that has to be redone each season."

He shrugged. "After I threaded my way back to the steppes and showed my master the hooves, he thanked me and placed me in his stables. I felt as if he'd crowned me prince."

Hope and caution warred in Martin's chest. The caves offered a way to get to Karele's father and return before the spring thaws. Only one thing remained. "What killed the horses?"

Karele's lips thinned in a grimace. "I don't know. Ablajin set a guard on the caves to guard against whatever might come out of them, but nothing ever came."

12

UNDER THE SEA

AMOS TEK STOOD on the elevated foredeck of the *Penance*, his weathered sailor's face wet and boyish, grinning each time his craft fell from a swell. "This is paradise, lad."

Errol didn't agree. The waves chopped in gray-green swirls in the temperamental winter weather, and the peaks and valleys of the sea weighted and floated his stomach by turns. The zingiber root took away enough of his nausea to keep him from throwing up, if just barely. Even so, he knew he wore the washed-out pallor of a sea traveler trying very hard not to be sick.

"You have a strange notion of it, Captain." His words hit the air as a series of growls. If he relaxed the clench in his midsection enough to speak normally, he would puke.

Tek turned from his enraptured consideration of the sea to face him. "Ah, lad, you struggle against Deas's creation." He leaned forward to tap Errol's forehead. "The problem be here, not here." He touched his stomach.

Despite his doubt, Errol attempted to feign interest. The conversation kept him distracted. "How so?"

Tek laughed. "A ride on a ship is like a ride on a horse, or a run through hills. It's not a floating house, it's a horse made of wood and sail. You're sick because you be fighting that in your mind, expecting stillness and solidity when you should be moving with her." He pointed down the length of the ship. "Walk to the other end, lad. Embrace her."

Errol let go of the rail, took a few steps before the boards beneath his feet slanted at an unexpected angle, and stumbled. Tek appeared at his shoulder to steady him. "Use your senses, lad. The wind and the waves will tell you how she's going to move."

Errol closed his eyes, felt the wind coming in from his left, from the east, heard the pop and snap of sailcloth in response to the gusts, felt the swell of the ocean and the ship's responding tilt before she righted herself. In each case the ship responded a heartbeat afterward, a moment of time in which he could adjust.

"That's it, lad," Tek laughed. "Dance with her."

Errol moved back and forth across the deck, his senses tuned to the rhythm of the wind and water. He came back, aware he'd been unconscious of his stomach. "Why didn't anyone tell me that before?"

Tek threw his head back and laughed. "I lay trapped in port for years serving my penance before Deas allowed me to sail again. There in my cabin, I could do naught but think about the sea. Betimes I thought about why one person got sick and another didn't."

"Why were you a pirate?"

Tek's face stilled until his sun-browned skin might have been part of the ship he commanded. "When someone goes to the shadow lands, lad, they tell their story a hundred times. A thousand. It be part of the law there. If anyone asks how you came to Haven, you have to answer." The captain laughed. "And they make sure to ask you."

Errol let his confusion show, and Tek clapped him on the shoulder.

"The people of the shadow lands have a keen ear, lad. They know the truth when they hear it. After I tried a few times to paint my deeds in better colors, I found the truth to be less uncomfortable than those cursed blank looks they gave my lies."

He gave Errol a shrug. "The truth is, I loved the sea and hated service. I was willing to raid other ships so that I could live my way."

They stuck to the coast, passing along the western shores of Gascony and Basquon until they were half a day north of the strait that separated Illustra from Merakh. There, Tek gave the order to heave to.

"Why are we stopping, Captain?" Errol asked.

"It be time for us to sail southwest and we need to fix the sail to quarter against the wind."

"I don't understand."

Merodach stole up beside him. "The captain wants to make sure we avoid any contact with Merakhi longboats."

Errol's heart fluttered. "It's still winter. They couldn't be this close to the kingdom yet."

Tek laughed as he fixed the wheel. "Never gamble your life on what your enemy is supposed to do, lad. The watch captain be right, but there be other reasons as well. The current into the mouth of the strait from the Western Ocean is quick and perilous. Sailors hereabouts call it the Wash. The entrance acts like a funnel, and the shores of Basquon are littered with the wreckage of the unwary."

The thick canvas rippled against the lines as the *Penance* came about to quarter against the wind instead of sailing with it. Tek leaned against the rudder, and the ship slid sideways through the current heading southwest. The change in motion interfered with Errol's newfound sense of stability. "How long before we clear the Wash, Captain?"

Tek looked at the sky. "The airs are light, lad. Probably two days at this rate."

Merodach looked back to the east, his ice-blue eyes intent. "I think we should head due west, Captain."

The captain snorted. "Landwalkers. We'd have to tack back and forth to do that, and we'd lose at least a day."

Merodach pointed east, and Errol caught a different scent on the wind. "There's a group of Merakhi longships out there, Captain. They haven't seen us yet. We should try to keep it that way."

Tek peered east, shaking his head. "Your eyes may be sharper than mine." He looked up at the crow's nest. "Eyes aloft! Give me a look east, Noddy."

The man in the half-barrel, younger than Errol, held his hands to his forehead, shielding his eyes against the glare. "No sign, Captain."

Tek shook his head, showed no inclination to change course. "My charge is to get the lad to Ongol and back before spring, Master Merodach. Impossible as it is, I'm going to give it my best. We'll stay the course. The coastline be safer than the deep."

Merodach's normally impassive face registered his disagreement. Errol wasn't the only one to notice. Rale, on the far side of the quarterdeck, eyed the blond-haired watchman, who paced and scanned west at intervals before confronting Tek again.

"They are there, Captain. Turn west."

Tek snorted. "And how can a landwalker see something that a sailor in a crow's nest cannot?"

With an almost audible click, the pieces in Errol's mind to the puzzle that was Merodach came together. He stepped close to the silver-haired watchman and pulled a deep breath through his nose. "Are you sure?"

Merodach nodded.

Errol touched Tek's shoulder to get his attention. "Captain, have Noddy check again, please."

Tek sighed but voiced the order aloft. His eyebrows pinched when Noddy didn't immediately reply.

"Possible masts to the east, Captain."

"Possible? Curse your hide, Noddy. Do they be there or not?"

A thin face peered down from the perch. "They be points at the horizon. I can't be sure."

The sailor's confirmation, however weak, decided matters. "Change course, Captain," Errol said.

Tek shook his head, but the wheel spun in his hands. "I hope you know what you're doing, lad. Ships don't venture into the deep willingly."

Errol turned to Merodach. "How long do we need to head west to keep from being seen?"

Merodach eyed him, his pale face impassive. "Half a day."

"Make it so, Captain," Errol said. "I have found Captain Merodach's instincts to be flawless in the past."

Tek muttered something salty under his breath. "You be in charge, Master Errol. Caution be wise."

Merodach moved to stand alone at the starboard rail. Tek and his crew went about the task of changing the sail to suit their new heading. Errol walked on rolling feet to join the watch captain. Merodach acknowledged his presence with a nod but kept his gaze to the sea.

"You're a reader," Errol said.

Merodach's expression might have been characterized as a grin had there been any humor in it. "What makes you think so?"

"The fact that you can see ships from the deck of a ship that a sailor in the crow's nest can't."

Merodach shrugged. "I've always had uncommon vision."

Errol nodded. "No doubt."

The tall captain of the watch sighed. "What gave me away?"

Errol thought back. "You kept showing up at just the right time. At first I thought you'd been following me, making sure I was safe, but after Windridge there were times when I was in danger and you weren't anywhere around. Luis said he couldn't cast to see if I was alive while I recovered at Rale's because I was so close to death. If you didn't know I had survived, there was no way for you to follow me to Longhollow or know I'd signed on with Naaman Ru's caravan."

He turned to face Merodach head on, but the captain continued to watch the ocean. "But right as I was about to escape and Ru was going to kill me, you showed up to make sure I got away. How much wood did you go through to find me again?"

Merodach nodded. "Quite a bit. I thought I could keep you safe, but being a reader and a captain of the watch weren't enough. In Valon, I was outmatched. You're lucky to be here."

Errol didn't feel lucky—herded seemed a better description, like a cow to slaughter, or a sheep, maybe. "I don't understand how you found me at all. How did you even know to look for me?"

Merodach's mouth twitched, almost smiling. "The archbenefice and the primus are uncommonly wise men, Errol. When it became obvious Rodran would have no heir, they sent Martin and Luis to find the next king, but they didn't stop there. When Illustra's omnes were killed, the archbenefice had Primus Sten cast for the next one. Sten said it was a waste of time, since every boy in the kingdom gets tested at the age of fifteen for the reader's talent and every one of those is tested for the ability to be an omne, but Canon is a man of great faith. He refused to believe that Deas would allow the kingdom to descend into chaos because we couldn't confirm a cast."

"So . . . they knew about me, that I was an omne?" He reached out to steady his stance as the ship bucked. "But the primus seemed so surprised when Luis told him what I was."

Merodach smiled. "You showed up early. Strange, isn't it, that the search for a king and an omne should end up in the same little village at the same time." He gave Errol a penetrating look. "Too strange."

A warning like a trickle of ice water ran down his back. "What are you trying to say?"

"No one knows who is supposed to be the next king, Errol. No one. It might be you."

He shook his head against the temptation behind Merodach's words. He ached for Adora with an intensity that twisted his guts and made him yearn for life. "The herbwomen said someone has to die. Liam will live. He will be a king for the ages."

Merodach's light-blue eyes weighed him. "Why are you so afraid to hope?"

Errol left the rail of the ship, answering over his shoulder as he walked toward the stairs leading to his cabin and the staff he'd left there. "Because there's so much to lose."

He spent the rest of the day on the deck, working the forms, trying to ward off the impossible longing Merodach had placed in his heart. When he fell into bed hours later, sleep took him as soon as he closed his eyes.

He woke to the sound of screaming. Hollow thumping on the deck above punctuated the high-pitched wails of dying women. He shook his head, trying to clear the fog of sleep and confusion. There were no women on the ship. He rolled to the floor and took the stairs two at a time as sailors and guards swarmed out of the quarters with him, scrambling for weapons.

The rising sun lit the port side of the ship in warm yellow light, illuminating the backs of men holding pikes arrayed along the starboard side. A scream jerked his gaze aft to see spray flying from a shape out of a nightmare. Light flashed from fangs as a sailor swung his pike to strike. The monster twisted in midair to avoid the slash, and cruel teeth clamped onto the seaman's forearm. The thing dragged him screaming overboard. The water frothed red as other monsters gathered to share the kill.

Tek's voice cut across the bedlam. "Get back from the rail! They be clumsy out of the water."

Sailors and watchmen backed away, closing ranks. Errol slid his hands along the metal staff, searching for the point where it balanced in his grip as he watched the rail. The screams abated. Then without warning a monster flew over the rail, shedding a halo of mist to land in front of Errol. From the neck down it looked almost like a sea lion, though longer and narrower through the body with flippers that ended in glinting talons.

It looked at him.

Monster? What had he been thinking? The creature in front of him defied description—not human, surely not with that body, but its delicate face and luminous eyes spoke of intelligence.

Tek's voice registered in the background of his thoughts, but he couldn't make out the captain's words. The creature came toward him, the woman's face, narrow but strangely beautiful, delving, knowing him. Teeth bared, its scream like the sound of breaking glass, it lunged.

And stopped, pinned to the deck by a crossbow bolt. Merodach leapt forward, his sword striking the creature's heart. The thing took a long time to die, thrashing against the deck, trying to free itself.

A scream jerked him from his fascination. A creature had a sailor down. Despite the sword blows, it gnawed its way up the sailor's leg, ignoring his screams and struggles, until he stilled. Rale, brandishing a heavy cutlass, chopped through the tough neck of the monster.

"Throw the bodies of those things overboard," Tek yelled. "They'll not attack if they know they're going to die."

Two splashes hit the water, and the screaming of the creatures faded to stern. Tek turned the tiller over to the first mate and descended the quarterdeck to the waist of the ship. He barked an order toward the crow's nest. "Noddy, keep a watch for froth."

Gorge filled Errol's throat as he surveyed the carnage. "What are those things?"

Tek didn't answer, calling to a pair of hands instead. "Kagan, Weld, wrap Millon's body for burial. We'll lay him to rest as soon as I'm sure we're clear of the tiamat."

Errol had never heard the word before. "It looked . . ."

Tek sighed. "Yes, lad. It looked like a woman. That's what make the tiamat so dangerous. They can spin and dodge a sword stroke and haul a man to his death or they can land on the deck and freeze you with a look until they rip through your guts with those teeth."

Rale nodded. "You seem to know a lot about these things, Captain."

Tek took no offense. "Aye. Only a pirate, or a reformed pirate, would know what lurks in these waters. Why do you think kingdom ships stick close to the shore? Magis's barrier extends out into the ocean for a ways, it does, but outside the circle of that protection, there are dangers in the sea."

A knot of revulsion formed in Errol's chest. "Ferrals."

Tek nodded. "Aye. The tiamat be an ancient corruption of the malus." He scratched his head. "Of course, I never took the opportunity to ask a churchman. They might disagree with me."

"I doubt it," Rale said. "Will they attack again?"

Tek shrugged. "This time be different. The last time I sailed toward Ongol we didn't encounter tiamat until we were on the south side of the Wash. They be much closer to Illustra than before."

Errol understood. Rodran had died. The corrupted things on the earth and in the sea were creeping closer to Illustra, testing. How long would it be until the foul offspring of the malus realized the barrier was gone?

"Do they always scream before they attack?" Rale asked.

Tek shrugged. "I can't say *always*, but the two times I've sailed these waters, they have."

"Let's hope so," Rale said. "Otherwise you're going to have a difficult time manning your ship, Captain."

Tek lowered his voice. "That be why I brought extra crew and supplies. The monsters and the sea took half my men the last time I came here. I be hoping to lose less this time, but the ocean and its inhabitants be hard to tame, they do."

Rale gave Tek a hard look. "Is this why you confessed to a nuntius before we left, Captain?"

Tek nodded. "Things be in Deas's hand, they do, but we be swimming with the sharks now, and worse, make no mistake. I wanted Brandy to know I loved her as much as I loved the sea."

The plainspoken finality in Tek's voice opened a hole in Errol's middle.

Rale brushed the captain's admission aside. "I've spent a lifetime learning to judge the truth behind a man's words, Captain Tek. The tiamat aren't the worst of it, are they?"

Tek lowered his voice as he shook his head. "No. By the seas they are not."

With a grumble, Tek left the tiller in the hands of the first mate and waved Errol and his captains to the lower deck and into his cabin. There they circled around a broad weathered table darkened with age and cluttered with maps and charts. Symbols and abbreviated inscriptions Errol couldn't identify etched the parchments, and he fought the urge to take up a map and stare at it as if his reader's talent could provide him with some interpretation.

Tek ignored the chair behind him, and the rest stood as well. Each man wore his tension in his posture, as if they might come to blows in an instant, but none seemed as taut as Rale. "I'd like to know why you saw fit to withhold this information from us until now, Captain."

Tek, shorter than Rale by well over a hand, drew up. "Because I be captain, chosen by lot, and while we be on the water the mission be in my charge, watchmen or no." He pointed at each of them. "Unless any of you think to guide us through these waters."

Rale appeared to consider the idea, but at his silence Tek continued. "The last time I be in these waters, the sea spawn took a third of my men. I'd heard tales of the creatures, but the reality of them took us by surprise. Still, we passed through."

The horror of the tiamat filled Errol's mind. "Why would you ever brave this place after having heard the tales?"

Tek's sea-green eyes caught Errol's, and the captain's laugh sounded like waves breaking on shore. "The rarest spices in the world don't come from Merakh, lad. The people of the river want the world to think that, but they come from Ongol. The captain that finds a direct route to their land at the end of the world will be a rich man indeed."

He sighed, but the smile on his face never wavered. "In those days I wanted wealth above all else. Piracy or trade was all the same before the king's ships finally caught me and sent me to Haven."

"You should have been hanged," Merodach said.

Tek laughed. "Probably, but they did a rare thing at my trial. They cast lots to determine my punishment." He shrugged. "Deas spared me, and the cast banished me. Then I found a different way."

Rale's voice cut across Tek's, like a cloud obscuring the sun. "If the tiamat didn't stop you, Captain, what did?"

Tek's smile fled. "The maelstrom."

The captain pronounced the word on the tip of his tongue, giving it a Soeden sound. Merodach was the only one of them who appeared to understand and nodded. Rale caught the gesture.

"Explain," Rale commanded.

"There are areas in the gulf between Soeden and Frataland where the channel narrows," Merodach said. "The tides collide with the snows' runoff from the mountains, creating whirlpools. Each year, they catch some fishermen unaware." He looked at Tek. "But those are hardly more than rowboats."

Tek puffed. "Aye. Well, there's a maelstrom ahead where an island off the coast of Merakh narrows the sea down to a channel, and it nearly took my ship."

Rale shook his head. "Why not just sail around the island and avoid it altogether?"

The sea captain's eyes widened. "Do you not think I tried? There are worse things in the deep than the tiamat. Imagine a whale corrupted by the malus, man. No ship can withstand that. No, I will not chance that deep again."

"Then how do we get through?" Errol asked.

Tek paced his quarters. "I spent ten years in Haven considering that maelstrom, lad." He reached up to brush his hands across a thick beam. "I built this ship with the whirlpool in mind. She's two spans narrower across the beam, and her masts can hold more sail. The wind off the maelstrom will carry her through . . . I think."

Errol's stomach churned at the thought. "When will we get there?"

Tek laughed as if he hadn't told them they might all die aboard his ship. "Ye'll have no worry about advance notice, lad. The mael-strom be as loud as an avalanche. You can hear it two leagues away."

Errol thought he might throw up then and there.

He awoke one morning two weeks later, sweating in the summer of the southern continent and groggy from sleep haunted by the clash of armies. As he rubbed the sleep from his eyes and the ache from his temples, he realized the tumult of his dreams still pervaded his hearing like an omen of conflict. When he went on deck he discovered a small crowd at the forward rail, looking off in the distance.

Tek greeted him with a wave and a smile. Errol found the captain's enjoyment of perilous situations unnerving. Though he liked Tek, he would have preferred a seaman who exhibited more caution.

The roar grew by the minute, though the maelstrom remained beyond their vision. How could anything be so loud? He looked over the rail, but all he could see were the distant mountains of coastal Merakh and the island just west.

"You won't be able to see anything for a few hours yet, lad," Tek said. "We're still too far away, unless you want to go aloft."

Errol's stomach inched upward toward his throat at the offer. Tek nudged him and placed two small balls of waxed wool in his hand. "When we get nearer the whirlpool, you'll want to use these, lad, unless you want to come through the other side deaf as an anvil."

"Will we come through, Captain?"

Tek's perpetual squint lessened, and his jaw worked from side to side. "You be the only one to ask me, lad. I think we will, but I be a liar if I promised it, and Deas himself knows what we may run into on the far side. From here on I be no more experienced than the greenest deckhand."

Errol glanced aloft, saw a pair of sailors in the rigging, adding sail. "How will you pass orders to your crew?"

"You be thinking. That's good. We've worked out hand signals, though the most important command has been given. The maelstrom raises a powerful wind. It should be enough to pull us through and out the other side before the whirlpool sucks us down."

The ship seemed to lurch under his feet. "Should be?"

Tek laughed, his eyes alight. "The sea is a fickle mistress, lad."

The roar grew throughout the day. By noon Errol was forced to squeeze the sticky wads of cloth into his ears. Swells rocked the ship with a nauseous rhythm no amount of zingiber root could alleviate. Errol looked over the aft rail, squinting in surprise. Rings of waves like ripples in a pond stood in the water. The impossibility of what he saw drove him to rub his eyes, but the standing waves remained.

He could see the maelstrom now, a giant whirlpool with a heart of black descending below the surface. Mist and wind lashed the ship as Tek took the rudder and aimed for the heart of destruction.

Tek had gone mad. He must have. The captain's unnatural thirst for danger had finally driven him to insanity. Errol moved with the pitch and roll of the ship to claw his way aft toward the wheel. Wind whipped Tek's hair about his face, and he roared with maniacal laughter. Errol slithered along the deck as the ship raced toward doom.

He reached the captain just as a sickening jolt threw the ship sideways with the creak of timber and fittings stressed to the breaking point. Tek threw the wheel over, his arms straining to change course. His mouth chewed curses Errol couldn't hear as the wheel pulled back to its previous heading.

Taking the ship back toward the whirlpool.

Errol gathered his feet underneath him and made a sliding dive for Tek and the wheel. He used the wheel's handholds to pull himself to his feet, struggling with the ship's captain to force the ship to a new course. Slowly it moved, taking them away from the vortex.

Too slowly.

Hands covered his and Tek's. He blinked away salt water to see Rale and Merodach straining to help, necks cording with effort.

Groaning with protest, the ship found its course and rocketed away from the maelstrom and out into eddies. Wind filled the sails, and the water gradually smoothed. Errol flopped on the deck and rubbed his aching arms. Water dripped from his hair into his eyes.

Sometime later, when the roar had died enough to permit conversation of a sort, Tek turned the wheel over to the first mate and took a seat beside Errol. "You have the makings of a sailor, lad, despite your tender stomach. You were the first to realize I needed help with the wheel. With the time you bought, we were able to hold until your friends could help force the ship to its proper path."

Weak laughter shook Errol, threatened to pitch him into hysterics. "I thought you'd gone mad. Until the ship pitched I thought you were trying to kill us. I meant to take the wheel from you, not help you."

Tek's laughter drifted up to fill the sails. "It would have been a glorious end, lad, but I be wanting to see my Brandy again if I can."

13

ON THE EARTH

COLD AIR, CARRYING FROST, drifted down from the ring of mountains that bordered the Arryth, the broad expanse of farmland that ran the length and breadth of Gascony and extended into northern Basquon and Talia. The wind lifted Adora's hair and brushed her forehead with winter's caress. Barren grapevines and trees decorated the hillsides, their splayed branches resembling dark twisted bones raised in protest against another snowfall. She hated cold weather and the travel preparations it required, but she welcomed the chill like a long-absent friend. Deas was with them, it seemed; the winter proved to be as deep as everyone in Erinon had hoped.

The winding route Liam had chosen passed through a gap in the hills of Basquon, and they descended to the town of Marinne. A low wall of red stone, more decoration than defense, surrounded the burg, and inside the gates, crowds of men—from downy-cheeked youth to grizzled grandfathers—drilled under the guidance of brazen-throated instructors. The large open area had been divided by weapons: pikes, swords, and crossbows.

They slowed to survey the crowd, and Adora pointed to a man instructing a cluster of men and boys with swords. "I know him."

Liam followed her gesture, then nodded in confirmation and held up a hand to bring the caravan to a stop. "Nob."

The quartermaster bobbed his head, the tufts of his red hair ruffling. "Yes, Captain?"

"How long will it take to top off the supplies?"

Nob rubbed the bald crown of his head. "It's only been two days since we replenished them." At a look from Liam, he shrugged. "Of course, it wouldn't hurt to grab a few bags of beans, and the cheese is better here in the south, but that takes no more than an hour."

"I hate beans," Rokha muttered on Adora's left. "Tell him to buy some decent meat."

A hint of suspicion tickled Adora at Liam's questioning glance. His eyes glinted knowingly beneath the cascade of blond hair. Even so, she nodded.

"See to it, Nob," Liam said. He turned to Adora. "May I ask how you know this man, Your Highness?"

"I think you know, Captain." She pointed to the dark-skinned Basquon. His long hair shot with gray swayed as he tapped a man on the leg and demonstrated a proper lunge. "That's Count Rula."

Liam's blue eyes radiated his interest. "Yes, the captains talk of him. Five times they've offered him a captaincy in the watch, but he's always refused. Indurain says he's the finest instructor in Illustra."

"And what is your interest in the count?" Adora asked.

Liam's frank gaze made her uncomfortable. She was unused to that look. No one had regarded her that way since Rodran. Men usually viewed her with some mixture of affection and desire, but Liam looked at her as he would any man under his command.

"I wish to train under his instruction."

Adora dismounted, gave her reins to one of the guards, and approached the count with Liam and Rokha beside her. The stares of his men warned Rula, and he halted his lesson with an oath and turned. "Whoever you are, this interruption is most . . ." The irritation melted from his eyes, replaced by recognition. "Your Highness," he said with a deep bow. "This is an unexpected pleasure."

Adora nodded, amused to witness the brief lapse in Rula's legendary courtesy. "Count Rula, it warms my heart to see you again."

Rula smiled, showing white, even teeth. "You should know, Your Highness, that long-stemmed roses are becoming rare in the estates around my own. It seems that a new expression has taken hold among the young nobles." The count took her hand and brushed it with a fatherly kiss. "An expression of extreme passion." He laughed. "You and Earl Stone have done the impossible—you've managed to teach Basquons a greater depth that love and passion can take." He looked around, searching. "I don't see him. He is well, I trust?"

The mention of Errol brought an almost physical ache, but she masked the response and inclined her head. "He is, and I pray he will remain so." She turned to Liam. "May I present Captain Liam of the watch?"

Liam stepped forward, and Adora watched as the two men weighed each other.

"I have heard of you, Captain, through my old friend Reynald. He speaks very highly of you." Rula's eyes narrowed. "The hills of the Arryth are beautiful, but there are dozens of routes through this part of Illustra. What coincidence brings you through Marinne just when I happen to be organizing the forces here?"

Liam nodded. "Happenstance, perhaps. I am escorting the princess to the shadow lands on a mission to secure their alliance. You are the foremost instructor of the sword in Illustra. I want you to come with us and train me on the journey."

Rula gaped.

Adora jerked in surprise. "Captain Liam, Count Rula is responsible for organizing our forces here in the Arryth. He is, as you've mentioned, invaluable, and you are asking him to forsake that duty to be your personal instructor? Why?"

Liam remained as impassive as ever. "To give Illustra a greater chance of survival."

Rula faded from her awareness as realization hit her. Liam knew. Somehow he knew what the herbwomen, Radere and Adele, had prophesied: either he or Errol must die. *Deas, have mercy.* Liam believed it was going to be him. Sudden anger spread warmth through her cheeks. Why did there have to be a choice? Couldn't Deas make up his mind?

"I'm sorry," Rula said. "As Princess Adora has explained, my responsibility is here. Training one man, however gifted, cannot take precedence over training thousands."

Liam didn't respond, but he continued to gaze at Adora. She shook her head. Did all men have this perverse sense of doom, or was it limited to Errol and Liam? As soon as the thought bloomed, she berated herself for its unfairness.

A sigh that was almost a groan deflated her, but she signaled Liam her assent. "Tell Nob we'll be spending the night here." She turned to Rula. "Count, I regret that I must request your company on our trip to the shadow lands. You are uniquely qualified to render the assistance required."

Rula bristled, his eyes darkening. "Your Highness, are you telling me training one man is of more import than equipping the defense of Illustra?"

She nodded. "Yes, Count, I am telling you exactly that."

He stiffened and his voice held ice. "I must decline, Your Highness. Unless that fractious council of nobles has given you the authority to force my cooperation, I will do as I have been previously ordered."

Adora pointed back to her mare. "If you will accompany me, Count Rula, I will be happy to satisfy you. I have the letters in my pack."

Minutes later, Rula bowed once more as he returned the letters to her hand. "Please accept my apologies for my impertinence, Your Highness." He straightened, favoring Liam with a speculative look. "I would not intrude in matters deemed sensitive, Your

Highness, but your request and the letters of authority you have to enforce it raise more questions than they answer. May I ask why training one man will be so critical to Illustra's survival?"

A brief shake of Liam's head stilled her response. With a gesture, she demurred on the question. "Your loyalty to Illustra is beyond question, Count, but it is wiser not to discuss some matters where so many may hear." She hoped he would be satisfied by her assertion of royal privilege.

Rula refused to be put off. He knuckled his mustache in thought. "In war there are few circumstances where the might of a single fighter attains such paramount importance. However, if the armies are evenly matched, the skill of one man may carry the day."

His gaze moved back and forth between the two of them. "I know something of the river kingdom, Your Highness. The Altaru River winds for a thousand leagues through the desert. You might as well attempt to count the sand as number the Merakhi, and the steppes of the Morgols run to the east without end. Either kingdom has us outnumbered. One man, however skilled, is insignificant."

"The only time one warrior carries such importance is during the challenge of single combat." He shook his head. "Your Highness, this is not a tale for the storybooks. There is no reason for our enemy to agree to single combat. Please let me train my countrymen."

Adora turned her back on Rula's plea and put the letters back in her pack. "Please let me know if I can render any assistance as you turn your duties over to your subordinates, Count. I would appreciate it if you could begin Captain Liam's training this afternoon. We will need to resume our journey to the shadow lands in the morning."

Rula bowed, his posture radiating indignation, and left.

Weak sunlight, yellow but without the ability to warm, lay across the courtyard of Count Michela's mansion in the rich quarter of the town. The wan early-evening light reflected from the red tiles of the roof like an omen of bloodshed. Liam stood with his practice sword in the ready position with Rula circling him, searching for imperfections in his stance, like a jeweler scrutinizing a stone. Adora looked on, Rokha at her side.

Rula made a minute adjustment to Liam's form. Adora couldn't tell the difference. She looked to Rokha, who shrugged and shook her head. The count armed himself and took Liam through a series of attacks and parries, his stare boring into his student the whole time. After ten minutes the pace quickened until the clack of practice swords sounded like the frenzied beat of a drum. After another ten minutes, Rula backed away, sweating and breathing hard. Liam still looked fresh.

"Exactly what is it you expect to learn from me, boy?"

Liam didn't hesitate. "How to be unbeatable."

Rula blew air through his lips like a horse. "I can't do that unless I can put you against someone better than you." His face tightened. "And the only one who might have fit that description is dead."

Liam pursed his lips. "We'll have to find a substitute, some way of approximating a more skilled opponent."

Rula nodded, turned to Adora. "Your Highness, how many members of the watch did you bring with you?"

"Nearly two hundred, divided by ranks."

Rula glanced at the sky. "We have an hour yet. Let us begin with a pair of the lieutenants, shall we?"

Rokha disappeared through an arch of the steep-roofed mansion and emerged a few minutes later with two black-garbed watchmen—Lieutenants Jens and Falco. The men might have been brothers. Both were fair-skinned and dark-haired with rich blue eyes. Rula armed them each with a practice sword and positioned them on opposite sides of Liam.

The lieutenants shifted their feet, nervous. At Rula's signal, Liam darted to one side, circling away from Falco so that he faced Lieutenant Jens alone.

"He shouldn't have been able to do that," Rokha murmured. "Nobody his size moves like that." A flurry of blows, and a grunt echoed from the stones as Liam attacked and the lieutenant retreated, trying vainly to bring Falco back into the fight.

Liam pressed, circling to keep one lieutenant pinned behind the other. A few seconds later, it was over. Jens was disarmed and Liam faced Falco alone.

"Halt," Rula said. With a bow of thanks and a wave, he sent the watchmen back inside. He squeezed his eyes shut and pinched the bridge of his nose. "Captain Liam. There is no one better than you in the kingdom, probably not in Merakh either. Once more I ask, exactly what kind of opponent do you expect to meet?"

Liam took a deep breath, looked toward Adora before answering. "Something from legend."

Rula stared unblinking, then turned to Adora. "I have heard whispered rumors of what you saw in Merakh, Your Highness. Am I supposed to give credence to nightmares?"

At Adora's nod, Rula shook his head and turned to walk away. After a few steps, he paused. "I will serve however you command me, Your Highness, but I cannot train him to fight an opponent I know nothing about."

Darkness descended on the courtyard, but Adora made no move to go inside. Liam stood, sword in hand, as if waiting for an answer.

They departed the next morning—with Count Rula—and began the long descent down the Arryth toward the coast. Once the Apalian range was behind them, they turned east, cutting across the lowlands of Talia.

Count Rula, his expression thoughtful, kept to himself as they moved from the snow-laden mountain roads to the tracks soggy with winter rain farther south. He sat his large piebald gelding, his eyes intent on nothing, tugging his mustache at intervals. When they stopped two hours before sunset at the village of Tolve, the second day into the coastal plain, he disappeared into the carpenter's shop.

Early the next morning Adora emerged from the inn to see Rula overseeing the assembly of a wide circular platform. When he was finished it resembled a round stage with a large hole cut in the middle. Rula retrieved a practice sword that looked half again too long for him and gestured Liam into the center of the platforms.

"This should prove interesting," Rokha murmured.

Adora understood what Rula attempted without explanation. By using the height advantage of the platforms and a longer sword, he attempted to approximate the physical characteristics attributed to the malus that killed King Magis.

"Will it work?"

Rokha shook her head. "I don't think so, at least not the way Rula uses it now. That length of sword the count holds will be difficult to move." As if her words were prophecy, Rula signaled the start and was disarmed moments later.

Even so, they packed the platforms onto a wagon and rode southeast. Rula resumed his vacant-stared contemplation. That night he directed a pair of lieutenants to mount the platform and fence against Liam, who stood on the ground in the center. Despite the advantage in leverage and reach, the guards failed to win more than one bout out of five. After three days, the ratio had fallen to one bout out of ten.

"This isn't working," Liam said after his latest victory.

Rula yanked on his mustache. "Don't point out the obvious to me, Captain. It makes me cross."

Liam nodded, his face calm. "I think we should put another man on the platforms."

Rula shook his head. "We could put men up there until they collapsed under their weight or you lost every bout; it wouldn't help. The malus are monstrous. Training you to fight three men at once isn't the same as training you to fight one monster twice as big as you are. The moves are different."

They skirted the coast for three more days. On the fourth, outside the coastal fishing village of Andria, they found themselves riding against a tide of humanity. Farmers and fishermen led wives and children along the road away from the sandy marshland. Wagons and two-wheeled carts piled high with meager belongings and dirty-faced children maneuvered across the ruts and ridges of the winter road. Curses accompanied broken axles or delays. Fear lined faces that refused to make eye contact.

Liam, riding a big bay on Adora's right, moved his mount to intercept a blocky farmer with dark hair and haunted eyes. The man, as broad across the shoulders as Liam, recoiled as if he'd been struck.

Liam held up both hands. "I'm not going to hurt you."

The farmer shrank back. The children in the cart behind him began to cry. Adora urged her mount in front of Liam's. "Goodman, are you well?"

Rokha dismounted and joined Adora, her pack in hand. "His arm is broken. I need to splint it."

The farmer's left arm made an odd angle halfway between the shoulder and the elbow. Rokha poured milky liquid from a stoppered bottle into a cup and mixed in an equal amount of water. She offered it to the farmer, who stared at her blankly. "It's going to hurt when I set your arm. This will dull the pain."

He didn't respond.

Adora laid her hand on his good arm. "Drink it."

The farmer nodded, drained the cup. Rokha ripped cloth into strips.

"Look at me," Adora said. "What happened?"

He blinked. "It came out of the marsh by the sea, killed all the animals. It took Arlo. It ate him."

Adora leaned in, tried to keep the farmer's attention while Rokha set the arm. A spasm of pain wrenched his face, laid bare the horror beneath the surface for an instant before his expression went numb again.

"What came?" Adora asked.

The farmer gaped. "It took Arlo. I tried to stop it, but I ran out of arrows. It dodged them. It took Arlo."

Adora steeled herself. "Who's Arlo?"

"My son. I tried to get him."

Rokha finished tying the splints on the farmer's arm, then pulled Adora aside. "You won't learn anything from him. The shock is breaking his mind."

"We need to know what happened," Liam said.

Rokha shook her head. "You won't get it from him."

They moved from cart to cart, family to family. By the time they were done interviewing the villagers, they knew little more.

The villagers passed and the road emptied. "I know your mission is urgent, Your Highness," Liam said, "but this section of Talia is remote. If this is a preliminary thrust from Merakh, we need to know about it."

He sat his horse as before, expression grave, but his arms corded with tension, as if eager. Adora nodded her consent. "We'll investigate, but I don't want to get sidetracked, Captain. And I don't want to lose men. If it's the Merakhi, we'll send a message to the closest garrison."

"It doesn't sound like any Merakhi I've ever seen," Rokha said.

They rode south for a league and entered a deserted village filled with bodies of men and animals and signs of hasty departure. Chairs, toys, and other discarded pieces of life lay in tracks of churned mud that led out of town. A flap of wings and the screech of a chicken sounded to their right.

Liam dismounted, drawing his sword. With brusque gestures, he ordered all of the watchmen except for the lieutenants and some trusted soldiers to withdraw and ready bows.

"Is that wise, Captain?" Rula asked.

Liam paused, considering. "Perhaps not, but I'm sure it's not Merakhi. The villagers would know."

A muscle jumped at the base of Adora's throat. "I think we should leave, Captain. If it's not the Merakhi, it's not urgent. Let the garrison handle this. They have the men and the time."

Liam turned, sword bared. "Highness, we must know what

we fight. Merakhi soldiers won't be the only thing we'll face. There will be—"

The sound of splintering wood and an approaching scream came from their left.

"It's heard us," Rula shouted. The horses shied, scenting. Lieutenants Jens and Falco barked orders for the rest of the watchmen to dismount.

It came for them, gray-haired and red-eyed, its maw dripping blood from the chicken it held in one fist. The other hand held a rusty scythe. Seven feet tall and wiry, it moved with a speed that brought Adora's stomach to her throat.

Liam moved out in front. Twenty paces away the thing stopped, confused, snout snuffling the air. Its eyes moved across the watchmen arrayed to meet it, and it hunched over.

"It is unused to confrontation," Rula said.

Adora nodded.

"I don't think that will stop it," Rokha said. "It's a ferral— intelligent enough to fight or recognize its masters, but insane."

As if her words released the creature, it roared and charged. Liam moved forward, away from the rest of the watchmen, to meet it.

14

GIBBET'S TALE

ADORA'S STOMACH CONTRACTED in fear, leaving her middle empty with panic. The spawn veered away from Liam, its eyes raging, burning at the sight of the horses. It circled, devouring the distance with a loping gait, using its legs and one arm. The other arm lifted the scythe, the long moon-shaped arc of steel ready to strike.

Rokha cursed, her voice tight, and drew her sword. The watchmen tried to drop back to intercept it, but the spawn outflanked them. Their mounts reared and bolted, scattering. With a leap that carried it ten paces the creature landed on the slowest and the horse went down screaming. The scythe cut through the horse's belly and the animal's scream became a shriek of pain.

The thing stooped to feed, and the watchmen closed in, swords out. On Adora's left, Rula uttered prayers and warnings like imprecations. "It's too fast. Foolish watchmen, thinking with their swords." He set an arrow, drew the string to his cheek, and let fly.

The broadhead slammed into the spawn with a meaty *chunk*, and its muzzle opened in a roar of pain. The red eyes focused on the watchmen surrounding it, and for the briefest moment, they might have been lucid. Then it charged, the scythe swinging, moving so quickly the hiss of displaced air became a whine.

Lieutenant Falco caught the first blow, tried to twist to catch the weapon in a bind, but the spawn jerked the scythe free and seized the watchman's throat. Lieutenant Jens leapt, launching an overhand cut for the spawn's arm. A stroke that should have severed the limb opened a mere gash, but the creature dropped Falco and turned to face the new threat. Soldiers Kith, Spania, and Mast attacked from behind, each thrusting while Jens pulled Falco away.

The spawn screamed in pain and anger as sword points punched through its hide. It bolted away from the blades back toward the village, its maw covered in blood and slavering.

Toward Liam. The sight of a single man diverted the creature, and it veered toward him.

The creature's first blow whistled and blurred toward Liam's neck. Adora watched in the space between heartbeats as the spawn swung, and Liam's sword appeared as if by magic to parry, but the blow shook him. His sword quivered and his arm threatened to buckle as the spawn pushed, striving to force the hook of steel into the watchman's throat.

The creature's eyes widened in shock, but instead of attacking, Liam broke the bind and stepped back, his feet twitching to secure his footing. Enraged, the spawn launched a series of blows that should never have been parried yet were.

When the thing launched itself at Liam, trying to overwhelm him with its greater mass, he stepped aside and brought his sword up, the point catching the creature in the chest. Its weight forced the point through its spine, and a foot-long length of steel emerged from the thing's back.

They all moved forward to gather around the corpse as Liam placed one booted foot on its chest to yank his sword free.

Rula elbowed his way through, his tanned face livid and his mustache quivering in anger. "What, by everything that makes sense, did you think you were doing?"

Liam dipped his head in acknowledgment. "I needed to know what we face, Master Rula."

"What we face?" Rula yelled. "It's a spawn. You're cursed lucky to be alive!"

Liam shook his head. "Not so. I had an opportunity to observe the creature before it attacked me. I knew the thing to be stronger than I, but not faster." He shook his sword arm. "Though, I confess, I wouldn't want to fight one of those things every day. I appreciate your concern, but if I cannot defeat the offspring, then how will I defeat the sire? The spawn afforded an opportunity for me to gauge the strength of our enemy."

Rula spluttered, chewing through curses that slid from Liam's calm demeanor like so many feeble attacks. At last he turned to Adora. "Is he always like this?"

Adora's heart still skipped like a calf within her chest, but she managed a nod. "I'm afraid so."

The count rolled his shoulders. "Humph. Talians and Basquons are freer with their feelings. This unflappable logic is disconcerting."

Liam turned to her. "Your Highness, this kind of spawn has never been seen in Illustra before, and I doubt the creature swam the Forbidden Strait to get here."

Adora nodded. "Perhaps it traveled along the coast from the steppes."

This earned her a shake of the head. "That's doubtful. There would be no reason for it to choose to come inland here rather than farther east in Lugaria. Someone brought it here by ship and released it into the swamp."

Rula squinted but gave a brief nod. "To what end?"

Liam pointed at the surrounding buildings. "To clear out everyone who might witness what came after the creature."

Rula's hand found his mustache. "You think the Merakhi are coming through here?"

Liam nodded. "If they establish a foothold now, they'll flood through the passes of the Arryth and into Gascony as soon as the snow melts."

Adora noted the look on Liam's face just before he turned to gaze south. She interposed herself between him and Rula. "Our mission lies in the shadow lands. Any delay is unacceptable."

Liam averred. "Your Highness, we must determine whether or not the Merakhi intend to make a thrust here." He shifted to address the watchmen. "Gather the horses. We'll move south as soon as everyone has a mount."

Heat filled Adora's face. "Lieutenant Jens," she snapped, "you will disregard the captain's last instruction. Designate a man to ride to the garrison at Falia and bring them here with all haste. After that, he is to ride east to rejoin us."

She spun on her heel toward Liam. "Captain, I would have a word." Without waiting for an answer or checking to see if he followed, she strode away from the group. Inside, her heart beat like a smith's hammer. The mission to the shadow lands had been given into her hands, but if Liam stood his ground and refused to recognize her authority, she would be little more than decoration for the rest of the journey.

She couldn't hear footsteps behind her, but she forced herself to continue walking, head up and back straight, until she reached a count of twenty. She exhaled, her sigh whispering as she released the tension between her brows. When she turned, Liam stood waiting no more than two feet away, his face unreadable.

The sense of his presence almost weakened her resolve. Even though he waited for her to speak, it seemed more as if he granted her permission than followed her direction.

"Captain Liam, the mission is in my charge. Please refrain from countermanding my orders. We will leave as soon as we retrieve the horses."

She stepped to the side to slip past him, but he shifted to block her without appearing to move. "Your Highness, it is necessary to gauge this threat. There may be other spawn in the area. The opportunity to face the weapons of the enemy before we meet in pitched battle is invaluable and should not be lost."

Adora tried not to growl. "Allow me to interpret your statement, Captain: 'There might be other opponents for me to practice on, and I would hate to miss the chance to do that.'"

Liam shrugged. "I think that's what I just said."

She shook her head. "No, Captain. We are going east." She held up a finger. "One, I am not going to risk delay of the mission." Then she added a second finger. "Two, I will not jeopardize you or allow you to jeopardize yourself. For all you know the spawn might be part of a trap."

His face hardened. "I must be able to practice against them. I must!"

Darts pierced her heart, but she could not afford to be soft, not now. "I know why you are so determined, Captain, but the herbwomen said *one* of you must die." She pulled a shuddering breath into her lungs. "And it might not be you. You may end up being the one who lives."

His chiseled face softened, and she could see in those blue eyes he knew what saying those words cost her. With a nod he turned and strode to stand before the watchmen.

"I need a man to ride and notify the garrison, lead them here, and then rejoin us," Liam said.

When Lieutenant Falco raised a trembling hand, Liam came as close to anger as she had ever seen. "Lieutenant, you will ride in the cart until I am satisfied you're healed from your wounds."

He pointed to a rangy Lugarian named Gibbet. "If the Merakhi have breached our shores, we must know it. Stay with the garrison troops only long enough to bring us a report. Do you understand, soldier? No heroics."

Gibbet saluted, his deep-set eyes grim in his swarthy face, before mounting his horse and thundering away. The rest continued the mission at the pace set by the quartermaster's wagon.

Rokha rode with Adora at the head of the train, and for a while neither spoke. "You took a huge gamble back there, Your Highness."

Adora noted she hadn't called her Princess. "For all we know it could have been a trap."

"It's doubtful the Merakhi would have thought to need one. This portion of Talia is sparsely populated."

Adora nodded, felt the unasked question hanging in the air. "The mission was given to me. I will not turn it over simply because Captain Liam wants to practice his swordplay in the swamp."

This brought a warm laugh. "You become more worthy of Errol every day."

Heat flushed her cheeks and flowed across her skin like a plunge into a hot bath. "I like the sound of that."

"If you keep this up, he will have to do something even more heroic to deserve you."

The jest chilled her laughter. It came too close to her conversation with Liam. A brief pounding of hoofbeats sounded before he appeared at her side and rode with them, his face as beautiful and closed as always.

Or nearly so. It seemed he had lost some of his customary stoicism, but when he spoke, he stared straight ahead, as if he were addressing the Talian landscape. "Your uncle did me a great honor when he raised me to a captain of the watch." He stopped, as if needing her permission to continue.

His hesitancy made her nervous. In her experience, men only spoke in this fashion when the weight of their secrets became too much to carry. She wasn't sure she wanted to share Liam's burden, but the tension in his face compelled her.

"I understand, Captain, that the heads of the watch were anxious to promote you. If my uncle hadn't done it, I am sure someone else would have."

He nodded, mere acknowledgment. "He insisted on making me captain of his guard and took me into his confidence. In the days before his death, when he still possessed the strength to conduct the affairs of the court, he had me stand beside him. After each audience he would ask me my opinion.

"At first I refused to offer it, but he prompted me with some very direct language." Liam's eyes widened at the memory. "I told him how I would have conducted it differently. Then he would either agree or educate me."

He turned to meet her gaze at last. "I've had many teachers, Your Highness, but only two took me into their confidence in such a way, my father and your uncle. Do you know why he would do such a thing?"

Adora shook her head, unable to discern his meaning.

He nodded without expression and made no further attempt at conversation but continued to ride at her side as if expecting more of an answer. Somewhere in the recesses of her mind, pieces of information shifted, trying to connect . . . and failed.

She wanted to take Liam's question at face value, to believe Rodran's insistence on his promotion was merely the king's desire to show his gratitude before he died, but such a display of sentimentality didn't fit the uncle and king she knew.

After a lengthy silence, with a sigh and a bow, Liam turned his horse to return to his place with Lieutenant Jens.

"What do you make of that?" Rokha asked.

She bit her lip. "I've spent my entire life at court. My uncle trained me to read people the way scholars read books." She nodded toward Liam's retreating back. "That one is closed to me. He was raised by the solis, and those two herbwomen knew more about the kingdom's need than anyone else, yet Liam rarely mentions them. It's as if they never existed, and he's never spoken of what they taught him. I can't shake the feeling he's searching for something, but doesn't want to say what."

Rokha nodded. "If it were any other man, I wouldn't trust him."

Adora waved the implied question away. "His character is above reproach." She exhaled a long, slow breath. "But I must admit, his actions scare me."

They rode north out of the Talian delta and then turned northeast to skirt Gyarlo Sound, the deep inlet that separated the southern regions of Talia and Lugaria. They ascended into the foothills, and as the climate chilled, their horses struggled through a mix of slush and mud on the roads. They slogged from village to village, their progress measured in miles instead of leagues, but the worse the roads grew, the lighter the watchmen's spirits became.

Jens's smile split his craggy face into a happy leer. "If a small party like ours makes such slow progress, think of what this would do to an army."

Falco nodded and coughed. Lurid bruises still ringed his neck from his encounter with the spawn. "It's a shame we can't keep the roads like this. The Merakhi would run out of food before they made it out of Talia or Lugaria."

Adora puzzled at this. "What makes you so sure they will land there, Sergeant?"

Falco nodded. "West of Madera, the Basqu coast is cliffs, Your Highness. There are a few beaches on the west coast where ships could land, and the kingdom keeps garrisons at each. The pathways from there up to the land make any assault a suicide mission. Ten men could hold off a hundred."

Adora reflected on everything she'd heard about the populace of the river kingdom—ten men might have to.

Two weeks later, at an inn located in the village of Banat half-way through Lugaria, Adora clutched her side and shook with laughter as Count Rula regaled them with the tale of two foolish lovers, complete with gestures and improvised dance steps. As his audience roared over a particularly frivolous caper, Rokha's tense hand on her shoulder pulled Adora's gaze from the count's foolery, and when she saw Gibbet, the laughter drained from her.

The big watchman, nearly as broad across the shoulders as Liam, swayed on his feet where he stood by the entrance, his eyes scanning the interior. Rents in his clothing showed dried and fresh blood, and his dark beard highlighted the ashen pallor of his skin. Gibbet came to the large trestle table, walking with the stiff-kneed gait of a man weary to the point of unconsciousness. Jens and Falco escorted him, not touching him, but half a step behind in case he should fall.

Liam stood as they approached, pulling an empty bench from a nearby table. "Falco, escort the villagers to the door. Say nothing. There are too many ears here."

Rokha snorted. "He has a funny idea of 'too many.' Every village in the southern provinces is emptying out."

Adora couldn't help but agree. Besides themselves, there were no more than half a dozen people in the large common room. At a word from Liam, Rokha left to retrieve her kit.

Gibbet sat with a thump and stared at the tabletop until Rokha returned. When he started to speak, Liam forestalled him, nodding instead to Ru's daughter, who probed the extent of his injuries. Gibbet endured the examination, his face impassive.

"He needs a few feet worth of stitches and a couple weeks' rest, but there's nothing life threatening," Rokha said.

Gibbet winced as if he'd been rebuked.

Liam gave one sharp nod. "Report. Leave nothing out."

The watchman flinched under Liam's gaze and paused to squeeze his eyes shut before fixing his stare to a spot over Liam's shoulder. "As ordered, I rode back to Falia to alert the garrison to a possible Merakhi incursion. The weather turned rainy, but my mount was surefooted, and I arrived at the garrison in two and a half days. The commander was hesitant to believe we had encountered spawn, but after I showed him what had been done to Falco's weapon, he marshaled two-thirds of his men and we descended back into the Talian delta.

"The road into the next village north of our first encounter was littered with the belongings of villagers, as if their haste had become urgent. Though we saw no hint of an enemy, the commander ordered the garrison to dismount and form lines. We advanced with a squadron of pikemen backed by archers."

Gibbet paused, swallowed thickly. "I stayed on horseback considering the need to bring news back to the mission."

The light outside faded to pitch and the tavern lanterns suddenly seemed insufficient.

"The pikes entered the village in a semicircle, with the archers enclosed within. Nothing stirred except flies on the remains of farm animals, so we prepared to pass through to investigate the swamps. The commander ordered the horses brought forward so the men could remount at need." Gibbet stopped, his eyes losing focus and his mouth working as if he'd forgotten how to speak.

Liam's voice cracked like a whip. "Soldier, you will finish your report."

When Gibbet didn't respond, Liam struck him open handed across the face.

The blow cleared his gaze, and he swallowed. "The attack came before the horses arrived. If the Merakhi commander had waited until the men were in the process of mounting, we would have been wiped out in minutes. Spawn, like the one we fought before, swarmed out of the buildings, though we heard no signal."

"How many?" Liam asked.

"I estimated a score, though their speed made counting difficult. The haste of the attack took the archers off guard, and the first flight failed to slow them. The pikemen stood their ground as the spawn closed. They braced the pikes against the ground with one foot to take the impact, but most of the spawn jumped over the lines at the last second, and the foul creatures were loose in our midst.

"Arrows fell on us from the edge of the village. The archers drew short swords to defend, but the spawn cut through them. The garrison commander ordered half the horses forward into the hail of arrows to try and give the archers and the pikes enough room to fall back and reform the lines.

"Our losses mounted, but the men maintained order. One pike would engage the spawn, keeping it from leaping while the rest would surround it. In that way the battle began to turn, though we lost a third of the men before we could fall back. Then the Merakhi charged into the village to keep us engaged."

"They couldn't afford to let any of you escape," Rula said.

Gibbet nodded without making eye contact. "The garrison commander sent the light horse in slashing attacks to free the archers and pikes that survived, but the charges kept coming, preventing the men from regaining their mounts.

"The Merakhi broke through our flank, and we were cut off

from the road back." Gibbet paused. "The battle became desperate on both sides. The Merakhi outnumbered us, but the garrison was better trained. We . . ." Gibbet panted, lost in his memory. "We might have won. We were surrounded and numbered no more than three score by then, but the tide might have been turned. A single sword could have swung the balance."

Gibbet looked Liam in the face. "The commander formed us into a wedge, even the archers that remained. Arrows fell among us like hail as we punched through the northern end of their line. At the commander's order, the men wheeled to each side to buy me enough space to ride away."

Gibbet swallowed and his eyes became haunted. "I rode from the battle with the commander's dying shout in my ears. A squad of Merakhi horsemen pursued me. My mount showed signs of coming up lame, putting my ability to make the safety of the Gyarlo garrison in doubt, so I staked the horse when night fell and walked back to their camp."

His face became grim and eager. "Their lookout was not prepared for me to circle around and come at him from the west. No alarm was raised, and I killed the rest of the squad as they slept. I notified the next garrison of the incursion and caught up to you as quickly as I could."

His eyes focused, and he looked at Liam with accusation in them. "I should have stayed. One man could have meant the difference between victory and defeat."

The muscles in Liam's jaw clenched at the unspoken rebuke.

"Battles may be won through heroics, lad," Rula said, "but wars are won through wisdom."

Gibbet squeezed his eyes shut. "They were wiped out to a man because I fled." He glared at his superior. "Would you have left, Captain?"

A muscle in Liam's neck twitched, but he did not turn to Adora as she expected. He merely sat, withstanding Gibbet's accusation.

Adora nodded to Rokha, who poured a vial of blue liquid into a tankard of ale and placed it in Gibbet's hands.

15

ICE

WIND HOWLED THROUGH the narrow strait sailors called the Soeden Cut, whipping the furled canvas on the ship's useless arms. Sleet and ice lashed the upper deck in horizontal slashes that flayed the skin of any crewman or passenger foolish enough to set foot out in the open. Their ship lay at anchor ten leagues east of Steadham for the fifth consecutive day, trapped in the strait between Einland and Soeden, waiting for the storm to pass.

Martin stalked the quarters he shared with Luis, Karele, and Cruk in the stern. "How much longer can this last?" He didn't expect an answer.

"Probably no more than a week," Cruk answered. At a look from Martin, the watchman shrugged. "I didn't spend my whole life in Erinon. I was raised in Dannick, not too far from the coast."

Martin nodded. He'd forgotten.

"It would seem the weather has a double edge," Luis said. "The harsh winter that delays the Morgol advance breeds the same storm that halts our progress."

Karele shook his head. "The extra snow in the passes will take longer than a couple weeks to melt. This is to our advantage."

Martin refused to be encouraged. "If it ever stops."

Three days later the wind dropped from a howl to a moan, and Captain Piet Vitus unfurled enough sail to resume their journey toward the Bellian inlet, tacking back and forth in the strait.

Martin relieved his frustration at the protracted delay by accompanying Karele into the hold where the little man tended the horses. He rubbed the nose of a chestnut stallion, the scent of Karele's liniment heavy in the air. "How will we get them through the caves?"

The master of horses shrugged. "I don't know. We will have to trust Deas."

Martin stared, his incredulity warring with his liturgical training. "That's it?"

Karele's mouth twitched to one side. "That's all there's ever been, and for a solis, that's all there ever is. When Aurae told me to go back to the steppes, he didn't give me instructions. Bringing a gift of horses was my idea. We may not be able to get them there alive." He patted the deep-chested chestnut on the shoulder. "That would be unfortunate. These stallions would make fine breeding stock for my father."

Two weeks later they moved into the Bellian inlet, and their progress slowed further while Captain Vitus repeatedly sounded the water for depth. Martin stood next to Cruk as he gazed over the port rail with a clouded expression. The normally taciturn captain pointed to a broad river just visible to the north. "We sailed that way, up the Perik until we couldn't go any farther, every ship the kingdom could put on the water filled to overflowing with men." He sighed. "Strange how hot blood feels when it hits your skin." He turned to face Martin, his plain face slack. "We can't win."

The temptation to despair dragged at Martin like an anchor scraping the bottom of the sea. "If we could win on our own, it is doubtful we would need Liam's or Errol's death to save Illustra."

Cruk shook his head. "I can't imagine a foe stupid enough to be bound by single combat, Pater. That's for the tales."

Martin nodded. "Yet if the histories are to be believed, that's how Magis secured the barrier."

Cruk's shoulders bunched under his cloak as he gnawed his lower lip. "And you think the malus will be stupid enough to do it again?"

The answer opened a path to hopelessness, but he refused to follow it. "It may be this war will be the end of Illustra, but my heart tells me that Deas will not allow his creation to succumb completely to the malus. There may be lands beyond the oceans that are untouched by evil, and our resistance may yield an outcome beyond what we can witness. Deas has not told us the outcome of our struggle, only that it is ours to fight."

Cruk turned from his doleful regard, but his face failed to register hope.

For seven days they crept up the inlet until ice blocked their way. They reversed course and plowed through the slate-gray water until they came to the last set of docks they had passed. They unloaded without conversation, the weather and their mood too grim for farewells. Heading east, they rode their prize horses into Hest, a fishing town that squatted on the inlet with buildings that matched the color of the water. What wasn't gray was snow or smoke.

"We'll need provisions," Cruk said. He led them through a market that seemed well attended, given the weather.

Martin pulled a gold pouch from beneath his cloak and handed it over.

Cruk pointed south. "There used to be a decent inn half a mile that way—the Bent Anchor. I'll meet you there." He turned away. Perhaps no one but Martin noticed the dullness in the captain's eyes.

Martin led Luis and Karele south through the press of buyers and sellers. By the time they reached the inn, the crowd had thinned, but not as much as he'd expected. The innkeeper would have possessed the sharp, dark features typical of Bellia if the temptations of his larder had not been more than he could resist.

He didn't bother to meet Martin's gaze. "Rooms? We haven't had any rooms since Rodran died. Every minor noble east and north of here claims them on their way through." He shook his head in disgust. "I book one in, and before I can turn around someone of higher rank has kicked them out of their lodgings."

Martin pulled his symbol of office and his letter from the archbenefice and placed them on the bar in front of the innkeeper. The man's shoulders slumped. "I don't know where a benefice ranks, Your Excellency. You'll have to sort that out with the nobles."

"No need," Martin said. "Just give us any room that will accommodate four. We'll be leaving in the morning."

The innkeeper sighed as if Martin's gesture hadn't helped. "Aye, they all leave in the morning, trying to get as far from the steppes as possible. I'll be going west myself as soon as the passes start to clear."

"That's cutting it pretty fine."

The innkeeper nodded. "I'll need every gold crown I can get. I saw what happened during the Steppes War. I don't intend to starve when the price of food starts reaching for the sky."

They moved out from Hest the next morning with sixty leagues remaining between them and the Sprata Mountain range that kept Illustra in relative safety. They journeyed east through clogged roads and ascended the foothills through progressively emptier towns. Supplies became scarce, but Martin's letter of authority and the unspoken threat of Cruk's sword ensured them plenty of provisions. A week out of Hest they stopped at a ridge overlooking a small village of steep-roofed cabins tucked into the nooks and crannies of the mountains.

"Change comes slowly here, it seems," Karele said.

Cruk pointed to the buildings built into the hillsides. "It's deserted. There's no smoke from the chimneys. That doesn't make sense."

"Why not?" Martin asked. "These people are closer to the steppes than any of the others."

Cruk grunted. "That's what protects them, Pater. The Morgols would have to backtrack a long way to get to a little place like Monsberg. If you were looking for plunder, would you bother searching out a little village like this? These people should have realized they were safest right here." He shrugged. "Even if most of them didn't, you always have a few holdouts, the stubborn or the old, who refuse to leave their homes." His fingers brushed his sword. "No one's here."

They rode in, stopping at each house along the way to allow Cruk an opportunity to search it. They were all the same: emptied of personal belongings, food, and livestock, and devoid of life. An eerie sense of something out of place gnawed at Martin, growing with each abandoned cabin they passed.

The snow swallowed the sounds of their passage, and his unease grew. In the middle of Monsberg, a small post pointed up a narrow lane to a cabin a bit larger than the rest, the post identifying it as the Frozen Arrow, the village inn. Martin dismounted in the deserted stable yard, but besides the fact that the inn was deserted, nothing seemed out of place. "Tidy."

Cruk nodded approval. "Bellians are a very orderly people."

A creak, sharp in the still air, yanked their attention to a door swaying slightly ajar.

Cruk drew his sword. "There's no wind." Martin did the same, feeling ridiculous, and Karele nocked an arrow to the short bow he'd procured in Erinon.

They stepped onto the porch to the sound of footsteps retreating along the floor inside the inn. Cruk pushed the door open with the point of his sword, crouched and ready to strike, but the room beyond appeared empty. They passed through the kitchen, where pots, pans, jars, spices, and anything else small enough to cart away had been removed. The cook fires had long since burned themselves out, leaving nothing in the arched fireplaces but cold, dead ash.

A clatter beneath them pulled Martin from his inspection. "Someone's in the cellar."

It took them a moment to find the stairs and another to find a torch. At the bottom of the roughhewn steps, a thin, shadowy figure darted behind a giant ale cask. Cruk snorted as he followed. He emerged a moment later gripping a skinny, underfed boy who shivered in fear or cold.

"I have the strangest feeling I've done this before," Cruk said. For the first time in days, Martin saw him smile. The boy yelped and struggled to free his arm, but Cruk didn't appear to notice his efforts.

Martin laughed. The boy looked nothing like Errol, aside from being dark-haired and skinny, but their circumstances unleashed a cloud of memories. "Go easy, Cruk. There's no telling what struggles this one's had, and I've underestimated such before."

Cruk's eyes softened. He pulled the boy around to face him. "Aye. Boy, no one wants to hurt you, but we need information. If I let you go, will you stay put?"

The boy nodded, his mouth gaping and his brown eyes large and round.

Martin gestured up the stairs. "I'm Pater Martin. Why don't we go up where we can have light and fire? What's your name, boy?"

"Owen."

As they started up the stairs he asked, "Is there any food left in Monsberg, lad?"

He shook his head. "Not really, Pater. They cleaned the village out when they left. I found some old carrots and beets at the bottom of Jesper's vegetable bin and some bread at the baker's that wasn't too moldy."

Cruk grunted. "You found the ale readily enough, boy. I can smell it on you."

The boy shrugged. "Loren's main cask was too big to haul. He'll never miss it."

Upstairs they set a fire. Once the boy determined the captain meant him no harm, he stuck by Cruk so closely the watchman had a difficult time coaxing flame from the damp wood.

"Owen," Martin called. "Let's give Captain Cruk some room to work. Have a seat. I'd like to talk to you." He patted the chair next to him.

The boy inched away from Cruk and squirmed into the chair, his bony knees drawn up to his chin, looking ready to bolt at the first loud noise.

"Where is everybody?" Luis asked.

The boy reached out and rubbed Luis's dark olive skin, his eyes wide. "They left."

Martin stifled a sigh. "Why didn't you go with them?"

"I got into Loren's ale and fell asleep. When I woke up the next day, they were all gone."

Cruk struck steel and flint, and sparks jumped into the tinder. "Every village has one." He growled a curse. "What's wrong with people?"

Owen hunched his shoulders, pushed farther back into the chair. "Is he mad?"

Martin squeezed a bony shoulder. "Yes, Owen, but not at you. Did the villagers leave because of the Morgols?"

"No, Pater. It was the bezahl."

"What's that?"

Cruk snorted. "A mountain spirit, Pater. It's a myth."

Owen nodded. "That's what Heinid said, but then it came out of the cave and ate all her goats in one night. The only thing it left was the hooves."

Karele jerked. Martin pulled his cloak closer despite the healthy blaze coming from the fireplace. "What happened next, Owen?"

The boy leaned forward. "Everyone started arguing about what killed the goats—some people accused other people, some said it was Morgols looking for meat. They didn't believe me at first when I said it was the bezahl."

Martin started. "How did you know?"

"I saw it come out of the cave beneath mine, Pater. It kept coming, not every day, but more often. Bold, Jesper called it."

"When did it first come out of the cave?" Luis asked.

Owen shrugged. "Maybe three moons ago."

"Right after Rodran died," Cruk said.

"Don't you live in the village?" Martin asked.

Owen shook his head, then fixed his eye on the floor beneath his feet. "They don't like having me around, so I stay in my cave most of the time." He looked at Martin and the rest of them, then rolled his shoulders. "It's not so bad, and the bezahl can't get to me."

Cruk fingered his sword. "How well do you know these caves, lad?"

Martin jerked his head in denial. "No, Captain, we will not."

Cruk looked his way, his face etched with implacable necessity. "We need a guide, Pater."

Martin pointed. "We have Karele."

Karele cleared his throat. "Owen, the four of us have to do something very important, something that will help a lot of people, but it means we have to go all the way through the caves to the other side."

Owen nodded. "You mean to the steppes. I can show you."

"Enough." Martin slapped his palm on his chair. "I forbid it. We will give the boy provisions and money to go west to the next village."

"And then what, Pater?" Cruk asked. "As soon as some cutpurse or swindler sees he has gold, the boy will end up in the gutter with his throat cut."

Owen gulped, his throat apple bobbing and his eyes wide.

"I think Aurae has placed him with us," Karele said.

Martin cut the air with his hand. "I don't believe you."

Karele nodded as if acknowledging his doubt. "Shall we have the secondus cast for it?"

"Boy," Cruk said, "how many different bezahls have you seen?"

Owen's face scrunched as he thought. "Just one, I think. It has a white patch on the shoulder."

Cruk nodded. "Simple enough. We use one of the horses as bait and kill the spawn when it comes for it."

"Aren't you the one that says no fight is simple?" Martin asked.

He nodded. "Yes, but I'd rather fight that thing on open ground in daylight than in the caves."

The boy shook his head. "But it won't come out until dusk, Pater. It doesn't like the light so much."

Cruk squeezed his eyes shut. "Nothing's ever easy." With a sigh he left the fire. "We might as well make it tonight. C'mon, boy. I need you to show me this cave. If we're going to lay a trap, we'll want to make it easy for the bezahl to take the bait."

Owen led them to a high meadow bordered by a frozen lake that butted up against the shadowed crags of the mountain range. A pair of openings showed in the sheer face, the lower one two paces across and twice as high and the upper one little more than a hole.

"You live there?" Martin asked.

Owen nodded. "It's not so bad. It opens up farther in, and it's warm enough out of the wind." He shrugged his thin shoulders. "I only use it to sleep in when Loren gets mad. He's been mad a lot lately."

Cruk turned to Karele, his face subdued. "You know the horses better than I do. Which one are you willing to lose?"

The solis's face grew somber, but he gave a nod, chose the slender roan, and brought it to Cruk.

The watchman for once didn't try to bait him. "If I can keep the bezahl from taking the horse, I will."

Karele nodded. "On the steppes, if a man gets caught by a winter storm unaware, he will not hesitate to kill his animal so that he will have heat and food to survive the night. To succeed, we must live. Don't take any undue risks, Captain."

Cruk staked the horse where the meadow sloped down to the lake. "We'll want to make the thing fight uphill if we can." He looked at the gray sky overhead. In the last hour it had darkened from steel to slate. "I need to hurry."

He mounted and made for the nearest stand of fir trees a few hundred paces away. After long moments punctuated by the sound of chopping, he returned with a dozen branches, trimmed and sharpened to a point. Cruk placed one in Martin's hands. "I've never fought a myth before, but I'll try to keep it occupied so the rest of you can ride up and skewer it." He gave one each to Luis and Karele. "Don't close with it, and don't get fancy. Stick it, get another lance, and stick it again."

Martin's stomach tightened. Cruk hadn't offered a secondary plan.

They formed a broad ring behind the roan and waited.

"Wait in the village, Owen," Cruk said. The boy nodded, but he moved a few paces behind the ring and stopped.

The roan pulled at the stake and whinnied, high and afraid. Martin's horse tossed its head and snorted, catching a scent. He stared at the cave opening that yawned like a giant maw in the mountain face.

Then it came, lumbering on cloven hooves with surprising speed.

"Deas have mercy on us," Luis breathed. "Look at the size of the thing."

Martin had expected, hoped, the bezahl was nothing more than an oversized ferral, but this was different. As big as a draft horse with the legs and curled horns of a ram, the black-furred spawn scented the air with a nose like a bull. It swung its heavy head back and forth on its thick neck, scenting. When it caught the smell of the horses, it lifted a powerful muzzle and roared, showing pointed teeth like daggers.

It came for the horse with ponderous strides. Martin gripped his sharpened stake as if it would protect him. "At least it's slower than the horses."

Cruk circled around at a gallop, his lance couched beneath his arm. He hit the bezahl from the side, the impact nearly throwing him from his horse. The tip of his stake struck the hide of the bezahl and broke, leaving an impression on the spawn's hide but no blood. The creature snapped at Cruk's mount as it raced by, missing by the merest fraction.

It continued its advance. The roan reared, pulling at the stake, screaming. Cruk circled around once more, drawing his sword as Karele angled in. The solis looked pitifully small on his mount and even smaller against the spawn. He leaned forward, the sharpened stake held in one hand, shouting encouragement to his horse.

The lance struck the bezahl in the head, just below the eye. The force of the blow set Karele wobbling in his seat. Nightmarish teeth raked the hindquarters of Karele's mount, and the horse squealed in pain. Still the spawn bore no mark.

Motion from the corner of his eye startled Martin. Sprinting for the roan across the snow, Owen held a knife in one hand and one of the sharpened stakes in the other.

Martin kicked his mount, his throat closing around the warning he wanted to yell but didn't for fear of alerting the bezahl. "Move, you stupid nag."

Cruk's sword flashed in the fading light, his face ruddy and sweating with desperation. The edge struck the spawn's horn, ringing, and succeeded in drawing the spawn's attention. Cruk veered away faster than the bezahl could follow. Owen's dagger sawed at the rope holding the roan to the stake, the thin cords of muscle in his arms working.

The horse reared, breaking the last few strands, and thundered off. Martin's mount closed on the spawn's blind side. If he could draw it away, he could circle around and pick Owen up. They would worry about the bezahl later. He couched the pole in the crook of his arm, leaned forward into the thrust.

Nothing could have prepared him for the impact. How had Karele stayed in the saddle? Martin's teeth banged together, and his head snapped forward on his neck. Spots swam in his vision as he yanked the reins to the right, away from the creature. After a dozen strides he wheeled, searching.

Screams echoed from the mountains to be swallowed by the snow. "No, Owen. No!"

The bezahl, confused by too many targets, lumbered to a stop, testing the air, its broad wet nose swinging back and forth, snorting mist. Owen crept behind and thrust his lance against the creature's backside. The spawn bellowed, and a trickle of blood flowed from the vulnerable spot Owen had found.

But it smelled him now.

Owen dropped the lance and ran, his feet churning snow across the meadow. The bezahl lumbered as it turned, and in that moment Owen opened space between himself and the spawn, but the bezahl was faster.

Cruk's mount charged in from the side, striking the spawn, but the creature ignored the attack in favor of prey it could catch. Luis struck at the head, but the spawn took the blow on its curved horn and continued. Martin angled his horse to circle around, hoping to lift Owen onto his saddle before the spawn caught him. Out of the corner of his eye, he saw Karele angling in from the opposite side, attempting the same.

They were too far away. The creature was nearly on the boy now. With a backward glance made of terror, Owen gathered his legs beneath him and dove.

He landed on the ice-covered lake, bouncing and sliding across it like a stone skipping across water. Its footing suddenly unstable, the bezahl slipped. Owen came to his feet and shuffled farther across the ice, the bezahl following.

With cracking sounds, like boughs of a tree breaking under too much snow, the spawn broke through, its bellow outraged and confused before the water cut it off.

It never surfaced.

Owen circled the hole, a dusting of snow blowing over it like a shroud, and came off the lake. Cruk hoisted the boy to ride in front of him on his saddle, his face inscrutable.

He motioned over his shoulder. "I'll get the roan."

They returned to the village to regroup, all of them silent. Luis and Martin built a roaring fire in the inn while Karele and Cruk tended the horses. As night fell, they made dinner from their provisions with generous tankards drawn from Loren's main barrel.

Martin allowed Owen half a tankard before switching him

to water. "Don't start down that road, lad. You won't like where it takes you."

Owen nodded and cast a glance at the other men around the fire who were still quiet. "Are they mad at me, Pater?"

Martin chuckled. "No, Owen, just tired. What possessed you to attack the bezahl that way?"

Owen shrugged his bony shoulders. "When the lances bounced off and then Captain Cruk's sword did the same, I knew you wouldn't be able to kill it. Then I thought about the lake. Jens, the miller, had a bull that wasn't right in the head. It wandered out onto the ice one winter and broke through. I figured that might work for the bezahl. Plus, I felt sorry for the horse."

Karele laughed, his eyes moist. "The horse is yours, Owen. Since you saved it, and possibly the rest of us, I think it small recompense."

The boy looked confused. He reminded Martin so much of Errol it hurt. He tousled the brown hair. "Karele means we owe you a debt for killing the spawn. Would you like to have the horse?"

Owen nodded, his eyes round. "I don't know how to ride."

Cruk cleared his throat, but when he spoke his voice was still thick. "I'll teach you to ride, boy, and anything else you'd like to learn."

Martin scrubbed a sleeve across his eyes. "It would seem Deas is giving us a second chance to do things right."

Luis nodded. "I assume that means that you've come to accept Owen as our guide?"

"Yes. The lad is brave and quick on his feet." He turned to Owen. "Do you know a way through the caves the horses can use?"

"I think so, Pater," Owen said. "But the caves change sometimes. After the mountains rumble, the passages are different. Some are blocked and others are opened."

Cruk sighed. "Earthquakes. Let's hope we can get through without getting trapped by one."

Martin stifled a feeling of dread at the thought of incalculable tons of rock above him. Men of his bulk didn't belong in the narrow passages and files underground. "How long will it take us to get to the steppes, lad?"

Owen's features scrunched as he thought. "I don't know, Pater. I made it in a fortnight, but I don't think the horses will be able to go so fast."

They entered the mouth just after dawn the next morning, walking the horses laden with their meager stores and a small mountain of improvised torches. The mouth of the cave bit off the light of the world outside, and darkness closed around them.

Cruk led the way. A few paces in, his horse shied, pulling at the reins, and he covered his nose with his heavy cloak. "Augh! The smell alone would keep the Morgols away." The torches revealed a pile—the skeletal remains of the farm animals from Monsberg.

Martin pointed ahead. "There's light up there."

Owen, walking next to Cruk like an additional shadow, nodded. "That's the moss. It grows where there's water."

They sidestepped their way across the fissures and cracks to the sound of trickling water until they came to a slanting rock face that glowed with pale light.

"Amazing," Luis said. "It's not moss, though. It's lichen."

Karele, however, had moved ahead to examine the floor of the cave. "This may not be as difficult as I had feared." He moved two dozen paces ahead and turned to face them. "The bezahl must have had a route through the caves from the steppes to Bellia. As big as it was, we should be able to follow its trail." He raised his torch.

The flickering light illumined crevices and stones that littered the floor of the cave, but even so Martin could see hints and suggestions of unnatural smoothness. Long ago, before earthquakes changed the track, the tunnel would have run unerringly to the east, a road under the mountains. "The malus made this. This part of the range must be more unstable than the mountains south of here."

They pushed on, led by torchlight and the eerie glow from patches of lichen. At times, enormous blocks of stone, some of them squared on one end, blocked their path, and they slowed to coax the horses up and over them. Before long, Martin lost his sense of time.

They continued until Cruk found a defensible spot to make camp. A ramp of stone lay off to the side, and Cruk backed the horses into a niche in the rock. Owen helped the watchman feed the animals before joining Martin, Luis, and Karele by their torch.

Cruk joined them a few moments later. "If there's another bezahl in here, we can inch back farther into the crevice. We'd be trapped, but at least we'd be out of reach."

Martin pulled the damp air of the cave into his lungs. When he let it out, his spirits felt as deflated as his lungs. "The bezahl's forays into Bellia are troubling. It is as if the spawn sensed Illustra's barrier was no longer present. The kingdom may find itself under attack at every border as spawn blunder their way in."

Karele shook his head. "My intuition tells me these are isolated cases. The akhen of Merakh and the Morgol theurgists will call the spawn of the earth to them and then marshal them in the field to fight us."

Cruk grunted his displeasure. "If it's all the same to you, I think I'd rather have them wander into the kingdom. A column of bezahls would make tatters of any army."

They slept in single file in the niche with the horses, as Cruk stood watch at the mouth of the crevice. Owen stayed with him for a while, and Martin could hear the captain telling the boy stories of the watch over the sound of the horses' quiet breathing. Owen's voice punctuated the exciting portions of the watchman's tales with squeaks of astonishment, followed by Cruk's laugh.

Martin smiled in the darkness and focused on the pair. Their laughter helped keep the world from closing in on him.

16

REFUGEES

ADORA SURVEYED THE COUNTRYSIDE as they rode northeast from the village of Banat toward the split of the Sprata River, one branch hugging the western slopes of the mountain range, the other flowing east into Haven. Miles of desolate plains stretched to the west and uncounted leagues of forest to the north. For centuries the church's excommunicates, those cut off rightly or wrongly, had been forced to make the trek to enter the shadow lands or die in the attempt.

Months prior, on Tek's ship, Martin had shared with Adora every detail of his trip, which she now communicated to Liam. He wore his silence like an accusation as she spoke, but she refused to acknowledge it. A lifetime of watching her uncle rule the kingdom had given her the training required to make the decision to send men to their death, but she ached inside. One watchman in battle would be equal to five ordinary men. Gibbet might have made the difference in the battle with the Merakhi, but the kingdom couldn't have afforded to offer him that chance.

Liam nodded. "We'll continue north so we can skirt as much

of the plain as possible. The river will be cold, but not so high as in spring." He paused. "Is that acceptable, Your Highness?"

Adora caught the subtle irony behind Liam's question, refused to rise to the bait. "I trust your judgment in this completely, Captain."

Ten leagues from their destination they entered the tiny village of Waterdown, whose reason for existence seemed to be a certain kind of wood that grew in that part of the world and nowhere else. The inn matched the village's size, forcing most of her men to sleep in the stable.

The innkeeper, a surly hatchet-faced man named Kol, who'd never ventured beyond the horizon, greeted them with narrowed eyes, his posture closed and unwelcoming. "Where might you be coming from?" His voice barked in the small space of the main room.

Adora kept her expression from growing cold. Some men came out of the womb with persimmons on their tongue, but most had a reason for their actions. "Our origin and destination are our business, innkeeper, but I assure you, we're honest folk."

Rokha eyed him, her lips pursed in a sour expression. "He's as thin as his name," she muttered. "Never trust a skinny innkeeper; it speaks poorly of the food."

"Are you kingdom folk?" Kol asked.

Liam and Rula caught her eye. "We are, good innkeeper," Adora said. "Though I'm curious why you would ask."

His expression remained as if he didn't believe her. "Seen too many people skirting the village, coming from the east, flitting through the trees like specters."

"Have you spoken to any of them?" Rula asked.

Kol huffed. "Didn't you listen? They're avoiding the village like we're riddled with plague. But you can see them at dusk circling north or south, moving west by twos or threes." His expression darkened to match the scruff of his beard. "We get the occasional runaway from the shadow lands here, but there's never been anything like this."

"When did you first notice them?" Adora asked. She kept her

face and voice smooth, but inside her stomach fluttered like a restless bird. Something had gone wrong in Haven.

Kol shrugged as if the question held no importance. "Three, maybe four days ago. We sent word to the garrison at Sligo, but that's fifty leagues away. Even if they send troops, they won't get here for another week."

He spat on the rough boards that made up the floor. "By then we'll be drowning in fugitives." Kol stopped to eye the men with Adora. "If you're kingdom soldiers, it's your responsibility to help us. The kingdom is supposed to help its people."

Adora turned away from his complaint. She'd met his kind before. No amount of protection or reassurance would suffice. His perpetual frown of disapproval had worn permanent ruts of condemnation in his face. Instead, she turned to Liam, seeking to rebuild his trust. "How long do we have until dusk?"

He nodded as if he understood her plan and approved. "An hour, perhaps a little less."

"I think it would be in our best interests to seek out some of these people and discover what compels them into the kingdom." She submitted the idea with a glance to Liam and Rula. "Do you agree?"

They nodded, and their company left the inn and split in two before meeting east of town at sunset. Liam went north with three lieutenants, while Adora went south with the count and Rokha.

Even before they entered the woods Adora could see shadows of men, women, and children moving toward the setting sun, some leading horses, others bearing burdens.

Rokha gave a low growl. "Refugees. Fleeing the shadow lands. Grim tidings."

Adora's breath stopped somewhere between her lungs and her throat. "Perhaps not," she whispered. "Let us see what they have to say."

Rokha kept pace with her. "Don't fool yourself, Your Highness. War has already come to them. Somehow, the Merakhi have learned of our hope for alliance and they've adjusted. Our efforts to make them split their forces have failed. They'll push everything west." She pointed to three figures made dim by the woods and failing light, a man on foot accompanied by a woman on a mule. "Them?"

Rula nodded. "A reasonable suggestion, but don't draw weapons. Let's not give the man any reason to believe we're a threat to his wife."

They threaded their way through the woods, angling to intercept. When the refugees stepped into a clearing, they were there waiting. But on seeing them the man mounted the mule behind the woman and swatted its hindquarters with his sword. The animal loped away, the man turning to watch them until the trees blocked their view.

Rokha shook her head. "They fear for their lives."

"As well they should," Rula said. "Have you never seen the ceremony for excommunication? The guilty are banished to the shadow lands with whatever they can carry on horseback. To return is to die." He gave Rokha a level stare. "I know of only one excommunicate who remained to live in the kingdom."

"And you knew where he was all along," Rokha said.

"Your grandfather and I came to regret Naaman's banishment." He sighed. "But there's no undoing the past. When your father killed his brother, your grandfather lost both of his sons. We allowed Naaman to roam the kingdom as a struggling merchant—" he paused—"at first for the sake of the infant he carried, then for the girl, and later for the woman."

Rokha nudged her mount over and enfolded her uncle in her hug. Adora met Rula's gaze over her shoulder and smiled. It took a long time for Rokha to let go.

They tried twice more to engage solitary travelers into speaking, but without success. It appeared the fear of acknowledging their identities was at least as great as the dread of what drove them. Short of holding them at sword point—an idea that Adora considered and then discarded—there would be no conversation. They moved out of the woods and placed themselves on the road, hardly more than a track now, east of the village and waited for Liam and his party.

The sky faded from rose to purple before they arrived, leading a man on horseback. The man looked vaguely familiar, but the scorn twisting his face confounded Adora's memory and she failed to retrieve his name. Far from being frightened of the watchmen, he appeared almost eager to draw swords with them. Adora dismissed him as a fool. Even an idiot could feel the threat emanating from Liam, who rode at the man's left. At best the watch captain resembled a lion at rest.

When they came within a dozen paces, the man's eyes widened, and he jerked in the saddle, appearing to resist the impulse to bow.

Adora pointed to him as she addressed Liam. "He knows who I am. I don't know what words have passed between the two of you, but if there is any potential threat in him, be aware."

Liam nodded but didn't draw his sword.

She looked on the stranger again. The man's dour expression had yet to put lines on his face, but he wore it as if he would never wear another. Adora tried to imagine him as he might have been.

Memory returned the name, and she inclined her head. "Lord Waterson."

The twist lessened a fraction before becoming even more pronounced. "That title is no longer mine. It was stripped from me by Arwitten's abbot in Einland. I am Marcus now."

"Your pardon, Marcus. I would not have you escorted thus if the matter were not urgent," Adora said.

Liam raised his hand. "You misunderstand, Your Highness. It was he who sought us out, naming us for what we are."

Waterson exhaled through his nose. "Watchmen are impossible to miss. They always look ready to kill something."

Liam ignored the interruption. "He requested leave to speak to the head of our party. Not knowing his history or intention, I thought it best for us to accompany him thus."

She nodded. "What would you say, Marcus?"

His sneer, self-mocking now, came back in full force. "I would say that the shadow lands are doomed without kingdom help, Your Highness."

The mountains wavered in the distance, as if they'd become nothing more than fabric in the breeze. She clutched the pommel of her saddle, forcing herself to stay calm. "Please explain."

"Very well. The council informed the guard of the bargain struck with the priest, Martin Arwitten. We were told to watch the gap for your coming. On the word of that priest"—he spat the word—"we mobilized the shadow lands for war. Despite what you may think, Highness, most of the people of Haven were born there. They've never known anything but the peace that comes from Illustra's ignorance.

"Three weeks ago the canis came pouring through the cut, overwhelming my squad."

Adora shook her head in denial. "How can that be? Martin told me of your vigilance."

Waterson's look of disdain deepened. "Did he happen to mention that the spawn avoid the sunlight?" At Adora's nod, Waterson barked a bitter laugh. "Not anymore. They came for us at dawn, when we'd already pulled the guard. They cut through Haven like a sword. The few of us who survived fled north with packs of the spawn in pursuit, alerting the villagers, driving them from their homes."

"That would explain the refugees," Rula said, "and why they feared to speak to us. They still think they're under a death sentence."

Waterson shook his head in disgust. "They are, kingdom man. We all are. Excommunicated or not, we've come to Illustra from the shadow lands." He paused to give a meaningful glance to the watchmen around him. "Any one of these could draw their sword and cut me down right now. Ha. The church might even give you a reward for doing it." He unstopped a waterskin and raised it in a mocking toast. "Thus is the light of the world preserved."

Adora flinched at the bitter sarcasm in the excommunicate's words. "You're wrong, Lord Waterson. No man here will draw on you." She gestured east toward the barren plain. "Your council told you of our agreement, and you meet the only surviving relative of the king, yet you doubt our intention. Why else would I be here in this desolation except to cement the alliance between Illustra and Haven?" She almost laughed at his shock and disbelief.

"You lie. It's just more kingdom trickery."

Her voice crackled with ice. "You forget yourself, Waterson, and I have no need to lie to one such as you. As you've said, if I wish it, your life ends at a moment, but I do not lie. Merakh prepares its invasion, and the kingdom needs allies. In exchange for your help we have agreed to recognize Haven as a sovereign nation. Do you understand, Waterson? Your entire country will be free."

He gaped at her. "They can't get to you. Our country narrows into a deep defile at the north. The horde of spawn that chased us has cut the access. You'll have to go south across the length of the plain and meet them by ship. If they're coming to you, they'll be on the coast."

Deas have mercy. Waterson didn't know what he'd said. He couldn't. There would be no meeting with Merakhi longships filling the strait. If the shadowlanders tried to board ships to flank the spawn, they would be obliterated by Merakhi longboats.

"There is a way." Liam's voice sounded distant despite his proximity. "The ferrals will not expect an attack from their rear. If we can diminish their numbers, they will not be able to hold the defile closed."

Waterson looked at their company in disbelief. "For somebody as big as you are, you have remarkably few brains. How many men do you have here?"

Rula shrugged. "About two hundred."

Waterson shook his head. "It can't be done. You've never been to Haven. You don't even know the lay of the land."

Adora pointed a finger at Waterson's chest. "I will not surrender an entire country to be slaughtered. Is there anyone in the shadow lands who means anything to you, Waterson?"

At his nod she pressed on. "They will die without our help.

Merakhi longships fill the strait. Do you think this sudden attack by the dogs is a coincidence? The malus have discovered our plans for alliance and they mean to destroy the people of the shadow lands. They're caught between the spawn and their army." She eased back in her saddle and forced a confident smile onto her face. "We have two hundred of the watch and a guide with intimate knowledge of the shadow lands to show us the way."

Waterson's face went flat. "No."

"I'm not accustomed to taking *no* for an answer, my lord."

"I'm not your lord. I'm not anyone's lord. I'm Marcus, and I'm my own man. And right now I'd rather have one of your watchmen cut me down than to be dragged back to fight a horde of spawn." He twitched his reins. His horse, penned in still, shied to the left.

"Not even for the return of your lands and your title . . . my lord?" Adora asked.

Waterson's head snapped up, eyes wide as a succession of emotions chased each other across his face: surprise, hope, anger. He muttered a string of curses that barely reached her ears. Adora thought she heard her name more than once.

"You don't have that power," he said finally.

She gave a derisive laugh. "It's wartime, my lord." She took pains to emphasize his title. He knew he was being manipulated; his face showed it. "The council of nobles has given me all the power I need."

His fists clenched while Adora held her breath. Then his mouth pulled to one side as he spoke to Liam and Rula. "I hope at least one of you is a tactician. I can guide you through the pass to the northern end of the defile, but I can't tell you how to win against those kinds of numbers."

He turned back to Adora. "That was as ruthless a piece of manipulation as I've ever seen, Your Highness. Your uncle would be proud."

The words cut, but Adora smiled as if she'd been paid a rare compliment.

17

UNDER THE EARTH

THEY JOURNEYED under the Sprata Mountains for what they estimated to be two weeks. And then, finally, Martin saw a splinter of light that didn't come from torches or lichen. Daylight. The urge to rush to it after so long underground overwhelmed him, and a wordless cry of relief burst from his throat. He dragged his horse forward, crowding the front of the group where Cruk and Owen picked their way toward the exit.

But as Martin approached the crack of light, it didn't grow any larger. When he bumped into Cruk's unmoving figure, he saw why—the exit was blocked. A plinth of stone two spans across filled the space, leaving a gap hardly bigger than his leg.

"Is this the way out, Owen?" Cruk asked.

The boy's head bobbed on the thin stalk of his neck. "But this stone wasn't here before."

Luis nodded, his bald head catching the light from Cruk's torch. "That would explain why the bezahl began frequenting the Bellian side of the mountains—the steppes were denied to it."

Martin eyed the wan winter light coming through that crack

with longing, tried to ignore the urge to pry his way through that crevice by strength. "Owen, is there another way out?"

The boy shrugged. "I don't know. There might be."

The cave ended in a broad cavern, the ceiling overhead lost in darkness the light failed to reach. Cruk and Owen took the torch and left to search for another route. Martin watched the light from outside wane from light gray to charcoal to black. For the first time since they'd entered the cavern he had a sense of the time of day.

Hours passed as they waited with the horses for Cruk and Owen to return. Martin knelt to say vespers before digging into their provisions. In the recesses of his mind and heart there was nothing but silence. "What does Aurae tell you?" he asked Karele.

The master of horses shrugged. The darkness and confinement of the caves didn't appear to bother him. Peace settled over the solis regardless of circumstances, and Martin envied him. He'd felt Aurae in the shadow lands and again on the ship at Rodran's death, but aside from that, it was almost as if he'd imagined its presence.

"I think if Aurae speaks to me," Karele said, "you will hear him as well. You've been chosen as solis to bring the truth of Aurae to the Judica."

Martin didn't share his optimism. The darkness assumed an almost physical presence while they waited for Cruk and Owen to return. The last trickles of water lay too far behind them to offer light or sound to alleviate the deprivation of his senses. Only the occasional sigh from Luis or Karele reminded him he was not alone.

Finally the bobbing approach of orange-yellow light and the sound of steps signaled Cruk's and Owen's approach. Defeat wreathed the watchman's face in lurid flickers. "There's no way out." He cast a quick glance at Owen as he swallowed a curse. "If I had thought further ahead, I would have brought more rope. We could have used the horses to try and shift the stone."

Martin took the torch from Cruk and examined the exit. The

stone hadn't fallen there as the result of a cave-in. "The Morgols put the stone here to keep the bezahl from attacking their herds."

Karele nodded. "My father would go to even greater lengths to protect his horses."

Martin clambered onto the top of the barrier. Perhaps they could enlarge the mouth enough to get around the stone. That would still leave the problem of getting the horses out, but they could deal with that later. He checked the roof of the cave and discovered it to be as solid as the floor.

He returned to the circle, gave Cruk the torch. "We have to go back."

Cruk grunted. "It will be a miserable trip. We've used up well over half the stores and torches."

Martin's heart protested. "We'll be trapped in this infernal darkness?"

The watchman shook his head. "There's no danger of that. Owen and I will find the way out, but the trip back will take longer and we'll all be lighter at the end of it." He cast a meaningful glance at Owen, who sat dozing by his side.

Martin understood. The boy, thin as he was, couldn't afford to go long without food. They would have to limit themselves to severe rations so Owen could eat, but their central problem remained: They still needed to reach the steppes and find Ablajin.

Karele met his glance with a shake of his head, his sharp features and dark eyes somber in the dim light. "Aurae told me to seek out Ablajin, but didn't specify the path. I assumed this was the route to take. I'm sorry."

The oppressive darkness tempted Martin toward blame. He swallowed his comment to Karele with an effort. Recriminations would not serve them. "If we have to return, let's be about it. Perhaps the route back will go more quickly."

With a nod toward the boy sleeping on his arm, Cruk demurred. "Morning will be soon enough. The boy and the horses could do with a night's rest."

Martin stifled his protest and rolled himself into his cloak.

Frantic shakes startled him awake the next morning, and he bolted upright, panting in the dark. The passage outside showed an almost imperceptible lightening of the sky. Full daylight was still some time away. Cruk gripped his shoulders with a grip that threatened to turn his flesh to jelly.

"Owen's gone."

Martin started to speak, to offer reassurance, but Cruk gave one savage shake of his head before the words left his mouth.

"It's been over an hour. He's not just somewhere relieving himself." In the torchlight, worry and anger chased each other across Cruk's plain, lumpy face, and his short beard quivered each time he took his lower lip between his teeth.

Martin searched for some encouragement. "Perhaps he woke early and decided to search for another way out. He may have already found the passage we need."

Cruk snorted, impatience lining the sudden tension through the watchman's neck and shoulders. "That's just it, Pater. He has." He took Martin over to the stone that kept them captive. Then he opened the stubby fingers of one huge fist to reveal a scrap of the gray cloak Owen wore. "I found this by the crevice, caught on a jagged piece of rock." His hand closed over the scrap as if it were precious. "Owen is on the steppes."

Martin turned and slid down the face of the stone until he sat on the impossibly smooth floor of their cave. "How long can we wait before we run the risk of not making it back?"

Cruk sank down on his haunches. "Not long. It isn't just the cave. We'll have to find food once we get back to Bellia, and there isn't any in Monsberg."

The watchman hadn't answered him, which meant he probably didn't want to. "How long, Cruk, at the uttermost?"

"Water's not a problem, but a week will see the end of the food." Cruk lifted his head to meet Martin's gaze. "It will be a hungry trip back."

The image of Owen's face and Errol's, so unlike, merged in Martin's mind. "We'll wait for a week."

Three days and nights dragged by as they lay entombed in the rock, waiting for Owen's return. They measured the passage of time by the sliver of light that came through the space around the stone.

On the morning of the fourth day, Martin awoke to a thin reed of noise from beyond the stone. The whinny of horses brought an answering call from their listless mounts, followed by the grunting of men.

Nearly an hour later, the stone moved, scratching and scraping along the floor of the cave. Cruk drew his sword, but Karele shook his head in denial. "If they have enough men and animals to move the stone, they have too many to fight."

A passage a pace wide opened to the left, and a voice rasped a command in the Morgol language. When Karele answered back in the same tongue, the tone softened, became questioning.

Karele turned to Martin, not smiling but looking relieved. "We are ordered to come forth. They are of Ablajin's clan, but we must tread carefully until I can speak with my father. Show no weapon or fear, and do not let yourselves be provoked."

And with that, Martin followed the master of horses out into the light.

The snatch of a childhood prayer on his lips, he squinted out over the Morgol steppes. Though the sunlight was filtered by cloud cover, he could scarcely keep his eyes open. The wind, dry and bitter with cold, pulled the prayer from his lungs, dispersed it across the tough yellow grass and stone that constituted the landscape.

He shivered and pulled his cloak more tightly about him, a move he saw Cruk and Luis copy. Laughter met this, harsh amusement from short, stocky men with a yellow tint to their skin and dark, wispy facial hair; men who looked like they'd sprung from the implacable countryside.

Karele stepped forward, as short as the Morgols, but without the look of stone in his face or eyes. He bowed, his greeting in the Morgol tongue slipping from him as easily as if he'd never spoken another.

A Draw of Kings

The laughter stopped, and the response came back, questioning and cautious. Karele threw an arm back toward Cruk, beckoning. The captain came forward with the horses, surrendering the reins. He took the first one, a deep-chested black stallion, and brought it into the midst of their enemy, no trace of fear in his voice or manner. Warriors who held drawn short bows parted for him as though he had the power to command, but they did not lower their weapons.

Karele stood by the horse, not holding the bridle, merely resting his hand on the stallion's shoulder. He rubbed the horse's nose with affectionate strokes, then shifted to the front, still speaking, his hand tracing the deep muscled chest. The Morgol guards lowered their bows as he slid his hands down the legs. At some signal Martin couldn't see, the horse shifted, turning to the side. Karele continued his commentary, his tone clearly extolling the horse's virtues.

Martin couldn't understand his speech, yet his blood responded to Karele's cadence, and images of speed filled him, stoking a desire to ride. The Morgols nodded in agreement. Then the healer handed the reins back to Cruk, exchanged the stallion for a strong-withered mare. Martin turned his attention from Karele to the Morgol warriors surrounding them. Many of them had stowed their short bows to holders on their backs. They no longer looked upon Karele as an intruder or enemy.

Karele presented the remaining horses, stroking the legs, running his hands along the strong backs, tracing the powerful hindquarters. As he finished with the last, one of the guards stumped forward on bandy legs to run his hand up the back of the animal in front of Karele, raising the horse's coat, then plucking at it, his movements and voice disdainful.

Martin understood the gesture without translation. Such short-coated horses would never thrive in the fierce weather of the steppes. Karele nodded, then left the horse and the circle of stone-faced guards. Sallow hands darted for sabers that rested on each hip before his intent became obvious. One man, the leader, drew, his face stern, affronted. Karele pushed his hands forward toward the nose of one of the Morgols' long-haired ponies.

The mount tossed its head, then quieted. Karele dug his hands deep into the coat, nodding toward the mounts they'd brought. He came back into the circle, paused to bow from the waist toward the Morgol leader whose horse he had dared to touch.

Cruk's hands still hung loose and relaxed at his sides, but he held his weight forward on his feet. Wind tugged at Martin's hair, found passage down the neck of his cloak.

"What happens now?"

Karele shrugged. "It's up to them. I told them the horses are a gift, but I didn't say for whom. I'm waiting for them to ask. Once they do, they're honor bound to guide us to the recipient."

Martin surveyed the faces around them, faces as bleak as their surroundings. "What's to keep them from simply killing us and taking the horses?"

The healer looked shocked. "Anathema. A gift of horses is the highest honor to the Morgols. Taking them for themselves would be tantamount to forsaking their entire society."

Cruk's growl cut through the cold behind him. "Where's the boy? If they've harmed Owen, healer, no amount of horseflesh reverence matters."

The Morgols reacted to Cruk's tone, their open expressions sliding away to be replaced by their former implacability.

Karele sighed. "The nomads don't kill children, Captain, but if it will keep you from setting them on their guard . . ." He turned, and a stream of words in the Morgol tongue spilled from him. Martin caught Owen's name among the pile of nonsense syllables.

The lead guard answered, stealing glances at Cruk as he did so.

Cruk unclenched his jaws enough to ask for the translation.

Karele shrugged. "Owen was taken back to their camp. When they found him, he was weak from exposure; they did not wish to further expose him to the wind off the steppes."

The leader of the guards interjected with a string of words that finished with a questioning tone.

Karele conversed with him briefly, then turned to Martin and smiled. "Our gift has been accepted. They will take us to my father." He sprang onto the back of the nearest horse. Martin mounted and moved his horse close to Karele's.

When the Morgol captain gave orders to his men, Karele shook his head and spoke in a diffident tone. The eyes of the Morgol leader grew wide and his tone doubting. Karele placed his hands on the space between his mount's flickering ears and recited something that put Martin in mind of the rite of compulsion. Satisfied, the Morgol leader signaled, and the Morgols turned their horses to start across the plain.

"What was that?" Martin asked.

Karele shrugged. "They intended to return the stone to block the passage. I took an oath on my honor as a master of horses that the creature inhabiting the caves was dead, drowned in a lake on the far side of the mountains."

"And he believed you?"

The healer smiled. "There is no greater vow among the nomads. Of course, all of our lives are forfeit if I turn out to be wrong. Let's hope there was only one of those things in the caves."

Martin drew a breath sharp with the distilled cold of winter. "They are a strange and complicated people."

Karele nodded. "Did I not tell you that there was much about them worth redeeming?"

The healer's passion for the nomads moved Martin, but hundreds of years of combat and strife lay between the two kingdoms. "I'm not contesting your words, but how can we overcome the influence of their theurgists?"

Karele rode in silence before he sighed with a small sound like winter's chill whistling through the long grass. "I don't know."

18

FATHERS

AGAINST WIND that bent the long yellow grass of the steppes until it lay nearly flat against the frozen pack of the ground, they rode at a slow canter interspersed with quick trots for the better part of the day. "I thought the steppes would be covered in snow," Martin said, the flesh around his mouth thick and stiff from cold. The Morgols' expressionless faces were beginning to make sense. Toward evening, with the sun nothing more than a ball of heatless light above the mountains behind them, they finally reached the Morgol camp.

Young men with dark wisps of down on their faces took their mounts. Martin smiled at the short, round-faced adolescent who took his reins as though approaching a ghost. The boy started, stumbling over a small fold in the earth, and almost broke into a run.

"What tales do they tell of us, I wonder?" He hadn't meant the words to carry, but Karele picked them up.

"Men of the kingdom are painted as giants, living in a land of warmth and water." He waved a hand. "There's not much of either here. The steppes are a place of dry, barren cold." Martin thought he spoke almost fondly.

The Morgols led them to a large tent with smoke drifting from a hole at its apex, and they followed as their escort shouldered aside a thick flap of hide and entered into blessed warmth.

Karele rushed toward a figure seated by a brazier as though he meant to embrace him, but at the last moment the solis slowed, became tentative. "Baabgai Ablajin." He knelt, not looking at the impassive man above him. Karele's adoptive father looked like every other Morgol, perhaps even more stoic.

"Son, it is death for you to return," Ablajin said.

Martin jerked in surprise. This was not Merakh. Tradesmen did not ply routes to the steppes. A Merakhi might have reason to speak the language of Illustra, but it surprised him that a Morgol would, unless . . .

Ablajin turned to face them. "My son convinced me of the wisdom of learning your tongue." It seemed the planes of his face might have softened into a smile. "Before today, I questioned the time and effort spent doing so."

When no one responded, he turned to Karele and uttered a string of Morgol, gesturing toward Martin and the rest. Karele shook his head, replying in the same tongue.

"My son says you do not answer because you are unsure of your welcome. Please, come and sit."

Martin stepped forward into the ruddy warmth of the tent and seated himself near a brazier surrounded by a thick pile of furs. He didn't recognize the animal, but the stiff hair prickled his skin through his clothes.

Karele seated himself cross-legged and bowed from the waist. "Father, I have brought you a gift of horses."

Ablajin nodded, his eyes somber. "So I have been told, my son. Were these different times, I would hold a feast for such a gift to honor you and your friends."

Martin responded with a bow of his head. "What times are we in, um . . . ?" He stammered, searching for the correct address.

Ablajin smiled at his discomfort. "In the tongue of the Jhengin, I am a jheng. You may call me chieftain. It is close enough to the idea to suffice for informal gatherings such as this. The times I refer to are war. We are at war with your kingdom."

Karele shook his head in denial. "No, Father. While the winter holds we are not. The hooves are silent and will be until they ascend the pass."

Ablajin sighed and stared at the base of the brass brazier. "Things change, son, and not always for the better. The theurgists have taken control of the clans. The council of chiefs no longer commands the horsemen." He raised his head, lines of wariness etched around his eyes.

Another flap opened to admit a gust of cold, and a squat man with burning, haughty eyes. Streaks of red, poorly healed scars, ran the length of each jawline. Half a dozen men with bared sabers followed him. "What he says is so." He turned to Karele's father. "You have brought the enemy into your tent? Have care, Ablajin. A jheng is not above the word of the holy."

Ablajin's gaze burned in protest, but when he spoke, his voice carried resignation more than anything else. "Is not a man, any man of the plains, allowed to see his son and his son's companions, Oorgat?"

The theurgist snapped his fingers, and the guards used their sabers to prod Martin and the rest to a standing position. "I will test their intention, Ablajin. When I uncover their purpose, I will kill them and set you to the question."

Martin gaped as his native tongue rolled from the theurgist's lips. Oorgat faced him. "Yes, I know your speech, as do all the holy. Your kingdom will soon serve us."

Ablajin stood, squaring his shoulders. "I have accepted their gift of horses, Oorgat."

The theurgist shrugged. "What is that to me?"

Ablajin's eyes flared, and even Oorgat's men looked uncomfortable, but the guards, each of them as cold and unyeilding as iron, prodded Martin and the rest of them from the warmth of Ablajin's welcome out into the dusk. They herded them to a small, lightless tent where they were tied to the central support.

Oorgat smiled down at them from the entrance. "The cold of the steppes is holy. It often induces men to confess and save themselves the trouble of the question."

The flap closed behind him, leaving a gap through which the wind cut like the naked edge of a dagger.

Cruk sat on Martin's left, Luis to his right, and Karele behind. Martin, facing the flap, pulled his knees up and tucked his head as far down as he could. The fact that his bulk shielded Karele from the worst of the gusts failed to cheer him.

A sour grunt came from his left. "I don't think this is the welcome you envisioned, healer." Cruk's voice sounded as if he chewed his words and found them distasteful, but now it shook as well, perhaps with cold.

"We can't stay like this," Karele said.

"I don't think we've got much choice in the matter," Cruk pointed out. He grunted. "I haven't been able to do much with these ropes."

"This is the testing," Karele said. "The Morgols use the cold to gauge a man's strength. In an hour, after the sun has gone down, it's going to get very cold in here."

Martin's breath misted despite the fact he still held his head as close to his legs as possible. They were going to die.

Cruk snorted. "What would you suggest?"

Martin felt a tug on his bonds as unseen hands groped, inching their way around the pole.

"Whose ropes are lowest on the pole?" Karele asked.

"How are we supposed to know that?" Cruk snapped.

Karele sighed. "Reach down with your hands. If you feel ropes, someone is beneath you. If you feel earth, you're on the bottom. We don't have much time. We have to stack ourselves. Whose ropes are on the bottom?"

"M-m-mine," Cruk stuttered through his usual growl.

"Move your hands up and tug on the ropes above you."

Martin felt a pull against his wrists. "Those are mine."

"Good," Karele said. "Martin, you should be able to slide

around until you're mostly sitting on Cruk. We need to share body heat. Luis, you're on top. See if you can get your legs underneath you and stand. The tent pole tapers as it goes up."

Pants of exertion filled the tent as the four of them strove to move into pairs. Martin thrashed like a netted fish until he ended up half on Cruk, half off. It was the best he could do.

"You've lost weight, Pater," Cruk said. "Thank you."

Martin managed a weak laugh at Cruk's wry tone. Out of the corner of his eye, he watched Luis struggle against numbness and cold to stand. He shimmied, working his bonds back and forth up the pole.

A relieved sigh came from the reader. "Much better. Why did they tie me so tight?"

Karele's lips thinned. "The theurgist spotted you as a reader. He probably wanted you to lose your hands."

Luis's voice, when it came, sounded worried. "How could he recognize me? There was no test."

The healer's sigh added to the chill of the tent. "Theurgists are a mix of skills between the readers of the kingdom and the ghostwalkers of Merakh." He drew breath as if he were about to go on but stopped.

"What are you not saying?" Luis asked.

The whistling of the wind invaded the silence of their tent, and the stillness grew against Martin's shoulders like a weight. What did Karele fear to reveal?

"If we live to wake in the morning, you must prepare yourselves." Martin barely heard him. "The theurgists are unwilling to open themselves to the spirits the Merakhi channel freely. They . . . they use children," Karele said. "Morgol's theurgists train a child from birth to accept the touch of those spirits. Using the child along with their innate skill, they try to see into the future. They maintain the combination gives them the power of divination."

Martin's tongue, thick with dread, made a hash of his words. "Who would surrender their child to such a fate?"

"They use their own." Karele's pause hung in the air. "Usually."

Cruk's voice rasped like a saw on stone. "Usually? You let us bring Owen here knowing this? We should have left him in his village. Oorgat will use him as a tool." Cruk jerked against his bonds as if he longed to strike the healer.

"I inquired," Karele said. "Aurae gave me no word one way or the other." He hung his head. "I thought he would be safe."

"I don't believe you know Aurae," Cruk said. "I think you're a trickster, a jade. What's your game? What betrayal do you have planned?"

Martin's voice erupted from his throat. "Captain, you forget yourself. He saved your life! Karele is head of the solis. Aurae is real. I have felt it." He deflated, remembering. "Karele redeemed my vow to Errol, brought us out of the river kingdom. You ask too much of him. No one is infallible."

Cruk shook his head in denial. "I can't let it happen again, Martin. I can't. Oh, Deas. I told myself we couldn't afford to get involved, that one drunken boy wasn't worth the risk of exposing who we were." His voice broke into splinters. "Don't you understand? I could have stopped Antil anytime I wanted. You and Luis were at the cabin, but I was there every day, in the inn, listening to Errol scream whenever Antil beat him."

Luis's voice, husky with cold and silence, mixed with the wind. "We all failed him in our own way, Captain; there is no one here who did not."

Cruk turned red-rimmed eyes to Martin, his face swollen with grief. "We have to save Owen, Martin. If we don't, we don't deserve to win. I don't want to live in a kingdom whose peace is bought with the lives of children."

Pain filled Martin's chest, as if the broken pieces of his heart struggled to keep beating. "We have no choice in the matter, Cruk. Some will die in our fight, and those of us who live will carry the cost in our hearts."

Cruk shook his head. "Not Owen. He's not a part of it."

Luis nodded. "Then we have to find a way to live until morning. I suggest we move as close together as possible."

Martin tried to stay awake, told himself that as long as he kept sleep at bay, death couldn't take him, but the cold lulled him, betraying his senses. False warmth spread its way up his legs and his eyes closed.

Morgol guards hauled him roughly to his feet, and it took a few minutes to realize his bonds were gone. He beat his hands together, trying to restore feeling. Pain flooded into them, and he breathed a sigh of relief. The morning sun glinted from the eastern edge of the plain, barely halfway over the horizon as he huddled with Cruk, Karele, and Luis in front of the assembled men of Ablajin's clan and the hungry glare of Oorgat. A girl of about nine, her eyes blank and unseeing, stood in front of the theurgist.

"Kingdom men," Oorgat spat. "They huddle even in the absence of wind."

"Yet they survived a test many of our own have not," Ablajin noted.

Hatred flared in Oorgat's eyes as he rounded on the chieftain. "It will not avail you, jheng." He spat the word as if it were an insult. "They have survived the cold only to enter the question. Once I have discerned their purpose against our land, I will give them to the winds."

Martin leaned toward Karele. "Give us to the winds?"

The solis shrugged. He curled against the cold, but his posture suggested he regarded it more as an inconvenience rather than a mortal threat. "It's a Morgol expression for quartering. They tie each limb to a different horse facing the points of the compass. Then they have the horses run." One corner of his mouth twitched to the side. "It's pretty gruesome."

Oorgat smiled as he turned to one of the guards. "Bring the foreign boy." He eyed Karele. "Today I will begin his training so that one day he will be my approach."

19

DIVINATION

CRUK'S GROWL, low and rumbling like an animal about to attack, set the theurgist back. He waved to the guards. "Watch him."

Ablajin's snort set the ends of his mustache waving. "He does not even have a sword, Oorgat. Are you afraid of one who huddles like a woman?"

The guards brought Owen from wherever he'd been kept. Martin noted the Morgol clothes. The boy looked comfortable and completely unafraid. When the guard released his arm he went to Ablajin.

Oorgat snapped his fingers. "Come here, boy."

At a nod from Ablajin, Owen went to Oorgat. "Would you like to help me?" The theurgist's smile stretched his face like a mask, and Owen withdrew from the leering expression.

"How?"

Oorgat shot a look filled with malice toward his captives and Ablajin. "I merely want to ask some questions." The theurgist pulled a rod from within his furred cloak and drew a circle around himself on the ground, being careful to close it.

"He thinks to guard himself against the spirit he seeks to call." The solis shook his head. "They do not understand. The malus will take whoever opens themselves to it. It is a question of the will, but they have drawn their useless circles in the ground for hundreds of years."

"Thank you for the explanation, healer." Cruk's voice rumbled like an earthquake. "But shouldn't you be doing something to save the boy?"

Karele refused to take offense. "I have been, Captain. Since Oorgat brought us out, I have not ceased to inquire of Aurae."

"And?" Cruk prompted.

The solis gave a brief shake of his head. "I don't know. Something here feels strange. I have striven to call Aurae and received no response, but the air feels odd, as if Deas is holding me back."

"What happens if Oorgat convinces Owen to accept the spirit?"

Karele's lips thinned, and his brown eyes darkened until they were almost black. "The malus will have him."

Oorgat faced Owen, his gaze hot, intent. "Why did you dare the mountain passage, boy? Everyone knows the remnant lives in the cave."

Owen shook his head. "Not anymore. We killed it."

Oorgat laughed in derision, faced the men. "Do you hear him? They say they killed it. Don't be ridiculous, boy. Its hide sheds spears and arrows like a mountain shedding snow in spring."

Ablajin spoke. "Yet they are here, Oorgat. Who is to say they did not kill the beast?"

The theurgist reddened. "I say. Hold your tongue, Ablajin. This is the work of the holy."

The chieftain shook his head. "I am jheng of the Wind Riders. It is my right to speak."

"How did you kill this thing, boy?" Oorgat asked.

Owen shrugged his small shoulders in the oversized fur of his cloak. "We used bait to bring it out of the cave. The arrows and sword just bounced off of it, so I got it to chase me out onto the lake. The ice was thick enough to hold me but not the bezahl. It broke through. It was too heavy to swim."

Oorgat's face opened in astonishment as Ablajin translated Owen's story to the horsemen around them. It was obvious he believed Owen's story and just as plain he did not want to. Ablajin and the guards looked on the boy with respect bordering on admiration.

With a sneer, Oorgat leveled a finger at Ablajin. "Do not think this will save you." He reached out with a thin, yellow-tinged arm and grabbed Owen, pulling him close. "What did you use for bait?"

The white showed around Owen's eyes, and he struggled to break the theurgist's grip. "We used one of the horses."

Oorgat threw the boy to the ground. "Horse killers. What more do you need to hear?"

The looks the guards gave Martin carried death. On his right, Karele shuddered as if someone had taken his cloak. He stepped forward. "I would speak to the men of the steppes."

"You will be silent, horse killer," Oorgat said, "or I will slay you before your time."

Karele ignored him, turned to the guards assembled there. "I am a master of horses." He pushed back his sleeves to reveal the shape of a hoof print on the inside of each forearm. "Do men of the kingdom wear these?" He raised his arms as if he could defy the brunt of cold and judgment and turned a circle so the multitude clustered around could see the tattoos. A stream of Morgol flowed from him.

When he finished, he turned to Martin. "I may have just signed our death warrant."

Rustling flowed through the crowd as one horseman after another placed a hand upon his sword. The faces, hundreds upon hundreds, remained as implacable as ever, but feet shifted and hands that weren't holding weapons flexed as nervous tension moved through the Morgols.

Martin swallowed. A dozen different emotions crackled across his senses. "Deas have mercy, healer. Nerves were stretched taut already. What did you do?"

Karele squinted against a gust of wind, and for a moment he looked like one of the Morgols. "I demanded a vote of swords to determine whether or not I can speak on Owen's behalf." He turned to face Martin squarely. "The theurgists and the clan chiefs rule, but the power of the steppes lies in its horsemen. They all know this. I invoked an ancient tradition to bypass the theurgist's power. He cannot deny me.

"Of course, if enough of them vote point down, they will kill us outright. We won't be allowed to utter a word."

Oorgat's eyes bulged and streams of what sounded like Morgol curses echoed against the dying wind. More than one warrior's gaze went flat, but Martin could not tell whether it was in agreement or offense. Something in his chest tightened, as if a fist had reached in to take hold of his heart.

When Oorgat paused, Ablajin stepped forward and proceeded to display a skill for speech and oration that rivaled Martin's own. Though Martin couldn't understand a word, he recognized a master at work. Ablajin's cadence and tone rose and fell as he built to his conclusion. He paused from time to time, never so long as to lose his audience, only long enough to bind them closer to him. By the time he finished, most of the warriors were leaning toward him, awaiting his command.

Oorgat's eyes raged with venom. The theurgist screamed.

Karele explained. "He demands a down vote. It would seem he believes having us killed outright is safer than letting me speak on Owen's behalf."

Ablajin stepped forward. His voice was raised, but it no longer resonated with persuasion. With an almost negligent wave of his hand he uttered a single phrase, then stepped back.

Karele chuckled. "That was brilliant. He told them he trusts his horsemen with his life, and a decision like this is a small thing compared to that."

Martin nodded agreement. "I would like time to speak with your father, if we survive."

Those assembled drew sabers, offered a salute to Karele that took in Martin, Cruk, and Luis, and then pointed with the tip, some up, some down.

Karele's face knotted. "I didn't expect that. It looks close. Oorgat's influence in the clan runs deeper than I suspected." He licked his lips. "They'll have to count."

The men divided themselves with the prisoners between them. One by one a man from each side came forward and the pair marched off to a separate area where they sheathed their weapons.

An hour passed, and the procession of men continued. Martin took the measure of the men remaining and turned to Karele with a smile. "We've won."

Cruk's voice rode across the chill. "Aye, but that only means the healer gets to speak. I don't think Oorgat is going to let a temporary setback discourage him. The theurgist means for us to die, and he doesn't look like the kind of fellow who changes his mind."

Karele turned to him. "Captain, if there is treachery after the vote is decided, you must make sure no harm comes to Ablajin."

"Why?" Cruk's lumpy face twisted in unbelief. "I don't like Morgols, and I know they don't care for me. I've got a few scars I could show you to prove it."

Martin took a small step to interpose himself between Cruk and Karele. The watchman's dislike for Karele could threaten their alliance and even their survival. "Captain, the solis's request is not lightly made. If Oorgat sees he cannot win, he will try to kill his most powerful adversary." Martin's gaze bored into Cruk's as if he could dismantle his resistance. "If Ablajin dies, we die."

Cruk's mouth compressed. A moment later he nodded. "I have no weapon."

Martin almost laughed. "You are more dangerous unarmed than most men would be with all the weapons they could carry."

The watchman hissed. "Somebody's going to try to stick me again. That kind of thing makes me irritable."

The counting continued until the line of men with their swords held point down had been exhausted. With a snarl Oorgat stepped back, motioning for Karele to step forward and speak. Ablajin came to stand by Martin. "My son will speak in our language. Few warriors know the tongue of your kingdom. I thought you would like me to translate."

Martin bowed. "I am honored, chieftain. I must confess that many of my preconceived notions were wrong."

Ablajin smiled, conveying a wry sense of humor. "We are a people, much like any other, and a people must have traditions of courtesy, however different, to govern their interactions."

Martin felt his eyebrows creeping upward in surprise. He sensed in Ablajin an advanced intellect, despite the chieftain's lack of formal education.

Karele bowed to each quarter of his audience and began.

Ablajin leaned in, pitching his voice so that Oorgat could not hear. "He begins by telling how the four of you came to find the boy Owen in a deserted village on the sunset side of the mountains." He paused. "Now he is talking about how you planned to come to us through the passage my son used to leave us."

A catch in Ablajin's voice at this last broke yet another of Martin's notions.

The chieftain's face hardened, and he darted a grim look at Cruk. "He says the large one staked a horse as bait. That was poorly done. Horses are prized—better to use a goat."

"There were none," Martin said. "It was use a horse or use a man."

After a moment Ablajin gave a terse nod. "Still, many of the warriors would have chosen to use a man." He pointed. "Now he says . . ." Ablajin stopped, his mouth hanging open. When Martin moved to speak, the chieftain raised a hand for silence.

He spun to face Martin. "Is that true? Did the boy really risk himself for the horse?"

Martin nodded. From deep in his chest a thrill of pride in Owen spread warmth out to his chilled arms. Oddly, he thought also of Errol, and the warmth deepened.

Still speaking, Karele strode forward to draw Owen out from

his guards so that the men could see him. Confused but compliant, Owen shuffled forward in his oversized fur boots. The lad looked ridiculous, but when Karele raised his arm, every warrior in the camp cheered. Ablajin joined them.

"You lie!" Oorgat spat. A ring of guards drifted forward to flank the theurgist.

Karele yelled above the din, and Ablajin's voice whipped across Martin's hearing as he translated. "He claims one of the men with him is a reader, a theurgist of the kingdom. My son says he can prove to any man that what he says is true." Ablajin turned to face him, his expression a mixture of disbelief and amusement. "Do you really possess the talent?"

Martin shook his head. "Not me, him." He sent a small gesture in Luis's direction. Ablajin caught it, his eyes narrowing. "I know a little of the importance of such a one. Tell me, quietly, who you are."

Martin paused. Cultured manners and intellect aside, this man was the kingdom's enemy. In a matter of weeks he might lead one of the clans across the mountains to attack Illustra. But he could think of nothing to do but trust.

"The reader among us is secondus of the conclave. His name is Luis Montari. Cruk is the large fellow with the frown. He is a captain in the watch. The watch is—"

Ablajin waved. "My son has told me of your land and those who guard its king. Who are you?"

"My name is Martin Arwitten. I was once a benefice of the church."

Karele's father kneaded his cheek with one hand. "My son was ever impulsive. I almost had him killed once before he became my master of horses. Oorgat is desperate. If he finds out who you are, he will become more so."

A change in the voices around them alerted Martin.

Oorgat shrieked a command, and the circle of men around him drew and charged.

"Down!" Cruk's voice shattered the air.

Hands pushed Ablajin and Martin to the ground in a heap. Grunts and yells followed. Ablajin yelled and fought to push Martin off.

Martin rolled to see one of Oorgat's men above him, sword raised. Ablajin's kick took the man in the groin. A split second later a foot of steel erupted from the man's chest. A hand grabbed the dying warrior as he fell, tossed him aside. Cruk's bloody face appeared. He tossed them a pair of Morgol sabers even as he spun.

Ablajin grabbed one and whirled it twice around him in a blur while Martin levered himself to his feet. Three of Oorgat's guards were down, but the rest were coming on, intent on reaching the chieftain. A pair of clansmen attacked the theurgist's men from behind.

Martin spun with saber in hand, looking for attackers, but for the moment, the space around him cleared. Every Morgol held naked steel, but only Oorgat's men fought Ablajin and a few of his men. The rest of the Morgols watched, wary and crouching.

Cruk stood like a boulder against the tide. Morgols flowed around him. Any who came too close were cut down.

Martin backed to Ablajin. "I can't tell friend from foe."

The chieftain parried a stroke that would have split his head and lunged. "Those with the red sash are Oorgat's men."

Martin ran in and cut one down from behind. He wound up next to Karele, his head swiveling, searching for the next threat. A man approached Ablajin from the rear, crouching, moving without a sound, his sword almost within reach.

Martin drew breath to yell, knowing he was too late. The saber rose.

A blur of arms and legs hit the man from the side, taking him down. Ablajin started in surprise and took the man through the throat. Owen, wearing blood and a smile, disentangled himself and stood.

Martin turned, searching for enemies, but the fight was over. A pile of bodies surrounded Cruk, who stood eyes wild, as if he expected the entire Morgol nation to attack. He edged through the jumble of arms and legs to join Martin. "Where's Oorgat?"

"And Luis."

Ablajin stepped apart to address the massed horsemen who still stood with bared swords eyeing each other, unsure. "Would you follow a man who attacks during a vote of the Wind Riders? Put up your swords. Bring Oorgat to me."

Karele's translation was interrupted by a voice calling from the nearest tent. Luis stepped out and pointed inside. Ablajin said something crisp, and a pair of men entered the tent, dragged out an unconscious Oorgat, and dumped him at the chieftain's feet.

Luis walked up wearing a sheepish grin. "I saw the theurgist slip away when the fight started to turn. I went after him and hit him over the head with a bronze urn."

Ablajin snapped an order, and they dumped water on Oorgat. He woke sputtering threats. "What did you hope to gain, theurgist, by killing me?" Ablajin asked in Illustra's tongue.

Oorgat spat. "Uluun promised me the Wind Rider clan if I could depose you. These pink-skinned foreigners offered an excuse as well as any other."

"Who is Uluun?" Cruk asked.

Lines of worry creased Ablajin's forehead. "Clan chief of the theurgists." He put the edge of his sword to Oorgat's throat. "Why would Uluun want me dead?"

Oorgat laughed. "Why should the Wind Riders be any different than the rest? All of the clans are now ruled by the holy." He shook his head in derision. "You are the last of the clan chiefs, Ablajin. All have died at our hand, and there is nowhere for you to go. When winter breaks and we put the pink-skinned to the sword, Uluun will have the other clans kill you and your men." His eyes grew cunning, and he pointed at Martin and the rest of them. "If you surrender to me, I will let you leave with these soft ones. Else, I will call the spawn to take you."

Ablajin's gaze grew thoughtful. "I would know why Uluun killed all the clan chiefs. We agreed to war."

Oorgat laughed. "Uluun's child saw betrayal. One of the chiefs will fight against him, but the child could not tell him which one."

Luis nodded. "The theurgist's art is murky. They seek answers to questions of the distant future. Even with the knowledge of the malus, the outcome is suspect."

"Stupid kingdom man." Oorgat's face wrenched into a sneer of contempt. "Uluun saw your land overrun with the warriors of Merakh and the men of the steppes. There will be no escape for you."

Ablajin pulled the edge of his sword from the theurgist's throat, and Oorgat continued, "You show some sense at last, Ablaj—"

Oorgat's last word changed to bubbling as Ablajin's sword sliced through most of his neck. The theurgist tottered and fell into a puddle of his own blood, the look of surprise slowly fading from his eyes.

The chieftain turned to Karele. "You are a son to make a father proud. Your unexpected arrival revealed Uluun's plot against me." He turned to address Martin and the rest. "Please join me and my companions in my tent. There is much that needs to be addressed." He turned and called to the crowd of men. Twelve stepped forward. The rest milled for a moment, but it looked as if most of them were headed back to their dwellings.

"What does he want to discuss?" Martin asked Karele.

Ablajin turned at the question. "How to get my clan into your kingdom before the snow melts."

Wild hope burned to life in Martin's chest.

20

TOWARD THE DEFILE

A RARE EAST WIND blew from the shadow lands and the foothills of the Sprata to fan the doubts Adora concealed with a straight back and a fierce smile. This far south the breeze carried as much threat of rain as it did snow.

She rode at the head of a contingent two hundred strong, Liam and Rokha on her right, Count Rula on her left, and Waterson out front. They all watched the cloud cover as if it had the power to bestow victory or defeat.

Liam and Rokha wore similar expressions; neither looked happy.

"Snow would be bad," Liam said.

Rokha nodded. "Rain would be worse."

"I don't understand." Adora hesitated to admit ignorance within Waterson's hearing, but she required comprehension. "I thought snow or rain helped the smaller force."

Liam chewed his lip, still staring in thought at the bank of clouds building like a wave to the east. "Normally you would be correct, Your Highness, but for the enemy we will face."

Rokha's expression became sharp, like a blade. "Those canis Waterson spoke of will hardly notice the poor footing caused by the weather. Horses' hooves are clumsier in the mud than the pads and claws of the spawn."

Adora followed their gaze skyward. "And we're already outnumbered," she said as a weight of stone settled in her stomach.

The next day they prepared to ford the Sprata. The clouds to the east roiled and hints of thunder fell on her ears like omens of destruction, but the air remained dry. Waterson led them to the northernmost part of the tributary leading into the shadow lands. He dismounted at the bank, searching.

The need for haste gnawed at Adora's middle, as if ferrals had somehow found their way inside her. "Why do we delay, Lord Waterson?"

Waterson's mouth pulled to one side, accentuating the cynical grimace of disdain he constantly wore. "It's winter, your worshipfulness. The water's cold. If we don't find the right spot, the horses won't be in any condition to carry us to safety if we get surprised."

Adora's face flushed. They stood at the entrance of the shadow lands in an attempt to salvage the alliance that might save her kingdom, and without a spawn in sight, Waterson spoke of retreat. "Do you mean we should flee, Waterson?" Her voice tightened at the end, became sharp.

He smiled at the absence of his title. "That's exactly what I mean, Highness. If that storm breaks at the wrong moment, we won't be a couple of ladies with swords, two hundred watchmen, and a fool excommunicate—we'll be food. I don't like the idea of being food."

"We're not returning to Illustra without the alliance," Liam said. He didn't bother to address Waterson directly or raise his voice. He might have been speaking of a piece of iron that needed quenching, but there was no mistaking his resolve.

Waterson shook his head, muttering imprecations under his breath. He continued north along the bank. The river flowed low and clear close to the edge, but skims of ice remained in protected shallows.

"Here." He pointed to a pile of rocks that might have been left by children playing castles. "The water is hardly knee-deep, and the crossing is level, though there are slippery spots."

For a moment his face lost the tortured grimace that mocked himself and everyone around him, and he turned to address Adora as if he were still her subject. "Are you certain you mean to do this thing, Your Highness?"

At Adora's nod, he sighed. "Then we should begin the crossing now. We'll be lucky to get all the men and wagons across before nightfall." He turned to Liam. "You'll want to make certain preparations. If the canis come upon us at night, no skill or luck will save us."

Her horse flinched at the cold, but Waterson had been true to his word—the water never made it to Adora's stirrups. The horses plodded through the crossing, hugging the northern edge of the river where it split to run through the shadow lands and along the eastern edge of the barren plain. The passage amounted to little more than a gap in the foothills that separated the shadow lands from the easternmost provinces of Illustra. As they passed out of Illustra, the air warmed.

Waterson saw her expression and smiled. "Look there, Your Highness."

He pointed north. A spur of mountains rose, peaks clawing at the sky and running to the east as far as the eye could see.

"Across those mountains lies the southern edge of the steppes. That range protects Haven not only from the horsemen but from their weather as well. Winter in the shadow lands is milder than in Illustra."

Liam spared a glance for the mountains before turning to survey the landscape. "How far are we from the defile?"

Waterson's blue eyes tightened beneath his thick brown hair. "The northern end is perhaps five leagues."

Liam nodded, then pointed north. Perhaps a league away, a

forest of pines nestled up against the beginning of the mountains. "Take us there."

As they rode, Liam drifted back, speaking with the lieutenants and the sergeants. A hundred paces from the trees, he held up a hand, and as one, the watchmen dismounted. Axes and swords were brought forth, and the majority of the men made for the trees while the remainder set picket lines and tents. By the time the cook fires were ready, a small mountain of lances as big around as a man's forearm were piled at four points around the camp. By the time supper was served, a palisade of sharpened stakes as thick as a prickle hog's hide encircled them.

Waterson stood in the center of the enclosure, staring in wonder at what had been erected in less than two hours. "If they are as good at fighting as they are at setting camp, we might live. I don't say we'll win, mind you, but some of us may live."

Rula laughed. "You may perhaps underestimate Captain Liam, still, Lord Waterson." He pointed at the barrier of sharpened stakes. "Those will serve a second purpose. Each man will carry one with him to fight the spawn, and the remainder will travel in the wagons. The men were instructed to cut stakes light enough to be used as lances."

Waterson snorted. "Men haven't used lances in battle since infantry started poking holes in their armor with crossbows."

"Ferrals don't use crossbows," Rula said. "The watch trains with every weapon known, old as well as new. With luck, their first charge will take a hundred of the spawn."

Adora watched as a glimmer of hope flared and then died in Waterson's eyes. "I've never been possessed of luck."

After sunset, Adora chased slumber in the tent she shared with Rokha, who lay at peace next to her while she rolled, changing position every few seconds.

"How can you even pretend to sleep?" she complained.

Rokha turned toward her in the darkness. Adora thought she could just make out a hint of the other woman's smile by the sliver of moonlight.

"All the choices have been made, Adora. Is there anything to this point that you would have done differently?"

She stilled. There were certainly things she wished had gone differently, but every command given had been based on Illustra's desperate need. There hadn't been any options. "No."

Rokha's smile grew. "Is there any decision about tomorrow that needs to be revisited?"

Adora sighed. "No."

"Then sleep, Your Highness. A rested arm swings a faster sword."

Despite Rokha's admonition, Adora woke the next morning with the grit of sleeplessness against her eyes. When she rolled from her tent, the black-garbed watchmen had already dismantled the barrier of protective stakes that had guarded them during the night. Liam strode through the camp, speaking with his men, inspecting the quartermaster's wagons, searching the ground for prints.

Rula approached carrying two bowls of porridge and a pair of full waterskins. "It's not what you're used to, I'll warrant," the count said. "But it will keep you from going hungry without slowing you down if it comes to fighting."

Adora nodded toward Liam as she lifted a spoonful of thick gruel. "How long has he been at it?"

Rula's mouth pulled to one side. "I can't say. I woke before dawn." He shrugged. "Old men have little need of sleep, but he had already risen. I saw him checking the men. I think he's spoken to every man in the camp this morning, asking after their equipment or horses. By Deas, the man is a natural general. I've seen watchmen twice his age gaze after him with something close to adoration in their eyes. He's almost more than human."

The count's glowing account brought Errol's description of Liam to mind, and with it the herbwomen's dire pronouncement.

Her heart fell. "Liam and Errol aren't very much alike, are they?" She'd spoken it to herself, but Count Rula turned to face her.

"No, Highness, they are not. These men will fight with Liam to the death because they know he is one of them, however more exalted." Rula's eyes grew distant. "Errol is something else, Your Highness. I'm not sure I can put it into words."

Her eyes stung and tears threatened to overwhelm her. For reasons she could neither identify nor verbalize, she needed to hear the count describe Errol, needed to know the man she loved held some measure of regard with someone who knew both men. "Please," she said, "try."

Rula caught the catch in her voice, gave a solemn nod. "All right. Liam is almost more than human. He does everything well, and better than well. He could have bested Naaman with a sword. I'm sure of it now. He's like no one else.

"With Errol, it's different. It's as if he's so human, he's almost every man. Unassuming, almost ordinary, and yet despite the terrible price he pays in injury and sacrifice, he finds a way to win."

Rula's voice thickened as tears spilled from Adora's eyes. "Liam is a man anyone would be honored to die with, Highness, but your Errol is a man people die for."

She stared at the ground and nodded, the motion scattering tears, as if she were planting seed for a hope of spring.

At a signal from Liam, the men mounted. A stern-faced sergeant with a shock of white hair against olive skin brought her horse. Rokha, already astride her dappled stallion, trotted up, her eyes fierce in the early light. "Come, Princess. Today we finally strike a blow for the kingdom."

Despite herself, Adora smiled. "I didn't know you held such love for the kingdom."

The half-Merakhi woman laughed, deep and vibrant, and the men close by turned to stare. "I don't, Highness, but I've come to favor you and that underfed boy you've fallen in love with." She tossed her wealth of glossy black hair over one shoulder. "And there are other reasons to fight as well." Her voice smoldered.

Ah, Merodach.

Adora mounted the bay gelding and set the horse on a pace to catch Liam and Count Rula, but when she pulled even with the captain of the watch, he objected.

"Your Highness," Liam said, "it is in your power to refuse, but I would request that you ride toward the back, with the supply wagons. We are less than a day from the northern end of the defile. If you ride in the vanguard, I cannot vouch for your safety." His lips pursed. "As has been pointed out to me, a leader should command from the rear."

Adora struggled not to take offense at his dismissal. Liam was almost always right, and he knew it, a trait that annoyed her. "Then should you not be at the rear with me, Captain?" She allowed herself the pleasure of putting extra emphasis on his rank.

He shook his head. If he caught the gibe, he gave no indication. "Not so. As you pointed out, I am captain. I cannot direct the men without an accurate idea of the lay of the land, which I cannot get through a subordinate's report. In addition I am more suited to this position than you. Your swordsmanship has improved under Rula's tutelage, but you are still the weakest blade present."

Why, of all the impudent, disrespectful . . . She drew breath to retort.

He held up a hand. "But there is another more important point that you must concede, Your Highness."

Her teeth clicked shut around her anger. "And what would that be?"

He turned his blue eyes on her, his blond mane shifting with the motion. She didn't love him. No one but Errol would ever do for her, but by the three, he was beautiful.

"You are indispensable to the mission," Liam said. "You must live to cement the agreement with the shadowlanders. Without you, the alliance will fail."

Again. This untutored peasant from a backwater village had outmaneuvered her again. With a stiff inclination of her head, she slowed her mount until she rode in the company of the supply wagons. Rokha hadn't bothered to accompany her.

The sun moved along its inexorable path through the southern part of the sky, illuminating a ridge of low mountains extending from the Sprata to the east toward the sunset.

Waterson appeared at her side. The expression of self-mockery had returned to twist his features.

"Should you not be riding toward the front, Lord Waterson?" she asked. Frustration served to make her tone frosty, and she shook her head in apology almost immediately. "Forgive me, my lord. I am unused to this."

Waterson's mouth pulled to one side. "I'm not sure how one becomes accustomed to battle, but to answer your question, I have told your captain all I know of this part of the shadow lands. I've only been this way twice—once on entering the land and once on leaving it."

They crested a low rise, and the defile, which had looked distant only a moment before, sprang forward. Hills ran west to east in an unbroken ribbon except for a narrow passage weather or water had created.

The winter air, cool and dry, afforded her an unhindered view of the defile. No more than a couple hundred paces wide, it was bordered by steep cliffs. She drew a shuddering breath. Though she'd rarely left the isle, Rodran had insisted on including military history in her education, and now that knowledge pressed against her, tempting her to despair.

"Oh, Deas," she breathed. "They're trapped in a killing ground."

Waterson looked at her and nodded. "The defile runs for two leagues or more. A few hundred of the demon dogs could hold it against an army, and we will face a thousand or more. And the spawn are hard to kill. I've seen a canis pincushioned with a dozen arrows come charging on."

Adora peered into the heart of the defile, straining to catch a glimpse, but the shadows cast by the steep walls prevented her. An impossible hope flared like a candle in her heart. "I don't

213

see them. Perhaps your countrymen are overcoming them as we speak."

Waterson bit his lips and gave a slow shake of his head. "Look there, Your Highness." He pointed to the sun directly overhead.

"But how . . ." She stopped as realization silenced her. There shouldn't be any shadows in the defile. The floor of the passage should have been visible. She peered at the passage again, saw those shadows stir, boiling like a pot of water over a fire.

Liam held up a hand, passing orders to the lieutenants, and a ripple of movement followed as ten score watchmen deployed, fanning out in a long double line that stretched to either side. The supply carts creaked forward, their beds filled with the extra lances.

At a signal, the line moved forward at a trot, the jangle of tack and weapons loud. A soft breeze blew from the defile and she caught a whiff of corruption, like the smell of a gangrenous wound.

Waterson stiffened. "Your captain plays a dangerous game, Highness."

His tone held both disapproval and grudging admiration, preventing her from discerning his meaning. "Explain."

"We are still a league distant, and the dogs have yet to notice us. This trot will alert them. Long before the horses can charge, the spawn will know we are here."

Adora's hands twitched on the reins. Safety or not, she could not bear to stay in the back to watch decisions made without explanation. She drove the gelding forward at a canter until she drew even with Liam's muscled stallion.

"Captain Liam," she called. He looked at her without fully turning his head. "Won't this alert the spawn and take away your element of surprise?"

He nodded, face tight, but didn't speak, his gaze boring forward, unblinking.

She reached across her horse to grip his arm. "Explain yourself, Captain."

He pointed at the seething shadows within the defile. "The canis are wild and fierce, but they are incapable of forming a battle plan."

As he spoke, howls drifted to her, diminished by distance but clear enough to chill the pulse of her blood.

"There is only one reason I can discern for their frenzied activity, Your Highness." His gaze caught her now, azure and cold. "The shadowlanders are trying to break through."

Hot bile burned the back of her throat and she fought to keep her stomach under control. Her allies were caught between the spawn and the Merakhi. "How soon can we charge?"

"Soon, Highness, but I must hold something in reserve for the mounts. We cannot spend them completely in the charge, or we will fail to get clear."

"Will we get clear?" Adora winced at her question. It sounded too much like an omen of failure.

Liam shrugged. "I will be able to answer that better in a few minutes." He raised his hand, circled it twice in the air above his head and thrust it forward.

The column moved ahead at a canter, the distance to the spawn now less than half a league. Other sounds came to her now, misplaced threads in the tapestry of noise woven by the baying of ferrals—the clash of armor, the piercing scream of men, and something more.

She watched as the ferrals caught a scent or sound of the threat at their backs. First one, then another peeled from the snarling mass to check the air, confused.

At her side Liam tensed, a human bowstring ready to fire. When the first dog peeled away from the pack to charge, he thrust his arm forward.

The column sprang to a gallop.

21

BLOOD COURSE

WATERSON'S HORSE APPEARED at her side, and his hand snaked out to grab her reins, slowing her. Fear and rage heated her face. "What do you think you're doing? Unhand me!"

His face darkened. "And let you die? Look in your hand."

Adora glanced down, saw the rapier Rula had given her in one hand, the reins in the other. What had she been about to do?

"Do you want to help?" Waterson screamed at her.

She nodded.

"Then put away your sword and follow me." He moved to the nearest supply cart, grabbed three of the wood lances, and signaled her to do the same. The trimmed branches, between three and four paces in length, threw her off balance, and she struggled to manage her horse and the weapons at the same time.

A concussion deeper than sound alone pulsed through the air, and she turned to see the first line of watchmen enter the end of the defile and hit the spawn. The bays turned to yelps and screams as ferrals and men collided, but the watch refused to engage, and the attack peeled away.

The dogs, driven mad by bloodlust and pain, rushed to pursue

216

the first line, and the second line hit them, lances taking many of the dogs in the side before they wheeled their mounts and returned, with the spawn struggling to follow.

Adora looked at the sharpened end of a lance. No, not sharpened, barbed. She spurred her mount forward, tossed one of the lances to Liam, another to Rokha. Canis dragging lances that wouldn't come loose came baying after the watchmen. But they were slow.

Liam turned, a fist in the air, his face scowling with impatience, waiting for his line to rearm. Then they charged once more.

The wounded spawn, eyes red with hatred, bayed and fled. The watchmen ignored the fleeing canis, concentrated on the spawn coming from the defile, and braced for impact.

Adora could make out men on the other side of the pack now, dim figures with short desperate moves within the canyon—they appeared to be fighting the dogs as well.

She returned to the cart for more lances, but when she saw the diminished pile, her mouth went dry. Would there be enough?

Ferrals came again from the defile, but many appeared to be injured and seemed fearful. With a shout, Liam ordered the formation to charge. A dozen men on each flank drew swords to protect the sortie. Most of the dogs turned in retreat.

Horses with empty saddles ran across the field, fouling the battle line. Waterson tossed a lance to the closest watchman and pulled his horse close to hers, shielding her.

With a shout Adora imagined could be heard half a mile away, Liam called for a change in formation. It seemed he hoped to draw what was left of the dogs and finish them off. The watchmen packed themselves in a double ring around Adora and Liam. The outer ring held lances at ready. In the gaps between them, the men of the inner ring fired arrows at any of the spawn that came close. And then it was over. With a clear line of retreat, shadowlanders poured from the defile, running to clear the way.

Adora gaped.

One shadowlander, his horse hobbling, made for them. Dust

caked his face, and blood ran from a jagged rip down his jawline. Adora pulled her horse next to Liam's.

The man looked at the ring of black-garbed watchmen. "Who is in charge?"

Adora pointed to Liam. "Captain Liam of the watch runs the battle line, but the mission to secure the alliance with Haven is in my care. I'm Adora, niece to King Rodran."

The man bowed in his saddle, spraying droplets of blood on the ground. "I'm Hadrian Alba, commander of the vanguard of the army of the council of the solis."

"How long will it take to clear the defile, Commander?" Liam asked. "And what can you tell me of the battle on your rearguard?"

"Nearly a hundred thousand people fill the canyon, Captain," Alba said. "Though we are outnumbered, the rearguard will hold. The land narrows leading into the defile on the southern side as well, so the Merakhi cannot use their greater numbers to flank us." Alba pointed to the cliffs at the top of the canyon. "We must get my men up there."

"Why?"

Alba gave Adora a vicious smile, stretching the blood caked on his face. "We've rigged the passage. At my order, my men will cause an avalanche that will seal off the canyon. The Merakhi won't be able to follow us."

Liam nodded his approval. "Is the canyon rigged at both ends?"

Alba shook his head.

Liam clenched his jaw. "Which end?"

"This one."

Adora watched as Liam digested the news, staring toward the defile that spewed soldiers and civilians like so much debris in a flood. Carts clogged the canyon as people pressed to escape. Movement through the passage looked on the verge of grinding to a halt.

"The Merakhi will chew into your soldiers all the way through the passage." Liam snapped an order to the nearest lieutenant of the watch, a gangly redhead. "Royce, gather two squads of men and follow me. We'll need ropes."

Liam turned to leave, but Alba grabbed him by the arm. "There's more, Captain." He ran a hand through sweat-stained hair. "The Merakhi have brought spawn with them. Some of them can fly."

Liam's jaw muscle jumped at the news, but his voice was controlled when he spoke. "Alba, set up a defensive perimeter around the mouth of the canyon. There are still canis about. Use the rest of your men to move your people out of the canyon as quickly as possible. Lieutenant Royce, you're with me."

Adora kicked her mount, prepared to override Liam's inevitable objection to her presence. Yet when she pulled alongside, it was Rokha who approached her, pitching her voice so only Adora could hear.

"You would jeopardize the mission, Princess?"

Adora stiffened at the rebuke but refused to be swayed. "There is more than this mission at stake." She nodded toward Liam. "If he dies, the hope of all Illustra dies with him."

Rokha's brown eyes flashed. "You think he is to be the soteregia, then?"

She shook her head. "It doesn't matter what I think. The herbwomen said both he and Errol had to be there. Liam must live through this, and if anything happens to you on the heights, there will be no one to tend his injuries."

Rokha opened her mouth to respond but just shook her head and motioned Adora toward Liam.

"You've given this thought?" he asked.

She nodded, trying to keep the flush of embarrassment from her face. "You may need more than one healer. There is more than just the mission to the shadow lands at stake here."

He nodded, but whether in comprehension or acquiescence, she didn't know.

"I hope you know how to climb, Your Highness."

She glanced at the towers of rock that defined the walls of the defile and gripped the reins. Heights unnerved her. Under Rokha's scrutiny, she forced her expression toward neutrality.

They dismounted at the foot of the plateau, where a crack in the stone a pace wide ran from top to bottom. One of the watchmen, a sandy-haired Gascon, whose thin frame belied his whiplike strength, began the climb trailing a skein of rope after him. He ascended the wall at a steady pace, his movements confident and sure. In minutes his outline diminished to a black speck against the russet stone.

Adora swallowed. Somewhere beneath her stomach, a tremble started, threatening to move to her arms and legs. She jerked at a touch on her arm.

Rokha smiled, eyes gently mocking. "If you can kill two men to gain your freedom, you should be able to face down a pile of rock. Just don't look down."

Surprised laughter burst from her, but the sound turned tremulous. Liam signaled men to go up one by one. Halfway through, he nodded toward Rokha, who brushed Adora's elbow as she left.

Then he sent the rest of the watchmen until only he and Adora were left. With a nod, he held the rope out to her. "You begin. I will come behind. Keep your eyes on the rock in front of you and the climb above."

A part of her wanted to protest that she did not need his safeguarding, but the vertical stretch of stone yawned before her, dizzying and threatening to dash her against the base of the plateau. Not trusting herself to speak, she nodded.

The rough fibers dug into her hands. A year ago they would have blistered in moments, but months of work with the sword had placed calluses in her palms and secured her from such hurts. On her right hand, anyway. Less than halfway up, the skin on her left hand broke, and the rope tore into the flesh beneath. With a growl, she braced her legs against the sides of the column and wrapped a bit of cloth around her palm. Ooze and blood wet the fabric.

Then she looked down.

Without warning, vertigo assaulted her and the world pitched sideways, her feet slipping from their hold on the rock. She squeezed her eyes shut as terror claimed her. Desperate to still the sensation of falling, she wrapped her arms and legs around the rope as soft whimpers clogged her throat.

The touch of a hand on her foot sent her into a panic, and she screamed before a voice intruded on her awareness.

"Highness, lift your head and open your eyes."

Adora pulled her face out of her arms and forced her eyelids to unclench. A blur of rock, nothing more than a violent swirl of color showed before her. Tremors shook her, and her hands slipped a fraction. Liam's hand clamped like a vise on her thigh, halting the slide.

"I can't get the world to stop spinning."

Liam didn't respond, and an irrational fear blossomed in her heart that he no longer shared the rope with her, had never been there at all, and she would eventually tire and fall to her death.

She peered down through slits. He wasn't there.

Sobs choked her.

The rope jerked, and her sobs threatened to grow to a wail. "I'm here," Liam said. His voice sounded close, as though his mouth rested scant inches from her ear. An arm powerful enough to bend iron closed around her waist, pulling her into a rough embrace.

"Put your arms around my neck."

"I'd have to let go of the rope to do that."

The arm compressing her midsection squeezed tighter. "Do you think I would dare let you fall? Errol would beat me black and blue with that stick of his."

A laugh, hysterical at the edges, slipped from Adora and echoed from the rock. She opened her eyes just enough to verify Liam's presence and threw her arms around his neck. He grunted at the sudden shift in weight and began climbing his way upward.

"Let me know if your arms get tired," he said into her ear. "I'll stop so you can rest. We should be at the top in a few minutes."

She nodded, smearing tears into his neck with her nose. Fatigue was the least of her worries. Enough panic-driven energy throbbed through her veins for her to hold Liam for hours if need be. Noises drifted to her from the floor of the canyon below as shadowlanders poured from the passage and soldiers screamed, urging them to move faster.

"We're almost there, Your Highness."

A shriek sounded above her, the noise tearing the wind as if a hawk had been given a human voice. Liam cursed, set his feet. One arm found her waist, moved her to his left hip. A second later the rasp of steel sounded as he drew. The thrum of a half dozen bows sounded, and the creature screeched again.

Adora forced her eyes open to see a monstrous shape coming at them, talons extended, mouth agape with pointed teeth, as though a bat had somehow managed to mate with a bird of prey. It dove in close, then wheeled away as Liam flicked his sword at it. Adora caught a glimpse of crazed yellow eyes, filled with insanity and intelligence. A flight of arrows kept the thing at bay as Liam sheathed his sword and pulled his way to the top of the plateau.

Adora rolled away, her hands embracing the security of the dirt and rock beneath her. A hand gripped her wrist, pulling her upright.

"Get up, Princess," Rokha said. "We're going to need every sword."

Adora lurched to her feet, weaving like a drunkard in the aftermath of her vertigo. Around her, watchmen battled flying spawn that filled the sky with talons and teeth. She yanked her sword loose as she stumbled. A shriek behind her caught her off guard, but before she could coax her feet to turn toward the threat, Rokha leapt, her sword whistling through the air above Adora's head.

The cry of the spawn turned into a wail, and the thing fell at Adora's feet, its wings beating the ground before going still.

Pairs of watchmen filled the northern end of the plateau, fighting back to back. None of the men were down, but those who'd been the first to climb bore grievous injuries. Dead spawn lay everywhere.

Adora spotted a shock of bright red hair. Lieutenant Royce fought with Liam, the two of them working their way to the cliff's edge, where ropes and nets held tons of rock. Liam's sword disappeared and reappeared in time to the lightning-fast flicks of his wrist, and a trail of dead and dying spawn appeared in his wake.

Adora felt a tug at her back and sensed Rokha's intention. They trailed after Liam, the cloud of spawn growing thicker as the bulk of the Merakhi army approached. The chasm that defined the passage yawned open just ahead, and she stopped as vertigo threatened to reclaim her.

"I can't," she yelled.

Rokha beckoned the nearest team of watchmen, who wove their way toward them with a flurry of sword strokes. At a signal Adora failed to see, Rokha and one of the watchmen swapped places.

"Do not fail to keep her safe," Rokha said. Her voice carried an edge to match her sword.

Adora's arm began to tire. Fear could only drive her for so long. "Who are you?"

"Sergeant Kirik."

Adora searched her memory, pulled the face of the squat Bellian before her. Kirik didn't boast the quickest blade, but he possessed the stubborn endurance common to his people.

"I don't know how much longer I can go, Sergeant."

Kirik put two fingers between his lips and whistled another pair of watchmen toward them. "Rest, Your Highness," Kirik said. "We will form the points of a triangle around you. When you've recovered enough to swing your sword again, one of us will rest in your place."

Squatting in the rock and dirt, Adora watched as Liam stalked the edge of the plateau, his eyes on the battle raging in the defile. He stood next to a large pile of rock, bound with a net of ropes. His attention on the floor of the passage never wavered, but his sword seemed to move of its own volition.

Time dragged by. Adora rose, ordered one of the watchmen guarding her to rest, and then rested herself when her turn came around again. Still Liam watched the edge. She lost count of the number of times she'd switched and had just sat again on the dirt in tearful fatigue when the air stilled with an abruptness that snatched her head from its resting place on her arms.

The last of the spawn twitched in its death throes at Liam's feet.

Adora's lungs heaved, and her arms hung like dead weights at her side. A carpet of dead ferrals covered the cliff top. "What kind of enemy do we face that they would throw away so many?"

No one answered. She forced herself to the edge, heedless of the dizziness that threatened to claim her, drawn by a change in Liam's posture. The captain signaled Lieutenant Royce, who moved to the other end of the netted rock the shadowlanders had placed above the defile to secure their escape.

The pair of them swung, swords flashing in the air, and the ring of metal against stone knelled a thrill of victory through Adora's chest. A cascade of tumbling rock poured into the passage, gaining momentum. Through the sound of its thunder, the shrill cries of dying men, animals, and spawn could be heard. And still it went on. Adora exulted. They'd done it. The army of the shadow lands had been secured.

Liam spun from the defile, turning Adora's cries of victory to ashes in her mouth. Far from expressing satisfaction or victory, his expression was set in lines of determination and his eyes flared with dire resolve. He walked past her toward the rope leading back to the floor of the canyon without a word.

Rokha trailed in his wake, her lips pursed in bitterness, her healer's kit in her hands. "I'll need your help. Some of these men should be tended before they attempt the descent. Watchmen are thickheaded. You'll probably have to use your authority to make them accept treatment."

Adora grabbed Rokha's arm as she came within reach. "What did he see?"

Rokha's brown eyes, so dark they were almost black, found hers. "The shadow land's army is gone. The vanguard is all we will have to take with us back to Illustra. The rest died in the passage fighting to get their people free."

Adora gaped, her mind refusing to accept Rokha's pronouncement, but Ru's daughter went on. "We've gained little more than a multitude of refugees."

22

ONGOL

TWO WEEKS AFTER their escape from the maelstrom, the landscape to port began to change. Errol watched sand and rock give way to scattered trees that grew more dense with each passing league. Soon the vegetation became an impenetrable morass.

The air turned heavy, laden with water, and heat that had been oppressive became unbearable. Crew and passengers alike shed tunics to go about bare-chested. Sweat ran as freely as water in the quiet air. Where before the sails had billowed and popped, now they seldom bellied and often hung limp before filling again.

Then the wind stopped altogether, stranding their ship in the calm as if it were dry-docked. Tek stared at the slack canvas that hung lifeless from the masts and chewed his sailor's vocabulary through gritted teeth. The coast lay less than a mile distant, teasing them. After two days in which tempers grew thin, Tek called a conference on deck.

"We're becalmed, gentlemen, and no doubt."

Rale nodded, the motion sending drops of sweat onto the deck to join similar splatters from the rest of them. "The question is, will we stay that way?"

Tek shrugged. "There be no way of knowing for sure. My charts and maps tell no tales of anything past the whirlpool." He sighed. "But the sea itself gives us a sign and a bad one at that."

"How so?" Rale asked.

"No boats, man." Tek pointed. "We haven't seen a fishing vessel or any sort of boat since we started along the western edge of the continent."

"The tiamat and other sea spawn could explain that, Captain," Merodach said. His skin had turned darker under the sun's onslaught, and his ice-blue eyes seemed lit from within.

"Aye." Tek scratched his chin. "But we've seen no sign of spawn for days. I think we be at the end of the wind, and it be gone for longer than we can wait for it to return. We need to put ashore."

Rale turned to scan the coastline. "We don't know where we are, Captain."

"How were we ever going to know?" Errol asked. The heat lent his question a harsh edge.

"By the rivers, lad," Tek said. "Soon or late, rivers run into the sea, and when they do, people build cities there."

"Or fishing villages, at the least," Merodach said.

Rale looked at him, his heavy brows raised. "Errol?"

He started. "What?"

His teacher chuckled. "The Judica placed the mission in your hands. What should we do?"

He looked across the security and safety of the ship's rail to the wall of green that crowded the coast. No road or path or even animal track led from the beach. If they landed, they would be as lost and without bearings as they were on the ship, but they'd have no shelter.

"If the decision is up to me, I say we wait three days. If there's still no wind, you, Merodach, and I will put ashore with all the provisions we can carry and move south until we find people. When we do, I hope to Deas they're Ongolese."

The ship drifted south with the current while they waited for the return of a wind that never came. Time slipped by in a sodden haze until dawn of the third day. With reluctance chewing at him, Errol gave the order to board the ship's solitary rowboat, and they set off for the coast.

Merodach pulled the oars with the fluid motion of one born to water. "My family lives on the coast of Soeden," the watchman said. A ghost of a smile played at the corners of his mouth, and Errol marveled again at the change Rokha had wrought in the formerly stoic watchman.

"Do you miss them?" Errol asked.

Merodach's eyes gazed off into the distance. "Watchmen give up their family for the honor of protecting the king. Since the first watch donned black and forsook their kin, all watchmen go by a single name. It's a sign of our unswerving commitment to the crown."

"Until the Judica voted to split the watch to start guarding the benefices."

From his seat on the rear thwart, Rale growled his opinion. "Weir's doing. If the watch had been kept intact, Sarin's murders might have been prevented."

Merodach dipped the oars in the water and pulled as he shook his head. "I doubt it. Hundreds of years of peace made the watch as complacent as the Judica. Few of us protested the church's move. Most believed the next king would come from the rank of benefices."

Rale drew a sharp breath before he sighed. "Illustra has lost much."

Merodach nodded. "And there will be more to lose. Even if we win."

They beached with the grinding noise of wet sand scraping wood. Errol's first impression of the jungle was a riot of smells as sea detritus mixed with the odors of decaying foliage and a thousand blooming plants.

The first mate held the boat steady as Errol and the captains jumped in knee-deep water and waded ashore, shouldering the packs that held their rations. Rale put a foot on the gunwale and fixed the first mate with a level stare. "Tell Captain Tek to maintain his position for a month. We'll either return or send word if we are able."

The mate's mouth pulled to one side in a smirk. "Oh aye, I'll tell him." He pushed off with the oars and started back to the ship.

Rale watched with a sour expression. "Which is not the same as saying Tek will actually do it."

Errol fidgeted under the weight of his pack as Merodach led the way down the beach. Months of food and fighting had made him tough, but the two captains of the watch were still larger and stronger, and he resorted to using the odd metal staff Martin had found as a walking stick.

An hour or so later, they stopped so Merodach could scout the way ahead. Errol shrugged off his pack with a sigh of relief and ate a portion of his rations. With nothing better to do, he pulled his staff to his lap and examined the ancient find. The ends narrowed to a point, yet despite what should have been a fragile spot in the weapon, it showed no sign of breaking or even chipping, as wood would have. He ran his fingers along the metal, marveling again that it could feel smooth and yet always offer a sure grip despite the presence of rain or sweat.

He scrutinized the length. There was not a mark on it. Impossible. He distinctly remembered parrying any number of thrusts from swords made with forge-hardened steel.

The sounds of the jungle faded from the forefront of his awareness as he handed the staff to Rale, who took it with an air of avid curiosity and worked a set of moves. The buzz of displaced air filled the beach.

He was soon drenched with sweat and stopped to wipe his brow. "Ten years ago I might have beaten Cruk with a weapon like this. I've never seen metal like it. Not steel, it's lighter than ash or even aspen, and it settles in the hand as if it knows how to fight." His hands caressed the staff before giving it back to Errol with obvious reluctance. "That's quite a weapon, lad. I wouldn't place money on anyone against you with that in your hands."

Errol's desire to spar, to prove himself against the best, had left him, burned away by the procession of men he'd killed in Merakh. He frowned, trying to remember just when he'd lost the need to match his skill against others. With a grunt, he levered himself to his feet, shifted to the firmer footing of wet sand close to the water, and began to move.

The inactivity of ship travel had left his muscles tight and resistant, but they relaxed when he stopped trying to force the staff and simply flowed through the moves Rale had taught him so long ago. After a few minutes he closed his eyes. Peace covered him, and his awareness heightened. The murmur of waves caressing the shore mixed with the cries of animals shielded by the jungle. The taste and smells of the sea and earth blended in his senses. His feet found sure purchase in the grit of the cool wet sand, and the wind kissed his face.

And always he moved, flowing like water as the wind parted and rejoined. Why would he ever want to fight when he could simply dance like this?

Merodach's return, footsteps whisper light on the sand, became part of his awareness, yet he continued. From behind closed lids, he sensed no urgency in the watchman's demeanor, only the steady breath of his lungs mingling with the breeze. At last Errol grounded the staff and opened his eyes with a smile, content in the moment.

The Soede nodded. "I hope no one ever beats you, Errol. There may be men more deadly, but there are none more beautiful."

Errol shouldered his pack to follow Merodach, but a call from the water stopped them. The rowboat approached the shore again with Tek, the first mate, and a pair of crewmen driving the oars. When the boat slid up onto the sand, Tek hoisted a heavy pack and jumped lightly into the surf to join them.

His weather-beaten face crinkled into a sheepish smile. "I be thinking that if the Ongolese are close, this be as good a route as any a merchant could wish, rivers or no."

Rale fixed him with a businesslike stare. "We're on land now, Captain Tek."

Tek's mouth pulled to one side and ducked his head. "Say

no more, watchman. You be calling the orders till we be back aboard ship."

"Not me—him." Errol looked to see Rale pointing his way. Not a trace of irony or amusement betrayed itself on Elar Indomiel's face. His teacher really meant for him to take command.

Errol sighed as he squirmed under the weight of his pack. It seemed as if it carried more than just physical burdens. He looked back at his footprints at the water's end. The waves had already erased most of the evidence of his presence. Tek, Rale, and Merodach stood looking at him as if he were actually in charge.

"Let's go."

They marched south toward a line of craggy hills whose rocks bore ancient evidence of fire. Nothing grew on the scorched slopes, and the smell of sulfur drifted in wisps from fissures in the ground. The beach ended at a sheer cliff that extended into the water. Merodach, from his vanguard position, said this was as far as he had scouted and gave Errol a questioning look.

At Errol's nod they began to pick their way upward toward a saddle in the ridge above them. It looked absurdly high, but no path or road or even animal track presented itself, only stretches of black rock pocked by holes.

Errol stooped to pick up a piece that had broken off and grunted in surprise at its light weight.

"It's volcanic," Merodach said. "As it cools it leaves those holes. There's more air than stone in your hand." He smiled at Errol's expression. "We have them in the far north of Soeden."

When they crested the hill an hour later, they surveyed a different world. The lifeless expanse of rock gave way to plant growth on the southern side. Grasses and weeds dominated at first, but farther down the slope, broad-leafed ferns and trees grew thickly enough to block their view. In the distance, they saw a fishing village wrapped around a crescent lagoon. A solitary ship, a Merakhi longboat, stood at anchor, but nothing moved on board.

"There be a mystery," Tek said. "Nothing that delicate could make it through the maelstrom."

Errol shrugged, more concerned about being spotted than how the ship had gotten there. "There must be another route here."

Tek's eyes narrowed with a speculative look. "Aye, lad, and if I can find it . . ." He gave his head a little shake. "That be a voyage for another time."

They threaded their way down the mountain toward the jungle, the smell of vegetation and animals growing with each step.

Tek drew his sword with a rasp. "I don't mean to tell you your business, lad," he said to Errol. "But strange places often hide strange animals. A beast of the verdant can kill us just as dead as a spawn."

Merodach's blade caught the light, and Errol gripped his metal staff, point forward. As they entered the shrouded darkness of the jungle, a cascade of sound and smell struck with the force of a blow, and he strained his eyes to adjust to the sudden gloom. Hints of motion at the limits of his vision set him scanning their surroundings with jerks of his head in a futile attempt to see everywhere at once.

A startled yelp escaped him when Tek grabbed him from behind and yanked him backward. Errol landed on his backside at the same time Tek's sword flashed, its stroke joining the hiss of a coiled snake on the jungle floor.

A serpent head two hands across flew into the growth to leave the rest of the body, as big around as Errol's thigh, writhing on the path.

Tek pulled him to his feet with a chuckle. "That be one story I did not credit 'til now." His face split into a sheepish grin. "They say its coils be strong enough to kill a cow and its jaws wide enough to swallow a child." He shrugged. "Or a small man."

Rale nodded. "I suggest we keep an eye on the canopy as well."

The muscles in Errol's neck grew fatigued with his attempts to see above him and all around as well, but they descended toward the deserted village without further incident. He, Rale, and Tek stopped within the vegetation's cover as Merodach stepped forward to search the village.

Errol made out bodies and clear signs of fighting. When

Merodach returned, Errol expected he would suggest they skirt the village, but the grim Soede surprised him. "You need to look at this."

Errol followed, his back straight and tense, through the maze of wooden huts. Before they reached the center of the village, he'd stopped to examine a half dozen bodies, all wearing the white of Merakhi soldiers, all of them janiss, elite fighters.

None of the bodies were Ongolese.

"It was a trap," Errol said. "These men were lured here and slaughtered." He caught Merodach's eye. "Are there any bodies that aren't Merakhi?"

Merodach gave him an approving glance even while he shook his head.

"How many of them died from arrows?"

The Soede's approval grew. "Almost all. Only a few bear sword cuts."

Rale brushed past Errol with a curse. He knelt at one of the bodies and lifted one of its hands, then laid a hand on the corpse's brow. "He hasn't stiffened yet." Rale glanced at the sun. "He's been dead less than three hours, but it's impossible to tell in this heat just how long." He scanned the jungle. "We've probably been seen."

Tek's hand leapt to his sword.

Merodach motioned for him to put it away. "There's more on the other side." Then he moved away as if Rale's pronouncement did not concern him.

Errol walked through the dead with his qualms nipping at his heels. Why hadn't he cast to see if entering the village was safe?

Did it matter? There had been no other choice. The book of Magis was in Ongol, and this route had been their only way in. What was the point in casting when all other options had been stripped away?

An additional two score Merakhi dead lay on the stretch of ground between the edge of the village and the jungle. Most of them had fallen from arrows in the back—arrows that were no longer in evidence.

Merodach held up a hand, and they stopped. Without apparent transition two score Ongolese appeared, each holding a bow. The man at the fore, who appeared to be the leader, wore three stripes of red on each cheek and towered two hands over Rale. Huge scars, pink and livid against his dark skin, bore testimony to horrific injuries suffered in the past. Every man wore evidence of similar indignities or worse. A warrior gazed back at him with a single eye, the other lost in the mass of puckered flesh on one side of his face. The leader barked an order in a tongue like nothing Errol had ever heard before.

Merodach turned to face him. "I hope you picked up something of their language while we were in Merakh. Their leader doesn't seem to be the patient type."

A dozen bows came up, and the warriors stepped forward to surround them. Errol grunted in cynical amusement even as his stomach tried to hide behind his spine. He'd witnessed what Ongolese fighters could do in Merakh. Even without the bows, he and his friends wouldn't stand a chance.

Tek's voice growled something from behind Errol. The array of deep-chested warriors surrounding them laughed, but the leader frowned and barked an order. The bows dropped, but hands still rested on swords.

Rale turned with an expression of forced calm on his face. "You speak their language, Captain?" At Tek's nod, he asked, "What did you just say?"

Tek smirked. "I said a lion such as he would gain little honor by slaying a mouse such as me."

Rale darted a glance at the fuming Ongolese leader. "In the future, Tek, you will clear your comments with me before speaking. Understand?"

Tek smiled and pointed at Errol. "I thought he was in charge."

Rale's eyes, hot with tension, found Errol. "Well, lad?"

The leader shifted his weight, showing signs of impatience. Errol concentrated on keeping his movements deliberate. "Captain Tek, please convey our respects to the Ongol leader. Tell him that we too fight the Merakhi." Errol darted a glance at the leader. "Be brief."

Tek let loose a stream of rich, rounded syllables that put Errol in mind of food and hospitality. The line of Ongolese warriors gave appreciative nods at hearing their language, but the leader's posture remained tense. He jabbed a crooked finger at the four of them as he began to speak.

Errol waited for Tek to translate. The sea captain grimaced. "He says that mice are vermin and should be exterminated before they have a chance to multiply." Tek coughed. "Maybe I shouldn't have made that first comment."

The momentary favor they'd gained from Tek's knowledge of the language appeared to be slipping. Errol nudged his arm. "Tell them I am looking for one named Hadari, who used to be chief of the guard for the Merakhi ilhotep, and that I owe him my life."

Rale whistled. "Boy, that's a dangerous move. We don't know if these men view Hadari as a friend or an enemy."

Tek nodded. "I do hate to agree with the watchman, lad, but he's got the right of it. Best to let the information out slowly."

Errol looked at the soldiers, their black skin shining in the sun. He sensed tension in the set of their legs, preparation for attack. "We're out of time, Tek, and the truth will have to come out anyway since finding Hadari and the book is the purpose of our journey."

The sea captain wet his lips, relayed Errol's message in a series of staccato bursts as he squinted, searching for the right words. The leader's hand jumped to his sword hilt, and he drew the large curved sword, his face storming.

Errol took a step back. "Are you sure you said it right?"

Tek nodded. "Aye, lad."

A voice cut the air, crackling with command, and a man stepped forward, two circles of white decorating the area underneath each eye. The leader bristled at the tone, took another step toward them with his sword drawn. Errol swallowed at the size of the blade. Thick and heavy, it looked more like an executioner's axe than a sword, but the Ongolese looked muscled enough to wield it like a rapier.

The man with the spots barked a short command, eyes blazing. The leader stopped as if he'd struck a wall. With a snarl, he backed up, his neck corded with frustrated violence.

An ache in his chest reminded Errol to breathe again. "What did they say?"

"I can tell you most of the words they said, lad, but I can't explain it. I know their language from my travels, but there be undercurrents here that defy me."

Rale shook his head.

Errol kept his eyes on the two Ongolese. They looked ready to draw weapons on each other. "Just tell me what they said."

Tek ducked his head. "The one with the white spots be a holy man of some type, I think. Something about your friend's name gave offense to Red Stripes there." Tek cracked a lopsided grin. "He seems to be a chief of sorts. I don't think people that offend him live very long."

Errol sighed. It seemed Tek's ability with the language might not be as helpful as he'd hoped.

Tek pointed. "White Spots stepped in and claimed us. We seem to be under his jurisdiction now."

The chief still had his weapon drawn. He didn't look to be a man who relinquished authority with grace. Errol didn't care much for their chances if the chief decided to defy the holy man's orders.

"Now what?" he asked.

Tek shrugged. "You be as informed as me, lad. I think we have to wait for White Spots to decide what to do with us."

Mere heartbeats later, the holy man snapped an order, and four warriors came forward with thick leather thongs and tied their hands behind their back. Then they left the village moving northeast through the jungle at a pace that winded Errol and left Tek gasping and red-faced.

White Spots called for a rest after the ship captain fell facedown the second time. The closest warriors slapped Tek's legs and made comments that set the Ongolese to laughing. Except the chief.

The holy man came forward with a waterskin and offered them each a drink. Tek's eyes widened as the liquid hit his tongue, and he gasped. Errol took a cautious pull, though he could detect no hint of fermentation. The drink flowed across his tongue with hints of mint and peaches and something bitter, like tea but far stronger. His heart thrummed as his fatigue disappeared.

The holy man leaned forward as Errol drank, towering over him. "Hadari's name is strong, pale one. Most revere him." He inclined his head toward the chief. "But not all."

His voice, deep and rich like the volcanic soil that nourished the jungle, gave his words an unfamiliar lilt that Errol struggled to follow.

"You understood us the whole time?"

"You may call me Adayo." The holy man nodded with a smile. "I speak Merakhi also. You run well for a pale one. Your companions are not so well-suited for the journey as you. What is your name?"

Errol looked in Adayo's face as his lips formed his answer, but he clamped his jaws shut against his response. An avid desire lurked behind the intense brown of the holy man's eyes. If they meant to take them to Hadari, why were they bound? What need required running men through the jungle until they dropped from exhaustion? Months of moving by horseback had sapped his ability to run easily, but his condition still surpassed the rest of the party. Of the three, only Merodach remained upright. Tek and Rale sat on the hard-packed earth, heads down and breathing hard.

The holy man peered at him, waiting.

Errol stared back, considering. Every people expressed the talent differently. Illustra had readers who cast lots, while the nomads produced theurgists and the Merakhi had akhen, ghost-walkers. How did the talent manifest itself in Ongol? What would Adayo do with his name?

"Tell me, Adayo, if you're taking us to Hadari, why are we bound?"

The man's smile never wavered, but tension entered it, and his eyes flashed with disappointment. "Hadari's name is known to the Merakhi, and reports have come to us of northerners aligned with the sand people. You may harbor the burning ones, though you show it not."

Errol shook his head. "The burning ones?"

Adayo nodded. "There are those among the Merakhi who allow spirits to inhabit them." He shook his head and sniffed. "They carry the smell of fire, like the burning mountains."

"Malus." Errol traced a path with his hand from the top of his head to his stomach. "Is this why you want to know my name?"

The holy man nodded and smiled, but it held only resolve.

Errol bowed. "Please forgive my hesitation. I do not know what is possible for you. I would prefer not to surrender my name until I know it's safe to do so."

Adayo nodded. "You are wise, pale one, but until I am sure of you, you will be bound." He turned and called an order to the circle of warriors, and they resumed their passage through the forest.

Strengthened by repeated doses of the holy man's drink, they kept a steady jog that ate up the miles, but always Adayo urged them to greater speed. By the time the green of the forest canopy began to darken toward gray with the inexorable descent of the sun, the holy man's frustration became obvious. In fact, everywhere Errol looked, the men of Ongol evidenced signs of agitation. Red Stripes—the war leader, Errol had come to learn—entered a heated argument with Adayo, an argument the war leader punctuated by stabbing the air with his sword. Errol saw many of the warriors nodding agreement out of Adayo's line of sight.

The holy man's voice rose, quieting the sounds of the jungle. He turned to Errol. "We must not tarry here, pale one. We are too close to the boscage of the ancients. If the short one cannot keep up, we will have to leave him."

The specifics of Adayo's warning escaped Errol, but there was no mistaking the tone he used. The Ongolese had been on a customary path close to danger, but Errol and his companions had caused an unexpected delay. Now they stood at the edge of something even these oversized warriors feared, something that came out at night. Errol didn't bother to speculate. The reaction of the Ongolese warriors told the story.

Spawn.

He stood, squared up to face Adayo. "How far do we have to get by sundown?"

Adayo's brows furrowed beneath the smooth skin of his shaved head. "At least two more leagues, pale one, and brother sun will be lost to us in less than an hour."

Errol glanced at Red Stripes. The man stood, sword drawn, ready and eager to spill blood. With a gesture he pointed the tip of his massive sword toward Tek.

Adayo turned to Errol with a shrug. "Phamba says that we should spill the blood of the slow one to buy us enough time. On this point we agree. It is death to remain this close to the ancients after dark."

Errol shivered in the heat. "These ancients are the spawn of the malus?"

Adayo give him a tight-lipped smile. "You are wise, pale one, to see so clearly. They seldom venture from the plain." His mouth stretched, showing white, even teeth. "Unless they scent humans."

Errol gestured with his tied arms. "Untie us. The white-haired one and I will help our brother make the distance."

Adayo smiled as if Errol had given him a gift. "And what token will you provide that I may trust you?"

"My name is Errol Stone."

Adayo's smile grew, and he bowed. With a cry he turned to Phamba and shouted in Ongolese. Then he cut their bonds. With his face close to Errol's he breathed his words like a blessing. "Now, pale one, we must run if you would live."

23

THE CITY OF FIRE

ERROL'S LUNGS HEAVED as they strove to make the distance that would grant them safety from the spawn. Leaves as large as his torso whipped across his face as he struggled to keep the pace the holy man, Adayo, and the chieftain, Phamba, demanded.

Tek's weight, shared with Merodach, added no more than perhaps ten pounds to Errol's burden. The sailing captain remained fit, despite his years of land-locked exile, so he was still able to do his part, but the speed the Ongolese required threatened to undo them all. A few paces behind, Rale ran with the determination of one who had decided his heart would burst before he quit.

Tek tripped, then fell, taking Errol down with him. Phamba growled and pulled his sword, advancing on the gasping figure of the ship's captain.

Tek stared up at the broad gleam of the blade, panting. Waiting. "Tell Brandy I loved her as much as the sea."

Errol scrambled to put himself between Phamba and Amos Tek.

"Move, lad," Tek said. "I can't make the run. I've turned my ankle. It won't bear my weight."

"Then we'll carry you," Errol said without looking back. "Get

239

up on your good leg so you can wrap your arms around Mero-dach's shoulders and mine."

Adayo drew his sword, mirroring Phamba, the tip coming within inches of Errol's chest. "Stupid pale one, would you die for him?"

"We won't die."

The holy man turned his head and spat. "The ancients will devour you if you do not cross the river before sunset. At night, this jungle belongs to them. He will not make it." He gestured with the blade. "Move, pale one. Better I kill your comrade quickly with the sword than leave him for the twisted ones. They keep their prey alive as long as possible while they devour it. Would you wish that for him?"

The holy man's simple description sent pulses of fear down Errol's spine. "Then leave us. We will make the crossing or not, but I won't leave him."

Adayo shook his head. "You do not have that choice, Errol Stone. You have given me your name, your complete name. By the law of our land, you are mine to command." The holy man's gaze bored into him, and the blade neared his throat. "I ask you again, would you die for him?"

Movement at the corner of his eye pulled his gaze. Guards held Merodach and Rale, a blade at each man's throat and a point at their belly. Errol tried not to shrink from Adayo's threat. Rale and Merodach offered no help, their eyes, one pair blue like the sky and the other gray, were resigned. He swallowed. Were either of those captains in charge, Tek would be dead already. They were men of the watch, accustomed to sacrifice—theirs or someone else's.

He couldn't do it. They might all die for the sake of a gimpy sea captain, but he would not be the means of a friend's death.

Fury contorted Adayo's face. "Move, northlander. Move if you would live."

"No."

Adayo raised his sword.

"Enough," Phamba said.

Adayo whipped toward Phamba. "He has not said."

Phamba shrugged. "It does not matter, holy one. He has chosen. Would you strike him down because the words do not follow our tradition? He is not Ongolese."

Adayo pulled a breath that would have burst the lungs of a normal-sized man and nodded. Phamba signaled a pair of warriors who came forward to lift Tek and support his weight. Errol darted looks at Tek, then Phamba, then Adayo.

"A test?"

Phamba stepped forward. "Yes, little one." The wave of his arm took in the warriors surrounding them. "We have lost many to the Merakhi that have come in the guise of friends."

Errol goggled. He had a difficult time imagining anyone foolish enough to attack these giant men of the south.

Phamba shook his head. "Do not be deceived. The sand dwellers carry a strength that is more than human, and they are growing. Already some of their speakers, those you call ghostwalkers, match us in size as the spirit corrupts their fleshly vessel."

Errol squinted. "But how did you know we weren't Merakhi?"

Adayo sheathed his giant sword. "The ghostwalkers have the means to appear as men of the north, but they would never hesitate to kill one of their own if it meant survival for the remainder. You refused to abandon your comrade."

"The people of the river would have killed him themselves," Phamba added.

Errol adjusted his estimation of the Ongolese chieftain. There were layers there. "So you understood everything we said?"

Phamba's grin warmed him like an unexpected burst of sun on a cloudy day. "People speak more freely when they think they cannot be understood."

"The ancients?" Errol asked.

Grins slid from the faces of the Ongolese. "Real enough," Adayo said. "But the river that denies them passage is just over the next hill. The offspring of evil do not care for the water."

"And Hadari?" Errol asked.

"I told you the truth, pale one. He lives in the city of fire just beyond the river. Now, we must hurry. The threat of the ancients is a truth, and I'm no longer young and foolish enough to tempt their jungle after dark."

They continued at a walk. Merodach and Rale closed in next to Errol as they followed the Ongolese who carried Tek to the river.

"Well done, Errol," Rale said. He kept his face forward as he spoke, but Errol could see the gleam of pride in his eyes. "The outcome would have been different had I made the decision. The Ongolese were looking for a different type of sacrifice than the one I would have offered."

Merodach nodded. "Or I. We swore never to outlive the king again."

"But Tek's not a watchman," Errol protested.

"When he joined our mission, he accepted the same responsibility," Merodach said. "You are to be kept alive at all costs."

Merodach didn't elaborate, and Errol didn't require it, but inside, so deep in his chest he could pretend it didn't exist, burned the hope that somehow he might live through whatever lay ahead.

They crested a hill and descended toward a broad sluggish river that flowed to the southeast, separating the jungle from a broad plain. In the dying moments of the sun, orange light flared and shimmered in reflections from a hundred domes beyond the water.

Errol stopped to stare in admiration.

"It is not so large as Guerir," Phamba said. "And I am told that Erinon is larger still, but I have never heard of a city that is more beautiful than Gomibe."

They crossed the water on large flat-bottomed boats as the sun set, washing the plain in crimson. By the time their crafts bumped the pier on the opposite side of the river, they needed torchlight to guide them into the city.

The streets of Gomibe proved to be wide and well lit, its denizens wearing loose-fitting clothes dyed in bright colors, with blue, green, and red predominant. Yet the men and women Errol saw hurried about tasks wearing expressions that seemed at odds with the cheerful aspect of their city.

"A city preparing for war," Rale said.

"Truly," Adayo said. "In truth, we cannot—"

"Do not," Phamba interrupted. "That is for the mfalme."

They ushered them deeper into a city designed in a series of concentric arcs with roads radiating from the nexus like rays of the sun. As they drew near to their destination, one of the men ran ahead. At the center of Gomibe, they came within sight of a large low-domed building that could have held the entire village of Callowford. An entryway jutted out from the side, and a quartet of guards bearing grievous scars stood watch. Phamba and Adayo stepped forward side by side and bowed.

"We bring one who speaks for his country, Captain."

The man they addressed, a heavy-set mountain with a brooding countenance, eyed Errol and the rest of the party with disapproval. "He is poorly dressed for an emissary. And his manners are lacking if he comes to the city of fire without the speech of his host on his tongue."

Errol stepped forward and bent at the waist until his torso was parallel to the ground. "Your pardon, Captain. I only met Hadari a few months ago, and there was scant opportunity to learn your language."

The captain raised an eyebrow at him. "He comes to us with names of power on his tongue. How do you know Hadari, northlander?"

"He was chief of the guard while I was imprisoned in Guerir."

The captain shifted his attention to Adayo and Phamba. "He is plain spoken for a pale one. Usually their answers shift and slide like a serpent in the water. Did they pass the test?"

Phamba stiffened at the question. "They would not be here else."

The captain ignored Phamba's reaction. "The mfalme will see them." He wrinkled his nose. "But not while they have the smell of tar and salt water on them." He raised his hand, and a pair of Ongolese women, tall and sloe-eyed, came forward to take charge of them. "See that they are bathed and dress them in something more appropriate."

An hour later, Errol tugged at the fabric again. The loose-fitting clothes of the Ongolese rested against his skin in unfamiliar ways, and he squirmed, trying to adapt. His face still held the fire of embarrassment at being washed by the women of the mfalme's staff, his consternation a source of much amusement.

He stood next to Rale and Merodach, who were likewise attired. The two men looked comfortable in the strange clothes. Perhaps their training within the watch had given them the ability to ignore such external distractions. The mfalme's chamber lay at the center of the low-domed building. Errol entered into a throne room unlike any other.

The Ongolese ruler held court in the middle of a garden; an opening in the dome's center revealing the star-filled sky. Palms reached upward, flanked by ferns, and the air carried the heavy scents of a myriad of flowers. Blooms in a riot of color were visible in the yellow torchlight.

They followed their escort along a path that wound toward the center of the garden, where the mfalme sat in a high-backed throne made of wood so dark it was almost black. Ongol's ruler sat unmoving beneath a large covering made from the skin of some animal that had carried white and orange stripes in life.

The man on the throne loomed tall as all the Ongolese, yet he carried enough bulk to appear squat. Torchlight gleamed off a scalp that held no hint of hair, but his eyebrows were full and thick above eyes as dark as obsidian. Though much of the mfalme was hidden, his body showed evidence of horrific conflict. His left arm ended just below the elbow, and his right foot, poking from beneath the coverlet, was nothing more than a stump of puckered scar tissue. Ongol's king was severely crippled. Errol tried without success not to stare.

The mfalme leaned to his right to speak in a voice as deep as the earth, spasms of pain twisting his scarred face as he addressed one whose unscarred body stood in sharp contrast to his own.

Hadari.

Errol's heart pounded at the sight of his friend, but Hadari deferred acknowledgment. "The mfalme says you have noted his medallions." The king's mouth stretched the memory of a wound that laced his jawline. Hadari continued. "Speak. Should the Ongolese not fight the ancients?"

Errol bowed. "Forgive me, mfalme, but the ones you fight are kept from you by water on all sides. Why do you fight?"

The mfalme nodded and answered Errol's question directly.

"You are wise, northlander. Few of my own men would ask, since we have always fought. Many do not think to question what has always been done. The ancients occupy the verdant in the center of our land, but though they are numerous and do not die from their years, they cannot breed. So we fight them. Already their numbers are half what they were ten generations ago." The Ongolese ruler's face stretched in a parody of a smile.

"We are patient," Hadari said. "The women informed the mfalme you bear medallions of your own on your skin. Surely you understand this."

Errol grasped for a way to explain the scars Antil had given him. Hadari leaned over to whisper to the mfalme, pointing toward Errol. At a nod from the ruler, the big man came forward to lift him as easily as a child and pull him close.

His voice, deep as the waters of the ocean, rumbled in Errol's hearing. "I have hoped for your safety, brother. In Merakh I learned you are wise, and now I find you are fortunate as well." Hadari placed him again on the interlocking sandstones of the floor. "Allow me to present the ruler of Ongol, Mfalme Mulu Robel." He turned back to Errol. "That you have dared the journey speaks of great need."

Hadari did not ask the purpose of their journey, but the question lay between them, and within the moment, Errol's discomfort grew. He pitched his voice so that it would carry to the throne.

"The church of Illustra has asked me to bring the book of

A DRAW OF KINGS

Magis home." The book held the sacred history of the church. In its absence the church had depended on an exclusively oral tradition since Magis's death hundreds of years ago, a tradition that had slowly departed from the truth. The benefices of the church wanted the book—thought for generations to have been destroyed—with a desire so deep and desperate, they were willing to hamper the war effort to secure it.

Hadari stepped back, and for the first time his face became closed, unreadable.

Bring him forward, my friend," the mfalme said, his voice so slurred by the scars and pain, the words were almost unintelligible. "Dire messages dampen the heart." He sighed, his chest expanding and deflating like a bellows. "Let us welcome our guests with food and drink as we speak to their need."

Hadari bowed and clapped hands twice the size of Errol's, and serving men and women materialized a moment later with dishes of meat and fruit. At Hadari's direction, Errol, Rale, and Merodach arrayed themselves around Ongol's king on deep cushions.

A servant fed the king a cluster of grapes as he spoke again. "My trusted one has told me of your experience in the prisons of the ilhotep." He nodded toward Rale and Merodach. "Your companions wear the look of men accustomed to command. Does your kingdom have so many such as these that they can afford to send them away?"

Errol looked to Hadari, unsure of how to answer.

Hadari wore a reassuring smile. "Speak freely, my friend. This is not the court of the ilhotep."

"The truth, Your Majesty, is that many of my countrymen do not think we will survive the war. I'm told the Merakhi outnumber us three to one."

The king nodded. "The sand people are uncountable."

"And they have the spawn of the malus to aid them," Errol added. "Adayo called them the ancients." Mulu Robel nodded for him to continue. "The leaders of the church of Illustra sent us to bring the book of Magis home."

"You would serve them, Errol Stone?" the king asked. "Hadari told me these men bound you with compulsion."

A stab of bitterness twisted in his side, and he closed his eyes, concentrating on letting it go. "No, Your Majesty, I do not serve them, but I would like for the book to survive."

"Are you a servant of Deas, then, my brother?" Hadari asked.

Silence stretched across the moments as he looked into Hadari's eyes, searching for an answer. In his peripheral vision, he could see Rale and Merodach where they sat, not watching him but wearing the stillness of men possessed by singular focus. Hadari's eyes held him, showing neither judgment nor expectation but refusing to let him go.

Did he serve Deas? *Yes.* He couldn't deny it. His actions had been guided as surely as if he'd been nothing more than a sheep sent for slaughter. But Errol sensed Hadari searched for a different answer. He wanted to know if Errol was a willing servant.

Fatigue and despair so deep he thought he might crumple beneath their weight enveloped him as if the burden of the kingdom had become a physical thing that rested on his shoulders.

"I am His servant, but I am so tired." A cry tore its way from his chest, and his vision blurred as tears smeared the torchlight. Hands lifted him, and he found himself enfolded in Hadari's embrace. Sobs wracked him as he clung to the Ongolese warrior, his misery blowing through him like a gale. When his grief had run its course, Hadari set him back on his feet, his eyes fierce, proud.

Mulu Robel regarded Errol from within his scarred visage, his expression unreadable. "I am sorry. I cannot send the book back with you."

Errol jerked his gaze from the floor. The king's tone and expression carried many things—sympathy, sadness, regret, but also resolution. The mfalme would not change his mind.

Mulu Robel's face shuddered, and he jerked his good hand up to summon four broad-backed warriors who appeared to shoulder the burden of the king and his throne by means of rods threaded through holes in his chair. "You and your countrymen deserve an explanation, Errol Stone." His voice became increasingly formal. "Such discussions must wait until morning to be better understood. Relax and enjoy the peace of the gardens of Ongol."

Errol thought he heard a catch in Mulu Robel's voice, but the mfalme's tortured speech was still unfamiliar to him. Despite the king's blessing to enjoy the gardens' peace, he sought his bed soon after.

A hand shook him, and he rolled, panicked, into a fighter's crouch, his eyes searching for his staff. A voice murmured in his ear. "Quiet, brother," Hadari said. "I have much to show you if you would understand."

Errol released the breath he held, then nodded to show he understood. The night outside the arched opening of his window lay black and still. "What time is it?" he whispered.

Hadari stepped back, his feet bare and soundless. "Four hours until dawn. Come. As the mfalme's aide, I am given authority to move at will through the palace, but the privilege does not extend to you. I have arranged the guards to allow us passage, but we will still have to be cunning."

"What is it you want me to see?"

Hadari's eyes grew somber in the torchlight. "The mfalme's courage and Ongol's weakness."

The undertone of caution in Hadari's voice brought gooseflesh, and Errol darted a look outside. "Will we have time?"

Hadari put a hand on his shoulder. "They are one and the same. Follow and be silent."

They threaded their way through the palace, pausing often until the sound of the guards' footsteps receded beyond hearing. After nearly an hour they ascended a set of broad stone steps that led to a circular balcony decked with planters of broad-leafed ferns and blossoms. Hadari stopped and pointed to the chamber beneath them, leaning close to whisper. "This is where the mfalme sleeps when such comfort is not denied to him."

Errol searched the cavernous room, but aside from obvious luxury of the deep cushions, the fountains, and the plants, the king's sleeping quarters were empty. "Where is he?"

The skin around Hadari's eyes pinched as if the Ongol guard fought to keep some obscure pain at bay. "He will come. We need only be patient."

Moments passed, and Errol found himself swaying on his feet, his eyes aching for slumber. Then, so softly he might have imagined it, came the whimpering of an animal in pain. Hadari's hand closed on Errol's shoulder.

Four women, tall and lithe, carried the mfalme toward his cushions, their motions as gentle as if the Ongolese ruler had been fashioned from spun glass. Despite their care, Mulu Robel jerked and moaned with each movement. Errol stared, his face burning at the tapestry before him. The mfalme wore only a loin cloth, the horrific extent of his wounds laid bare to see. Besides the missing hand and foot, the Ongol ruler wore deep trenches of scars that ran the length of his torso and limbs. The skin next to the half-healed wounds pulsed with the mfalme's heartbeat, and each pulse tore whimpers from his lips.

The women laid him on the cushions as they would a babe, and proceeded to wash him with cloths that filled the room with the heavy scent of belladon.

Hadari led Errol away and back to his room. Once there, he secured the lock and leaned out of the window to check for unwanted ears before speaking.

"Now you know our greatest weakness, my brother. The mfalme is trapped, his body a prison of unrelenting pain. Slowly, like the ocean eating away the stone of seaside cliffs, the mfalme's agony diminishes his mind. The belladon gives him some relief, but in order to rule he must forego the drug during the day."

"How does he stand it?" Errol asked.

Hadari shook his head. "The rule of the mfalme is absolute until he dies. He has no choice, or so it would seem."

The truth of the king's pain sickened Errol, as if he'd seen the mfalme tortured and locked in stocks from which he could never escape. He shook his head in confusion. "How is this a threat to Ongol?"

The sound of footsteps outside cut off Hadari's answer. Errol leaned out of the archway to see a pair of guards patrolling the grounds nearby. Without answering, Hadari left the room.

Errol woke the next morning after a series of startled jerks thrust him from sleep. The early-morning air, cool compared to the sultry heat of the previous day, brought him to awareness.

As he stepped from his quarters still wearing the brightly colored robe the mfalme's servants had given him the previous day, one of the king's guards stepped into place beside him. Errol didn't recognize him, but the calm assurance and the impressive array of weaponry he carried proclaimed him a palace soldier.

"I am instructed to bring you to the mfalme upon your rising," he said.

Errol gestured acquiescence. "Is it permissible to bring my countrymen as well?"

The guard nodded. "Indeed. They are already with him."

They turned toward the exterior of the palace, the side facing to the north, where steps carved into the thick rocks of the dome spiraled upward toward the cerulean sky. Minutes later they approached the summit, where the king sat on his portable chair surrounded by four huge guards. Errol concentrated on keeping his gaze from the colorful blanket that hid the worst of the mfalme's injuries.

Tek stood to one side, his ankle heavily bandaged. Merodach's face glistened with sweat in the early-morning sun, testimony to the means of the ship captain's arrival. Each man, from king to sailor, nodded a somber greeting to Errol and turned back to the north. Hadari, standing on Robel's right, stepped to the side to allow Errol to stand between them.

The mfalme nodded greeting, then pointed north. Rich green

cropland extended north from the king's city for a distance of some three leagues before the jungle asserted its claim on the foothills beyond.

Errol blinked. Then he shielded his eyes with one hand as he scrubbed sleep away with the other. A line of black, like a splash of dried blood, stretched across the jungle in the distance. Beyond the line lay nothing but dead rock and barren earth that continued until the haze of distance obscured it.

"You see it?" Robel asked.

Errol nodded.

"The withering started a few months ago." His huge shoulders shrugged beneath the brilliant colors of his blanket. "The lore of our kingdom is different than that of Illustra or Merakh. In Ongol, the akanwe—those born with the talent to be readers in your kingdom or ghostwalkers in Merakh—strive to understand the land. It is given to them to understand how to keep the plants and animals of Ongol in health." Mulu Robel turned to him. "Have you not wondered how we are able to flourish outside the protective influence Magis bought for your kingdom? Our akanwe have strengthened our kingdom against the death the fallen ones sought to send against us."

"But now you're losing," Errol said.

Robel Mulu shook his head as if casting away his pain. "The death of your king tipped the scales in favor of the malus. The time approached when I would have had to surrender or watch the entire width and breadth of Ongol die, lost for all time. . . ."

He breathed deeply and stared into Errol's eyes, as if willing him to understand. "But no longer. When Hadari came to us with the book of Magis, the advance of the withering halted."

Now Errol understood. "You think it's the book."

The mfalme nodded. "To surrender the book to you, Earl Stone, I must be willing to surrender my kingdom along with every living thing within it."

24

THE WITHERING

ERROL STARED ACROSS THE DISTANCE at the lifeless boundary that denoted the border between what remained of Ongol and the creeping death where the malus of Merakh held sway. "How long will your kingdom last if Illustra falls to the Merakhi?"

Mulu Robel smiled, his eyes filled with hopes and doubts too numerous to define. "The mountains between Ongol and Merakh constrain the number that can be sent against us, and the giant whirlpool has never been conquered until you came through it. Only the trip through the Eastern Ocean lies open to them, and it is long and perilous. The men of Ongol are the mightiest warriors alive. As long as the withering is halted by the book, we will hold."

Errol shook his head. "Against the malus, Mfalme? Once they have enslaved and corrupted Illustra, do you think they will be content to leave you in peace? Have they offered you any hope of such an outcome?"

The mfalme's eyes grew troubled, but when he spoke he didn't answer. "And will sending the book of Magis, the holy object capable of halting the spread of the withering, north with you make us any safer?"

Errol groped for an answer. He'd come to Ongol believing the book would be in Hadari's possession and that his friend would readily surrender it in order to heal the church. He was unprepared to argue for its return. Why wasn't Martin beside him? The former benefice wielded persuasion the way Liam handled a sword.

He needed time to persuade Mulu Robel, but more than that, he needed an answer to the Ongol king's belief that Magis's book could somehow protect his kingdom. Errol pointed to the stretch of death in the distance.

"Can we go there, Mfalme? I'd like to understand this threat better."

Mulu Robel nodded. "I understand, Earl Stone. You seek time to convince me to surrender the surety of my kingdom. I tell you plainly, I cannot be persuaded, but I will guide you to the withering myself. Let us go down. The horses of Ongol are not so fast as those of Merakh, but they endure, my friend. We will harness the best to my chariots and be there well before sunset."

Errol rode in a chariot behind a warrior named Sumeya. His torso tapered down to a waist that appeared all the smaller for the muscle he carried. Every line and movement carried a promise of deadly quickness, but he smiled without ceasing, and despite the concentration their pace required, he managed to supply Errol with his entire family history, including wartime service, weddings, and blood feuds. He pronounced Errol's name with a hitch between syllables that no amount of coaching or correction could cure. His family, those currently living, appeared to number in the hundreds.

"Tell me, honored Err-ol, do you have a large family? Tales of the northlanders are rare in my country."

Errol felt the question slide between his ribs like the thrust of a knife. "I don't have a family." His mouth twisted around the words as Antil's face, wearing hate and vengeance, rose in his memory.

Sumeya diverted enough attention from driving the chariot to lay a weighty hand on Errol's shoulder. "Orphans are rare in Ongol," he said, "but not unheard of. Was there no one, Err-ol, who could tell you who your father or mother was?"

Errol's laugh, short and quick, took Sumeya by surprise. "I know who my father was. He disowned me at birth. After my adoptive father died, he took my name and made me an orphan."

Sumeya's face registered shock and horror, robbing the warrior of his ability to speak. In the intervening silence Errol lost himself in the rhythmic hoofbeats of the horses that brought the line of death ever closer.

"He is evil, Err-ol. To reject a son is *karat*—a death to the family." His face broadened with the advent of inspiration. "I will go with you to your kingdom and help you kill him."

Errol started. Sumeya's offer appeared sincere. The gesture warmed his heart even while it made him feel exposed, as if someone had come upon him bathing in the Sprata. "I cannot kill him, Sumeya. It is forbidden. He is a holy man."

The Ongol warrior snorted. "No, Err-ol. Here in Ongol we would kill anyone who committed such an offense, holy men included."

Errol nodded. "Alas, Illustra is not Ongol."

Sumeya returned to his duties as Errol's charioteer for the space of a league before turning to offer another suggestion. "We should bring this evil man here to Ongol, where you can kill him."

Sumeya's deep brown eyes were wide above his hopeful smile. Errol fought to suppress a laugh that might be misinterpreted. "I am grateful for your offer, Sumeya, but I do not want to kill him."

The instant the words left his mouth, Errol realized they were true. He did not desire Antil's death. The mere thought of Callowford's priest made him weary, but the idea of killing a man who was probably incapable of defending himself filled Errol with repugnance.

"Holy men in Illustra are not warriors, Sumeya. Killing him would bring me no honor, only shame."

Sumeya took this in with the studied intensity of a child. "You are wise, Err-ol. A warrior's honor is more important than his vengeance. Here in Ongol, our worst criminals are shunned. They are not recognized and none are allowed to acknowledge their presence. Your father, he would be one of these. He is not worth killing." He nodded to himself as if satisfied with his conclusion.

Errol breathed a sigh of relief that the uncomfortable topic seemed at last to be at an end. They rode the rest of the way accompanied by the sound of hooves and wind, the sense of dying things growing in Errol's mind until it filled him.

They passed into the strip of jungle that separated the farmland of Ongol from the stretch of death that had come from the Merakhi border. The sickly sweet stench of decaying plants and flesh assaulted him. Animals had been caught in the withering as well. He closed his eyes as Sumeya slowed the horses along the track leading north.

Moments later the Ongol warrior's hand found him. "There is something strange here, Err-ol."

He opened his eyes to look around, tried not to breathe through his nose. *Strange?* The air itself carried blight, but Sumeya hadn't spoken of the withering. Something pulled Sumeya's gaze ahead, and his body carried the tension of one prepared to draw weapons in earnest. They broke from the strip of jungle, and Errol saw what the Ongolese with his height advantage had noticed seconds before.

Tall figures stood on the path that stretched toward the mountains, figures that stood at ease next to their oversized horses, figures that waited in patient expectation.

Merakhi.

Errol did a quick count. There were only ten.

"I do not like this, Err-ol," Sumeya said with a shake of his head. He urged the horses to move faster, until they passed Mulu Robel's chariot and joined the rest of the escort who had placed themselves between the Merakhi and the mfalme. "I am of the blood to be akanwe, should I choose. There is wrongness in them. They are . . ." He paused, searching for the words that would match the look of revulsion in his eyes. "They are overgrown."

Errol looked again. The Merakhi were still two hundred paces away. Yet even at that distance something nagged at his perception. With a start he realized they stood beside their mounts.

"They are as big as Ongolese—bigger, I think."

Sumeya nodded. "These Merakhi, they have been altered, Err-ol. Sinew and bone! Their flesh screams with it."

Emptiness opened in the pit of Errol's stomach. "Why are they here?"

Sumeya shook his head. "I do not know. This is my first trip to the withering."

Mulu Robel's chariot slowed, then stopped as the king's driver prepared to turn. With a shake of his head, Robel pointed forward, and the horses threw their heads as the driver turned them to face the Merakhi once more. In the other chariots, every Ongol who wasn't driving drew his sword.

Errol's chariot drew close enough for him to address Robel. "Your Majesty, you cannot mean to let them approach."

The mfalme nodded. "I would know the mind of my enemy. It is my hope they can be persuaded to cease their war with us."

"Then you are hasty, Mfalme," Rale said. "If they attack, your guard will be hard-pressed to keep them from you, and your death hands them the kingdom of Ongol. Civil war is as beneficial to them as conquering you, and less trouble."

Mulu Robel stiffened at the correction. "Nevertheless, I mean to speak with them. My guards are the greatest warriors alive. If they cannot protect me against ten foes, then my kingdom is lost anyway."

"I will accompany you if you wish, Mfalme," Errol said, "but we must be cautious. The malus cannot be killed. If they attack us, they have little to lose except the service of the ones they have possessed."

Hadari, in the chariot between Errol and his king, nodded and smiled. "Have I not said you are wise, brother? My counsel is the same. Let us withdraw from this place."

The mfalme cut the air in denial. "We are armed and they are vastly outnumbered. If we turn and flee, my entire kingdom will know of it. I will not unman the people who must fight for me." He turned to face the waiting group of Merakhi. "Courage, friends."

"I agree," Tek said from the chariot he rode. "The malus feed on fear. Don't show them any."

Hadari leaned toward Errol, his voice dipping. "Now you know the threat to Ongol, brother. The mfalme has been here before. The Merakhi offered him healing, but he refused." Hadari's eyes tightened. "But his pain grows. I am afraid, brother."

The Merakhi approached until they were twenty paces short of the Ongolese arrayed in their chariots. The shirra at their waists looked like playthings, toy swords for amusement. A man, with jet black hair and a lean, wiry build that put Errol in mind of a viper, stepped forward and offered an ingratiating smile and bow to the mfalme.

"Revered leader," he greeted, his mouth splitting into a smile that showed too many teeth. "We meet again. Once more I am sent by the exalted one, the omniscient ruler of Merakh, to offer a treaty of peace and more."

Mulu Robel's nose twitched as if he'd caught the scent of corruption. "Your ilhotep brought war upon my people and took our women and children"—he glanced toward Hadari—"to be his slaves. But I am told this 'light of the stars' is dead at the hands of his council. What of your new leader, this 'exalted one,' Chort?"

Chort's eyes vibrated, and his expression became cruel, his grin widening. Errol brushed a hand against the skin of his throat. The Merakhi, grown abnormally large under the influence of the malus, could kill without weapons. The teeth within those oversized jaws could rip out his throat.

"Belaaz, the holy one, rules in Guerir," Chort said, "and he is merciful. I am empowered to secure peace with you, honored mfalme, peace between our two kingdoms that has not been known in five generations."

Longing bloomed on Mulu Robel's face. Errol gripped the strange metal staff and set his feet. His movement brought Chort's gaze to him, and a spasm twisted the Merakhi's face.

Mulu Robel's response rumbled from somewhere deep in his chest, thick strains of emotion cracking his voice. "What does Belaaz seek in exchange for this peace?"

Chort stood without acknowledging the question, his eyes fixed on Errol and a rictus of hatred twisting his mouth. Merodach inched closer, his sword back in its sheath. His hands held his bow with a borale, one of the wicked-looking arrows, fitted to the bowstring.

"Chort!" Mulu Robel called. The Merakhi started, his eyes blinking several times in quick succession. "What is Belaaz's price for peace?"

Chort bowed, the bend of his back and the spread of his arms insouciant. "My ruler desires nothing more than justice, noble mfalme. To such end, he has suspended the ilhotep's war that has raged with Ongol for so many years."

He stepped forward and cut his eyes toward Errol, his voice dipping into a singsong cadence. "Belaaz has declared these men standing with you, noble mfalme, to be under suspicion for the murder of the ilhotep." Chort licked his bared teeth like a tiger ready to strike. "He would give much, much even beyond peace, for their return to Merakh to face justice."

Ongol's king nodded as he rubbed his jaws with his good hand. To all appearances, Mulu Robel considered Chort's offer worthy. Hadari whispered in the king's ear, his gestures sharp, urgent. The rest of the Merakhi, grotesquely large, moved forward as if to hear better, but they fanned out as they came and their hands rested on their weapons.

Robel cut off Hadari with a wave of his hand, then raised his head. "Much, you say. I have the riches of Ongol and the love of its people. What more can you offer?"

Chort's expression grew cunning. "You have wealth and respect, noble one, but I can offer you what none other can." His gaze lingered on the robes and blanket that hid the mfalme's deformities. "Behold."

Chort thrust out his hand and beckoned to one of his men with a jerk of his head. "Your gift, Mfalme." The man drew his sword and struck Chort's hand, severing the first two fingers in a spray of blood. Instead of wrapping the wound, Chort displayed the hand for Robel to see. In moments the blood flow lessened, then stopped altogether. As Errol watched, the stubs of the Merakhi's stricken fingers lengthened, shedding flakes of dried blood, until Chort stood, flexing his hand in proof. The severed fingers still lay at his feet.

Errol glanced at Hadari as comprehension stabbed him.

Robel stared at Chort's hand like a condemned man offered pardon. "Will you remove the withering?"

Chort's eyes grew wide in feigned innocence. "It is not the holy one of Merakh who has sent this blight, Mulu Robel, but rather the foul northlanders in Illustra."

Robel pursed his lips in thought. "You would swear this on your life?"

The Merakhi's eyes grew bright. "I do swear this."

Mulu Robel's good hand clenched the front rail of his chariot, his face taut. "Sumeya! Come forward."

Beads of sweat appeared on Chort's forehead. "What is this?"

The mfalme's smile grew vicious. "The war between our countries has deprived Ongol of its akanwe, Chort, as you know. There are none left, but today is Sumeya's twentieth naming day." His eyes narrowed. "And he has the talent." Grief etched Robel's face as he shook his head, staring at Chort's restored hand. "I know Merakh is the source of our blight. A liar can never be trusted, no matter how great his gift may seem."

Chort snarled. "Do you think you can survive, worm? You and

your petty warriors have managed to kill a few of our creations and you think to match *us*? I will keep you trapped in that useless body for eternity and laugh as you howl in your torment." Wheeling to face Errol, he drew his sword. "Kill him!"

Ten Merakhi charged, swollen and huge under the influence of their malus. Chort feinted toward Mulu Robel, then vaulted over the king's chariot. His jump carried him toward Errol's spinning staff. Before he landed, an arrow cried, and a whirling shaft of black tore the Merakhi's throat away.

Screams of pain and fury merged into a cauldron of sound. Robel's guards formed a ring around their king. They were the strongest warriors in the world.

And the Merakhi were beating them.

Sumeya took a sword cut along his thigh. He rolled into his fall, striking for his opponent's middle. The Merakhi leapt over the stroke and landed behind, his sword thrusting. Another scream tore the air, and the Merakhi stilled, an arrow jutting from his eye.

The remaining Merakhi focused their attack on Merodach, trying to still his deadly arrows. The watch captain backed away, and the Ongolese guards formed an arc with the mfalme and the northlanders behind it. Another arrow screamed and another Merakhi went down.

Then they broke, running back up the blackened hillside for their horses. Merodach's borales followed them, striking. Not every arrow killed, but every Merakhi was marked.

Mulu Robel thrust his hand at the fleeing figures. "Hunt them down. No prisoners."

"There's no need," Merodach said. He might have been discussing lunch. "The arrows are poisoned." He pointed. "Look there."

One by one the Merakhi fell, twitching where they hit the lifeless earth before they too grew still.

Errol's hand ached, and he willed his fingers to loosen their grip. He pulled air into his lungs with desperate gasps as if he'd fought Chort's men alone.

"We do not use poisoned arrows," Robel said. "It is considered unworthy to defeat an opponent in such a way."

Merodach nodded, his blue eyes glinting in the bright sunlight. "If I could poison every malus-possessed Merakhi in the world, I would do it without hesitation. They are not opponents, Mfalme Robel—they are blight."

The Ongolese warriors still standing nodded their agreement. After a moment's hesitation, Robel did as well. "I regret my decision has cost the blood of my guards, but we have learned something of our common enemy, Errol Stone."

Errol jerked. "What might that be?"

"The ancients, those you call the malus, are not without number. They are limited to inhabiting those who have the same talent as the readers of your kingdom. Even among the Merakhi, they do not have an unlimited number of willing hosts, else they would have fought to the last man in their attempt to kill you."

Errol nodded. The king's logic made sense, but another possibility occurred to him. "Or it takes time for the malus to force the host body to such size. Belaaz was no taller than I when we fled Merakh."

Something, a hint of intuition or a breath of wind, told Errol now was the time to speak. "If the Merakhi defeat Illustra, Mfalme, they will swallow Ongol soon after."

Robel nodded. "It is so."

Errol took a deep breath. "The book of Magis is crucial to our kingdom, Mfalme. If I fail to return with it, many will lose hope."

The mfalme gave a small shake of his head. "You are asking me to sacrifice my kingdom to the withering."

Tek limped forward from his position at the rear of their party. Warm air moved like an exhalation of heat across his face, stirred his sweat-stained hair for a moment. "Beggin' yer pardon, King Robel, but I don't think so."

"Then how do you explain the halt of the withering with the arrival of the book?" Robel asked.

Tek rolled his shoulders like a ship riding a wave. "It's not the book holding back the blight of the Merakhi," he said. Then he pointed at Hadari. "It's him."

25

A CHANGE OF WIND

MULU ROBEL leaned toward Errol, his expression bemused. "I understand not how you northlanders express humor. Is this a jest?"

Tek's sea-weathered face wore a knowing smirk as he continued to point at Hadari.

"I don't think so, Mfalme," Errol said, "but I'm not sure. Captain Tek comes from the shadow lands."

Robel's eyebrows rose at this. "I have never met one of the banished before. I thought to leave their land of exile meant death."

Rale shrugged. "Times change, Mfalme. A man who needs allies must be willing to set aside previous judgments."

Ongol's king nodded and turned to Tek. "Can you offer proof of your claim, northlander?"

Tek lifted a shoulder. "We be on the edge of the withering here. Come and see, but proof be in the mind of the man." The captain walked back to the edge of dying plants that lay like a cut across the jungle. Robel's chariot driver edged closer as the rest of the party walked behind him.

Tek strode up to a tree precisely on the withering line—its

leaves blackened to the north but hale and green to the south. The captain reached out and took hold of a large leathery leaf, half black and half green.

Errol watched, his eyes growing wide, as green infused the black part of the leaf, slowly giving life back to the whole until no hint of death remained.

"It is not possible," Robel gasped. "Even the strongest of the akanwe could not do such a thing. What talent did the gods give you, sea captain, that you are able to do this?"

Tek's deep green eyes glinted in the glare of the Ongol sun. "There be no talent sufficient to repair this ill, my king. No reader, theurgist, ghostwalker, or akanwe be strong enough to undo this bane of malice."

"You're solis," Errol said.

"Aye," Tek said. "I be." He pointed to Hadari. "And so is he."

"Solis?" Robel asked. "Explain."

Tek nodded. "The solis hear Aurae, the spirit of Deas, for whatever purpose Deas intends."

He looked at the men of two kingdoms who stared at him in wonder, and his mouth pulled to one side in a self-deprecating grin. "I be as much surprised about it as you. Outcast as a pirate, I floundered in the shadow lands until a breath of inspiration led me to back to the shore, clueless but compelled. The ship I built there sat at anchor for years before circumstance thrust me back into the waters of the world again."

Mulu Robel beckoned, and Tek pulled the regenerated leaf from the tree and put in the mfalme's good hand, where his fingertips brushed it as if in unbelief. "Hadari, can you do this thing?"

The big man stepped forward. "I do not know. I never conceived of such ability."

"Come. Try."

Hadari took a blackened leaf in his hands. Green spread from his touch for a moment before the leaf broke away from the stalk.

"What happened?" Robel asked.

Hadari shook his head, not answering.

Sumeya stepped forward, tugged Hadari to the side, and pointed to a leaf that still retained a hint of green at the base of its stem. "This one," he said.

Hadari took the leaf in his hands, and once again verdant health flowed through the veins until the whole was green. Hadari let go as if the leaf were made of gossamer and might tear free, but the tree held on.

Sumeya turned to the mfalme, his broad face split in a radiant smile. "His healing must work with the remnant of health within the plant to succeed."

Robel eyed the plant, his jaw working. "Can it be done? Can the withering be removed?"

Sumeya nodded, his gaze dancing. "I believe it can, Mfalme. The work will be slow, but I will work with Hadari to determine where to use his power."

The king of Ongol turned to Tek, his eyes wide with wonder. "For this, I will make you second in the kingdom if you ask it of me."

Tek sketched a clumsy bow. "I be a simple reformed pirate, Your Majesty, meant for my Brandy and the sea."

Mulu Robel nodded as if he'd expected no less and turned to Errol. "The book is yours, with one condition."

Errol waited, not daring to hope. "What might that be, Your Majesty?"

The king of Ongol's face became almost pleading. "That you give my scribes time to copy it. I would know more of its contents."

He bowed as low as he could. "Gladly, Mfalme."

Three days later, they left the royal city with the book, bound once more and wrapped in oiled cloth to guard against the weather. As the growth in the jungle thickened, they forsook the king's chariots and continued on foot, the northlanders struggling once more to keep pace with their Ongolese escort. Adayo and Phamba halted two hours before sunset well back from the boscage of the ancients.

"The journey through the domain of the ancients takes planning," Adayo said. "I would not risk any of your party"—he darted a look at Tek's ankle—"by setting too swift a pace."

Errol glanced around the thick jungle, tried to take comfort from the dense growth. How fast would he be able to climb one of the trees? A morbid curiosity grew in his mind. "What form do these ancients take?"

Adayo's face, speckled by sunlight shining through the canopy of foliage, took on a grim cast, the lines of his face taut. "Ah, Earl Stone, you are unfamiliar with the beasts of Ongol. There are cats in your kingdom, the spotted ones. . . ." He stopped searching for the word.

"Lynx," Errol prompted.

Adayo nodded. "Yes. How big are they?"

Errol shook his head. "I've never seen one. They stay in the mountains of Frataland, but I'm told they might attack children or sheep."

Soft laughter accompanied Adayo's nod. "Imagine such a thing, its paw as big as your head, and weighing as much as Phamba and I together."

Errol gaped.

Adayo smiled. "Now imagine one of those corrupted by the malus. It holds all of the power and ferocity of the animal but with greater intelligence and an unquenchable thirst for human blood."

Errol's stomach dropped with a weight against the bones of his hips.

Adayo noted his reaction. "In the history of our kingdom, warriors have tested themselves against the ancients, striving to claim the verdant from them. We lure them into the jungle, where arrows and javelins may be used from cover, but at great cost. The men who survive such a hunt become heroes, only a little lower than the mfalme."

Errol swallowed. "Are we far enough from their plain?"

Adayo nodded. "The river lies less than a mile from here and they are too big to swim well. Tomorrow we must make haste past the boscage."

A fascination gripped Errol. "Do they not hunt during the day?"

"Never, but sometimes they can be seen sleeping beneath the solitary bringo trees that dot the plain."

"Perhaps we will see one."

Adayo shook his head. "That is a sight to be avoided, Earl Stone. Their vision is keen."

Tek cleared his throat from a few paces away. "They be gone, lad. There are no spawn left on the plain."

Adayo looked at the sea captain as if he were sunstruck. "The mfalme says you have powerful sight, northlander, but I will not put your pronouncement to the test. Caution costs us nothing."

Amos Tek nodded. "That be wise, but there are no ferrals left in your kingdom, Adayo. The malus have called their offspring east"—he turned to look at Errol—"to join the fight."

The truth of his words struck a chill deeper than a Soede winter into Errol's chest. What manner of twisted creatures would they be fighting when they returned home?

Adayo and Phamba jerked upright, their gazes searching back the way they'd come.

Errol followed their lead, his eyes searching but finding nothing. "What do you see?"

Phamba turned to regard Errol, his expression unreadable. "The wind has shifted, northlander. Zephyr has changed her mind. Our days will soon cool."

Errol wet his lips. "But that would mean . . ."

"Aye," Tek said. "Winter is breaking in Illustra."

Merodach and Rale bore twin expressions of tension and haste. "How fast can you get us back to our ship?" Rale asked.

"As fast as your feet can take you," Adayo said. "We'll leave in the morning."

Errol looked at the reddening sun as it began its descent toward the tops of the trees. "No. There are no spawn to avoid. We go now."

Adayo glanced at Tek before sighing into the wind. "Then let us run."

Martin sat heavy in his saddle at the front of the Wind Rider clan, his shaggy horse ignoring the chill wind that wormed its way into every rent and hole in his cloak. He rode next to Ablajin, who led twenty thousand fighting men along with their women, children, and belongings. Though the Morgol warriors spoke exclusively in their native tongue, Martin didn't require Karele's translation to catch their mood. Ablajin's men were unsettled.

Their worry showed itself in a dozen different ways—a squint of the eyes, hands that stayed near swords, mutters spoken at random. Karele, on the other side of the jheng, rode with one ear toward the men, his expression confirming Martin's fears.

"What do they say?" Martin asked.

Karele waited for Ablajin's nod of approval before answering, and Martin stared in wonder. As head of the solis, the spiritual head of the entire nation of the shadow lands, Karele held a position comparable to Archbenefice Bertrand Canon, if not king of Illustra. That he would submit himself to a clan chief of the steppes was surprising.

"They are afraid," Karele said. "And like men who fear something great, they express their dread by speaking of smaller concerns that offer them some measure of power."

Martin nodded, impressed once again by the depth of Karele's insight into the human spirit. "What do they speak of?"

Karele's eyes, dark beneath the loose hair that tumbled to his shoulders, squinted in shared worry. "They fear they will be ordered to fight against their kinsman, that they will be pitted against cousins or brothers-by-marriage."

Martin nodded. He understood, but he didn't know what

choice they had. "I understand their fears, Ablajin. When the time for battle comes, I will do what I can to keep them from such a fight." He knew it was small consolation, but he had nothing more.

Ablajin exhaled as if he'd held his breath for too long. "I am grateful." He turned his eyes to Martin and gave a quick nod, his coarse braid lashing against the wind. "But if we must fight against men whose names and clasps are known to us, we will."

Karele held up a hand. "There is another more immediate fear, and I do not think there will be any remedy for their unease." His breath plumed briefly in the chill. "They know that to cross into Illustra, they must pass beneath the mountains."

"Do the caves scare them so much, then?" Martin asked.

The solis shook his head. "It is more than that. They fear being unmanned in the sight of their wives and children."

Ablajin placed a hand on Martin's arm. "Few outsiders would know this of us, Holy Martin, but the essence of what it means to be Morgol is to be immune to fear. A warrior may weep at a loved one's death, or he may scream in pain, but for him to do either from fear is to bring shame upon his family and clan. Doing so in front of his wife and children is doubly damning."

"Even so," Karele said, "the fear of the caves weaves its way through their conversation, mentioned briefly before it stills the tongue, and there is no antidote or argument that will avail them." The solis locked gazes with Martin. "The caves represent the end of their way of life, and they fear what lies ahead. Victory means the subjugation of the steppes by Illustra, their former enemy, and defeat means death for them all and their nation ruled by theurgists."

Martin hung his head, staring at his thick hands upon the pommel of his saddle. His mind turned Karele's words over and again, seeking some balm that he might offer against these fears, but nothing came. "They are right, so far as I can tell," he said at last.

"I have thought so as well," Ablajin said. "Yet the future is difficult to see even for the theurgists, else Oorgat would not have died from a prophecy he brought to fruition. I choose to take comfort in the misty future. It may be that there are outcomes unknown to us. Who knows what kind of world we will wake to after the war?"

Martin stared at the clan chief in amazement. Where did a man of the steppes, raised within the apostasy of generational theurgy, find such peace? "If we survive this war, clan chief, I would offer you the hospitality of my kingdom."

Ablajin's face shone with surprised joy, his smile showing merry crinkles around his eyes. "My son has told me stories of the Green Isle where your king and church rule. I should like very much to see it."

Martin found Ablajin looking at him, his request plain. After a deep breath he told the clan chief of the isle and its peoples for hours as they rode, and Ablajin's questions showed both a child-like curiosity and a scholarly discernment that surprised him.

As the sun set they came within sight of the cave that would lead them beneath the mountains to Bellia, and the muttering behind them grew. Ablajin turned his horse to face the clan. The warriors, men ranging in age from a score to three times that number faced him. Their unease became a palpable thing, until Martin could almost smell it on the chill north wind.

"They will break," he said to Ablajin. He tried to speak without attracting attention. "The longer they stare at the cave, the more the fear of it grows upon them."

"You are right, holy Martin," Ablajin murmured in return, "but they must conquer it themselves. Any strength I give them through my words will not last long enough to bring them through to the other side."

The tension heightened until the horses, attuned to their riders, shied and fought the reins. Just when it appeared the entire clan might break and run, one of Ablajin's lieutenants, Ulaat, kicked his horse forward until its nose touched that of Ablajin's mount. Then he spun to face the assembly.

"Hooves and wind," the lieutenant shouted, his eyes tight,

"if a master of horses and four soft kingdom men can brave the dark, a Wind Rider can."

Ablajin's gaze sought Martin. "He means no offense, holy Martin."

Martin rubbed his belly. Months of travel and infrequent food had diminished his bulk, but he still carried far more padding than the Morgol riders. "I would be small-minded to take offense at the truth"—he gave his midsection a soft pat—"however indelicately spoken."

Slowly at first, but in a growing tide, the warriors of Ablajin's clan committed to braving the underground crossing. The clan chief nodded his approval, then cast a look at the dying light. "I think it would be best if we camped before beginning the passage." He glanced at the mouth of the cave and shivered. "There are some who may need the knowledge of sunlight to bolster their courage."

Ulaat passed word among the lieutenants, and the large octagonal tents were quickly erected. Cook fires sprouted like flowers on the plains. Martin cast about for Luis and Cruk, but his countrymen were not to be seen. He passed a hand across his heavy jaws. Cruk's decades-old enmity for the Morgols could prove to be a problem. He didn't think the watchman would do anything to jeopardize their newfound alliance, but it would be best not to leave the captain to his own devices for too long.

Luis presented a different problem. Day by day, his friend had withdrawn a little more into his thoughts, leaving Martin bereft of his counsel. Many times at night or early in the morning, Martin spied Luis casting in solitary locations, his face blank, lost in the question and answer that framed his craft, the calling that shaped him as secondus of the conclave.

Martin shrugged as if an unfamiliar and unwelcome weight had settled upon his shoulders. The failure of the cast of stones, the draw for the king they knew would come from Callowford, gnawed at him. How much more had it distressed Luis, who had shaped it?

Women and children stared at Martin as he passed by, their fingers pointing at his strangely rounded eyes or his girth, both equally rare on the steppes. On the northern end of the camp, he found them both. Cruk stood guard, Owen by his side, while Luis strove to carve a lot. Small white fissures laced the back of his chapped hands as he stroked the knife over the wood. Despite the chill, his motions were steady, and before the sun slipped below the horizon, a pair of spheres lay before him.

Luis regarded them as he might an enemy. Martin coughed, and the secondus jerked, scooping up his lots to deposit them in a rough leather bag, his face red.

"How many?" Martin asked. Worry sharpened his voice. Cruk turned at the sound.

Separated from the reader's trance that kept him from feeling the cold, Luis's hands trembled as he shook the bag. "Specify."

A sigh, bitter as the wind, escaped Martin. He knelt on the frozen earth next to his friend. "How many times have you cast the same question since the stones failed us?"

Luis didn't bother to raise his head. His shoulders lifted a fraction, then fell back into place as he drew from the bag. "More times than I can count."

Martin shook his head. "I doubt that. How many?"

The lots within the bag clacked softly as Luis rolled it across the ground. "Perhaps a hundred." He drew again, shook his head with a rueful smile. "But not always the same question. I even cast to see if I was still a reader. Then I tested to see if the question could be answered."

He looked at Martin at last, his eyes dark, haunted. "Both of those came up *yes*."

Martin balked at the torture in his friend's voice. "But there remains no answer between Errol and Liam." He'd meant to phrase it as a question.

Luis shook his head and drew again. "Illustra must have its soteregia, Martin." His gaze changed from haunted to grief-stricken. "What if the wrong man dies?"

271

He tried to block the possibility from his mind, but Luis's question wormed its way through his defenses, ate at his conviction until he doubted his faith. "Deas will ensure that does not happen," he said, but his statement carried no fire.

Luis continued to draw, sparing only the barest glances for the lots before repeating the process.

"Still?" Martin asked.

"Twelve times for Errol. Twelve times for Liam."

Bands of despair squeezed his chest, keeping him from drawing breath. Luis folded his bag and tucked it away before throwing the lots with a savage grunt out into the grass of the plain.

Cruk edged his way toward them, his face grim. "We have a more pressing concern." His voice shoved aside their concern. "The wind has shifted."

Martin stared, then rose to face south. A whisper brushed his face, startlingly warm compared to the north wind that no longer cut, that no longer kept the passes protecting the kingdom filled with ice. "It's coming now," he breathed. "War."

26

REFUGEE

ADORA PACED IN HER TENT, clothed in bone-deep weariness that made her light-headed even as it weighted each step. She locked her knees as reports continued to come in, none of them good. Rohka's and Rula's expressions were grim—Liam's was unreadable.

Now back in Illustra, their forces had enough food for a fortnight, perhaps two if adults went to half rations. The refugees numbered nearly fifty thousand men, women, and children—fighting men accounted for perhaps a fifth of that. Scavenger parties returned empty-handed. The villages, too small to feed such numbers even during harvest, had been emptied of people and provender.

Waterson entered and stood before her, his empathy surprising, considering the circumstances. He no longer balked at the use of his title but continued to speak his mind in blunt terms, even so. Under the circumstances, Adora found his harsh honesty refreshing.

His mouth turned down at the edges. "That didn't turn out well."

Adora couldn't tell if he referred to the overall mission into the shadow lands or the latest report from the scavengers. In the end, it didn't matter. Both were a disaster, differing only in scale.

Rokha laughed. "Maybe you should banish all your nobles, Your Highness. It seems to provide a perspective most of them lack."

Adora nodded. "I appreciate Lord Waterson's honesty, but I'd appreciate a supply of food for our return to the west even more."

"It's not going to happen, Your Highness," Rokha said with a toss of her head. "The villages are cleaned out. Only the most ignorant peasant could miss the change in the weather." She cast a glance out the open flap of the tent. Darkness veiled the landscape, but Rokha sighed anyway. "Rain would help. Nothing slows an army like nice deep mud."

Liam nodded his agreement. "Yet the fair weather offers some hope too. Our return will progress more quickly than it would otherwise."

Lord Waterson nodded. "True enough. We'll be able to get a few more leagues out of the horses before we have to slaughter them for meat."

Adora searched his face but found no sign of jesting or sarcasm. Liam and Rokha nodded their agreement.

Lieutenant Jens entered the pavilion and made his way to Adora and Liam, trying to make eye contact with both of them at once before settling for staring into the distance halfway between them.

"Your Highness, Captain," he bowed. "Our rear scouts have returned." He hesitated, his manner furtive. "There are only two of them."

Rokha growled out a curse that would have done the hardest sergeant proud, and Liam grew still. Adora made a summoning gesture with one hand. She tried to keep it from trembling. "Bring them in."

A pair of men shambled in. Both bore wounds that would require treatment; rents and tears in their clothing bore traces of blood.

Liam stepped forward. "Sergeant Ancois, report."

A blond-haired man with the chiseled features and strong chin of an Avenian stepped forward to essay a bow toward Adora. He stumbled, and pain leached color from his face. "Your Highness."

Adora bowed. Her training with healer Norv split her mind, allowed her to continue the façade of court protocol even as she surveyed his injuries, assessing which required immediate attention and which could wait. There were too many of the former. Ancois should have been in the infirmary, but watchman pride would never allow him to seek the healer's arts before giving his dispatch to his superior.

"Make your report as brief as possible, Sergeant Ancois," Adora said. "Time weighs against us." If she couldn't order him to the infirmary, perhaps she could hurry him there.

Ancois nodded. She might have detected relief on his pasty features.

"Of the score of watchmen who served as the rear scout, only I and Ianson remain. A dozen of us scaled the plateau to observe and harry the enemy in hopes of bringing report of their withdrawal from the shadow lands."

He blinked, swaying.

"They have spawn with them, Your Highness," he said, "creatures of vast strength that they are using to clear the canyon of the rock and rubble. The Merakhi are not retreating."

Adora shivered, then pulled her cloak more tightly about her in the hope it would be attributed to the cold, if noticed.

"How long before they have it cleared?" Count Rula asked.

Ancois shifted to face him. His face blanched with the effort. "Perhaps three days."

"They'll be on top of us in seven," Waterson said, "five if the weather holds. We can't stay here."

"Deas help us," Rula muttered.

"We couldn't remain at any rate," Liam said. Somehow he managed to look unconcerned by the sergeant's news. "The need for supplies drives us west as surely as the enemy's advance." He turned toward Ancois. "More troubling is their control of the spawn. The beasts possess greater intelligence than animals, but they're insane. That they can control them well enough to force them to labor troubles me."

Ancois nodded. "There was a man among the beasts, Captain." He shook his head. "But he was more than that. Though distance makes such calculations difficult, he had to be close to three spans tall. The spawn feared him."

Adora cut the air with one hand. "It matters little how they are controlled. We must either find a means to escape their notice or outpace their pursuit." She turned to the scouts. "Is there anything else of immediate concern?" At the shake of their heads she thanked them for their service and ordered them to the infirmary.

Jens approached, again splitting the difference between Adora and Liam for his bow. "There is a group of men and women outside demanding an audience."

A pain grew somewhere in the back of Adora's neck, then traveled into her head, where it exerted a viselike grip on her skull. Before she could signal her refusal or assent, the flap of the large tent flew back and a group of men and women, fronted by a Lugarian man and a Talian woman, marched in. They spread around her in an arc, unarmed except for the sternness of their expressions.

Adora kept her tone civil. Just. "How may I serve you?"

"Serve us?" the woman said. "Serve us?" The tone rose an octave.

"Easy, Marya," the man said. "We've been running at full retreat for the last three days. She doesn't know who we are."

The Talian whirled on him. "And she didn't bother to seek us out either, did she, Garet."

Adora straightened with an effort. The motion sent a stab of pain through her skull. "Am I addressing the council of Haven? Please accept my sincerest apologies. The haste of our retreat precluded meeting." She allowed a hint of iron into her voice. "Once again, how may I serve you?"

The woman's eyes, dark like her hair, blazed. "You can sign the writ of recognition the priest promised us, Your Highness."

She leaned forward. "The writ of recognition is meant to acknowledge your kingdom as a sovereign nation in exchange for the cooperation of your military forces." It might have been the fatigue that precipitated her response or perhaps a reaction to the Talian's manner, but she couldn't stop herself. "Forgive my blunt observation, but you no longer appear to have either."

With a brusque gesture she waved an arm that included her advisors. "At this moment we're discussing how to keep your people alive and out of the hands of the enemy."

Even Waterson and Rokha winced.

"Go easy, Your Highness," Liam said. "They have lost much."

Adora's eyes widened in spite of her effort to maintain a detached demeanor. She sighed. Had she ever been this tired? "Please forgive me, fatigue and disappointment weigh heavily upon me. Yet the question remains, to what end shall we sign the accords?"

Marya drew herself up, but Garet laid a hand on her arm, and she retreated to stand with the rest of the council, leaving him to face Adora alone. "Because it was promised," he said.

His appeal touched her where Marya's indignation didn't. She took a deep breath. "If we are to be allies, then I think it only fair for you to hear our deliberation, if you wish, but be warned, I'll put no restraint on my advisors' counsel just to spare your feelings."

"Agreed," Garet said. Behind him, Marya gave a single nod.

"Count Rula," Adora said, "what is your opinion on this matter?"

The count knuckled his mustache. With shoulder-length hair and the lean build of a swordsman, the count served as a continual reminder of his nephew Naaman Ru. In the presence of his great-niece, he exercised restraint. Rokha's fierce love for her father, in spite of his faults, and Rula's enmity toward him sometimes made for a tense atmosphere.

"The church will demand an accounting, Highness. The benefices are pragmatic. In the absence of an army, it would be more expedient to simply rule the shadow lands rather than recognize it as a sovereign country." He inclined his head toward Adora. "And they will expect you to know this as well."

Adora nodded. The count's thoughts mirrored her own. "So you recommend against recognition?"

Rula shook his head. "No. I merely state what I believe to be the church's position. As Rodran's sole descendant, it is your place to honor the intentions of the kingdom, inconvenient or not."

Adora shifted. "Lord Waterson?"

He stepped forward with a shake of his head. "You can sign the treaty if you want, Your Highness, but there's not much left of the shadow lands or their army." His mouth pulled to one side. "Unless you want to count me and a few thousand like me. I'm sorry, we're not enough to make a difference against the Merakhi. We're not enough to warrant a treaty." If his possession of a strange dual citizenship affected his response, Adora couldn't tell.

She nodded, tried to ignore the stricken looks on the faces of Garet, Marya, and the rest of their council. "Captain Liam?"

Liam stepped forward. Garet and Marya faced him and jerked in surprise.

The shadowlanders, their eyes wide, bent to each other, whispering as though something about the captain shocked them.

Liam waited until he had their attention, though they continued to stare at him in wonder. "Lord Waterson and Count Rula present cogent arguments, Your Highness. I might argue the kingdom should honor its promise, but doing so under the present circumstances offers little in the way of mutual advantage." He turned from Adora to the council. "The treaty with the shadow lands must be a secondary consideration to safeguarding the refugees with us. Do you agree?"

Garet, Marya, and the rest nodded assent, but every line of their posture showed wariness.

"The present need of our two peoples is to evade the Merakhi forces behind us." He turned to Adora. "Perhaps if the council could offer some means of accomplishing this, it would provide the justification Your Highness requires for fulfilling the kingdom's promise."

Garet and Marya eyed Liam with a mixture of wonder and distrust, as if he held the means of some secret they meant to keep hidden. Adora shoved that thought aside. She didn't have time for such ruminations.

She turned to the council. "Do you know what Captain Liam speaks of?"

Garet stepped forward, hesitant. "The council may have the ability to hinder the Merakhi in their pursuit."

"Are you saying you have the ability to mask us from the Merakhi and their spawn?" She didn't have the time or patience for word play. "Can it be done?"

Garet nodded. "It is possible."

Adora stood. "If you can do this thing, I will sign the accords. But hidden or not, we will begin our retreat in the morning. Food and survival lay to the west."

Garet and the rest of the council bowed to her, but she couldn't help noticing that they bowed more deeply to Liam.

The next morning, Adora and Rokha watched the chaotic mass of humanity from a small rise. The sun, two hours into the sky, warmed Adora's face, and a southerly wind foretold mild temperatures for the day.

They still hadn't broken camp.

Pain in her hands reminded her to unclench her fists from around her horse's reins, but a knot of frustration remained at the delay.

"They move like a bag full of cats," Rokha said. Every soldier, watchman, and guard in camp was positioned in an attempt to bring order to the throng of refugees as they began their journey west, but to little avail.

"At this rate the Merakhi army will catch us before we break camp."

"It's not that bad, Your Highness. Even within my father's caravan, the first day out from camp brought inevitable delay. If we managed to get under way before noon, we counted ourselves lucky."

She pointed to their right, where Nob, their quartermaster, jockeyed the few carts and the multitude of mules into order. "He knows what he's about. After today, those people will be ready to march with the dawn. You'll see."

She sighed. If Rokha saw no need to panic, there probably wasn't one. Lieutenant Jens approached, reined his piebald stallion to a stop, and gave a perfunctory bow. "Your Highness, the council has requested that we alter our course."

"Why?"

Jens balked at the question, and his gaze wandered the landscape instead of meeting hers. "They wouldn't give a reason, Your Highness. They only said it was necessary. Captain Liam has given his provisional agreement." He gave her a hopeful look.

"I'm sure he has," Adora said. Something in the request set her hackles on edge. "Where are we to go?"

"Northwest," Jens said. "Captain Liam and Count Rula say this will bring us to Escadrill."

"Wretched place," Rokha muttered, "but probably our best bet to obtain food before the stores run out."

Adora nodded. "Why do I get the feeling that there's something else at play here?"

She twitched the reins, and her mount came about to face east. In the distance, spread out in an arc facing the river, stood Haven's council, all twelve of them on foot.

"Everyone holds secrets, Your Highness," Rokha said.

"Lieutenant Jens," Adora called over her shoulder, "tell Captain Liam and the rest of the watch I approve of the plan to move northwest, and have them plot the quickest route to Escadrill." She turned to Rokha. "You know the town. Will there still be food merchants there?"

Rokha nodded. "It will cost you every gold crown those bandits can squeeze out of you, but I expect so."

At the end of the third day, Rokha voiced her approval at the distance they'd traveled.

"How far?" Adora asked.

Ru's daughter pursed her full lips before she answered. "About five leagues. Deas willing, we'll be able to maintain it."

Adora's heart labored under a weight of disappointment. "We have to find a way to go faster." She shook her head, trying to deny Rokha's assessment. "If we do not, we will run out of food, or the Merakhi column will slip past us to the south—assuming the council can mask our route—and block the passages into the Arryth." She beat a fist against her thigh in frustration. "I could make ten leagues on foot in one day."

Rokha sighed. "But you're not a creeping mass of humanity, Princess, and you wouldn't be able to hold that pace day after day. Look." She pointed to the wagons. "Every one of those wagons is filled with the very young and the old. Everyone without a horse—and that's most of them—must walk.

"Consider that an army takes time to move as well. Two hours after the vanguard begins the day's march, the rear is still motionless. The Merakhi army will not be so fast as you think. The larger they are, the slower they move."

"You called me Princess again."

Rokha shrugged. "You were being stupid."

On the fifteenth day, Nob came to see her. "We've got to cut the rations again." That he failed to duck his head or use her title told her the seriousness of their situation.

She winced. Bad news sent pain through her temples like one of Sevra's kicks. "How many days until we reach Escadrill?"

Nob smacked his lips as he thought. "Another week, Your Highness."

Rokha nodded confirmation.

Adora's stomach growled its resentments. She'd been subject to rationing just like everyone else. "Cut the rations for every man on horseback and every adult in the wagons—and cut them hard. Leave full rations for nursing mothers and children." She turned to Rokha. "Flog anyone caught stealing food."

Four days from Escadrill the slithering mass of humanity in the vanguard stopped. With a jerk of her reins, Adora pulled out of the middle of the formation and sought Lieutenant Jens. The people close to the front milled around like bees without a queen.

After a moment she spotted the watchman riding back to her.

"Your Highness." Jens bowed from his position in the saddle. At her apparent frustration, he hastened to explain. "We've encountered another band of refugees."

Adora's hands jerked in irritation. "You know what to do, Lieutenant. Assign the old and young positions in wagons and get someone to take a tally of their food stores."

Jens sighed. "That's just it, Your Highness. They refuse to give up their food stores." He shrugged. "More accurately, their leader refused."

Rokha snorted, and she eyed the lieutenant's sword until he blushed. "What do you think you have that sharp pointy thing at your side for?"

Jens answered her with a glare. "He's a priest. I work for the church, not the other way around."

Adora clenched her teeth, then thought better of it as pain lanced across her skull. "We don't have time for the niceties of church relations right now, Lieutenant. Where are these people from?"

Jens jerked his head in a nod. "The Sorland province, Your Highness, from the village of Callowford."

27

ANTIL

BANDS SQUEEZED HER CHEST until spots danced in her vision and dizziness threatened to pitch her from the saddle. Rokha called her name as if from a great distance. When her vision cleared, Lieutenant Jens had backed away. Her hands ached, and she looked down to see her knuckles standing out from their flesh.

"There's more than one priest in Sorland, Your Highness," Rokha said.

Adora whipped around to face her. "You doubt? Who else could it possibly be?" Her lips trembled, and tears of frustration and rage gathered and spilled from her lashes. "When has Errol ever been spared?"

Rokha reached over to grasp her hands, but Adora shook her off with a flip of her reins and dug her heels into the flanks of her horse.

Hooves thundered behind as Rokha and Jens struggled to catch her. The press of bodies prevented them. People turned at the sound of her approach, their eyes wide at the sight of her riding through the crowd, heedless of those scrambling to get out of her way.

At the front of the caravan, near a train of carts, shadowlanders and Illustrans came together like opposing waves, but in the morass of humanity, she could see no obvious center that would indicate Antil's presence.

A need for haste she couldn't control drove her forward.

She reached down to grab the nearest soldier and spun him by his arm. "Where is the priest?"

He gaped at her, then snapped to attention and pointed. "Over there, Your Highness, next to the largest cart."

Adora rushed for the wagons, squeezing her way past a burly pair of teamsters into the space where two of the watch confronted a man in a dirty cassock.

Antil.

She'd never seen him, had never wanted to see him, and deep in her heart had nourished the hope that he would somehow fail to escape the flood of Morgols who had poured into his province. Inside, she railed at Deas. Was there no wound too deep for Errol to suffer? Must he endure this as well?

"Antil." She waited for him to turn.

A hint of dimples in his cheeks was the only resemblance she could see. His nose had been broken at least once and his eyes were too haunted to compare, but the hair still held a hint of the deep brown where gray had failed to mar it.

Recognition spread across his face.

She must be sure. "Are you . . . Antil?" Almost she had used his title, but she would not cheapen the work of other men who labored faithfully for the church.

The man before her, the one responsible for Errol's pain, nodded.

She launched herself at him. He flinched, the whites of his eyes showing around brown irises. Her hands shook with rage, and the shock of blows shook her arms in time with her heartbeat. Blood poured from the ruin of Antil's nose.

A blur of color like a flash of lightning caught her arm, held it, and forced it down. The momentum of her swing carried her into Waterson's arms, and his hands tightened on her wrists, squeezing until her fists unclenched. She jerked and struggled, but he refused to let go.

"Unhand me," she screamed. "Do you forget who I am?"

Still struggling with her in his grasp, Waterson shifted to address Antil, who stood with his hands pressed against his face. "I think there's something about your presence, priest, that annoys the princess. You should probably contrive a reason to be elsewhere."

"Let me go!" Adora spat.

"Not likely, Your Highness," Waterson said. Strain touched his voice as she fought to get loose. He turned to Jens, who stared at her. "Get that priest out of her sight."

Jens grabbed Antil by the arm and began to lead him away, out of her reach.

Adora yanked to free her arm, but Waterson kept her pinned. He leaned close until she felt his breath on her ear. "If you have to beat this priest, for Deas's sake do it in private. All the discipline we've managed to impose on this rabble will fall apart if you continue."

Rokha leaned in from the other side. "Is this really the weapon you wish to use? Think, Princess."

As if a bucket of cold water had caught her unaware, Adora calmed. She relaxed her struggle against Waterson, who paused, wary, before releasing her. She straightened and adjusted her clothes before raising her voice to address Lord Waterson loudly enough for the retreating forms of Lieutenant Jens and the priest to hear.

"Lord Waterson, please convey Pater Antil to the rear of the caravan." She looked at the wagons and carts that clogged the road to Escadrill. "And assign these wagons to their proper place." She tried not to notice the peasants' fear as they scrambled to obey.

Walking with as much of her royal demeanor as she could summon, she remounted and rode back to the center of the train. Rokha pulled in alongside, her lips pressed together but not quite suppressing a smile.

Adora stared straight ahead, refusing to hold that gaze. "Does everything I do amuse you?"

Rokha shrugged and tossed her blue-black hair over one shoulder. "Not everything, Your Highness, but hitting the priest ranks high on the list." She laughed enthusiastically. "What did you hope to accomplish?"

She inhaled. "I wanted him to feel every stroke he put on Errol's back." Her breath escaped her in a sigh of powerlessness and regret. "I've lost my chance to avenge him."

Rokha's fresh laughter caught her off guard. "If so, you have a limited imagination for retribution, Your Highness." At Adora's look, Rokha held up a hand. "That's probably for the best, but were I the last princess of the kingdom, I could imagine many ways my power could be used to avenge someone short of death."

Waterson rode up to her a short time later, his eyes wary but his mouth pulled to one side in a mocking grin. "I'd forgotten how much I disliked priests," he said in a conversational tone. "That one managed to remind me." He bent from the waist to give Adora an exaggerated bow. "If the laws of the kingdom were different, I would owe you an apology, Your Highness. I don't think the church would be eager to defend that one. It's a pity I stopped you."

Adora watched Waterson's antics with the trace of a smile, still turning Rokha's suggestion over in her mind. "Lord Waterson, please convey my invitation to Pater Antil to dine with me tonight in my tent. It has been a long time since I have availed myself of the solace of the church. I find myself in need of her advice."

Waterson's eyes lit with savage amusement before he galloped off.

"Very good, Your Highness," Rokha said. Her alto voice purred with approval. "But what exactly do you intend to do with him?"

Adora pulled her lower lip between her teeth. "I'm not sure. Let's find out who Pater Antil is."

Later that day they entered the interminable track of forest that bordered the Stones River and stretched all the way to Escadrill. They pitched camp three days short of their goal. Parties were sent to procure firewood, and the wagon masters took the opportunity to replace or repair axles that required attention. As dusk deepened, Liam and the solis returned to camp with news written on their faces.

Adora took one look at Marya and suspected grim tidings. A glance at Garet confirmed it. Rula beckoned them to a large table, where a map of all Illustra was spread before them, complete with topographical annotations.

At a gesture from Adora, Liam leaned over the map, his thick finger pinpointing their position. "We are three days from Escadrill, Highness. Another two weeks from there to the merchants' center at Longhollow and another ten days to make the safety of the Arryth."

"What of the Merakhi?" Rula asked.

Garet cleared his throat. He shifted his weight from foot to foot and kept his gaze focused on the map as if he feared to meet Adora's eyes. "With the help of Aurae, we have masked our passage and sent their army south toward the swamp of southern Lugaria." His fingers tapped the area on the map in a brisk staccato. "Your Highness, we have managed to send them on a delayed route back into their own vanguard."

"But . . . ?"

Liam leaned forward, catching her attention. "Their army travels more quickly than we. If we do not split our military forces from the refugees, they will beat us to the Arryth despite their longer route."

"We would be trapped on this side of the mountains," Marya said.

Adora's face heated. "You're asking me to abandon the refugees of two countries to the Merakhi and the Morgols."

Liam shook his head. "If we don't beat the Merakhi to the Arryth, Your Highness, our presence will hardly help them. If we get there first, we can try to hold one of the northern passes open."

"If," Adora said, not bothering to hide the doubt in her voice. "Try." She turned on the members of Haven's council. "You are amenable to Captain Liam's suggestion?"

As one, each member of the council looked at Liam, looked at him in a way they looked at no other man or woman of the kingdom, and nodded. What hold did he have over them?

"And if we do not make it to the Arryth before the Merakhi or cannot hold a passage open for the refugees?"

Garet, still looking at Liam, nodded as if he were accepting a burden or condemnation. "Take what men we have left under arms, Your Highness. We refugees will follow as best we can."

Adora shook her head as a bitter chuckle escaped her lips. "No, my lord councilor. Martin Arwitten spoke at length about you and the rest of the council. Illustra cannot afford to lose you or the abilities you bring."

Garet and Marya looked stricken, their faces blanching until they matched the wan light of the lamps. "We cannot leave our people, Your Highness."

"But you expect me to leave mine? No. If I go, you must come with me. I will not leave behind a weapon that can hide us from our enemy at a crucial moment. I have seen what Solis Karele is capable of."

Again the council looked at Liam as if seeking his blessing or permission and then nodded acquiescence. "It shall be as you say, Your Highness." Garet shrank further under the weight of his abdication, and the fire highlighted crevices of worry in his face.

"Tomorrow, then," Adora said. "Those of the watch and what remains of your army will make for the Arryth." She sighed, then straightened. "Now, if you would please leave me, I have matters to attend."

The small crowd shuffled from her pavilion as though she

had placed them under judgment. Lord Waterson stood by the entrance, Antil at his elbow, waiting for permission to enter.

"Lady Rokha, Captain Liam, would you please remain?" She glanced at the priest. "I may find your counsel useful." Let the little toad interpret that how he would.

For once, Naaman Ru's daughter didn't laugh at her weakness, only nodded, checking the position of the sword at her hip.

She moved to a small table, hardly more than a couple of boards thrown across crude trestles, and bade the rest of them to join her. Waterson escorted Antil into the tent. The priest's eyes were filled with the fear of her until he saw Liam. With a wordless cry of joy, he closed the space between them to grip the captain by his arms.

"Liam, my boy, my precious boy, how are you?" He tried to give the captain a friendly shake, but only succeeded in rocking himself.

Liam gripped Antil's forearms in return, his smile easy and natural. "Well, Pater. I am well."

The display shocked her. How could Liam stomach to have that vile priest touch him, fawn over him like a dog eager to see its long-gone master? "Come, gentlemen," she said, her voice clipped. "I would ask you to renew your acquaintance while we refresh ourselves."

Waterson eyed the rations on the table. Despite the abbreviated area, there remained plenty of empty space. "I think refresh might be a bit generous, Your Highness. Perhaps we should say, 'fend off the worst of our hunger.'"

Rokha laughed and seated herself on Adora's left. Waterson sat on her right with Antil next to him while Liam filled the chair at the foot of the table.

"Liam is a captain of the watch," Adora said. "He was my uncle's chief protector prior to his death."

Antil puffed up as if Adora had complimented him. "I have no doubt of it, Your Highness. Since Liam was a boy, I have seen the hand of Deas on him."

Adora toyed with the undersized piece of cheese on her plate. "It's interesting you should use that term, Pater—the hand of Deas. I have heard many people describe Errol Stone the same way."

Antil's face flushed, but he refused to rise to the bait. "So the priest, Martin, told me."

Adora leaned back, warming to her task. "In fact, my uncle, King Rodran, elevated Errol to the nobility for his courage and service to the crown. Imagine that, Pater Antil, an *orphan* so distinguishing himself that the king made him an earl. That certainly sounds like the hand of Deas to me." She shifted. "What do you think, Lady Rokha?"

"Absolutely, Your Highness," Rokha drawled. "When Errol joined my father's caravan . . . Excuse my manners." She inclined her head toward Antil. "My father was Naaman Ru, the finest swordsman of his generation. Perhaps you've heard of him. Anyway, when Errol joined my father's caravan, he knew something of the staff, but even I was surprised at how quickly he became nearly invincible with it."

Antil ripped his bread in half, thrust a piece in his mouth as if he were trying to stifle his tongue.

Rokha leaned forward. "What do you think, Captain Liam? Is Errol not accomplished?"

Liam nodded. "The one time we sparred, he defeated me, though I have improved since then."

"There," Adora said. "You see, Pater Antil. You're a man of the church, after all. Doesn't that sound like the hand of Deas is on Errol Stone?"

He swallowed thickly, his eyes burning. "That Liam does not contradict you tells me you must be speaking the truth of his exploits."

Adora's face heated at the slight, and she reached for a sword she no longer wore. Across the table she saw Liam lean back with wide eyes.

"Priests," Waterson muttered into his wine. "Slow to admit a wrong, slower still to apologize for it. It's too bad Abbott Lugnar is dead. I would love to discuss some finer points of theology with him." He tapped his sword as he took another drink.

Waterson's aside gave Adora the time she needed to compose herself, and an unexpected opening. "Slow? No, Lord Waterson. Not all priests are slow. Some are very quick to act, and it is not always to punish a perceived sin." She leered at Antil. "Especially if they happen to see an exposed bit of leg or bosom. Wouldn't you say, Pater Antil?"

The priest's face reddened and boiled as he panted in his extremity. "Filth!" He spat. "Born in filth and baptized in the mire. Stone is nothing. Whatever fortune or circumstance has come to him will soon end. The higher his elevation, the greater his inevitable downfall. And on that day I will celebrate."

Liam, his face hard, rose from his seat. "Do not ever seek to speak to me or come into my presence again. Until now, I thought you only too zealous in the pursuit of your duties, but I see I was wrong." He strode from the tent without looking back.

Antil watched him leave, his mouth open in a soundless cry, stricken, as if his hope of salvation had left the tent with Liam.

Adora allowed herself a small smile. "It may be beyond my power to assign the penance you deserve for your deeds of spite and hatred, but as a member of the royal house, I have the right to retain my own personal priest, one of my choosing. It is an honor that has been bestowed upon benefices and even the occasional archbenefice in Illustra's long history. I choose to bestow it upon you."

She let her smile grow, allowed the pleasure at her inspiration to show without restraint. "You will be my confidant, Pater Antil. From this day forward I will confess to you every thought and deed of Errol Stone that has captured my heart."

She leaned forward, holding him with her gaze. "And you will listen, my priest. You will listen until you can recite them back to me word for word."

28

RETURN

ERROL STOOD ON THE DECK as the *Penance* creaked and groaned with the smallest of swells, its ribs loose and complaining after a second trip through the maelstrom. Errol chafed at the slower speed, but Tek refused to add more sail.

"She be bruised and battered, lad," the sea captain said. "Adding to her pain would be poor gratitude for her service." He shrugged. "Besides, I do not think we be wanting to swim in these waters."

They had traveled for weeks without a Merakhi ship in sight, but now as they sailed toward Illustra's western coast, the ocean current swept them east toward the Forbidden Strait between the kingdom and Merakh. Nervous, Errol pulled a pair of blanks and his reader's knife to cast for the presence of Merakhi ships.

"You needn't bother," Merodach said. The watchman's eyes held confidence but a hint of perplexity as well. "The closest Merakhi ships are just offshore of Bota in Basquon." He flexed his hands. "It took me a dozen casts to pinpoint their location."

Errol rolled his shoulders, shedding a burden he hadn't realized he carried until that moment. "The way is open. We can go home." He prayed Adora would be there waiting for him. They wouldn't have much time together before . . .

"I think we should find the reason behind this, lad." Rale chewed his lower lip in thought for a moment. "Good news in wartime makes me suspicious."

Merodach nodded.

Errol sighed his disappointment as he pulled a pair of blanks from his pocket to test the safest choice, but a sudden diffidence overtook him. How long had it been since he'd cast? He bounced one of the blanks in his palm, felt the open grain of the pine against his fingertips, before he returned it to its place inside his cloak. If Deas meant him to die, why bother casting for choices?

"Let's see what lies inside the strait, Captain Tek."

"Aye, lad." Tek spun the wheel, and the ship hauled over to starboard, the sails clapping with the direction change. "Hands forward on arms," Tek said. The mate relayed the order in his brazen-throated yell, and every man left on the ship came forward to man crossbows and longbows.

They anchored that night a mere five leagues from the strait, Captain Tek unwilling to brave the narrow entry in the dark. At dawn the next morning, they crept eastward, every man tense by his weapon.

"You know, lad," Tek said, "if we be spotted by Merakhi, we will have to make for the kingdom side of the strait."

Errol looked north toward the cliffs that towered over them, weather-smoothed rock running vertically until it ended in churning surf below. "How close is the nearest Illustran port?"

Tek's mouth pulled to one side. "Too far to be of any use."

A cry from the crow's nest startled him, and he jumped, his hands gripping the metal staff that never left his side.

"Masts ahead."

Merodach nodded as if he expected no less. "Unless casting no longer works, they'll be kingdom ships, such as we have."

Rale's brows lowered at that and his eyes grew dark. "It's a shame that death has put Weir beyond our reach. I wouldn't mind the opportunity to kill him myself."

The forest of masts grew closer until Errol could make out the composition of Illustra's navy. A more mismatched collection of ships would have been hard to find. Nearest to them, a single cog, the largest ship in sight, held its position just outside the mouth of the strait.

"That would be the flagship, lad," Tek said. "It be the fastest ship of the lot. Having it on the outside of the strait do not bode well for what be going on."

"What do you mean?" Errol asked.

Tek's gaze ran back and forth over the odd collection of ships. "They be hailing us. I think we better swing alongside and find out how bad things be."

The first mate relayed Tek's orders as the captain swung the wheel, and they slowed to a crawl and sailed to within a half dozen paces of the flagship. Sailors dressed in the red livery of Illustra's royal house used grappling hooks to bring the ships together, their movements crisp with discipline, but they didn't wear the look of men hopeful of victory.

The first mate of the other ship beckoned them aboard. "Welcome to the *Fearless*, my lords. We were told to watch for your passing. Captain Mederi awaits you in his cabin."

Tek winced at the name.

Errol judged the *Fearless* to be roughly one and a half times as big as Tek's ship, the forward and aft decks large and high enough to make a longship think twice about attacking. In addition, the masts were heavier and taller, capable of nearly twice the sail.

"Last resort," Rale said as he surveyed the vessel. At Errol's bidding he continued. "Weir spent decades consolidating the naval and shipping power of Illustra in his own hands. Without his ships the best the kingdom can hope for is to keep the Merakhi bottled up in the strait. Deas help us if they break through and sail up the western coast. Instead of fighting a two-front war, it'll be three, and that last one will be at our backs."

Captain Mederi's cabin was nearly twice the size of Tek's. Trestle tables nailed to the floor and covered with a pile of charts filled the space. Mederi, a gangly Talian with a large hooked nose and thinning black hair, rose to greet them with quick, jerky motions.

He shook hands with each of them, but at the sight of Tek, his face darkened. "I see you survived the mission to Ongol. Pity."

Rale's mouth pulled to one side. "You two know each other?"

Tek coughed into his hand. "It's an old misunderstanding."

Errol stepped forward, drawing Mederi's attention. "We don't have time to settle scores, Captain." He gestured toward the charts. "What's happening here?"

Mederi sagged as if his anger had been the source of his fortitude. "We're outmatched, but we knew that going in. The kingdom's aim is not so much to win the strait, but to keep the Merakhi from leaving it. We're only a league from Bota, the narrowest point." He pointed to an oversized chart showing the Basquon port and the portion of the strait they now occupied. "The longships have a shallower draft, so they can sail closer to the coast, but we've installed trebuchets on the cliffs to hurl anything we can find at them." He traced a finger between Illustra and Merakh. "What cogs we have fill the strait, driving the longships close to our shore, where the siege engines can pick them off."

"They'll catch on sooner or later," Tek said. He leaned over the map engrossed in the layout of the two navies. "Then they'll come at you in force or try to slip your blockade at night."

"Aye." Mederi gave Tek a grudging nod. "They started as much a few nights ago as soon as the moon became too dim to light the water. We barely held. They nearly sank two of the cogs. Fortunately, they had to withdraw, but we don't have replacements." His chest rose as he pulled the sea air into his lungs. "We can hold them once, maybe twice more. Then they'll be through and headed up the coast."

Tek nodded, his eyes intent on the chart. Small numbers next to sinuous lines indicated the depth in fathoms at the bottleneck. "There's only one thing you can do."

Mederi's face chilled. "They're not as honorable as you, Tek. They don't leave their prisoners on some Deas-forsaken island to wait for rescue. They kill them."

Instead of growing angry, Tek laughed. "You misunderstand me, Mederi. There be no surrender to the Merakhi. You'll have to let them sink your ships." He paused to run a hand across his grizzled chin. "And if they won't do it, you'll have to."

Mederi inhaled, his face thunderous. Then he caught sight of Tek tapping the chart and leaned over it. "Blast me, it might work."

"What might work?" Errol asked.

Mederi tore himself from the chart. "Narrowing the strait even more. If we sink the ships too damaged to be of use to us, the longships will be limited to the center of the strait." He turned back to Tek. "We still can't hold forever."

"No, Captain Mederi, you can't," Tek said. "But you might buy Illustra enough time for a miracle." He glanced at Errol.

Errol tried to ignore the implication of that look, but a small voice reminded him of who Tek was. The little sea captain didn't flaunt it, but he was solis. Errol didn't want to think of himself as a miracle—it meant death.

Rale leaned in. "What news do the ships bring from Erinon?"

Mederi waved an arm toward the strait. "The people on the Green Isle are no better off than we are here. Each vessel brings different tidings, but they all say the Judica is desperate. They've ordered the conclave to work without ceasing until the soteregia is found. The thunder of hundreds of casts fills the halls, but every one fails."

Mederi shook his head. "The latest news is the worst. The archbenefice is ill."

"How ill?" Rale demanded.

"He suffered a stroke. Bertrand Canon lies near death if he has not passed over already. I have withheld the news from my command." He spread his hands. "Our battle is hopeless enough."

Rale and Tek groaned, but Merodach stiffened and his eyes

grew moist. Deep within Errol's chest, the smoldering hope for the kingdom's unlikely victory guttered and blew out. Without Bertrand Canon to head the Judica and advise the council of nobles, Illustra was bereft.

"A ship without a rudder finds the shoals," Tek said.

"A double succession," Rale said. He shook his head. "Who rules?"

Mederi's shoulders lifted then settled before he answered. "Duke Escarion's voice carries the most weight with the nobles, and most of his orders get carried out. Primus Sten still heads the conclave. The last report stated that he continues to seek the soteregia, despite the failure of their craft."

Merodach shook his head. "It's not the craft that's failed, Captain. It's the question."

"How can that be? There is either a soteregia or there isn't."

Rale waved a hand dismissing the rest of the discussion. "We can't stay here, Captain. We need the fastest ship you can spare to get us back to the isle."

"I can't give you anything. If we intend to clog the shallows with wreckage, it'll take everything I have."

"We do be willing to trade," Tek said. "My ship be not so big as your cogs, but its larger than what the watchmen require to speed back to Erinon."

A lump in Errol's throat made it difficult to swallow. "You're going to scuttle your own ship?"

Tek rested a hand on Errol's shoulder. "She's been a fair vessel, lad, and more faithful than most, but even with dry dock she'll never be right again. This be the best service she can offer." He turned to Mederi. "I'll throw myself in as well, if you'll have me."

Mederi's face flashed from shock to grudging admiration. "I'd rather have you with me than against me, pirate though you are."

Tek laughed. "Reformed pirate."

Mederi inked a command to release one of his ships back to Erinon, and then he and Tek turned their attention back to the charts as Errol and the rest left the cabin.

They stepped aboard the *Waverider* an hour later, the smell of tar and naptha strong in Errol's nose. Scorch marks covered the topmost deck of the ship near the catapult fastened ahead of the foremast. In the distance, Illustran ships made for the shallow parts of the strait as smoke stained the early spring sky.

Two weeks later they slipped into Erinon's western port. As they entered the harbor, they passed ships headed the other way, ships that were hardly more than fishing vessels capable of offering little more than token resistance to the fleet of longships Merakh sent against them.

Errol pointed at one. "Can they hold?"

Rale's eyes reflected the gray-green of the sea. "If any man can wring victory from the strait, Amos Tek can." He blinked twice. "But no, they cannot hold. At best they can make the cost in lives and time too high for the Merakhi to be willing to pay."

"The malus don't have a price," Errol said. "We're going to lose."

Rale nodded, still looking across the harbor toward the docks of the city. "It seems to me we had this conversation once before, Errol. The only battle that's been lost is the one that's already been fought."

Errol's chest ached to ask Rale what he thought about the soteregia, but he was too afraid of the answer to voice the question. Deep within, surrounded by layers of distraction and denial, lay the conviction he must die. He didn't want to hear it confirmed by any of his friends.

As they glided to the pier, the sound of bells, deep and melancholy, drifted across the water. Errol didn't ask, and neither Rale nor Merodach offered an interpretation, but he knew the meaning.

A sparse collection of dockhands, remnants of a thriving concern, tied their ship to the pier and they disembarked. A pair of nobles, alike in face but different in coloring, stood on the weathered timbers of the pier to take their report—Derek and

Darren, the sons of Duke Escarion. At seeing Errol's face, they started in surprise.

"Well met, Earl Stone," Derek said. Darren nodded his agreement behind him. "Your arrival is an unexpected pleasure." The ever-present smile, gentle and mocking, was gone from Derek's face. Darren had always been quiet, but now his silence seemed weighed with grief.

He didn't want to ask. For as long as he kept the question to himself he could hope that it might not be true. Errol shook his head. That was a boy's way of thinking. Such hopeful denials wouldn't serve him.

"We heard the bells," he said into the silence. "How long ago did the archbenefice die?"

Derek's gaze went past him. "Three days."

"Who leads in his place?" Rale asked.

"No one." Derek hurled the words as if they offended him. "The benefices can't figure out which of them is supposed to be the salvation of the kingdom." Derek closed his eyes and sighed. "Every last one of them claims to feel the call of Deas to lead."

Darren put a hand on his older brother's shoulder. "Go easy, Derek. They are ordinary men caught in extraordinary circumstances."

"Then we need extraordinary men," Derek said, but the heat had gone from his voice.

Errol nodded. Illustra required heroes. Liam was one and Pater Martin another, but they were few, too few.

He shifted the pack that hung from his shoulder, tightened his grip on the metal staff Martin had given him. "I must go to the Judica."

The light of hope flared in Darren's eyes. "You were successful?"

"Yes."

A smile like a glint of sunlight grew on Darren's face. "Perhaps that will embolden the benefices to make a decision."

Errol shrugged, the weight of the book and its revelations suddenly heavy. "That depends on how they receive it."

29

KNOWABLE

THEY ASCENDED the rough granite steps that led from the docks to the royal compound, where the Judica, the conclave, and the watch made their home. Questions gnawed at Errol, queries he'd denied himself during his journey.

"Do you have any news of Princess Adora?" he asked.

"No." Derek shook his head. "Nor of Pater Martin."

Errol stumbled, and his foot slipped back to the previous step. "What of Martin?"

Derek grimaced, his hands fluttering in the air. "My apologies. You departed before he left with the secondus and Captain Cruk. They sent some messages back, but no one's heard from them since they passed into the eastern parts of Bellia." He tapped his head with one finger. "That small man went with them."

"Karele," Errol said. "But why Bellia?"

Rale made a sound behind him. "Caves. Martin seeks another way onto the steppes, but to what end I have no idea."

But Errol suspected. Karele's adoptive father, Ablajin, held authority of a sort with the horsemen. Had the horse master gone seeking to make peace? But why take Martin and Luis with him?

"If they have gone to the steppes, it is unlikely we will see them again," Derek said.

Errol wanted to argue, but his hope seemed too uncertain to offer.

As they entered the compound, word of their arrival ran ahead of them. Servants, nobles, and churchmen alike gaped in wonder, the faces sloughing off mourning as they passed. Their regard weighed on Errol like a millstone around his neck. Against the might of Merakh and the unlikely hope of Martin's mission, the recovery of the book seemed insignificant. What good would doctrine do against such odds?

Men in heavy crimson robes raced ahead of them toward the meeting hall of the Judica, but when Errol arrived at the official entrance, the guards bade him wait while the rest of the benefices gathered.

At last the way swung open to reveal a sea of florid faces wreathed in mixtures of hope and fear. The temptation to draw out the moment, to keep the benefices in suspense, washed over him for an instant, but only for a pair of heartbeats. He unslung his pack and with simple movements untied the oiled skin that protected the ancient book, the source of Magis's folly. A collective gasp filled the hall. Some of the older benefices wept openly, uncaring, while others reached toward him with outstretched arms as if they could touch the hope of their salvation despite the distance between themselves and the dais.

Errol noted the presence of Benefice Kell, who had brought the accusation against him of consorting with spirits and had unwittingly been the means of his survival. Thin wisps of his ancient hair wafted back and forth as he rocked on his feet, tears tracking down his face. Benefice Kerran, one of his few defenders from the first, looked upon him like a man given his greatest hope.

Kell came forward, stumping on his old man's legs until he stood within arm's reach of Errol. "I know you've no cause to look upon me with benevolence, Earl Stone, but I confess before

Deas and all these men that I was wrong to accuse you. Only Deas's chosen could have brought the book back."

It was meant to be praise; Errol knew that, but Kell's pronouncement stabbed him like an omen of prophecy. Deas's chosen would die.

The other benefices remained in their seats—held by reticence or protocol, Errol didn't know which—but Kerran came forward to join Kell on the dais, his hands extended.

Errol's fingertips caressed the thick leather cover of the book, brushed the brass binding that held it closed.

"The church and its Judica owe you much, Earl Stone," Benefice Kerran said. "How may we repay you?"

Errol surrendered the book with a pang of loss. Other than himself, Kell, and Kerran, no one stood on the dais. No one ruled. "Who commands in Canon's absence?"

Kerran sighed. "No one at the moment. The duties of archbenefice are carried out by an appointee chosen each week."

Again, the traditions of the church escaped Errol. Why did the Judica insist on doing everything the hard way? "Why haven't you told the conclave to cast for the next archbenefice?"

Kell and Kerran exhaled in unison. "It's not that simple, lad," Kell said. For once his weathered features didn't appear stern, only tired. "The corruption within the church carried out by Benefices Weir and Dane has taught us to be suspicious of each other." He snorted. "As if we weren't already."

Kerran nodded. "Also, there has been no omne to verify the cast. Suspicion runs to the conclave as well."

Kell put a hand on Errol's shoulder. He could feel nothing except earnest sincerity in the old man's touch. "You may be the weight that tips the scales, Earl Stone. You have returned the book to us, and you are the omne. As such, your integrity is unassailable. The Judica is in your debt." Kell leaned close, beseeched. "You could use that debt to force us into action."

He felt the extremity of Kell's need as Benefice Kerran nodded assent behind him.

"No." He tried to ignore the look of shock that twisted their faces. "It won't work. If you need me to tell the Judica what to do now, who will you turn to next—someone like Weir?

"Archbenefice Canon had the Judica and the conclave tested—each and every member, including the primus. You can trust each other." He shrugged. "You just have to make the decision to do it."

He favored each of them with a bow. "Benefices, if you will excuse me, I need to report to the council of nobles." He gestured toward the book. "And you have much to do."

Their gazes followed him as he departed, but he left without regret. If he allowed them to make him their leader, their reliance would lead them to helplessness.

When he arrived at the hall the council of nobles used as their meeting place, he was surprised to find a mere fraction of the men present who'd attended months before. Duke Escarion had eschewed the seat of authority on the dais. Instead, the space was filled with maps of the kingdom spread on a dozen trestle tables that had been shoved together in the center of the room. Every noble present clustered around as the duke used a pointer to brief them all. Rale and Merodach stood on each side.

"We've got every tub not committed to the Forbidden Strait ferrying men from Soeden to Einland." He shifted his pointer. "Most of the Fratalanders have already made their way south into Bellia. Those that remain are too few to threaten the Morgol army pouring through the gap."

A noble with a florid complexion and a bushy red mustache pointed to the inlet that reached far into Bellia. "Can we not hold the Morgols here? The landscape would pinch them into a longer column. Pikemen and archers would be able to stop their cavalry."

Escarion glanced at Rale, who pointed to a pair of markers just west of Bellia in Dannick. "It's a good suggestion, Duke Hoffen, but the men you need are too far away to get there before the Morgols."

A different noble made a strangled noise in his throat. "Do

you know what you're saying? There's nothing but rolling plains from there to the mountains of the Arryth. You've just surrendered Bellia, Dannick, and Einland to the Morgols."

Duke Escarion gestured at the map, pulling the noble's attention and ire away from Captain Rale. "Count Hessen, even could we hold the Bellian inlet against the Morgols, that portion of the army would be trapped by any force coming against them from the south." He smacked his pointer on the border between Lugaria and Sorland. "We know the Merakhi have already crossed from the shadow lands into this region. Were they to march north, any force in Bellia would be caught between them and the Morgols. They'd be totally wiped out."

The duke's words went into Errol's side like a sword thrust. He tried to keep his voice neutral, failed. "What of Princess Adora? Is she . . . Did her mission succeed?"

Escarion's expression was unreadable. "No, Earl Stone."

The room spun. Errol thrust out an arm, groped for the nearest shoulder to support his weight as the duke's voice came to him from a distance. "The princess and Captain Liam are unharmed, but the Merakhi landed a large force of soldiers and spawn on the southern coast of the shadow lands. Haven's army was wiped out buying their civilians enough time to escape. The princess and Captain Liam will meet our forces in Gascony."

"They aren't coming here?" Errol asked.

With a gesture to Rale and Merodach, Escarion shook his head. "We've already sent word for them to await our arrival. The Forbidden Strait cannot be held indefinitely. We must engage the Merakhi in the Arryth and hope we can defeat them before they can land a force behind us."

Errol looked into the shadowed gaze of the duke, tried not to see the despair Escarion fought to keep from his eyes. Around the tables, the nobles paled and most of them wore resignation. To win the war, they would have to engage a superior force from not one but two countries and triumph quickly. Then, assuming enough of their army survived such a victory, they would have to turn and defeat whatever force the Merakhi sent to attack them from the west.

"How soon do we leave Erinon?" he asked.

Escarion exchanged a glance with Rale and Merodach before he answered. "The captains will leave in the morning with the remnants of the watch still on the island. The rest of us will follow as soon as we can." He sighed. "We will have to convince the Judica and the conclave of their peril. They will not want to leave."

"I will depart with the captains, but I don't think you'll have a problem convincing the Judica, Your Grace," Errol said. "They have something they will dearly want to protect."

A whisper of breeze, no more than a suggestion of air movement, brought Antil's scent to Adora as they rode west. The odor nauseated her, and like rotted meat eaten unawares, everything about the man turned her stomach. Not for the first time she regretted her decision to make the bitter little man her personal priest. In the beginning she thought she might change him, might force him to see the nobility that lay within his son, but she'd underestimated Pater Antil.

No endorsement, however sincere, no matter the source, would convince him of Errol's worth. Antil's own self-loathing went too deep. Several times she'd found herself on the verge of striking him, only to stop just short, her arms shaking with the suppressed violence of withheld blows. Rokha, her jaws and shoulders clenched, had quickly left her company, only returning to her side if Antil rode elsewhere.

Adora could hardly blame her.

Weary of Antil's denials, Adora now considered a different approach. "Tell me about her," she said at last.

Antil looked at her with eyes that shared Errol's color but not his openness and squinted in suspicion. "You will have to specify, Your Highness. Callowford is a small village, but I am acquainted with more than one 'her.'"

That was another thing she despised about him; his corrections never ceased and the superior smirk that twisted his lips into a parody of a smile made her sword arm itch. "Pardon my mistake, Pater. I thought you to be a more discerning man." She smiled as his grin faded. "There is only one 'her' I have any interest in: Errol's mother. I want to know what my future husband's mother was like."

Antil set his jaws, didn't speak.

"Perhaps I didn't make myself clear."

"Your Highness"—Antil bit his words off one at a time—"I am your priest. You are not my confessor."

Adora forced a laugh, hoped it sounded genuine in its amusement. "I am not interested in the sordid details of your indiscretions, you miserable excuse for a priest. Errol is the noblest man in the kingdom, despite the treatment he received at your hands. Since there seems to be no such quality within you, Pater Antil, I can only conclude that his mother must have been a woman of extraordinary depth. I adjure you, as your sovereign, tell me everything you can recollect or surmise about her in as plain and honest a fashion as you can contrive. Leave nothing out."

His mouth gaped as she spoke, stretching in horror by the time she was done. "You cannot ask that of me. You cannot."

She slowed her horse and leaned a little toward him, her gaze burning with all the love and passion for Errol she held. "You are quite right, Pater. I do not ask it; I demand it."

He shook, but whether he struggled with her command or himself she could not tell. His head turned from her with a jerk, so when he spoke she had to strain to hear him. "Where shall I begin, Your Highness?"

To his credit, he did not spit her title like an epithet as he had so often in the past.

An unexpected twinge of pity for his self-loathing arose, moved her to speak softly. "What was her name?"

"Candide," Antil said. He stared at the reins in his hands. "And she fit it. She was sweet and pure."

"Hardly that," Adora observed softly, "if she would knowingly bed a priest."

She had the impression of movement, only that, before Antil's open hand connected with her face, the slap loud in her ears. Stunned past anger she stared at him, at the rage that twisted his features.

"You may kill me, Your Highness, but I will not suffer your insults of Candide. She was perfect in ways you could never hope to approach." His voice rose until he screamed as tears bunched in his eyes. "She burned like a bonfire on a moonless night until she died, was killed giving birth to that filth you say you love." He panted, defying her. "She loved me!"

Adora rubbed her cheek. He had pulled the blow. Sevra and her minions had given her worse. Insight flared in her, and she understood Antil. She didn't like him any better—far from it; he remained contemptible—but now she knew how to approach him.

But that would have to wait. Too many people had seen him strike her. Rokha and Waterson rode toward them with swords drawn. Even Liam had slowed to turn, unhooking his short bow and nudging his horse to ride back to her.

She sighed. He deserved death, but until Illustra found its king, the burden of mercy belonged to her. She jerked her reins toward Antil with her left hand. The priest gaped at her in surprise as she drew her sword and clubbed him across the temple as hard as she could. The shock jolted her arm, sending pain shooting though her elbow.

Antil's eyes rolled and he toppled from his saddle.

Her rescue party stopped in front of her.

Waterson sheathed his sword, glanced at the dimming sky overhead. "You have an unusual way of selecting campsites, Your Highness."

Rokha dismounted and sauntered over to stand at Antil's unconscious form. "I can pour some water on him, if you'd like to continue your conversation."

Adora nodded. Tired as he made her, she needed to verify her insight. It would be easier to do so now, while Antil's emotions were still raw and unbalanced. Later, he might manage to restore the judgmental stoicism he wore like a cloak.

He spluttered and coughed as he woke to Rokha's drenching. When he cleared his eyes, Adora stood waiting for him, her sword clenched in her hand, ready to strike again. Liam sat his horse behind her, short bow at the ready.

She took a deep breath and began, "Do not think to escape my questions by forcing me to kill you, priest. I have defeated and killed men who thought me defenseless. I have no reservations against beating you within a breath of life for your insolence."

He shook water from his hair. "What else do you want to know, Princess?" He growled the words, but underneath he sounded tired, defeated.

"When did you start blaming a child for a woman's death?"

He barked a laugh, and at first she thought he would deny the accusation in her question, but when he looked at her, his reserve had given way to sardonic admission. He gave her a condescending bow from his seat on the ground.

"Stupid question. When she died, of course."

Angered at his disrespect, she searched for a way to strike back, to keep him off balance. "Candide's death must have been convenient for you. You would have been struck from the priesthood otherwise."

Her arrow failed to find its mark. "I'd planned to leave the campaign. Traveling with Prince Jaclin offered a means to be paid while we looked for a place far enough from our families to hide." He looked at her as if daring her to insult him further. "Months before we came to Callowford, we'd snuck from Jaclin's column to be married by the priest of a small village in Gascony. We liked Callowford. Our plans were to simply let Jaclin and his men leave us behind."

Something was not right; this was not the story she'd heard.

"Your words have the sound of truth behind them, priest, but perhaps you could explain why your tale differs from the one you told Martin Arwitten?"

Antil regarded her from eyes narrowed to slits. "Do I owe the truth to a man who would strike me?"

Adora nodded, even as she ignored the irony in Antil's protest. "Do you owe the truth to me?"

He smiled, but his eyes mocked her. "Of course, Your Highness, I am your confessor, am I not?"

He tired her with his semantics, but she pressed forward, hoping to find some scrap of knowledge that would help Errol. "But you didn't kill the child."

Antil ran his tongue over his teeth and spat a piece of grass into the dirt. "I'm not a murderer, Princess. I gave the babe to Warrel." He laughed. "Beware, Your Highness. The boy is a curse. Everyone around him dies. Warrel's wife wasted away five years after he came to them. Then Warrel was crushed by stone." He smiled. "Perhaps you would do best to avoid him."

Behind, she heard Liam's growl. Even his patience was running low. She ground her teeth until her jaws ached. "Say his name."

He laughed at her. He laughed!

"I have been saying his name . . . Princess. Every time I speak of him as a curse or filth, I name him."

Rokha, still and unseen by Antil, delivered a savage uppercut to the priest's chin, the sound of his jaws meeting a sharp retort in the evening air. She bowed to Adora, her movements formal. "Your Highness, I crave your pardon for interrupting your conversation."

Adora nodded and gestured with one hand to tell Rokha her apology was unnecessary. Antil lay like discarded cloth on the ground.

"What will you do with him?" Rokha asked.

She rolled each shoulder, trying to shed the weight of her responsibility. "What had to be done since the moment we found him: take him to Errol." She forced the next words past a lump in her throat. "If he still lives."

"Errol lives," Liam said.

But when Adora turned to inquire how he knew such a thing, the captain of the watch had already moved away.

30

CONFLUENCE

MARTIN RODE AT ABLAJIN'S SIDE with Luis and Cruk trailing close behind. Since leaving the steppes, Cruk had encased himself in silence. He spoke seldom, but he looked often at the phalanx of Ablajin's men, clustered in a tight mass as they rode. Many times Martin could see his eyes darting, working back and forth, counting the men and their horses, as if trying to multiply their number by sheer force of will.

When the mountain range that ran south from the Soeden Strait down the Gascony border came into view, Cruk nudged his horse into a canter. He stopped next to Ablajin and gave an uncomfortable-sounding grunt.

Ablajin nodded to acknowledge his presence.

"There's going to be trouble," Cruk said.

The Morgol leader's eyebrows lifted in surprise, and Martin winced. No one would ever accuse Cruk of being diplomatic.

"How so, Captain?" Ablajin asked.

Cruk gestured first at the force behind them and then forward toward the mountains. "Deploying your men to fight here is risky.

It's a hard thing to ask a man to fight his countrymen, harder still if they're outnumbered twenty to one."

The Morgol chieftain nodded. "Holy Martin tells me you are the foremost tactician in the kingdom. I see he is correct, yet there is much about my people that you do not know. From the moment my clan allowed me to live after I killed Oorgat, they declared themselves enemies of our nation."

Cruk nodded. "Yet having a common enemy does not make them our ally. If I were the opposing commander, I would offer them a battlefield amnesty and kill them later."

Martin saw Ablajin's eyes widen as he turned to face him. "Your pardon, Martin, I underestimated the vision of your captain. Such a thing as he suggests would be unholy to the chieftains, but the treachery of the theurgists has no boundaries."

"What do you propose, Captain?"

"Once we pass through the gap into the Arryth, take your men south to the border between Gascony and Talia to battle against the Merakhi. I will send men with you to smooth the journey."

"A part of me had hoped to repay the theurgists in person for their treachery." Ablajin gave a somber nod. "But your plan is for the best." The corners of his mouth twitched upward. "How will you fight them, those people who were known to me?"

Martin understood. Ablajin asked for a measure of trust in return.

"Bows and pikes," Cruk said. "Men with longbows will cover squadrons of pikemen. If we can narrow the gaps, light cavalry won't stand a chance, especially fighting uphill."

Ablajin nodded. "It is a good plan. A Morgol's love for his horse will make him hesitate to charge a line of men with the long spears. Grouped together, they will make easy targets."

Martin looked to see Ablajin's gaze upon him, the brown eyes serious, his tone formal. "I would ask a boon for my people, holy Martin."

"If I can grant it, I will, Chieftain Ablajin."

"Provide a place for the women and children of the clan if

your battle is won. They will awake to a different world, and the steppes may be closed to them."

Martin bowed. "I will do everything in my power to make it so. They will be honored members of the kingdom, Chieftain Ablajin."

Two days later they rode through one of the gaps in the mountain chain that circled the Arryth, the fertile region of Illustra where generations of farmers had fed the kingdom everything from wheat to wine. Martin, his elementary education in warfare reawakened, could only stare at the hills sloping up and away from him on each side. He shuddered. Too wide. The gap, every gap opening west to Illustra's heart, offered too much access.

He pointed. "Will we have enough men to hold them?

Cruk roused from his inspection of the road ahead to spare a brief glance for their immediate surroundings. Owen rode in front of the watchman, snuggled into one burly arm, snoring softly. Cruk paused, his stare growing distant. "No."

Martin waited, but the captain seemed uncompelled to add anything further.

"How long can we hold?"

Cruk met his question with frank assessment. "Men can hold for a long time, Pater, if they know what they're holding for and have some hope of living." His hand idly stroked Owen's shoulder in a comforting gesture. "How much time will you need?"

Cruk's question hit him like an accusation from Deas. He didn't know. Again the thought came to him that there might not be an answer, that he and Luis and all the rest of Illustra were living on numbered breaths. He shook his head. *No.* The herbwomen had said there was a way.

But if they'd been Deas's chosen, the heads of the solis, why hadn't Deas simply told them what that way was? He laughed at the irony. Twice he'd been elevated to the red of the Judica, and yet he craved nothing more than another scrap of reassurance from two dead herbwomen.

"There may not be enough time," he said to Cruk.

The captain's mouth pulled to one side. It was hard to tell whether he was grimacing or grinning. "Every now and then I'd appreciate it if you would offer an evasion or two. You have a nasty habit of telling a man the unvarnished truth."

The expression slipped, then disappeared. "I heard you with the secondus. If one of them has to die to save the kingdom, there's a simple way to guarantee Illustra's safety."

Martin held up a hand, but Cruk ignored the plea.

"Send them both out to fight."

A breeze, channeled by the hills, lifted a stray lock of his hair as it caressed his face. On the surface, Cruk's solution offered a way for the kingdom to survive, but a foreboding grew in him as he considered the idea. The herbwomen had said one of them must die. That could only mean one of them had to live. But to what end? Neither Errol nor Liam had children. No matter which of them died, there would be no heir to maintain the barrier bought by the sacrifice.

He tasted Luis's despair. Cruk looked at him, waiting for an answer, but there was none to give.

They crested a rise, and the gap into the Arryth snapped into focus. Lines of men working on fortifications appeared. The sound of engineers calling out instructions drifted to them.

"Praise Deas," Cruk said. "Somebody at least had enough sense to begin preparations while we were gone."

The clatter of weapons startled Martin, and he turned his head to see workmen turned soldiers. Cruk chuckled. "Should have expected that, I suppose. Thousands of Morgols are bound to make anyone nervous." He turned to call to Ablajin. "Chieftain, would you have your men wait? I think we need to make some introductions."

A detachment of guards broke away from the squadron guarding the gap and rode toward them at an easy canter. When they neared, the detachment split into two groups: one composed of watchmen and irregulars, the other made up of grim-faced church guards in red livery. The church soldiers had weapons drawn, despite Martin and Cruk's presence at the head of the column.

Cruk muttered under his breath. "Not good." He pointed. "We've got a problem, Pater. Those church soldiers seemed to be more intent on you than the Morgols. Who have you annoyed now?"

"It could be almost anyone," Luis quipped.

Martin noted the soldiers in red hardly spared a glance for the twenty thousand Morgol warriors spread before them. Their attention clearly seemed centered on Martin. They came at him in an arc, hemming him in.

"I think this would be a good time for you to use some of your fabled oratory, Martin," Luis said. "They look very serious."

Cruk grunted as he adjusted Owen, who still slept tucked within his arm. "I've noticed a man with bared steel has a hard time hearing."

Ablajin nodded toward the approaching guards. "I will order my men to come to your aid if you ask it, holy Martin, but would not spilling kingdom blood jeopardize our alliance?"

Martin exhaled. "It would. Something must have happened within the Judica." At his side, Luis made a sound halfway between a sigh and agreement.

"At least they haven't put arrows to bowstrings," Cruk said. Martin nodded, but the edges of those swords appeared very keen.

At ten paces the church guard detachment stopped. Its leader, a blond-haired captain with a beard and mustache that blurred the scar running through his sharp Gascon features, pointed his sword at Martin.

"I adjure you by the authority given me by the Grand Judica, are you Martin Arwitten?"

The absence of the title of pater, or even priest, could not bode well. "I am."

The sword returned to attention but not to its sheath. "Martin

Arwitten, I am Captain Geraud. I am commanded to conduct you to the Grand Judica in haste. There you will answer for your deeds and serve whatever penance or penalty Deas and the Grand Judica deem fit to expunge your debt."

"Captain," Luis said, "does your charge include any others?"

The captain shook his head.

A trace of cold threaded its way across Martin's skin. The Grand Judica, the church guard had said. Not the archbenefice. "Who signed the writ?"

"Benefices Kell and Kerran."

He struggled to pull air into his lungs. "What of Archbenefice Canon?"

The guard blinked twice. "The archbenefice is dead."

Martin bowed his head and recited the panikhida. When he looked up he saw Cruk speaking with the detachment of watchmen and irregulars. Owen was now awake but still sat in the saddle in front of Cruk. A bluff-faced lieutenant nodded, moving with the brusque motions of one who feared displeasing a superior.

When Cruk returned to Martin's side, Ablajin was there to meet him.

He pointed to Owen. "What will be done with the child?"

Cruk stiffened. "I will see to the boy."

Ablajin nodded but raised a hand. "I would like to adopt Owen into my household. Among my people, he is already considered a man for saving his horse."

Martin put his hand on Cruk's arm, drawing the captain's ire to himself, but he refused to acknowledge the anger in his gaze. "Owen will need a family, Captain. And if the kingdom survives, it will need men who can speak to both peoples."

Cruk's internal struggle played across the lines of his face. For a moment it appeared as though his long history of stoic resolve would collapse. Tremors worked through his cheeks as his mouth twisted, framing objections he never uttered.

He lifted Owen and turned him so that they sat face-to-face.

Cruk rested a scarred hand on top of the boy's windblown thatch of hair. "Owen, I have to go places that won't be safe for you. Would you like to live with the chieftain's clan and learn how to take care of horses?"

The boy's face brightened, but he may have sensed a portion of Cruk's struggle. He didn't speak. His nod appeared to tear Cruk's heart from his chest.

"Well then," Cruk said, his voice thick, "I want you to be the best horseman you can be." He hugged the boy close, then lifted him to the ground. "Off with you now."

Owen scampered toward the rear of the caravan and Ablajin's household.

Ablajin's horse faced Cruk, and the chieftain bent in a deep bow that he held. When he rose, Cruk acknowledged him with a nod.

"The boy Owen will be as my own son, Captain," Ablajin said. He pointed to Karele a few paces away. "You know that I speak the truth."

Cruk breathed deeply. "I do." The strain of speaking threaded its way through his voice. "I wouldn't have let him go otherwise."

He turned to Martin. "I'll be going back with you."

Martin turned to Luis. The secondus returned the look with a lift of his eyebrows. "You know I will always be at your side, Martin." He reached into his cloak and pulled out a pair of blanks. "And the answer I seek is somewhere back there."

The church captain coughed. "If you please, Pater."

Martin nodded. "Though I wish the circumstances were different, it will be good to see Erinon again."

"No, Pater." Captain Geraud shook his head. "The Judica awaits us in Gascony. Erinon has been evacuated."

Martin ignored the panic worming its way through his belly. They'd known holding the strait would be next to impossible once Weir burnt his ships. With a mental shove, he pushed this latest bit of news into the corner of his mind where he kept all the other circumstances that defied his attempts at control.

"Where is the church setting its headquarters, Captain?" Luis asked.

"I am commanded to convey you to Gergy, the ducal seat of Escarion."

Cruk rolled his shoulders as he gazed at nothing, then nodded. "It's a bit close to the mountains, but retreat doesn't matter now. It's centrally located. We'll be able to coordinate as well from there as any other location."

Ten days and innumerable changes of horses later, they arrived at Duke Escarion's estate. The home of Illustra's most powerful duke—which Martin had visited several times over the years—resembled the man himself. Strong towers stood at the corners of a five-sided fortress, and though the architecture carried beauty of a sort, it lacked the ostentatious embellishments Duke Weir had favored. Escarion favored function over form. No trees grew within a half mile of the walls, but flower gardens inside the main gates and rich tapestries and carpets decorating its halls testified to Mickala Escarion's influence.

Cruk nodded his approval as they surveyed the castle from a low rise. "A defensible place, but if we can't hold the Arryth, it will hardly matter. They'll just surround it and starve us out, and a siege is a bad way to die."

"It was built for another age," Martin said, "before the provinces united. After Magis died, no one thought we would ever see the Merakhi back on our soil." He waved at the throngs of refugees heading west, leaving the duke's lands behind. "There aren't enough castles in Illustra to protect the people that have filled the kingdom. We must win."

Captain Geraud twitched his reins, looking uncomfortable. "If you please, Pater, the Judica is waiting."

When Martin nodded, the church guards drew weapons and surrounded him, forcing Cruk and Luis outside of the circle. They descended a low rise and crossed the half mile of field that teemed with more armed men than Martin had ever envisioned. Pikemen drilled under the strident direction of their commanders. A row of men with longbows stretched into the distance, drawing and releasing a cloud of arrows into the air. The flight arced almost lazily overhead before plummeting toward a red-cloth target spread on the ground.

It seemed a vast company, but Cruk's expression told a different story.

They crossed a broad moat, their horses' hooves echoing like the call of a drum. Inside the courtyard, the church guards dismounted, and the captain signaled Martin to do the same.

When Luis and Cruk made to follow, Geraud held up one hand. "My orders were to convey Martin Arwitten to the hall of the Judica alone and under guard." He ducked his head. "I'm sorry, Pater."

Martin swallowed, forced a reassuring smile to his face. "It's quite all right, Captain." He turned to Luis and Cruk. "You both know what to do."

Though his arrival hadn't been a surprise, guards kept him waiting outside the grand hall the Judica had claimed for its meeting space. When the doors opened and they escorted him in, each of the benefices wore the ceremonial red of their position along with the gold chain and symbol of their office, confirming his fears. The seating would be a formal one. Archbenefice Canon had confessed before he died, and the entire Judica knew Martin and Luis had cast for the king privately. That he had done so under the orders of the archbenefice would gain him no clemency whatsoever.

The only questioned that remained would be the penalty, or rather, how they would choose to enact it. The Judica had devised rather creative means of execution in the past.

Instead of raised seating, the benefices sat arrayed in a broad half circle of cushioned chairs running several rows deep. The most powerful members that remained after Bertrand Canon's purge occupied the front.

The doors banged shut, and a guard barred them from within.

A seat that would have been occupied by the archbenefice sat empty at the focal point of the arc, but on either side sat Benefices Kell and Kerran, old and young, benefices of the most powerful dioceses in the kingdom, both stern faced, both ready to pass judgment.

A functionary stepped forward, pulled the archbenefice's staff from its holder, and rapped it on the floor six times. Martin sighed. Had the count been held to three, he would have been allowed to speak. Six strikes meant the Judica had already voted.

"Benefice Kerran," Kell intoned. His voice carried the hollow timbre of the old. "Recite the charges."

Kerran rose and moved to face Martin a mere arm's length away. "Martin Arwitten, it has been charged and confirmed by lot that you cast for Illustra's king in contravention of the authority of the Judica. Further, it has been confirmed that, by your absence, you allowed the blame for this act to fall upon Earl Stone, placing his life in danger."

Benefice Kell's voice ripped through the hall. "How do you plead?"

Plead? Martin shook his head. They'd struck the floor six times. There was no plea. All he could do was confess.

"The charges are true."

Kerran nodded as if he expected no less. "And have you no extenuating circumstances to offer in your behalf, Martin Arwitten?"

If he wanted to save himself from the worst of their penalty, this would be his only chance. Canon had ordered him to find the next king. True, he should have reported the archbenefice's actions to the Judica, but he had still been a subordinate acting on the instructions of his superior, and the circumstances had been exceptional. And as for Errol being blamed for his actions, he'd left Erinon before the extent of the charges and their consequences had been known.

He wet his lips. These men were known to him. Once he had counted many of them as friends. Surely he could persuade enough of them to evade death.

A hint of breath, perhaps the guard's, stirred the hair on the back of his neck, and his panic cleared. *No.* He would not quibble. Only absolute truth mattered now, when the kingdom stood on the edge of its own demise. "I have nothing to offer in my behalf, Benefice."

Kerran nodded, his face somber.

"Then these proceedings are at an end," Benefice Kell said. "Pronounce sentence."

"Martin Arwitten." Kerran's voice filled the hall. As one, Kell and the rest of the benefices rose. A sea of red surrounded him. "To determine penance and penalty for your actions, the Grand Judica has sought guidance from the conclave."

Martin jerked in surprise. What? The Judica never cast lots to determine punishment.

"In accordance with the conclave's cast and the will of Deas, Eleison, and knowable Aurae, we pronounce sentence."

Martin blinked, his mind fighting to make sense of what he'd just heard.

"Martin Arwitten, you are commanded to don the crimson of the office of archbenefice and assume the responsibilities of that office until death severs you from the service of the church." The collected benefices including Kerran and Kell dropped to their knees. Kerran, his head bowed, pointed at Martin's heart. "You are adjured by Deas."

31

WAR COUNCIL

JUST BEFORE DAWN, Errol moved through the halls of Duke Escarion's castle with tentative steps, ready to spring away at the first sign of being recognized. His recovery of the book of Magis had robbed him of any hope for anonymity. Everywhere he went, servants pointed and whispered, ducking their heads and bowing as if he were royalty. Even other members of the nobility, seasoned men and women old enough to be his grandparents and know better, spoke to him in quiet, almost reverent tones, ducking their heads each time he replied.

He wanted nothing more than to slip away from the crowds of churchmen and nobles who packed the corridors, but the proclamations from the Judica made that impossible. After his unlikely elevation, Martin seemed intent on correcting perceived slights to Errol on behalf of his predecessor and Rodran.

Errol just wanted him to shut up.

With Adora still days away according to the latest messenger, the only honest company he cared for was Cruk and Rale. Merodach was straightforward enough, but the taciturn captain hoarded his speech the way a miser guarded his gold. Bemused, he turned a corner and nearly ran over the slight form of Mickala Escarion.

"Pardon me, Duchess," he said, stammering his words. He still struggled to reconcile this woman, who seemed no more than a decade older than himself, as the mother of Derek and Darren Escarion. "I should pay more attention to what's in front of me."

Her laughter brightened the hall like an additional torch. "You can be excused, I think. Do you require anything, Earl Stone?"

He nodded. "I've gotten turned around. Could you direct me to Captain Cruk? I believe he is in the nobles' hall."

She signaled the servant trailing behind her as she looped an arm through his with a motherly smile that belied her age. "Come, Earl Stone, I will conduct you."

He slipped into the hall used by the nobles to plan the campaign. It was empty now, or nearly so. Cruk, Reynald, Rale, and Merodach stood at the oversized table gazing at a huge map of the Arryth. They didn't appear pleased.

At the sound of the door, the four men looked up.

"I'm sorry," Errol said. "I didn't mean to interrupt. I'll come back later."

Rale shook his head, the suggestion of a smile playing around his lips. "Said the hero of the kingdom."

Cruk grunted. "Three times over." He waved a hand, beckoning. "Come here, Errol. Take a look at the midden we're wading through."

The absence of Cruk's customary title for him—boy—brought a strange pang of regret. Too much had changed and too fast.

"I'm not very good at reading maps," Errol said.

"We'll explain," Rale said. He traced a line of mountains that started just west of Steadham in the north, ran south along the eastern border of Gascony, and then ran west with the border of Basquon. "This line of low mountains is the front we must hold. If the Merakhi or the Morgols break through into the flatland of the Arryth, they'll push us all the way back to the Beron Strait."

Errol peered at the map. Notations marked each gap in the

mountains. He pointed at one of the numbers in red. "What do those mean?"

"That's the number of men we estimate are needed to hold the gap," Reynald said.

Cruk snorted. "The bare minimum."

Merodach nodded. "And that's for a single engagement. There won't be any reinforcements. The numbers are in thousands."

Errol added up the markers. The other men lapsed into silence as he did so and time stretched. He'd never been quick with numbers despite Naaman Ru's abbreviated attempt to turn him into a merchant. "We need a hundred thousand men?"

Cruk exhaled through his nose as if he smelled something foul. "No, Errol. We need more, a lot more."

"How many do we have?"

Rale squinted. "Seventy thousand, perhaps ninety with the Morgols Archbenefice Arwitten brought with him. Princess Adora indicates that she has another ten thousand shadowlanders. That's all there is, unless we start drafting old men and boys who know nothing about fighting."

Cruk gestured his disgust. "Always a mistake. That type of conscript is more of a hindrance in battle than an asset."

Errol stared at the map with its uncompromising reality and shook his head. It wasn't hopeless—it was worse. "What's happening now?"

Rale pointed to the southeastern end of the range. "Watch captains Indurain and Merkx are investing the Pelligroso Pass. The Merakhi advance force Princess Adora encountered should arrive there within the week."

Errol's stomach lurched. These men talked about thousands dying with little more emotion than they would spend discussing breakfast. "Can they hold?"

Rale shrugged. "We hope so."

He fought the panic that erupted in his stomach, threatening to bring his breakfast back up on him. They had invited him to look at the map, to think, not to fall to pieces like some scared village drunk. He stared at the chart. The oversized scale managed to convey the details of the terrain in terrifying clarity. The Pelligroso Pass resembled an extended passage rather than a gateway. That seemed important. There were regions of the Sprata that looked like that, the gorge for one.

He pointed. "How difficult would it be to get men, ours or the enemies', up onto the cliffs overlooking the pass?"

Rale nodded his approval. "It can't be done from their side, but the slope is more gradual from ours."

"Bowmen," Errol said. "As many as you can spare. If you—we—lose that gap, it won't matter if we hold the rest."

"What else?" Rale prompted.

Errol looked again. What was Rale fishing for? His plan would work. He checked that thought. No, his plan *should* work, but every fight he'd seen held unexpected elements. What would he do if the Merakhi somehow nullified his bowmen and came through the gap? "Here." He pointed to the western end, where the pass opened into the fertile lands of the Arryth. "Close the gap. Use soldiers, conscripts, anyone you can. If they're no good in a fight, let them fill the gap with enough earth and rock so that there won't be one." He shrugged. "At least they can narrow it to give us a better chance."

Rale looked away, seeking Cruk and Merodach. "Well," he said. "How do you vote?"

Merodach nodded. "Better than most. Captaincy."

"And you, Captain Cruk?" Rale asked.

"The archbenefice won't like it," Cruk said. "He'll probably have a fit. You know why we can't give him his own command."

Rale brushed away Cruk's argument with a wave. "Can we afford not to? We have few enough men who can think through the advantages of the terrain. Will Captain Liam remain here at Escarion while men of lesser talent command our forces?"

Cruk sighed. "No. It's one argument Martin will lose with him."

The import of their discussion became apparent. "Me? You want me to command?"

"Yes," Rale said. "Welcome to the watch, Earl Stone, I should say Captain Stone. It's more than honorary now."

Errol shook his head. "I've never commanded anyone in battle. I don't know the first thing about giving orders."

Cruk grunted. "Nonsense, lad. You placed your men and your fallback better than most anyone else. The part of command you're worried about is simple. Give an order, and if it's not followed, thump the idiot with your staff until he sees the error of his ways."

Captain Reynald looked at Rale, shaking his head. "Arwitten will flay the skin off us for this."

Rale shrugged and looked at Merodach. "I'm more than happy to put the question of Errol's command to the conclave."

After a moment in which he'd forgotten to breathe, Errol faced the white-haired captain. "You've already cast the question. How did you even think to ask that?"

Merodach nodded to Reynald. "When he suggested you for command, I offered to fashion the lots." He shrugged. "No other argument would persuade Martin to let you go, I think."

"Maybe not even that one."

Errol nodded, dumbfounded. "When? Where?" He shook his head. "Who?"

Rale made gestures with his hands that Errol supposed were meant to calm him before he pointed to the map again. "We're filling the gaps from the south up. We still have shadowlanders trickling in through the mountains in north Gascony, but we should be safe from Morgol attack for weeks yet."

He straightened and placed his big hand on Errol's shoulder. "As for *who*, your troops will be comprised of watchmen and irregulars." A hint of a smile curled his lips beneath his strong, broad nose. "And there are some pretty tough-looking *irregulars* who have been asking after you."

Cruk nodded. "The Soede leading them is the fattest swordsman I've ever seen, but he knocked a sergeant of the watch unconscious for making light of him."

Laughter, surprised and clean, gushed from Errol before he realized it. "I'll take them, all of them. They're not particularly disciplined, but they all know how to swing a sword."

Rale sighed. "Now to speak with the archbenefice."

Reynald tucked his hands into his sword belt. "Would you rather I did it?"

Errol's mentor shook his head. "No. Martin will discover sooner or later this was my idea."

Cruk laughed, raucous, loud. "Elar, you seem to have a gift for annoying the head of the church."

Rale gave him a tight-lipped smile. "I can't deny it."

"No!" Martin thundered. "I forbid it!" His gaze landed on Errol and Captain Rale like a whip. Errol winced as if leather had found his skin. "Are you daft? Are you insane?" Martin's voice rose with each question until his bellow filled the hall.

Rale winced but otherwise kept his composure. Errol saw the archbenefice ball his hands into fists. Bertrand Canon might have balked at physical violence; Martin Arwitten would not. Illustra's archbenefice took a deep breath, as if preparing for a renewed attack. "What makes you think—"

"We cast for it," Rale said.

Martin gurgled, his tirade cut off in midthreat. "Who authorized you to approach the conclave on this matter?"

Errol wasn't sure he liked Martin's soft-spoken tone any better than his screaming.

"Did you cast this?" Martin asked him.

"No, Archbenefice," Errol said, bowing his head.

Martin snorted. "Now he shows respect." He leveled that gaze back at Rale. "You do not have access to the conclave, Captain. No one does at this point except me, and I never authorized such a cast. So either you are lying, or you've managed to convince a reader to do this without my authorization. Either way, I am very displeased."

Rale nodded. "I understand, Archbenefice, but neither of those happened. Captain Merodach performed the cast."

Martin's eyes narrowed, and he pursed his lips. "Ah. I see." He turned to the chair where Luis Montari sat in silence. "Secondus, please confirm the cast."

Luis pulled a pair of blanks and his knife from his pocket. "What was the question?"

Martin's eyes lit with the possibility of hope. "Yes, Captain Rale, what was the question?"

"Whether Errol should take command of one of the gaps to protect the Arryth. Then we cast to see when." He shrugged. The motion brought a flash of annoyance to Martin's face. "Captain Merodach was quite thorough, Archbenefice."

A muscle in Martin's cheek jumped. "Yes. I'm sure he was."

A knock at the door interrupted Luis's twelfth draw. Nine times the lots indicated Errol should take command. Martin pointed to Rale, gestured for him to open the door. A low-voiced conversation took place between the captain and an animated guard.

Rale nodded and closed the door. "A messenger just arrived from Princess Adora," he said, facing Martin. "She will be at Escarion before nightfall."

Errol's chest struggled to contain the pounding of his heart. He wanted to shout in celebration and cry in relief. The conflicting emotions conspired to root him to the spot, staring in dumbfounded wonder at Rale.

But the captain's gaze found his, then darted away to Martin. "Pater Antil, the former priest of Callowford, accompanies her. She requests an immediate audience with the archbenefice and Earl Stone."

Errol's gaze locked with Martin's, but he could find no evidence of subterfuge there. Surprise wreathed the man's face, then embers of rekindled anger, coals that threatened to roar back to flame.

"You do not have to do this," Martin said to Errol again. "It is not required."

Errol turned that over in his mind, nodding at the sound of truth within it, but just because something sounded true, didn't make it so. "Did you have Luis cast the question, or did Aurae tell you I shouldn't meet with . . . with . . . him?" He couldn't bring himself to call Antil his father. As if he shrugged off a mental weight, he rejected Antil's claim on him. The priest was not, had never been, his father.

"Neither," Martin answered, "but I can inquire if you wish. If there is any mercy in Deas, he would not require it of you."

That drew Errol up short. *Mercy?* He'd never thought of Deas in that way. After having been driven like an ox before the goad for over a year now, that would be the last quality he'd ascribe to Deas.

"Is Deas really merciful, Pater?" Errol asked.

Martin stiffened, whether at the question or the lesser title, Errol couldn't tell, but a moment later, he nodded. "I believe He is."

"He doesn't seem so to me."

"Do you believe Him cruel, then?" Martin asked.

Errol shook his head. "I used to think so, but now it seems everything just comes down to what's necessary. Rodran died without an heir. So it becomes necessary to find a new sacrifice to renew the barrier." He avoided saying the sacrifice would be himself. The argument would be pointless.

"If it's successful, other people will see it as merciful," Martin said.

"I guess so," Errol said. That truth failed to touch or warm him in any way. He pointed to the broad doors of the archbenefice's offices. "We're here."

"I speak for the church now, Errol. There is no compulsion, literal or figurative, that requires this of you."

Martin's eyes were tear-filled.

Errol nodded. For a moment, he considered turning back,

but for too long he'd sought a family, seeking origins, hoping to understand himself. Despite it all, he remained hopeful that something good would come of this. He opened the door, followed Martin into spacious chambers, and stopped. Interim quarters for the archbenefice they might be, but they impressed nonetheless. A gilded chair filled a dais surrounded by rich red tapestries, and to one side an altar offered the archbenefice a luxurious backdrop to celebrate the sacrament. A setting more unlike Martin's cabin in the Sprata would have been hard to imagine.

An attendant helped Martin into his robes and slipped his symbol of office over his head. The transformation from hermit to archbenefice was accomplished, and Errol bowed as Martin Arwitten took his seat.

The attendant stepped forward. "Archbenefice, Her Highness and Pater Antil await your pleasure."

Martin looked at Errol before he answered. "Admit the princess. Inform Pater Antil that we ask him to abide yet awhile."

Adora entered. Errol's vision blurred, and then she filled his arms and he held tight, fighting to keep himself from crying aloud with relief. He tasted salt from their tears as her lips found his.

"You don't have to meet with him, Errol."

He kissed her cheek and brushed away the rest of her tears. "I want to know who I am."

Her fists knotted in his shirt. "I know who you are." She shook him a little. "And by now, you should know as well."

"She is right," Martin said.

Errol nodded, but said nothing. His desire to see Antil went deeper than logic or reason could define. He would because he must.

"He hates you," Adora said.

In spite of himself, Errol laughed. "I think I knew that."

Adora shook her head. "He changed his story from what he told to Martin—and . . . I believe him. He was going to leave the priesthood. The woman he loved, who died giving birth to you, was his wife."

Errol nodded. "Ah." It didn't really matter, but it was good to know. He turned to the archbenefice. "I think I'm ready now."

Martin signaled his attendant. "Escort Pater Antil into my presence."

Antil, dressed in the clean black robes of a priest, walked the strip of crimson carpet to approach the dais where Martin awaited. At the first step, he knelt on both knees. "As you have commanded, Archbenefice, so have I come. How may I serve?"

"Arise, Pater," Martin said. "My loyal servant and the kingdom's hero, Earl Errol Stone, has questions he wishes to put to you. I command you to answer him honestly and without reservation."

Antil's jaws clenched, but his head jerked in affirmation.

Errol considered his tormentor. Antil stood below him, yet even were they side by side, the priest would still have been shorter than he, but there were similarities between them he could not deny. A memory of dimples showed in Antil's cheeks, however long it had been since he'd used them, and the nose might have been the same had the priest not broken his more than once.

But there the similarities ended. Antil's expression was twisted, as if the circumstances that had taken his life from its desired path had bred a deep and abiding resentment that could not be overcome. What might have the priest been if his wife hadn't died? What might Errol himself have been?

Antil fidgeted, but Errol ignored his agitation, intrigued by the question. What would he, Errol Stone, have been? Loved? Probably. If a woman had loved Antil, there must have been something in him she found worthy. Errol might have grown up with a family, his real family, with all the warmth and security that went with it.

And what then? At fourteen, he would have been tested, discovered as an omne, and sent to Erinon to die at Sarin Valon's hand. Errol snorted, then laughed at the affronted expression that twisted Antil's face a little more.

The laughter in the presence of his enemy cleansed him. He would not waste his time or emotions hating Antil. He could not excuse the vicious little priest's behavior, but Antil's deeds no longer held him captive.

Did he want anything from him? The answer came to him.

"Do you have any living family?"

The priest's eyes widened at the unexpected question before he jerked a nod, but he didn't speak.

Martin's voice curtailed Errol's next question. "You are in the presence of one of the greatest heroes in the kingdom's history, Pater Antil." His voice hardened into steel. "I pray you remember that you are a representative of the church. This is Earl Stone, omne of the conclave, captain of the watch, and betrothed of her Highness, Princess Adora. Come, loosen your tongue . . . if you wish to keep it."

Antil bowed his head at the archbenefice's command, but his answer was sharp. "My father is dead, but I am told my mother still lives, along with a brother and a sister." He shrugged. "They both have children. I don't know how many." He bit his words as if they offended him.

"And where are they?" Errol asked.

Antil glared at his superior. "You speak of respect and yet you allow him to address me without my title?"

Martin's laugh, filled with derision, bounced off the walls, the echoes mocking Antil's protest. "Under the circumstances, Pater Antil, you are fortunate he doesn't take that stick of his and offer you the recompense you so richly deserve. I will not abide stalling. Answer the question."

"Here, in Gascony."

Errol lost track of his heartbeat for a moment. It returned with the roaring sound of blood surging through his veins. "Names. I want their names."

Antil glared at him as if he'd already guessed his intent.

"Answer please, Pater Antil," Martin said. "If you force me to send functionaries to dig the information out of the church archives, I shall become bilious."

The priest refused to meet Errol's gaze. "The family name is

Ariel." He made a gesture as if he were throwing something away. "Simple craftsmen close to the border with Talia."

Errol turned, gave Martin a formal bow. "Archbenefice, I would ask your indulgence."

Martin nodded. "Done." His eyes betrayed a sudden unease and something else Errol couldn't identify.

"If I should survive this war, I want to meet my family, but I want him forbidden to acknowledge me."

He faced Antil. "I'm sorry she died. I could say that it might have been Deas's way to spare me from the murderous plans of Sarin Valon, but I believe Deas will still demand my life. If it's my death you've wished, then I would say you are still likely to get it."

"There, Pater Antil," Martin said. "Though you have not asked it, you have mercy. Had Earl Stone demanded your life, I would have searched church law and tradition for a way to grant his request."

"May I withdraw now . . . Archbenefice?" Antil asked.

Martin smiled, but the expression held no warmth or humor. "You may, but stay close. There remains the matter of your penance."

32

SEARCH

SHE PULLED HIM CLOSE, unmindful of the arch-benefice or his attendants, and kissed him, letting her lips linger against his. The sensation of melting into him overtook her, and she felt his heartbeat as if it were her own. When they parted, his breath stroked her neck and ear.

"Make me your wife."

He smiled, equal parts eagerness and rue, and she realized he would refuse.

"Gladly, *maitale*." He kissed her on the forehead as if she were his sister. "If I live."

His tone said plainly he didn't expect to. "Would you deny me? After I have waited for you?"

His smile and dimples faded. "I will never deny you anything, my heart, but I think Liam will eventually rule Illustra, and I will not take you for myself for a night or two and deprive another man of his gift."

Her skin heated as though his denials had the ability to stoke her desire rather than cool it. "How do you know I will survive you?" She gestured to Martin, who tried and failed to keep the

334

knowledge of their conversation from showing on his face. "The ceremony need not be lengthy. He can marry us now."

Errol faltered, the deep blue of his eyes intent, his pupils dilating with a mix of emotions. She saw love and fear, but most of all she saw longing. With her hands tangled in his dark brown hair she pulled him close.

A pounding at the door startled them, and a moment later Captains Rale and Cruk came in, urgent and grim. *No. Please, no.*

He pulled away from her, not jerking as though ashamed, simply parting as if their need for him had been expected.

"Archbenefice," Rale said, "our scouts have returned. The Merakhi are farther north than we realized." He turned to Errol. "We need to march, or we'll lose the southern gaps."

Desperation flamed, prompting her plea. "Can he not wait a few days, Captain?"

Rale shook his head, but it was Cruk who spoke. "Not even a few hours, Your Highness. If we don't beat the Merakhi to the gaps, we've lost."

"Can't you send someone else?"

"All the captains are marching," Rale said.

"But night approaches," Martin said. She wanted to kiss the bulky old priest in that moment for sparing her dignity.

"There's enough moonlight to move by," Cruk said. "A few miles tonight might make the difference."

The archbenefice nodded. He had no choice, really.

The captains discussed specifics that fell on her ears like disregarded conversations in a crowded room. Then Errol simply bowed over her hand and kissed it, because of where they were and who she was, and left.

Except for her the room was empty. No. Martin remained, his attendant dismissed on some errand. Thick hands pulled her into an embrace that swallowed her. She stiffened, but the warmth of his arms eroded her resolve like a wave pulling sand from beneath her feet. Tremors worked themselves loose from her control until she could no longer keep them at bay. She clutched Martin's stole of office, and he held her until the wracking sobs subsided.

"Have faith, child," Martin said. "Deas hears."

She wanted to accept the hope he offered, but she'd lost Errol too many times. Try as she might, she could not refute his acceptance of death, and the shadows of hope people offered against it lacked enough conviction to contravene Errol's simple acknowledgment. The man she loved would die, required as a sacrifice by Illustra's need. There was no hope.

She left.

Rokha found her wandering about Escarion's palace, her emotions both numb and raw. Adora sought her gaze. "He's gone."

Brown eyes more used to laughter than sympathy acknowledged her. "I heard."

Adora lifted her head. "Why are you still here? You're a watchman."

The well-muscled shoulders, strong without being mannish, lifted in response. "I prefer my battles small and personal. Trouble follows you, Your Highness, the way it follows that crazy boy you love."

"I don't know what to do." Errol's absence created an emptiness she hadn't realized existed until she met him, and each time he left she became half a person. She hadn't felt this hollow since discovering her uncle Rodran had died. Old grief mingled with new. She hadn't even been given the chance to say good-bye.

She stopped. Oliver Turing's contorted face appeared, telling her to find her father. What had he meant? Prince Jaclin had been a stranger to her. She'd been scarcely four when he died, but even then he'd been a distant memory, campaigning at the kingdom's borders since her mother's death at her birth.

Her back straightened, purpose giving her strength. "We need to find my father."

Rokha's brows rose. "Why?"

Adora turned to face her. "Turing took my uncle's confession. I had no idea his chamberlain could function as a nuntius, but

Sevra killed him before he could give me the full message. He was only able to tell me to find my father." She shook her head at the rest of the memory. "I assume he meant the location of his grave."

"Shouldn't he be buried on the Green Isle?"

"I would think so. I didn't really know him, so I never asked about his grave. It seems I would have gone to his funeral or visited his grave at least once . . . but I have no memory of it. I was only four. " She smiled a sad smile at Rokha. "But I suppose the answer is just a few blocks of wood away."

"The archbenefice has restricted the conclave to questions of the succession."

"The new tremus is an old friend," Adora said. "I've known Willem since I was old enough to toddle around the palace."

They found him in his quarters in the lower halls of the castle. The dank air chilled her, but the sight of Willem, a lanky scarecrow in his blue reader's robe, warmed her, and his oversized hands pulled her into his embrace.

He looked around before he spoke. "How are you, Snub Nose?"

She pushed away. "I haven't been snub-nosed since I was twelve."

Willem sighed and rubbed his own beaklike appendage. "I know. You were so much cuter then. Now you're all willowy womanhood."

He was impossible.

"I need a cast, Willem."

The smile remained, but the eyes grew serious beneath the bushy eyebrows. "Every reader has been ordered to bend their efforts to finding the next king." He sighed. "The church's new archbenefice is disconcertingly direct. We are forbidden to do anything else."

Adora nodded, trying to look confident. "I think this may help you do just that." She outlined the circumstances of Oliver Turing's message.

Willem's long face pulled to one side. "That may be stretching it a bit, Your Highness. There's nothing there that gives me the latitude to disobey the archbenefice's directive. I'm sorry."

Rokha laid a hand on his arm and gave him a dazzling smile. "But wouldn't you say there is enough doubt to test Her Highness's request?"

Willem's face unknotted and he smiled. "Clever girl. It's really too bad we don't consider women for the conclave." He gave Adora a wink. "I think she's right—at least that's what I'm going to say if the archbenefice presses me on it."

"How long will it take?" Adora asked.

Willem shrugged. "That depends on how precise you want us to be, Your Highness. We'll narrow it to a specific province first and then work in progressively smaller grids. We can send you to the exact building so long as we have the time as well as readers familiar with the area."

"Erinon would be the most likely place to start," Rokha said.

Adora shook her head, moved by intuition. "He's not there. Oliver wouldn't have needed to tell me to find him if he were."

Tremus Willem shooed them from his presence. "This will take time, my ladies, and your startling beauty will only delay me. Come back in a few hours. Perhaps Deas and luck will be with us."

She bowed, indicating her thanks, and left, Rokha at her side. They ascended the stairs until she came out on the uppermost parapet of Escarion's castle to see the sun still floating above the horizon, a circle of dying fire. Far below her, figures milled about in preparation to leave. She looked from figure to figure, searching for a man of average height holding a gray metal staff. The wind, warm with the promise of spring, lifted her hair and fanned it out behind.

There was no sign of Errol.

"I'm standing here like some silly damsel from the tales," she said at last, "waiting for a last glimpse of my betrothed before he goes off to battle."

Rokha chuckled. "There is a lot of truth in those tales."

Adora bit her lip. "And sometimes the hero dies."

She hadn't thought the whisper would reach Rokha's ears, but Ru's daughter nodded. "Yet sometimes he lives."

She positioned herself against the early-evening light. He might not see her, but she would honor him even so. He deserved that much and more. After a few minutes, she turned to go in, but Rokha grabbed her arm and pointed.

Errol crossed the heavy-timbered drawbridge on his black horse, Midnight. Some instinct must have alerted him, because neither of them called, but he turned. Seeing her, he lifted a hand in a hesitant wave, then rode toward a mass of men waiting in the meadow.

She pulled a deep breath and let it out through pursed lips. "It's bad luck to watch someone disappear in the distance." With decisiveness she didn't feel, she made for the steps that led back down into the castle. "Willem will be waiting."

They found him in his workshop, standing at an elevated table with a pair of readers facing him. He appeared displeased.

One of the readers, who looked very young, ducked his head. "I'm sorry, Tremus, but that's all I know."

"I understand, Sando, but it is a reader's obligation to be a student of all things. Wood and stone, boy, you know less of your home than anyone I've ever met."

Sando ducked his head again. "I haven't been there since I was tested, Tremus."

Willem closed his eyes and sighed, his shoulders lowering a fraction. "Yes. Yes, you are right. Thank you. And there is none other in the conclave from that region?"

"No, Tremus."

Willem dismissed the readers with a motion of one oversized hand. "You may return to your duties."

He followed behind them and closed the door. "Once we had the province narrowed down to Basquon, it became increasingly difficult to find readers with intimate knowledge of the region." He sighed, his eyebrows drooping a fraction. "I fear I was harsh with Sando. Expecting him to remember details from his boyhood is unreasonable."

"I am half Basqu," Rokha said. "Might my knowledge help?"

Willem brightened. "It might. Come." He moved to a table that held a map of Illustra and pointed to an area where the Basquon and Gascony border met the Western Ocean. "How familiar are you with this area?"

Rokha's dark hair followed the shake of her head. "Not at all, I'm afraid. My family is farther east, where the border runs into Talia."

Confusion jumbled Adora's thoughts into a heap. "Why would my father be buried there?" She stared at the spot on the map as if she could force it to surrender its secret by dint of will alone.

"How closely were you able to narrow the location?" Rokha asked Willem.

"Down to the village of Tacita. Sando knows of it, but that was as far as we could go. Even as a lad, he went there seldom. A few buildings and a couple of remote estates are all he could recall." He lifted those expressive hands. "I'm sorry, Your Highness."

"On the contrary, Tremus. You've given me a chance to find my father's resting place and perhaps discover the secret behind Oliver's message." She turned to Rokha. "Will you go with me?"

Rokha laughed a deep velvet sound. "Was there ever any doubt?"

"How long will it take us to get there?" Adora asked.

Ru's daughter peered at the map. "That depends on how many people we take and how many horses you can commandeer."

A hawk-nosed watchman met Errol at the end of the drawbridge and drew his horse alongside to lead him out to the meadow. "I'm Lieutenant Pick. Captain Elar sent me to introduce you to your command, Captain Stone. Your troops should be ready to ride within the hour. Each man will be given enough food for a week. That should give the supply wagons time to reach your position."

"And which position is that, Lieutenant?"

"Cruor Gap, sir."

They stopped in front of a group of mounted men. Errol's first impression was that his command looked pitifully small, perhaps three thousand soldiers in all. He pointed to his troops. "How many men are we expected to face, Lieutenant?"

"Our scouts say ten thousand, sir."

Errol tried to keep his face neutral. They would be out-numbered by more than three to one. "Spawn?"

Pick looked confused. "Sir?"

Errol allowed his frustration to show. "Ferrals, Lieutenant. What did the scouting report say of any spawn the Merakhi have with them?"

Pick wet lips that had gone white. "Th-there was no mention of them."

Errol exhaled. "Please inform Captain Elar of our conversation and relay my suggestion he find scouts who can provide an accurate report. Now, tell me how my force is divided."

The lieutenant ducked his head as if glad to move on to a different subject. "Equal parts pikemen, archers, and swords-men, Captain Stone. I'm sorry to report many of the blades are irregulars."

Errol arched his eyebrows. "Did you spar with any of them, Lieutenant?"

"No, Captain. I did not think it prudent to expend my effort on such."

Errol laughed, and then saw how his laugh caught the lieuten-ant by surprise. "Some of those irregulars trained me, Pick, and I beat all five watchmen on my challenge."

Pick simply nodded, so Errol continued, impatient to see him gone. "Thank you, Lieutenant. You may return to Captain Elar now."

His troops were split into ranks by their weapons: pikes to

the left, swords in the center, bowmen to the right, each man standing ready by his horse.

Errol smiled for the first time since leaving the castle. The swords in front were known to him. A lump formed in his throat as nine men came forward and went to one knee, led by a Soede big enough to make three, possibly four, of Errol.

Despite himself he laughed. "Get up, Sven. You all look ridiculous down there."

Sven shook his head. "I wouldn't do this for just any man, my lord, not even Naaman Ru, but I . . . we heard what you did. Our swords are yours for as long as you want them." He cleared his throat, his extra chin moving with the effort. "That means we're yours."

Errol shook his head. The man's regard settled on him like a weight, bestowing responsibilities he didn't want. He searched for someone who might see him in a less exalted light, but the rest of them mirrored Sven's regard. Even Onan, who doubted everything the church claimed, looked up at Errol as if his mere presence guaranteed their victory.

He drew breath to dispel the stupid notion their regard implied, to insist they rise, but Conger, the ex-priest, stood and hurried to his side, leaning in to whisper to him. "Have a care, my lord. Every man here with a spit's worth of sense knows what we're headed into, but they've chosen to hope in something they think will see them through to wives and children after the fighting. That something is you. Your next word will confirm or destroy that hope."

Errol kept his face smooth, but he wanted to rail against Conger, to deny the truth the ex-priest spoke. He didn't want to be anyone's hope. The rest of his troops, all three thousand of them, copied the caravan guards' gesture.

He wanted to groan. What was he supposed to say to men who would most likely die before a fortnight passed? In the end, the words refused to come. He simply slid his hands down the metal staff and thrust it into the air. Thousands of voices roared their approval.

"That was nicely done," Conger said. "It reminds me of the time—I think it was three hundred years ago—Dorian, the one the Lugarian's call 'The Great,' had to lead—"

Errol sighed. "Conger, do we have time for this?"

The former priest scuffed the ground as he scratched beneath his arm. "Ah, no, probably not."

The troops still knelt, waiting. Errol looked at them with a weary sigh. "Please get up, Sven. You're too heavy to have all that weight on one knee."

The Soede gave a grateful nod, and Errol raised both hands to signal the rest of the men to rise as well, before he turned to Conger. "Does anyone know how to get to Cruor Gap?"

Vichay A'laras, who'd been tenth in Ru's caravan, stepped forward. "We all know the way, my lord, but I was raised in the southeast part of Gascony. I am more familiar than most."

"How quickly can you get us there?"

The setting sun, shining from behind Errol, lit A'laras's face with ruddy light, as if he'd already been wounded. "Four days."

A puff of air, sweeping in from the distant shore of the Western Ocean, lifted the hair on the back of Errol's neck, and a sense of urgency tightened his gut. "Can we do it in three?"

A'laras nodded. "There is a path over the Guerre Spur that will save us time." He shot a look toward Sven. "But we may lose some of the horses."

Errol understood. The rocky climb and Sven's weight would be too much for a normal horse. "Conger."

"Yes, my lord?"

Errol squeezed his eyes shut. "Stop calling me that unless there are people around I need to impress. Commandeer a draft horse. If anyone complains, tell them to take it from one of my supply wagons. We'll be on the road south. Catch up to us."

Conger nodded. "Yes, my, uh, Captain." He mounted and rode off toward the quartermaster's tent at a gallop.

Errol turned to Sven. "You'll be my second for the swords. I want you and the seconds for the pikes and bowmen to ride up front with me. We'll plan on the way." He looked at the rest of the ten. "I need someone to relay orders. Which one of you has the best voice?"

Diar Muen, the redheaded native of Erinon who'd been Ru's third, stepped forward. "I think I can do that job, Captain."

Errol nodded. Muen's clear tenor would do well. "Tell everyone to mount up. We ride by moonlight tonight and the night after."

In the end only Lord Waterson accompanied Adora and Rokha to Tacita. Each rode a horse loaded with provisions for the journey. "We'll be lucky to make it in two weeks," Waterson said. He gave one of the horses a disgusted slap on the rump. He gave Adora an accusing look. "You could have gotten us better mounts."

She nodded in acknowledgment of the simple truth. The stable master had even offered them to her. "And how would I justify taking them from men who need them in battle?"

Waterson shrugged. "By saying, 'I'm the princess and I want a better horse.'"

Adora closed her eyes for a moment. "Were you always this cynical, my lord?"

He smirked at her. His time in exile had clearly robbed him of all respect for the crown. "It's a recent development."

For two days they rode through and around a press of refugees—men, women, and children with a thousand different shades of fear painted on their faces. Much of the traffic headed west toward the coast, but a fair portion went in the opposite direction as temperament and rumor dictated.

"Fools," Waterson said. "No place is safe."

Rokha nodded her agreement. "All they know is their fear and the need to flee, even if they don't have a good idea of where or why. They're like animals running from fire."

Adora wanted to offer some argument to Waterson's and Rokha's judgment of the refugees, but too many times she saw terror on those faces, robbing them of reason.

On the third day they turned from the main road that led to the great cities opposite Erinon and headed southwest toward Tacita. The endless knots of refugees thinned to nothing within a few miles.

"Perhaps they're smarter than I thought," Waterson mused. "If we fail to hold the strait, Tacita will be overrun in a day." He pursed his lips. "And I'm headed straight for it. Perhaps I'm more stupid than I thought." He shook his head. "No. I knew I was an idiot for agreeing to come with you."

"You didn't agree," Rokha said. "You volunteered."

Waterson waved a hand in the air. "Semantics. A gentleman is honor-bound to offer his protection to his liege and a lady."

Rokha looked toward the sky and snorted. "You said pitched battle was an exercise in tedium and terror. You came because you wanted to."

He looked offended. "Please, Countess Rokha. It sounds better my way."

"I'm not a countess."

Waterson laughed. "Do you think Her Royal Highness will allow you to remain untitled after all your service to the crown?"

"Over my dead body."

"It may come to that."

Their banter grated on Adora's nerves. The mention of battle conjured images of the nightmares Errol must fight. "I am pleased you have joined us, Lord Waterson. An extra pair of eyes and another sword are most welcome."

Waterson bowed low over his saddle. "I'm grateful that you find my talents useful, Your Highness. I was just about to mention that I think we're being followed." He sent Rokha a smirk, clearly pleased to have been the first to mention it.

Adora searched behind her. The terrain, a series of low rolling hills that flattened as they approached the coast, prevented seeing for any great distance. "Are you sure?"

"Follow me and watch." He kicked his horse into a canter, but as they approached a stand of trees split by the road, he detoured around and returned to the rutted track farther on. He kept to his pace until they placed another low rise between them and the copse of cedars.

"Look at the sky."

They waited. A few minutes later a flock of gray-beaked rooks took to the air, their plumage dark against the blue. Waterson nodded, his face lacking all traces of the amusement it had worn moments before. "I hate being right. Your Highness, I would suggest you and Lady Rokha ride quickly ahead, but not too quickly. I'm curious to see who might have an interest in us. If they're trying to catch up to you, they won't be looking for me."

Adora nodded. "How will you find us?"

Waterson blinked. "Find an inn at the next village. Get rooms under the name of Tanner." He slapped his horse with the reins and rode south away from the road.

33

CLASH

BLINDING SUNLIGHT flooded the Cruor Gap. Errol squinted against the glare, searching for telltale shadows that would signal the Merakhi had beaten him to the gap, but he saw nothing.

"Diar."

The tall redhead, never far away, stepped closer.

Errol pointed. "Where are our scouts?"

"They aren't due back for another hour, Captain."

A premonition of danger rolled over him, chilling him as if he'd lost his footing and fallen into snow. He twisted in his saddle, searching for Arick, his second of the bowmen. The Avenian, tall with lean sinewy arms like the men under his command, sat his horse in a state of tense anticipation, his hands constantly checking his quiver.

Errol pointed to the walls that bordered the road through the gap. "Arick, get your men up there as soon as you can. If there are no Merakhi, push as far east as possible." The sense of apprehension grew. "Move quickly. They're close."

Arick relayed the order but remained behind. "What if they're already there?"

Errol chewed his lip. Urgency pressed on him, and he wanted to scream at Arick's men to run, but a moment's planning might be all they would have once the fighting began. "Pick a spot, Lieutenant, and concentrate your fire. Pile up enough dead to keep their cavalry and foot soldiers from making a decent charge."

Arick nodded his approval and moved away. Bowmen throughout the ranks rode to the base of the walls and dismounted, leaving their horses behind. Errol eyed the slope. On this side of the range the hills could be climbed, praise Deas, but sheer cliffs on the eastern side denied their enemy access to the heights.

The distant scream of a horse ripped through the air, and an invisible hand closed around Errol's heart. They were still hundreds of paces from the gap. He leaned across his horse, clutched Diar's arm. "Get the pikes to the gap now!"

Muen relayed the order, his voice cutting through the sudden din of voices like a trumpet. A riderless horse came through the gap at a gallop, hooves pounding the road. A thousand of Errol's men drove their mounts, whipping flanks with their reins in an effort to seal the passage. Bowmen scrabbled up the cliff, hands and legs pushing, moving too fast to see if the next handhold or foothold was sound. More than one fell screaming to the rocks below.

Errol tried to spur his horse forward, but Sven's hands on the reins prevented him. "The captain commands from the rear, my lord."

Rage mottled Errol's vision. "I can't command if I can't see what's happening." He pointed to a rise just to the right of the gap. "I'm headed there. I want the swords in the center on horseback in case the pikes can't hold. Muen! You're with me."

He jerked the reins from Sven's hands and dug his heels into Midnight's flanks as bile rose to his throat. The clash of men and weapons filled his ears as the first wave of pikemen arrived at the gap and dismounted, forming hasty ranks two deep—too shallow to withstand a real charge—and rushed forward.

The line bulged, thinning in the center, where ferrals on all fours darted in between pikemen. Errol watched Sven move a phalanx of swords into the middle, chopping with short, vicious strokes at the spawn that managed to get inside the reach of the pikes.

Men poured into the battle. Ferral howls of frustration, oddly human, filled the air.

Muen clapped him on the back. "We're holding!"

Errol nodded. Muen spoke the truth, but their casualties were horrific. They couldn't afford to trade death for death with the Merakhi. "We need those bows!"

From his vantage point, he spied the monstrous figure of a man in the midst of the ferrals, laughing. He topped the demon spawn by at least three feet.

Muen's triumph faded into horror. "Deas in heaven, how can we fight that?"

Errol grabbed him by the shoulder and forced him around until their gazes locked. "Can you climb?"

Muen gaped but nodded.

"Get to Lieutenant Arick. Tell him to train their fire on that giant and any others like him. They're driving the forces."

Muen stared through him, not moving. Errol whipped his hand across Muen's face. His head snapped to one side, red hair flying. "Move!"

Midnight leaped forward at Errol's urging. The giant Merakhi had the ferrals organized now, interspersing them with swordsmen who swung heavy-bladed shirra in wide arcs. The center of the line bulged again as Errol's swordsmen faced a combination of blades and teeth.

They had to straighten the line. The bowmen wouldn't be able to separate friend from foe otherwise. He searched for Hasta, the lieutenant in charge of the pikes. If they didn't reinforce the center, they'd lose the entire front.

He caught sight of the blocky Talian directing men on the left.

The noise of the battle deafened him, and he screamed in Hasta's face to make himself heard.

"Fill the center with pikes! Like a hedgehog!"

Hasta took one look at the bulge thinning their forces and nodded. At his command, the back ranks pivoted and wheeled toward the center. The pikes thickened until the demon spawn could no longer slip through.

The line straightened.

As it did a rain of arrows raked the Merakhi forces in a hail of death.

The Merakhi attack didn't falter—it melted in its tracks. A flood of shafts flew at the giant. With a roar of defiance, he sheathed his sword and grabbed a Merakhi warrior in each hand. As easily as Errol might lift a child, the spawn lifted the men into the air, using them as shields.

A dozen arrows thudded into the men, who jerked several times before going still. The remnants of the Merakhi force retreated, arrows chasing them the length of the gap. A long mound of casualties, a barrow of dead, filled the area between the cliffs.

Seconds Hasta and Sven came to him. Hasta, blood flowing from a shallow cut on his forehead, bowed from the neck. "Congratulations, Captain, on your victory."

Too many of the dead belonged to his force for him to feel anything more than relief, but Hasta's gesture required some response. "Thank you, Lieutenant. Please keep half the men in formation until we hear from Lieutenant Arick." He turned to Sven. "Deploy scouts. We need to know how far the Merakhi are withdrawing and the size of their force."

Sven nodded but hesitated. When Hasta withdrew, he spoke, keeping his voice low. "How did you know?" The big Soede waved an arm like a giant sausage toward the mound of dead that filled the gap. "If we'd been even an hour later, the passage would have been lost. Merakhi would be flooding into the Arryth right now. I heard the scouting report back at Escarion's. They said we had a week."

Errol squirmed as if his shirt no longer fit. "I don't know, Sven." He broke the gaze. "I just knew."

"Well, you kept us alive, my lord."

He shook his head. "Not all of us."

"Nothing could have changed that."

His sigh misted in the cool mountain air. "I am tired of people telling me how necessary dying is." Errol checked himself. He didn't have time to indulge in self-pity. With the immediate threat over, more and more of the men had turned, looking toward him with questioning expressions, waiting for orders.

He pointed. "Order anyone not on active duty to help clear the pass of the bodies. Burn theirs and bury ours back in the valley." He craned his neck, searching. "Find Conger. Have him say the panikhida and get the names of as many of our dead as he can. If we survive to return to Escarion, we'll notify the families."

Sven's frown bunched the flesh above his eyes. "Why not keep the bodies in the gap as a barrier to their charge?"

Errol gestured at the walls of the canyon. "Because we're at the western end. If we stay here, eventually they'll push hard enough to force us out of the entrance and into open territory. Once they do, our cause is lost. We must press farther into the gap."

The Soede ducked his head, embarrassed, a gesture that brought a smile to Errol's face. "I should have thought of that."

Sven left, mumbling to himself, and was replaced a moment later by Lieutenant Arick, his long nose twitching with excitement. "Magnificent! I never imagined such a victory."

The lieutenant's excitement annoyed Errol—their triumph had been too close and might well prove to be temporary. "Lieutenant Arick, congratulations on a job well done. Your aid was most timely."

Arick nodded his thanks at the praise, but his eyes tightened at the corners as he caught Errol's tone.

"Tell me what you saw of their leader," Errol said.

The lieutenant paled. "We fired enough shafts at him to kill a dozen men, Captain. I've never seen a man that big move so fast." He wagged his head back and forth. "I've never seen a man that big."

"It's not a man, Arick. It's a man possessed by a malus. It may get bigger."

His lieutenant nodded, dazed. "I fired at him as they retreated. Twice he snatched arrows from the air before they could find their mark."

"Keep your men on the heights, Arick, and keep them alert. They won't let us have that kind of advantage twice. As soon as the bodies are cleared, we're going to move forward and claim as much of the gap as we can."

Arick nodded and left. A notion occurred to Errol, and he called to the retreating figure. "Lieutenant"—Arick turned—"have your men take torches with them. The Merakhi may have spawn that can see in the dark as well as climb."

Errol turned, seeking a place to rest. Though he hadn't swung his staff once, fatigue threatened to drop him where he stood. How did Rale and Cruk stand it?

The village of Aresco had long forgotten its reason for being. Everywhere Adora looked, she saw signs of decline. Evidence of roads running in and out of the village lay before her, but missing stones at the edges—probably scavenged for fences—testified to the fact such thoroughfares were no longer needed. Even the buildings had a too-spacious look, as if they awaited the return of families and merchants to lend them enough life to offer hospitality.

Children scurrying through the oversized streets regarded them with curiosity, and more than one merchant or goodwife studied them with dread. Adora guided her horse up to a man whose countenance suggested more awareness than his fellows. "Can you guide us to the inn?"

He lifted an arm, but his hand didn't quite complete the gesture to point. Arthritis swelled his knuckles. "Go right at the next street."

She nodded her thanks. "If you have a healer, ask them for borage root oil. It will help the swelling in your hands."

He drifted away.

"These people are already dead," Rokha murmured. "If the Forbidden Strait falls to the Merakhi, this village won't even put up a fight." Her face closed in disappointment. "These people haven't even mustered the courage to run away."

"Where would they run?" Adora asked.

Rokha shrugged at the question. "The kingdom is larger than Gascony, and the world is bigger than Illustra and Merakh. There's always a place to run."

The weathered sign at the inn no longer indicated its name or purpose, and a layer of dust covered most of the tables in the interior. When they asked the innkeeper for a room, surprise interrupted the dispirited expression he wore.

Dinner consisted of tasteless cheese and bread. Adora sat in the common room watching a listless fire burn in the fireplace. "Does this await Illustra if we lose? Will the world simply lose its color and become a shadow of itself?"

"No," Rokha said. Her deep brown eyes clouded. "It will die altogether. The malus aren't coming to rule; they're coming to destroy."

The bland food and heatless fire depressed her. Adora shoved the remains of her dinner away. "We should wait for Waterson upstairs. I don't want to be recognized."

Rokha nodded and they drifted toward their room.

An hour later, as twilight lowered like a shroud, footsteps thundered up the stairs. Rokha grabbed Adora by the arm, thrust her behind as she drew her sword. "Stay behind me."

Waterson pounded around the corner at a run. At the sight of Rokha and Adora he stopped. "Company's coming."

Rokha spun to face her. "It's time to leave, Your Highness."

"In the dark?" Adora asked. Waterson's distress gripped her throat. He didn't usually care enough about anything to be this frantic.

Rokha nodded. "There are no allies here. These people don't care enough to help us or keep us hidden." She turned to Waterson. "How far behind are they?"

"Minutes, and both of them have better horses than we do."

"Both?" Rokha asked. She fingered her sword. "Let's just kill them and be on our way."

Waterson shook his head. "This isn't a fight we want, watch girl. There's something wrong with those two."

The inflection Waterson put on the word *wrong* raised Adora's hackles.

Rokha paled, her lips stark against pallid skin. "What did they look like?"

"They stopped where I left the road," Waterson said. "Then the woman dismounted." He shook his head, disbelieving. "Either she was riding a pony or she was close to seven feet tall."

"Malus," Rokha spat.

Weight settled into Adora's middle. What woman would have reason to give herself to a malus? Suspicion gnawed at her, but she pushed it away with an effort. Questions would take time they didn't have. "We have to get away from the village. They won't hesitate to kill everyone to get to us."

They grabbed their packs and rushed the stairs, heedless of the mild surprise on the faces of the villagers in the common room. A scream echoed from the street. Waterson signaled, and Adora dropped to the floor next to Rokha, hiding beneath the level of the dirty windows.

"The back," Waterson said. "Get to the horses." He threw the bar on the inn's front door. The boards of the threshold creaked under the tread of heavy footsteps, and a blow followed by the groan of protesting wood sounded behind them as they raced out the back toward the stable.

Adora followed Rokha into the courtyard at a run, the tendons of her right hand aching from the clench on her rapier. A stirring of shadow warned her, and she threw herself to the ground, rolling as the clash of steel rang in her ears. She came up, her sword ready, to see Rokha backpedaling beneath a furious attack.

Ru's daughter slipped a stroke by the narrowest margin. In

seconds she would be down. With her free hand Adora grabbed a handful of dirt and threw it at Rokha's attacker.

He flinched. Not much, but enough for Rokha to riposte and launch a desperate swipe at his head. Her attacker whipped his sword up to parry, too slow to block but enough to turn the attack so the flat of Rokha's sword instead of the blade took him across the temple, and he toppled like a felled pine.

Rokha panted, shaking and winded over the still figure. "Skorik." She snarled his name like a curse before moving forward, the point of her sword low, as if she contemplated what to do with him.

Adora struggled to pull air into her lungs. It couldn't have been more than seconds since they entered the yard, but it felt like hours.

Waterson burst through the door. He crashed forward, grabbing Rokha by the arm. "It's coming."

Rokha threw a curse behind her as they ran toward the stables. Adora grabbed a bridle and threw herself onto the first horse, smacking its rump with her sword, praying it would run away from the malus. A few hundred yards. That's all she needed to stop and get the bit in its mouth. Her mount pounded after Waterson's, and she offered thanks for its herd instinct. A horse thundered next to hers, and she looked over to see Rokha chop at the lantern by the entrance, spraying oil and fire onto the wood and hay.

Ru's daughter grimaced. "If we're lucky, the stable will go up." Her mouth grew tight "I hate killing horses."

Adora looked back to see flames racing across the hay to lick the dry wood of the barn. The sound of frightened horses pierced the air with their shrill cries. A figure, monstrous and threatening, stood silhouetted in the fire, and Adora bent over the neck of her horse, urging it forward.

Past the edge of town, Waterson slid forward on his mount's back to grab its muzzle and bring it to a halt. Adora's horse slowed, then stopped. She dismounted, sliding the bridle over its head to put the bit in its mouth, concentrating on the task to keep her hands from shaking. The horse champed as she remounted. She wrapped the reins around her fists as if the tight circles of leather could return the sense of security the monstrous form had taken from her.

They raced along the road southwest until the onset of dusk made their pace a hazard. Waterson, his features indistinct in the gloom, dismounted. The landscape rolled away from them, and clouds covered any hope of moonlight, or even starlight. A copse of trees, cedars by the smell, beckoned in the distance. Waterson ignored them, began walking.

"Aren't we stopping?" Adora asked.

"I'm not," Waterson said. "I'm going to get away from that thing even if I have to feel for each step in the dark."

Rokha nodded her agreement. "We don't know if they were able to follow us. The Merakhi say a malus is friends with the dark. I don't know if they mean the evil ones can see at night, but this is a poor time to find out."

An hour later, after they'd been reduced to Waterson's suggestion, a sliver of argent pierced through the thin clouds behind them. Light like a candle seen through a shroud illumined the road. They mounted and rode at a walk as Adora dozed off and on in her saddle.

When the garish light of day roused her, she found her horse trailing Waterson's mount, the lord holding her reins with one hand while he guided his horse with the other. Behind her Rokha lay stretched across her horse's back as if accustomed to sleeping that way.

Adora yawned, her jaws cracking, and Waterson turned to face her. "Good morning, Your Highness." Smudges like strokes of charcoal lay beneath his eyes.

"Didn't you sleep?"

He shook his head. "I can keep sleep at bay for a while, if needed, a leftover benefit of a misspent youth. The ability came in handy in the shadow lands when we guarded against the things that tried to come through the gap."

He frowned. "We have a problem. My horse is going lame. If we're pushed to it, it won't make a gallop. It needs rest." He laughed without humor. "Actually, it needs to be about ten years younger. Its teeth are shorter than a churchman's temper."

Her stomach growled. "Do we have any food?"

Waterson shook his head. "Only if you want to eat my horse." He shrugged. "It may come to that. I have no idea how far the next village is."

A soft beat of hooves preceded Rokha's presence. "This region is sparse. The soil's not right for farming. Mostly, it's used for sheep." She waved a hand at the scrub dotting the rolling countryside.

They limped into a village before noon with only the wind to greet them. Waterson dismounted. With careful movements, he ran his hands down the legs and lifted each hoof. The horse flinched as he ran his hand across the frog of a rear hoof. He pulled his knife and dug until a pebble came loose. He covered his nose against the stench.

"That rock has probably been in there for weeks." He kicked the ground in disgust as he looked around. "I doubt the farrier or blacksmith left anything behind we could use. If I could pack the hoof with moss, I might be able to ride her."

Adora dug in the pack behind her saddle and brought forth a bundle wrapped in waxed parchment. "There might be something in here that will help. Healer Norv taught me how to treat infections." She laid the packet on the ground and opened it. "I have urticweed." She shrugged. "It's mostly used to stop bleeding, but it also helps speed healing, in people anyway." She dug further. "I have veritmoss too. It's dry, but it might work if you wet it and pack it in."

"What's it do?" Waterson asked.

"It makes people tell the truth," Adora said. "And it usually makes them drowsy."

He grunted. "No telling what it's going to do to a horse." He held out his hand. "It's a good thing animals can't speak. I don't really want to know what a horse would have to confess."

Rokha tied her reins to the post of the nearest building. None of the rough dwellings were more than one story high. She stood on the rail and pulled herself up onto the gently sloped roof and disappeared. A moment later she reappeared, swinging down to land on her feet. "There's no sign of pursuit. I think we can spare a moment to see if anything useful was left behind."

Adora found little comfort in Rokha's words. No sign of pursuit might simply mean their enemies were just out of sight. Perhaps they had managed to kill the horses in the stable, but the malus hunting them would simply threaten villagers until others were provided. How much of a lead did they really have?

They departed moments later with Waterson on Rokha's mount leading his horse and the two women doubled up on Adora's. Rokha's search had yielded nothing, not even a stale crust of bread. A door creaked in the breeze as if lamenting the village's desertion.

34

BLIND

MARTIN ARWITTEN, newly anointed defender of the faith and archbenefice of Illustra, stalked the halls of Escarion. Anyone entitled to wear the red of the benefice or the blue of the conclave bypassed him with a display of dexterity normally denied such sedentary men.

Word had spread of his temper until even the servants avoided him.

Gone. Both of them, Errol and Liam, gone. One of them would be, had to be, the next savior and king of Illustra, and he'd somehow been persuaded to let them out of his sight, away from Escarion, where they could have been protected until the proper time.

Luis Montari walked beside him, his footsteps light, as though he bore no concern whatsoever over the fate of the kingdom. The secondus seemed to be the only man in Escarion who dared the archbenefice's presence. That fact annoyed Martin on some level he couldn't explain.

"They should be here, protected," Martin said.

"We cast the question, Archbenefice," Luis said.

Even the use of his title annoyed him. Had Bertrand Canon ever felt so powerless in the midst of his authority? "I have learned to be distrustful of lots."

Luis grimaced as though Martin had offered a personal rebuke, but after a moment he nodded and relaxed once more. "Then what did Aurae say to you when we sent Errol and Liam forth?"

Martin grunted. He hated arguing with the compact Talian at his side. He lost far too often. "Nothing. Aurae said nothing. I should have kept them here."

"If sending them out was wrong, wouldn't Aurae have told you?" Luis asked.

"You're a very annoying little man to have around."

Luis's face remained impassive.

Martin fidgeted as he walked. Hints of ideas, troubling notions he could share with no one else, bubbled through his mind. "We are blind, Luis. We fight a war that cannot be won without divine intervention, and at the same time the craft that has served the church for centuries has failed us at the most crucial juncture."

"I know. Martin, I'm sorry that . . ."

He put an arm on his friend's shoulder. "No. No. I do not chastise you. Rather, I ask why?"

"Archbenefice?"

"Why are we blind now and only on this one question?" He pointed in the general direction of the conclave's temporary quarters. "Our world still works in its fundamental ways. Every other question you cast yields an answer, but not that one."

"In some way our art has failed us," Luis said. "No. We have failed in our art." He laughed without humor. "Men and women all over the kingdom, from the poorest widow to the richest merchant, live searching for answers. I envy them. The answers have never been difficult; it's always been the questions I've struggled to find."

Martin nodded, reaching out to open the door. "I am sched-uled to address the Judica—" he sighed—"again."

Luis frowned. "You complain a lot for an archbenefice who's exercised more power than any in recent memory. The Judica has approved every motion you've put before it, and most without debate. That's almost sacrilege for a churchman."

Martin acknowledged the joke with a smile and its truth with a nod, but doubt filled him. Each of the initiatives he'd proposed before had obvious support from the book Errol had recovered from the Ongolese. "This one may encounter more resistance."

Luis's brown eyes showed his concern. "Do you want me to cast for you?"

A sudden diffidence grew in Martin at the request. "No, my friend. The proposal needs to be made whether they approve it or not. Let them tell me their answer in person." He stepped into the hallway. "But you can walk with me."

As they approached the temporary meeting hall, Luis continued to his quarters and Martin's page, a distant cousin of Duke Escarion, stepped in beside Martin. The lad, eleven or twelve, reminded him a bit of Owen, wide-eyed at everything, and coltish, with skinny arms and legs that moved more than necessary as he walked. A pang of loss and regret pulled at him before he suppressed it. Owen would be happy with Ablajin's clan. They'd already given him more love and acceptance in a few weeks than he'd received his entire life in Bellia.

"Are the benefices all here, Breun?"

An earnest nod that sent his brown hair flying answered him. "Yes, Your Excellency. They've been waiting for you."

That surprised him. "Am I late?"

"No, Your Excellency." The hair swayed in the opposite direction. "It's just now set to ring Nones."

"Well, let's not keep them waiting."

The boy tugged the door open with that same look of earnestness. Martin stepped through and walked between the rows of red-garbed men to the low dais and the seat that awaited him. With three raps of the staff, he called the Judica to order. "We are here met in the presence of Deas. Speak no word that is not true. Utter no truth that is not complete. You are adjured by the three, Deas, Eleison, and Aurae."

One of his first motions had been to rewrite the liturgies and protocols to remove the word *unknowable* from in front of *Aurae*. Sometimes he still stumbled over its absence. He seated himself on a chair built to impress rather than comfort and squirmed, but the seat refused to yield. He leaned forward, hoping the movement would be interpreted as earnestness. "My fellow benefices, I called you together in order that we may consider our plight and safeguard our posterity regardless of the outcome of this war."

Kell rose. "Archbenefice, surely you do not countenance the possibility of defeat."

Martin sighed. Kell's reaction summed up the opinion of many in the Judica. "I think we are unwise if we do not. I choose to believe that we will be victorious, that Deas will give us victory, but that choice is up to Him, is it not? The Merakhi have swept over the earth like a tide as they have before." He paused to let them recall the bit of history his words would surely bring to mind: Magis's sacrifice and death.

"We await the revelation of our own Magis," he continued. "But we cannot fully know the mind of Deas. What if he does not appear?" Now he needed to steer their thoughts toward his goal. "I believe the soteregia will be revealed, though he is unknown to us at present, but I would not have whatever remnants of the church that survive live in the darkness we have endured."

Benefice Kell stood again, the few tufts of hair that had yet to surrender their purchase on his head waving with the movement. "What do you propose, Archbenefice?"

Martin would have preferred to keep the Judica in suspense a moment longer, but he could not appear hesitant. "I propose that we commission every church functionary not occupied with the war to copy the book, and that those copies be sent forth with laymen appointed to keep them safe. The book must survive. We cannot lose it again."

The import of his proposal struck the Judica with the force of a thunderclap. Kell fumbled for his seat, and the benefices reeled in silence. Benefice Michay, whose jurisdiction included Escarion, gaped at him, his mouth moving without sound.

"You would trust the book of history to any peasant who knows how to read?" Kell asked.

Martin shook his head. Oratory would not avail him now. There could be no dissembling or maneuvering; Kell had stated the fear of the Judica in plain terms. "We, the Judica, must remain here, close to the fighting, in the hope that when the conclave, or Deas, reveals the identity of the king, we can crown him." He paused and let his gaze sweep the hall. "We have no surety that we will survive, but the book must."

"But to distribute copies must surely dilute the church's power," Michay said. Like every Gascon, his words leaned on each other, giving his speech a seductive rhythm.

Martin nodded. "I understand, and I agree that may be a possibility, but for centuries we referred to the loss of the book as 'Magis's Folly.' My benefices, can we afford to repeat his mistake? If the Judica becomes a casualty of war, the book must survive."

Grudging acceptance showed itself in the way each man sighed, nodded, or closed his eyes. Stubborn they might be, but each one of them had witnessed enough upheaval within the past year to recognize necessity, however grim it seemed.

"My benefices," Martin said as he rose from his seat and took the staff of office in hand, "I would put the motion to a vote. I propose to have the book of Magis, the history, copied and sent from here by horse and ship to every corner of the earth. If Illustra falls, the history of Deas, Eleison, and Aurae will survive. Please stand if you agree."

In the end they all stood, as he'd hoped they would. Many of them bore cheeks stained with tears of loss, and Benefice Ripani of Talia wept openly. "We have authorized schism within the church, Archbenefice."

"Perhaps not," Martin said. "It may be that if we embrace this change instead of fighting it, much may be saved that would otherwise be lost."

Ripani's jaws tightened. "It is devoutly to be wished."

Martin returned to his seat and opened the Judica for deliberation of other motions. Several benefices stood at once, asking for permission to set their concerns before their fellows. Martin would have laughed to himself were the situation not so dire. The Judica possessed topics without number that needed discussion. He inclined his head toward Benefice Michay. "Speak no word that is untrue or incomplete."

Michay, one of Errol's few supporters in the Judica even before that cause became popular, cleared his throat, his fine features and light-colored hair giving him a youthful air despite threescore years. "I hesitate to burden the archbenefice and the Judica with my request."

Martin cut him off with a chuckle. "You have been adjured. If you were truly hesitant, you wouldn't have popped out of your seat as if it held coals." The rest of the Judica laughed. Martin waved them to silence. "My fellow benefices, let us put aside our pretenses and speak honestly with each other. We're not fooling each other, and it is certainly true that we are not fooling Deas. Though I am sure it will surprise you, Benefice Michay, to hear me say it, speak plainly."

Michay nodded, his wry smile pulling his mouth to one side. "In truth, Archbenefice, I am hesitant to bring this particular petition before you since you have already addressed the matter."

A hint of foreboding sent prickles running the length of his arms. "What matter might this be?"

The benefice shrugged, his face lined with apologies. "The priest Antil, of Earl Stone's village, has sought me out as his advocate since I administered his orders." He shook his head. "Though I hardly remember the occasion."

Impatience gnawed at Martin's belly. He should have squashed Antil like a bug. Despite Errol's gesture of mercy, he should have had Antil thrown in the dankest prison Escarion possessed. "What does Pater Antil desire?"

Blond eyebrows drew together over gray eyes in puzzlement.

"I can only repeat what he has said, Archbenefice. He claims that Princess Adora has conferred upon him the honor of being her personal priest."

"This is true," Martin said.

"He has also said that you have forbidden him to leave Escarion."

"Also true," Martin said. "Please hasten to the point."

Michay nodded. "It seems that those two commands are now at odds."

The sense of foreboding in Martin's gut intensified. "Explain."

"Pater Antil says that the princess has left Escarion on an unexplained errand to the west."

Martin bolted from his seat, a burst of sudden anger heating his face. He snapped an order to the church guards at the door. "Bring him."

They blinked at him, obviously unaware of who he meant. "Bring who, Archbenefice?"

Martin gritted his teeth and squeezed his eyes shut in an effort not to yell. "Bring me that little toady of a priest, Antil. And I want readers, fast ones, here as well." He snapped his fingers. "Yes. Bring the secondus."

Martin fumed while he waited. *Gone.* All of them were gone. Illustra's survival rested on the edge of a blade, and the keys to its survival had mounted horses and scattered themselves across the province. He growled a few unarchbenefice-like phrases that would have shocked Cruk. Several members of the Judica looked at him with startled expressions, then averted their gaze. What was Adora thinking? This had to be Errol's fault. She'd never exhibited such erratic behavior before meeting the little urchin.

He checked himself—that was unfair. Errol Stone was no longer an urchin, and the fact that he possessed the ability to bring out the best and most extreme in people could hardly be cause to blame him.

A pack of readers moved into the hall, and minutes later Luis entered the Judica a few heartbeats before Antil arrived, stiff and formal, wearing his stoicism as if it could somehow keep him from the realization of his sins.

Martin surrendered his contemplation of Antil to address the readers. "Adora has left. I want to know where she is and where she's headed." The blue-robed men, friends he now snapped orders to, removed to a corner and conferred, blanks and knives ready.

Martin regarded Antil once more. "When did she leave?"

"About three days ago, Your Excellency," Antil replied.

Pressure built behind Martin's eyes, and he squinted against the pain. "And when did you bring your petition to Benefice Michay?"

A hint of a smile, small and vindictive, creased the callous lines of Antil's face. "This morning, Your Excellency."

Martin clenched his jaws to keep from screaming. "You let her go? And what were you thinking to wait so long before informing us of her departure?"

Antil's smile grew. "As you have pointed out to me, Your Excellency, I am but a lowly priest, perhaps the lowliest in your service. It is not my place to gainsay Her Highness." He pursed his lips. "When she did not return, I grew concerned that the princess might suffer for lack of her priest to torment. Nobles become irritable when they are deprived of their amusements."

Martin leaned forward from his seat to peer down at Antil. "And some priests as well." Martin waited for the jibe to hit home. Antil's face stiffened, resuming its masklike exterior. Martin leaned back. "I have decided on your penance, Pater Antil, a portion of it, at any rate. You will accompany a pair of guards to retrieve the princess. You are adjured to do everything in your power to ensure she returns safely to Escarion."

Benefice Michay stood, waiting to be recognized.

"Yes?" Martin asked.

"Pater Antil's story is known to most of us within the Judica, Your Excellency. I move we compel him to do as you have instructed."

Martin looked across the sea of red robes assembled before

him. "Please stand to indicate your assent to Benefice Michay's motion." A tide of crimson swelled upward.

He met Antil's wide-eyed stare, the look of a cornered animal, and sighed. "No, my brothers. Compulsion is wrong. Magnus used it in the extremity of his need. Unless the kingdom is threatened by a rogue reader, I will not resort to it." He called to Luis. "Which direction did the princess take?"

Luis turned the lot in his hands. "She's headed southwest, Your Excellency. We should have the village within the hour."

Martin nodded. "Pater Antil, you have your orders. You are adjured by Deas, Eleison, and Aurae. I don't trust you, so the watchmen will have specific orders regarding disobedience."

Antil's answering glare held rebellion.

35

ROUT

ERROL STARED into the bowl-shaped basin that interrupted the Cruor Gap. A half mile from the western entrance, the depression might have been big enough to contain a small village had it offered access to running water. Barren, it still presented a stern beauty to the eye. Three hundred paces away, on the other side of the basin, beyond reliable bow shot, Merakhi forces milled, seething like a cauldron over too much heat.

"This is as far as we can go," Arick said. He pointed, indicating the interruption in the cliffs that offered his bowmen a clear range of fire at the enemy.

Errol nodded at the obvious conclusion. Arick boasted few peers with a bow, but if Errol fell, leadership would have to pass to another, and the man before him was not a tactician. "What's our best estimate of their numbers?" He didn't want to ask the question. The forces opposite them easily surpassed the ten thousand they'd been told to expect.

Arick shrugged but his gray eyes squinted as he focused into the distance. "It's tough to say for certain, Captain. The gap narrows, and there are Merakhi and spawn filling it as far as we can see."

His reticence illustrated another reason Arick would not lead—the bowman found it difficult to commit to anything less than absolute surety. "Give me an estimate."

"Twenty thousand. Perhaps more."

Errol nodded. They couldn't afford to advance. To venture into that bowl meant slaughter. "Our numbers?"

To his right, Sven wiped his mouth. "Six hundred swords."

Errol took the news like a blow. He'd expected the swords to carry the heaviest casualty, but Sven's report distressed him. The pikes would have to spread to cover the additional ground.

Lieutenant Hasta threw back his shoulders. "We still have over two thousand men, Captain." His voice dropped. "But we're losing the pikes. I've got three score men who could fight if they had arms."

He nodded, acknowledging the lieutenant's familiar complaint. "Any sign of a resupply wagon?"

Sven shook his head. "No, Captain."

The Soede's voice sounded troubled. Errol couldn't blame him. The Merakhi could be filling the Arryth behind them for all they knew. He fingered the blanks he kept in his pocket, tempted to cast the question, but he doubted his enemy on the other side of the bowl would give him time. "Dispatch a couple of the men without weapons back into the Arryth. Send one south and one north. I want to know what's going on with the other gaps and if we have any hope of reinforcements. Take the rest of the unarmed pikemen and have them cut lances from any tree they find. We'll use them to reinforce the line."

He turned to Arick. "Do you have enough arrows?"

As expected, Arick shook his head.

"I dispatched the wounded back to the Arryth to make new ones, but the wood is green and heavy. We've searched the bodies to retrieve as many as we could, but we're still going to run short," Arick said. "What will we do then?"

Errol made an effort not to chew his words. "Throw rocks."

The cauldron of men and spawn across the basin boiled over,

spilling men and beasts into the bowl in preparation for another attack. "Get to your men, Arick. We'll pull our forces back to the narrowest part of the gap. That will take some of the burden off the swords."

Moments later they came like a flood.

Men and animals clashed, and the screams of the dying men mixed with the howls of wounded ferrals. Errol's men bunched in the neck of the passage, an opening barely a hundred paces wide, trapping the Merakhi as arrows fell like judgment. Three rows of pikes, backed by the swords, created an impenetrable barrier like a hedge of iron-tipped thorns. Muen's trumpet-like tenor blasted over the lines as he relayed Errol's and Sven's orders.

Then the rain of arrows withered. Errol searched the cliff, unable to see Arick or his men. Something had gone wrong. Dwindled though they were, Arick's supply of arrows shouldn't have given out for some while yet.

The Merakhi, unhindered by bow fire, thrust against the center. Then the ranks of the enemy thinned, and a monstrous figure marched forward with huge strides. The sword line bowed as the giant's massive shirra swept forward, snapping blades and felling men like blades of grass beneath a sickle. The line began to collapse.

Errol threw himself from his horse, the metal staff in his hand, and sprinted toward the line. "Sven! You're with me."

His lieutenant dispatched a Merakhi swordsman with a backhanded stroke to the neck and broke from the line to ride next to Errol. Blood flowed from a deep cut on the Soede's free arm. "Captain, you can't do this."

Errol pointed toward the malus. "If we don't stop him, we'll lose the line. Stop arguing and follow me."

He fought his way forward, striking back and forth, aiming killing blows at the exposed necks of his enemies. Blood, hot and sticky, covered his hands. Then he came face-to-face with the giant.

At the sight of Errol its mouth distorted, stretched into a cut of savage glee across the misshapen face. "I know you, little one. The bondage of Belaaz's court suited you better."

Errol tried to see through the influence of the malus to the man beneath, but the misshapen lumps on the Merakhi's face, as if some creature within longed to escape, prevented him. The eyes, filmed and putrid, stared at him without blinking. A bulge in the face shifted and then split, as if the skin could no longer contain the spiritual infection within it.

The shirra whistled as it cut the air, fast, too fast to avoid. Errol would have to parry. Even as he shifted to block, he knew the mass behind the blow would knock him off balance. And leave him open to the monster's follow.

He brought the staff up to block, pushing the metal with all the strength he held, trying to counter the impact. The clash brought only sparks from the weapons. Errol stumbled, righted himself as astonishment washed over him. That blow should have sent him sprawling.

The creature's mouth split into a snarl beneath a gaze that lashed him, leeching the warmth from his veins. "Our ancient weapon will not rescue you, little one. If I cannot break it, I will beat it from your hands and make your men watch as I eat your heart."

Errol backed away, the lines of battle flowing around them, the armies clashing to a draw as men and spawn fought. A wind, channeled by the narrow passage that led to the Arryth, cooled the sweat that bathed him.

The feel of the breeze brought a scream of rage from the malus-possessed Merakhi. "Do you think he will save you? He didn't even bother to save himself."

The shirra came for him, heavy as a headsman's axe and impossibly fast. Errol threw himself to the side, desperate to avoid the blow. The giant followed with an overhand strike, his mouth wide with glee. Errol rolled, and the blade struck sparks from the rock. Desperate, he raised his staff, frantic with the need to keep the malus from closing with him.

As if in a dream, over the giant's shoulder he saw a single shaft descending from the top of the canyon, heading for his enemy's head. But the malus noticed his stare and whirled, his sword spinning to take the arrow midflight. Errol thrust the point of his staff forward, his feet scrabbling as he tried to get his legs beneath him and rise. But he was too slow. The malus turned, his sword whistling, eyes dancing with the certainty of Errol's death.

Sven dispatched his opponent with a backhanded sweep of his sword and leapt, hitting the malus in the back, knocking the giant forward. Surprise filled the creature's vibrating eyes as the point of Errol's staff took the giant through the throat.

The Merakhi stiffened, falling backward as Errol's staff found its brain.

Ferrals howled, scampering to get away from the battle. Deprived of their support, the Merakhi line collapsed as men tried to retreat. Columns of pikes wheeled in from the sides, closing off the escape of the men and spawn who'd been closest. With grim efficiency the pikes advanced.

The battle moved away from Errol as the enemy retreated. Sven and Hasta pulled him back, their faces etched with relief. Errol pointed toward the cliffs. "Get a man up there. I want to know what happened to our bowmen."

Sven sent a swordsman scampering back to the ascension point before turning back to Errol, his mouth open. But he stopped short as the pounding of hooves sounded behind them. Errol turned to see a rider throw himself out of the saddle, stumbling across the rocks a dozen paces away.

Hasta stepped forward. "Sergeant Dyre, report."

The Bellian pointed, his eyes wide. "Merakhi forces are coming up from the south. They're in the Arryth."

Errol stepped forward. He would not retreat for a rumor. "You know this?"

Dyre nodded, his chin bobbing. "One of our scouts spied them from the cliff. They're driving a force of Illustrans before them." He swallowed, his throat working with the motion. "It's a rout, sir."

Despair settled over Errol like a shroud. The gap to the south could not be regained. "How long before they reach our position?"

"Tomorrow."

It would have to do. He turned to Lieutenant Hasta. "Have your men form up at the neck. Let the Merakhi think we mean to hold our position. As soon as it gets full dark, we retreat."

"Where will we go?" Sven asked. The Soede sounded as though his last hope had been slaughtered in front of him.

Errol fought a wave of helplessness so deep it threatened to drown him. He wanted to crawl into an ale barrel and hide there. "There's nothing defensible between here and Escarion. See to your men. Send messengers to the gaps to the north." He chewed his lip. "I want the two of you and Arick, if he's still alive, to meet me at the western entrance of the gap in an hour."

The Arryth lay spread before him, its verdant health dimmed by the cloud of dust raised by the fighting to the south. Sven and Hasta issued their reports: Their forces were down by over a third. Lieutenant Arick and most of the bowmen were dead, taken unaware by ferrals that had scaled the cliff.

Errol sighed. "I should have replaced Arick before the fighting started. I'm to blame for ignoring my suspicions."

"He died well," Sven said. "He was the bowman closest to you, there at the end."

"We needed him to live." He looked to Sven. "Have we recovered their bows?"

The Soede nodded, his extra chin moving in confirmation. "Aye, but we have precious few men left to man them."

36

THE BAS-RELIEF

FOR FIVE DAYS they'd ridden as if the Merakhi army hunted them from just behind the next hill, but the wind that broke winter's chill had carried no sound Adora could attribute to pursuit. Now the sun touched the horizon beneath a heavy cloud bank. Days of fitful sleep had left her eyes scratchy and dry in the light.

Waterson stiffened ahead of her and scented the air. "I smell the sea."

They crested a hill and came in view of a large village.

"Tacita," Adora said. Nothing moved over the village nestled in a broad arc of limestone that cupped the area in a protective hand, but a sensation of recognition nagged at her.

"Where do we begin?" Waterson asked.

The question slid past her, meant for her but without import. She knew this place. Rather, she felt as if she should know it. They dismounted, leaving the horses to graze and drink from a pond within the confines of the town. Adora walked past the buildings, the odd sense of familiarity growing within her. At a junction where a church rose opposite an inn, she turned without thinking, heading up an incline toward a large building, a mansion that overlooked the town.

Why did she know this place? A rock wall four feet high, assembled from the limestone that littered the fields, surrounded the manse. Weeds poked through cracks in the stones that paved a road toward the broad keep. Wide windows, huge targets for even a moderately skilled bowman, testified that the mansion's origin hearkened to a time of peace. Darkness filled those openings even as memories of life and light pulled at her.

Despite the immense solidity of the estate, everything struck her as too small, as if viewed from the wrong angle. They ascended a flight of rough-hewn steps leading to wide doors framed with massive oak planks.

Rokha drew her sword, her mouth tight. "I thought I saw movement at one of the windows."

Waterson grabbed the thick iron pull on the door and shoved. Hinges squalled in protest as the door swung open into the gloom. Heavy drops pattered, and thunder rumbled in the distance, heralding an approaching storm. "I'm not overly fond of invitations to ambush."

Adora tried to reconcile the impressions in her head that conflicted with her vision. "I know this place."

"You've been here before?" Rokha asked.

She had to nod. "But I can't remember when. At the far end of the room beyond this door, there's a fireplace large enough for me to stand in."

Waterson pulled his sword. "If we're lucky, we won't be attacked in here." He snorted. "Not that anyone who knows me would consider me lucky. You have a way of surrounding yourself with unfortunate men, Your Highness. You should consider moving in different circles."

Adora smiled despite the sorrow Waterson's banter woke in her. "I consider myself fortunate in my chance of companions, Lord Waterson."

For the space of a pair of breaths, Waterson's expression of self-mockery slipped from his eyes. The tightness around them relaxed, and Adora beheld the man he would have been had not circumstance betrayed him.

He bowed. "At your service, Your Highness."

She drew her sword and nodded.

They entered the next room. Waterson chuckled and pointed to a fireplace when a lightning flash briefly illuminated the space. "Not quite big enough to stand in."

"Not for an adult," Rokha said.

Their words took on a sepulchral echo in the empty space. Bits of broken furniture lay strewn here and there, but no lanterns or even torch material remained. Waterson led the way, moving with each flash of lightning. Adora followed, and Rokha protected their rear. The rain came in earnest, the sound mimicking the roar of the distant ocean.

"No," Adora said, obeying the impression of a memory. "Go left."

They departed the hall and followed arched corridors toward the back of the building. Despite Rokha's suspicion, nothing stirred inside, and no sound evidenced the presence of others. They arrived at a set of doors framed by large windows that led outside. Waterson pointed at the floor.

"Wait for the next flash."

In the harsh blue-white light that flickered across her vision, Adora could see two sets of footprints leading outside.

Waterson grimaced. "They got here before us."

"Impossible," Rokha said. "It has to be someone else."

Waterson gestured in the gloom. "As evidence goes, this is pretty hard to refute."

Adora frowned. Something didn't seem right. "No. They couldn't have beaten us here; they couldn't have known. I didn't even know where we were going until we arrived."

Waterson's chest inflated before he sighed. "I hope you're right, Your Highness."

He opened the door onto a torrent. Garish brilliance showed

a small stone church across a brief courtyard surrounded by a high stone wall. Waterson led the way at a run, stopping once they'd gained the protection of the overhanging roof.

"Do you remember this place, Your Highness?"

Adora nodded. She did, though the scale of the church seemed too small to fit her intuition. "I must have been a young child."

"The church would have been for the nobles of the house and perhaps for their staff," Waterson said. "I had one as well, though it was smaller than this." He moved through an archway into the sanctuary. It might have held thirty or forty people. Lightning showed through a far window.

"There's nothing here," Rokha said.

"There's nowhere else to go," Waterson said. "Check the floor."

They split up, their movements timed to the flashes of the storm. No footprints marred the dust of the floor. But when they returned to the narthex, they spotted tracks leading to an alcove with a dark-paneled door, nearly invisible against the aged wood paneling of the room.

It opened to reveal a set of stairs descending into the depths of the earth. Orange light glowed from a small torch set into a sconce on the wall. Waterson took it in hand, eyeing it as he might a viper. "It's just been lit."

More light glowed from beneath them. Adora's heart hammered against her ribs.

The stairs ended in a large oval chamber completely walled in with heavy blocks of limestone. By torchlight Adora could see niches fronted by faces cut in bas-relief, sculptures of men or women pictured in the flower of their youth. Some were children.

"It's a crypt," Waterson said. "There must be generations here."

"It is." A figure limned in shadow moved in the darkness. "There are. Welcome home, Your Highness."

Another silhouette, larger and armed with a sword, joined the first. "We despaired of your coming."

Waterson lifted his torch, and the shadows fled to reveal two normal-sized people. Adora's heart slowed from its frantic race.

They stepped forward and knelt to her. "Be welcome in Patria, the seat of your father."

She gaped.

Charlotte and Will, Oliver Turing's assistants, gazed up at her, awaiting her command, their expectation plain.

She dipped her head. "Oliver Turing died before he could deliver his message. All he could tell me was that I needed to find my father." She turned a slow circle, noting the number of tombs. "Why is he here? I always assumed he rested at Erinon."

Her news of Oliver Turing struck them, and they touched their heads together, mourning, before Charlotte spoke. "The decision to hide your father's body was made of desperation, Your Highness. The king and the church desired to erase his memory in case any of his sons survived."

Adora stiffened. *Sons.* It had been years since anyone had dared to remind her of her father's efforts to sire the future king. When it became clear Rodran would never produce an heir, the Judica had tasked Prince Jaclin with providing the scion Rodran could not. After the death of her mother, at Adora's own birth, the Judica feared nefarious forces were at work, so they sent Jaclin to roam the countryside in hopes of hiding the heirs he produced. But the Merakhi assassins, the ghostwalkers, had found them all. Only the prince's nickname, Randy Jac, had remained. She thrust the painful memories away. "Why would my uncle use a nuntius?"

"Because"—Charlotte smiled sadly—"he suspected something that he desperately wanted passed on, but the duke had him watched. Weir suspected the king of some secret knowledge."

"So Oliver sent you here?" Adora asked. Realization flooded through her like sunlight. "This was one of my father's estates. I played here as a child."

Will brought an unlit torch forward, touched it to Waterson's before moving to a niche hidden in the corner. "No one's been allowed here in almost twenty years. The entire kingdom thought it abandoned, a belief the king encouraged. I think you'll understand why."

Charlotte came forward, touched her fingers to the bas-relief in front of her father's tomb. "This is your father, Your Highness, as he looked some fifty years ago, when he was about your age."

Gasps from Rokha and Waterson echoed her own. She knew him.

Martin Arwitten, leader of the faithful, first among equals within the hall of the Judica, sat speechless. He cudgeled his brain, berating himself as a fool and a coward for not speaking, for not offering the nobles who remained, chief among them Duke Escarion, the solace and comfort of the church.

He gazed around the room, forced his eyes to see past his dread and fear, gauging these men. The faces surely wore expressions that reflected his.

"We are undone," Duke Batten said.

Several men nodded. One—Martin thought his name was Torin—filled a wine glass with careless movements, unheeding that it overflowed onto the polished wood of the table, and drained it. Bleary eyes testified to the number of times he'd made those same gestures already.

"We are not. Not while we have breath," Martin said. Inside, he snorted at the inefficacy of his words.

"The gaps are failing," Escarion said. To his credit, his tone did not accuse but rather informed, inviting strategy or suggestion. "Those possessed by a malus within the Merakhi army are able to control the spawn. We cannot stand against them. Our forces must retreat here to Escarion. We possess the high ground, Archbenefice, but the natural defenses here do not match those of the Arryth."

Martin nodded. He wanted nothing more than to shut himself in his rooms and leave the fate of Illustra to Deas, but some remnant of hope or will refused to let him surrender. He was probably a fool.

The map before him showed Escarion's lands. He traced the

rivers to the south with a thick finger. "The spawn we encountered in Bellia succumbed to the water." The nobles around him nodded in agreement, but their eyes betrayed their doubt. "And we must trust to Deas," he added, but his thoughts accused him as a deceiver.

Torin snorted, his lips flapping in the pause. "Show me some sign of Deas's favor." He stood, looking around the room as if searching for some evidence of deliverance. The count shook his head, wavering on his feet in time to each blink. He gripped a bottle of wine in each hand and staggered away. Martin envied him the luxury of his retreat.

Duke Escarion stood, signaling an end to the meeting. "We'll need sappers to take down the bridges."

He left with the other nobles in his wake, leaving Martin to sit in the empty room. The fire at the far end, set to drive away the spring chill, made joyful cracking sounds, and the flames danced as if happy to provide warmth.

The deep cushions of the chair invited him to remain, but the failure of their forces to hold against the Merakhi horde placed requirements on him. Not many, true, but certain tasks must be completed. He rose, took his staff in hand, and made for the door. His page, Breun, stepped in beside him, his round face curious and a little frightened.

When Martin turned from the wing of the castle that housed both the conclave and the Judica, the lad missed a step.

"Are we not returning to your quarters, Archbenefice?"

Martin shook his head. "I need to see an old friend, Breun. Come, we're going to drop in on Primus Sten."

"Yes, Your Excellency." Every line of the boy's posture showed he longed to ask why. Martin hadn't visited the primus since Sten had withdrawn from active participation in the conclave upon Canon's death. Luis and Willem had split Enoch's duties in his absence. The primus rarely left his rooms.

At the thought, a chill crept up one arm and down the other. *Like Sarin,* he thought. He waved his hand in the air as if he could physically brush the comparison aside. "I find myself in need of counsel, Breun."

The eyes widened in wonder. "You, Archbenefice?"

Martin chuckled in spite of himself. "Me perhaps more than any other, lad. The higher you rise, the greater your need for advice." He caught the boy's gaze. "I hope you will remember that."

"I will, Your Excellency." His hair flopped in agreement with his earnest nod.

They ascended the steps of the south tower. At his knock, the door opened to reveal the head of the conclave. At seeing Martin, Sten bowed. "Please come in, Archbenefice."

Martin bent in appreciation and stepped across the threshold. Sten had picked out his own room, a modest affair with a single window that faced south. A chair sat in front of it surrounded by the implements of Sten's craft. "Thank you for seeing me, Primus."

Sten noted Martin's inspection. "I don't really own that title anymore." His thin shoulders lifted beneath the weight of his heavy blue reader's cloak. "They're coming, but the lots are misbehaving, preventing me from determining exactly when. Perhaps it is me. I find it difficult to concentrate on the present or the future. I keep replaying the past, altering it within my mind to see how the present would change." He laughed. "We tried to prepare for this—the three of us, Rodran, Bertrand, and I—but the war didn't come in time. We aged until we became three old men guarding their secrets." He pointed out the window. "None of our machinations mattered in the end. Rodran couldn't father a child, and all the children we got from Prince Jaclin were killed. We turned the prince out to stud to save the kingdom, and it didn't help us at all."

He gave Martin a sad little smile. "All we accomplished was to deprive the princess of her father. The royal line failed, the church failed, and then the conclave failed. Luis blames himself, but the cast didn't work for me either."

Martin leaned forward. This was why he had come. "I need those secrets, Primus."

Sten's smile grew sad. "You know them already."

"Who is supposed to be king and savior of Illustra? One of you must have known."

Sten shook his head. "At the end we didn't even trust each other, not really. Bertrand and I saw how Rodran took to Liam, but the cast came up the same." He tottered to the chair that faced the south-looking window and took his seat with trembling, searching hands. He spoke to Martin as he gazed out across the meadows. "I think Rodran might have been the wisest of us all. Not once did he ask to have the question cast. Whenever we broached the subject, he just smiled and looked at Liam."

37

CHOSEN

ADORA HADN'T REALIZED she'd fallen until hands took her by the arms and lifted her. Inside she despised herself even as her heart beat its exultation. Liam was Illustra's soteregia, and Errol would live. The torchlight, seen through the film of tears that filled her eyes, flowed in her vision until the entire cavern danced in the orange-yellow glow.

"We promised Oliver we would stay until someone came," Charlotte said. "The villagers never knew we were here."

Her words washed over Adora, noted but having no impact. She stepped forward to her father's crypt, the father she hardly remembered, and pulled her dagger from her belt. Using the point like a chisel she beat and pried at the bas-relief, working to loosen the mortar that attached the likeness to the surrounding rock.

Waterson stepped in opposite her, working at the joints on the far side. "One of his sons survived after all." He sounded amazed. "How is that possible? Rodran searched the entire kingdom for an heir who survived the Merakhi assassins. There weren't any."

The herbwomen. "He was guarded," Adora said. With a grinding sound of rocks sliding against each other, the carving of Jaclin came loose. "The ghostwalkers never knew he was there."

"This is probably the only likeness of Prince Jaclin left in Illustra," Waterson said. "Nobody remembers him before age or the scars or without the beard. If Liam dies in combat without being crowned king . . ."

Adora shook her head. "He will not. Deas has appointed him to save us at the determined time." She wrapped the carving of the stranger, of her father, and of Illustra's salvation—and her own—in her cloak and turned to the four people who stood waiting for her command. "We have to get back to Escarion as quickly as we can. I have coin. We can buy horses on the way." Her mouth tightened. "I speak for the king."

They ascended the stairs, Charlotte and Will in front of Adora with Rokha and Waterson behind. Adora followed in the dim light. The sound of a blade biting into flesh warned her, and she threw herself to one side. A splash, hot and sticky, hit her in the face, and the flare of a torch made her wince. She came up, sword in hand, to mocking laughter. Will and Charlotte lay dead. A pair of blades, both stained red, pointed at her.

"Hello, strumpet."

Disbelief clattered through her mind. "Sevra." The face was that of Duke Weir's daughter, or it would have been, had it not grown hideous, surmounting a seven-foot frame. The duchess's eyes, so wide they appeared nearly lidless, stared and vibrated.

"We have unfinished business, little one," Sevra said. "I owe you a debt, and a Weir always pays in full." The sword bobbed in time to the words, the length of steel a hand longer than any other sword in the room.

"Skorik," Rokha said. The man with Sevra jerked as if stung. "This is treason."

The scar on his face contorted, but he gave no sign of being possessed. "No. This is vengeance."

Rokha laughed, but the sound held none of its usual warmth.

It crackled with derision like a whip striking flesh. "Because I found you an unworthy suitor? And this will elevate you in my eyes? You're a fool."

He spat. "I want no part of you, and your father is not here to protect you. You all should have died in Merakh."

Sevra cut Skorik short. "The day marches on, strumpet." She pointed the tip of her massive sword at the bundle that lay at Adora's feet. "I see you found something of interest. Did you really think Turing's last message escaped me?" She looked around the room, her lips curled. "So this is where they brought him." Her gaze narrowed into a look of deadly concentration. "Lift it, human. Let me see it."

Adora shot a look at Rokha. They faced only two opponents, and they held three blades of their own. Ru's daughter gave a slight shake of her head. Breathless, Adora bent, her movements slow and unthreatening, and lifted the stone with her father's image on it.

Sevra flicked her wrist, impatient, and Skorik thrust his torch forward to illuminate the stone visage. "A mystery. How quaint. Why would the image of a captain of the guard be in this abandoned place?" She stilled, and her eyes slowed their vibration. "There would be no need for you to come all this way for such inconsequence."

Duke Weir's daughter and the malus housed in her body leaned forward, still out of sword reach, to peer at the sculpture. "It is Captain Liam . . . and yet it is not." Her eyes widened. "I know this one. We hunted his offspring, my brothers and I." She gasped. "And one lived." Laughter echoed from the stones. "Oh, strumpet, you have given me a gift beyond measure. Almost I am tempted to let you live to see the disaster you've wrought.

"By guiding me here you've assured your kingdom's destruction." Like a monstrous child, she beat her hand against her thigh in glee. "Your Judica and conclave are blind. Had you made it back to them with this, they would have crowned him king and enabled him to rebuild the barrier. Taste it, strumpet! Taste the full measure of your failure. The strait is ours. In hours I will gather a force that will attack Illustra's men from behind."

"You would aid this?" Rokha said to Skorik.

His face contorted as conflicting emotions chased each other across his features. "I have chosen my side. Nothing I can do will undo it now."

Sevra looked at Rokha, her head tilted to one side in thought, with a smile that chilled Adora's heart. "We can use you, my brothers and I. Why not give yourself to us now, small one? You could have the power you've longed for."

Rokha laughed, brought her sword up, and turned to the ready position. "I don't think so."

The scrape of cloth against wood whispered in the silence. A ghost of movement in the shadowed interior of the church alerted them as black-clothed men moved in behind Sevra and Skorik.

Violence erupted as swords flashed everywhere.

Waterson dove, bearing Adora to the floor as Sevra launched a flicking attack that would have taken her in the throat. "Stay down." He grunted in pain but levered himself up to join against the pair.

She rolled, her vision registering the presence of a pair of the watch locked in combat, one against Skorik with Rokha, the other against Sevra with Waterson.

And Antil.

Already the priest bled from a wound in his side, but he launched blows that could not be ignored, giving the watchmen and Waterson openings to strike and dart back.

Rokha's voice cut the din, yelling instruction to the watchmen. "He prefers high-line attacks. Watch for a low feint."

Adora's sword lay just beyond her reach. Blows and parries whistled above her head, whining against the stones before returning to land against her hearing again. She crawled, belly down on the floor, for her blade. Sevra saw the movement and hopped back in preparation to aim a kick at her throat. Adora rolled, grasped the hilt, and swung.

And struck Skorik just above the heel.

Blood spurted from the severed tendon. Unable to maneuver, he went down beneath an onslaught of blows that took him in the side and neck. Naaman Ru's protégé died before he hit the floor.

Adora rose to see Sevra launch a counter that cleared the way to the door. Weir's daughter disappeared at a run into the fading light.

A rattling breath intruded on her awareness. She knew the sound, knew what it meant, but Waterson stood with Rokha, pressing the fold of her cloak against his shoulder, not his lung. A watchman huddled over a figure on the floor whose blood ran into a growing puddle at their feet. A hand twitched. Antil was still alive.

She wanted to stay away. Despite his service, she did not trust him. What revelation might he have kept in reserve? Adora forced herself to circle around and kneel by the pale, pale face. The eyes, not Errol's, looked up at her.

"I thank you for your service, Pater. Why?"

He struggled to pull a breath past the wound in his chest. "He . . ." He stopped, gave his head the barest shake. "No man—none—should have to bury his love." His face slackened. "He'll understand."

Antil grew still.

Adora stood, her gaze still fastened to the man she'd hated above any other. "He probably will."

The watchmen made to lift him.

Adora pointed to the stairs. "Place him down there with the rest. It's fitting." She gathered the bas-relief into her arms as if it held the power to keep Errol alive. "We must ride for Escarion now."

"A brisk walk at best," Waterson said, "with those sorry excuses for horses."

Errol leaned forward to give Midnight a reassuring pat. He wasn't sure who needed the gesture more, him or the horse. Illustran soldiers streamed from the Pelligroso Pass. Closer now, he could see they retreated in good order, what was left of them.

Half a league behind, a force of Merakhi filled the gentle slope that led into Gascony's heartland.

Sven towered over him on his left, perched atop the huge draft horse his bulk required. The lieutenant fidgeted, clearly uncomfortable with their plan. Errol couldn't blame him. Every time he thought of it, a muscle in his eye twitched. He cast a glance back at the wall of rubble and rock that trickled down, closing off the gap. On the cliff overlooking their position, men labored to dislodge more earth and rock.

"How long before it is ready?"

Lieutenant Hasta grunted. "Another hour at least."

The pace of Errol's heartbeat jumped. "It's going to be a near thing."

"Is this wise, Captain?" Sven asked.

Errol shook his head. "No, it's not even close. Wise would be tucking our tail between our legs and racing to Escarion as fast as our horses could take us." He sighed. "But if we do that, Captain Indurain's and Captain Merkx's force will be lost. Look." He pointed. Already the gap between pursuer and pursued had narrowed.

Hasta nodded. Errol had to give him credit; after his initial objections had been answered, he executed every order as if the idea had been his own. "Sergeant Cursus is almost there."

Errol watched as the horseman merged with the retreating force. "Let's hope Indurain and Merkx move quickly."

They waited, watching as the Illustrans moved farther out toward the flat ground that would give them better footing for retreat. A moment passed. Two. Then their path shifted, showing a subtle change that would bring them past the position Errol's force occupied.

"There it is," Errol said. "Get everyone in position. It's going to be tight."

Captain Indurain's force flowed past him. Every man bore wounds, gaping rents which left their owners pale and haggard beneath a veneer of sweat and dirt. Indurain and Merkx hadn't surrendered the Pelligroso easily, far from it. Even if they survived, most of their men would never fight again. As he watched, two more succumbed to their wounds and fell from blood-soaked saddles to lie dead upon the earth.

He squeezed his eyes shut, forcing his anger to serve him. "Have someone put their horses against the wall with the rest."

The watch captains diverted toward him.

Merkx bowed from his saddle. "My thanks, Captain Stone. They would have caught us after another three leagues."

Errol nodded. "Or less."

Merkx stiffened as if he'd been insulted. Errol held up his hand. "I mean no offense, Captain. It was easier to gauge their speed from here."

The Bellian nodded, mollified. He surveyed the rubble barrier Errol's men were building. "How can we help?"

Errol ached with the answer. A line of horses, all of the horses they could spare and then some, waited behind him. "We need to lure the enemy as high up the slope as possible. Let them think we've taken this gap and are going to escape to the far side. Slow your men. I have bowmen in place to keep the Merakhi off your back."

Their eyes widened in disbelief, accusing. Merkx started forward, his mouth open, ready to hurl accusations. Errol cut him off. "Desperate circumstances require desperate measures, Captain."

"Aye," Indurain said. "You would know this, yes?"

"I would."

The captains rode back to their forces, giving the order to slow.

Lieutenant Hasta coughed at his shoulder. "If they don't take the bait, Captain Stone, they'll have us all."

Errol nodded, acknowledging the observation without responding to it. "Where's Sven?"

The lieutenant's gaze became troubled. Instead of answering directly he pointed toward the cliff. The draft horse that had carried Sven to the gap was tethered to rocks at the base. Up above, the Soede walked across the stone, his feet searching tentatively. In one hand he held a length of iron scavenged from a farmer's cart. It looked almost dainty in his grip.

Errol spurred Midnight to the base. He stood in the stirrups, craning his neck to yell up the height. "Curse your fat hide, Sven. What are you doing up there?"

The Soede looked abashed, but resolution filled his face and posture. "You'll need every bit of horsepower you can get, Captain. A draft horse is too valuable to waste on an overfed swordsman."

Errol winced. "Without that horse, he's got no hope of escaping."

Lieutenant Hasta nodded. "He knows, Captain. He also knows that beast is worth five ordinary horses."

Twice he started forward to order Sven down the cliff. Both times he stopped, halted by the brutal truth of his insight. Stymied, he turned back to Hasta. "I want a horse left for him where it will be safe from the rockslide. If he manages to survive, he can catch up to us. I need my lieutenant." He turned Midnight to inspect the archers so Hasta wouldn't see the grief on his face.

Every man and bow was hidden behind the rocks that peppered the road beneath the cliffs. Grizzled veterans with hands like gnarled tree roots stood next to wide-eyed lads younger than Errol. Diar Muen came forward to meet him. Arick's replacement was more to his liking.

"You understand what needs to be done?" Errol asked.

The tall man nodded, stroking the longbow scavenged from the cliffs. The tinge of red in his hair proclaimed some trace of Erinon ancestry within. "Aye, Captain, we'll give those Merakhi something to think about. We'll mow them down like grass."

Errol nodded. "Remember what you're about, Muen. At this point, we need our men alive more than we need dead Merakhi. I want the Merakhi bunched up and held at bay until they mount an all-out charge. As soon as you see them massing, I want every man on his horse and out of here."

Indurain and Merkx approached him, their faces troubled.

"Our men are hidden in the gap, but we don't have enough mounts for all of them."

Errol nodded. "Have them double up with the smallest men of my command."

Merkx's face knotted. "Would it not be better for each man to have his own horse and make a run for Escarion?"

Errol understood the unspoken question and chose to answer it. "The spawn within the Merakhi army would run us down from behind long before Escarion. Do you agree?"

The Bellian's jaw muscles clenched as if he were fighting his answer. At last he nodded. "But if your plan fails . . ."

"If my plan fails," Errol cut in, "then we will lose my force as well as yours, which was lost at any rate." He turned to Indurain. "Do you disagree?"

The Basqu sighed. "No, I do not."

The sudden whistle of arrows cut the air like the cry of a thousand wounded birds.

Indurain pointed at the rain of shafts ascending in a shallow arc into the sky. "It seems we are past the point of debate." The arrows began their descent toward the startled Merakhi cries. "Good luck, Captain Stone. We'll await your signal."

He coaxed Midnight back toward the apex of the road, where he watched the vanguard of the Merakhi army halt. He nodded with satisfaction as the long stretch of men and spawn bunched together, shields raised to try and lessen their casualties.

A runner sprinted toward him as the deadly rain trickled. "Muen says they've finished, Captain."

Errol nodded. "Have the men wait for my signal. If we break too soon, the Merakhi will flank us by withdrawing to the valley."

The opposing army frothed like a river at flood, shifting as if they suspected another volley. Then, with a massive roar, they began their charge up the long slope. Errol stood in his stirrups and circled his arm, as if ordering a charge.

But instead of rushing to meet their opponent, every man

rushed from the gap back down the other side of the road leading to Escarion, out of sight of the Merakhi. Handlers stood
with the horses, waiting for the last of the men to escape. Errol
rode by, his throat clutching at the sight of a massive draft horse
and the thick ropes that connected it to the rocks at the base
of the cliff. Up on top a thick-bodied Soede stood ready with a
length of iron.

Lieutenant Hasta pulled his sorrel in beside him.

"Deas help us. I hope this works," Errol said.

The lieutenant gave a terse nod.

The first of the Merakhi entered the gap, a mix of men and
spawn howling for blood with every stride and leap. The handlers
loosed the horses, riding just ahead of them on the last mounts.
The animals, their noses filled with the scent of predators, needed
no other urging. They plunged forward, thick ropes snaking
behind them.

Errol and Lieutenant Hasta rode just ahead of the handlers.
The cry of terrified horses filled his ears, and he fought to keep
Midnight under control. A straggler went down beneath a wave
of ferrals, their teeth flashing white, then red.

A trickle of scree warned him, and he jerked the reins to the
left. Midnight shifted, a wrenching change in momentum that
almost unhorsed him. On the heights above, his neck cording
with effort, Sven strained to break a massive boulder loose from
the side of the cliff. With a crack like the bones of the earth
breaking, it came free, moving as if through water. Wherever it
touched, more rock and earth broke loose to join it.

Slabs of rock crumbled and shifted. The Merakhi forces at
the front tried to retreat, but the men and spawn behind them
advanced, filling the road as the side of the cliff gave way. Struggling to escape the path of the avalanche, Sven's draft horse pulled
a monstrous boulder.

Merakhi and spawn cried out, mouths and muzzles stretching
in panic as the avalanche grew, washing them down the slope,
burying them beneath tons of debris. The draft horse faltered,

its legs fighting to move but unable to budge the growing weight of rock against the thick ropes trailing behind it.

Ignoring Hasta's warning, Errol turned and raced back to the animal. The slide of rock grew closer as he dismounted and sawed at the thick hemp as he clutched the reins. Stones the size of his fists pelted him as he worked the blade back and forth in panicked strokes.

It snapped with a popping sound and the rough fibers lashed him. With a lunge, he threw himself onto Midnight's saddle. The river of earth and rock slowed. Where the road had been lay a vast hill of stones. He sighed, his hands shaking with relief. Nothing stirred.

"How many of them do you think we killed, Captain?" Hasta asked. The lieutenant held a waterskin toward him.

Errol washed the dirt from his throat. "Not enough. The survivors on the far side will regroup to pursue us through the valley, but we've given ourselves some time. I hope it's enough for us to make it back." He gave Midnight a nudge with his heels.

A voice ghosted to him from above. "Could you wait up for me, Captain? I'm not as nimble as those skinny pikemen."

He searched the trail.

"Where's the supply wagon? I'm hungry."

Errol looked up to see Sven scrambling down the cliff. He scrubbed away sudden tears that turned the dirt on his face to mud.

38

WITHDRAW

ADORA DUG HER HEELS into her mare. The horse rewarded her with a dispirited canter that lasted all of five strides before it settled back into a walk. Not for the first time, she regretted turning down the offer of better mounts in Escarion. Rokha and Waterson rode beside her without recriminations, but tension marked the way they leaned forward in their saddles as if they could somehow will their animals to greater speed. The two watchmen, Orban and Bartal, rode several paces behind, stoic despite the circumstances. No sign of censure or approval showed on their faces.

Waterson looked back, again. "I wish it hadn't rained. If we've lost the strait, we'd be able to see the dust from that many men and animals."

Rokha turned to look back, her deep brown eyes troubled by an obscure pain. "They're back there."

"How do you know?" Adora asked.

Rokha shrugged and shook her head. "I can feel them. That's bad, Your Highness. The last time I could sense the presence of so many malus, we were surrounded by them in Merakh."

Adora's stomach tried to trade places with her liver. "But that would mean . . ."

"That's right," Rokha said. "There are malus-possessed with whoever's back there."

She groped for some argument. "Could it be Sevra?"

Rokha paused, then shook her head again. "I don't think so, or rather, not just her. I never sensed her. It takes a greater number for me to sense them with my limited ability."

"How can you feel them at all?" Waterson asked.

Rokha nodded. If she took offense at his blunt question, she didn't show it. "Possession is similar enough to compulsion that I can pick up on it, but to sense either at a distance, there must be a great deal of it."

"I should go back and scout," Waterson said.

Adora cut the air with one hand in refusal. "No. Your horse is as spent as ours. If they spotted you, you'd never get away." She jingled her purse. "If I have to, I'll spend every last coin I have to buy fresh mounts at the next village."

"If they have them," Waterson pointed out.

They turned a bend in the road and once again came in view of the village of Aresco, but now nothing moved, and no sign of inhabitation presented itself. As they neared, Adora saw why and squeezed her eyes shut. Bodies, some of them too small to be adults, littered the streets, many of them cut down from behind.

Waterson waited until she regained her composure before dismounting and tying his horse to a nearby post, his face pale above the collar of his cloak. "I'll check the stables."

Rokha, her jaws tight, followed his lead. "Come, Your Highness. We'll check the houses. There may not be horses—" she looked around and sighed—"but there will probably be food and perhaps other supplies as well."

The watchmen looked at Adora as she slid from the back of

her horse, plainly waiting for orders. "Guard behind us. If you see anyone, don't wait to find out if they're friendly. Get us out of here."

Her mount hardly reacted when she cinched the long reins to the same column Rokha had used. A body lay sprawled on the threshold. Even in death the expression remained uncaring. "This is what we're fighting, isn't it? This disregard for life."

Rokha sighed. "It goes deeper than that. The malus at the heart of the Merakhi army don't just disregard life like a human would, they devour it. They prefer corruption over death." She shrugged. "Death is only a moment, after all. They take pleasure in it, but it gives them no lasting satisfaction." She pointed to a small wooden sign across the street that bore the mortar and pestle of a healer's shop. "Let's try there."

A rough wooden counter ran the length of one wall, behind which lay an assortment of jars. Rokha made for them while Adora searched the bins to one side. They were empty except for one, which held a few bunches of withered carrots. She held them up for Rokha's inspection.

"The horses will get more use out of those than we will. We might even get a gallop out of them if we have to." She put her hand into a jar and brought out a finger coated in a fine yellow powder. She licked it, then spat, her face red. "Curren, and it's potent. If we can get a bit of this in their hay, they'll think they are yearlings again, but we'll have to be careful. It makes them run hot. Too little water and we'll lose them."

There was nothing else. They returned to the street to find their horses gone.

Adora whipped her blade from its sheath, but the road to the west showed no signs of pursuit. Waterson came from the ruins of the stable, holding several sets of reins.

"The far end of the stable survived. I found a bit of hay and a watering trough out back. I think they'll run better on decent feed. There's a bag of oats that's not too far gone."

Rokha nodded. "We'll mix in some of the curren we found."

Waterson's eyes widened, but after a moment, he gave a grim nod.

Adora could feel the gazes of the dead on her, accusing. She shook her head, focusing her thoughts on one she prayed still lived. "Let's be on our way. Pursuit or not, we must get to Escarion."

The brisk trot barely stirred a breeze, but the horses managed to sustain a decent pace for the first time in weeks. When they stopped for a few minutes' rest, Adora fed them the carrots, and they whickered and snorted with more spirit than they'd ever shown.

Waterson climbed to the crest of a ridge behind them, where he lay watching, his body stretched on the downhill slope. After a few moments, Adora saw him jerk and slink away in an obvious attempt to avoid being seen.

"They're back there, all right. They don't have many horses, but they're moving quickly even so." He looked at Adora and Rokha, his eyes pinched. "I think they have ferrals with them. If the spawn see or smell us, they'll run us down. There's at least one malus with them."

"We knew that," Rokha said.

Adora pulled a shuddering breath into her lungs. "Let's get as much distance as we can out of the mounts before we give them the curren." She pulled herself into her saddle.

They raced east as fast as their mounts could take them, slowing only when one of the horses stumbled with fatigue. Waterson watched behind as Rokha scouted ahead, but the terrain betrayed them. Too often they were forced to ride around the hills to avoid being seen cresting the ridges.

The next morning, two of the horses went lame. No food or spice would coax them into anything more than a limp, their heads bobbing in time. Rokha and Adora dismounted. Waterson stopped to run his hands from shoulder to hoof. His mouth tightened. "They can't be ridden any time soon."

The watchmen dismounted and presented their reins to Adora

and Rokha. Adora shook her head in refusal, commanding with as much authority as she could muster. "We'll double up."

Bartal and Orban exchanged a glance before Bartal, the older of the two, spoke. "No, Your Highness. That is not an order we will obey. Once before the watch allowed their sovereign to die before them. We will not do so again." He held the reins out to her, his face as impassive in sentencing himself to death as it had been in keeping guard.

"I won't take them."

"You must," Orban said. "We will not ride. If you refuse to do so, then we all die needlessly. Rodran is dead. You are the last of the line."

She shook her head. "You know that's not true." The temptation to bring out the bas-relief made her hands itch.

"What may be true is for the Judica and the conclave to decide, Your Highness." He stepped forward to loop the reins of his horse around her wrist and went on in a lower voice. "Besides, we do not intend to die. A watchman can cover nearly as much ground in a day as his horse."

Bartal handed his reins to Rokha. Then the two watchmen faced the rising sun and set off at a jog. Adora watched them, dumbfounded.

Waterson spoke in a slow drawl. "If you want to continue the conversation, Your Highness, we'll have to mount up and ride after them. I'm not much of a runner."

They passed the watchmen a couple of hours later. The next day, the malus behind them faded from Rokha's awareness, and the following morning they crossed the river that marked the western border of Escarion.

Errol wove his way through the thick columns of men moving north and entered an area cordoned off by black-garbed members of the watch. There was no tent or pavilion available for the meeting of captains. He stepped into the seclusion of the barn and nodded in response to a salute from the pair of watchmen who guarded the privacy of the meeting, their gesture still strange to him.

Cruk and Rale stood at opposite ends of a table consisting of three planks of wood scavenged from one of the doors. An iron hinge askew and black with age still clung to one of the boards. A map of Gascony covered the table. Darkened spots on the map might have been ink, or perhaps blood.

"How did we lose the Pelligroso?" Cruk asked. His arm was bandaged, and his voice, always harsh, carried accusation.

"It hardly matters," Rale said before anyone could speak. He tapped the map. "We have to man the next best defensible line."

Cruk refused to be put off. "It matters. I don't fancy repeating a mistake." He turned toward Indurain and Merkx, where they stood on Errol's left. "What happened?"

Indurain sighed. "The blame cannot be denied. Captain Merkx and I were appointed to hold the southern end of the range. In this, we failed. The Merakhi brought a beast against us, a spawn I had not heard of before. It was no mere ferral. The head was armored with horns like a ram, though it bulked larger than any of our horses."

"Bezahl," Cruk said.

Indurain licked his lips. "It cut through our lines like a blade slicing gossamer. Arrows, even swords, would not draw blood. Lieutenant Gale sacrificed his horse to get close enough to the fell creature to jump on its back. He thrust his dagger through the thing's eye, killing it, but the spawn crushed him in its death throes."

Merkx nodded. "Our lines were ragged, but we restored order, thinking we had taken the worst the enemy had to offer." He drew himself up. "The malus commanding their army mocked us even as they withdrew, shouting in a strange tongue, and five more of the beasts, hidden until then, charged our line."

"Water," Cruk said. He looked toward Rale. "We encountered one—I had hoped the only one—on the eastern edge of Bellia. The bezahl can't swim."

Rale grimaced and his brows drew together over his broad nose. "The spring melt will keep us safe everywhere except on the south. The only river on that side is the Clearwash, and it sits in sight of Duke Escarion's fortress. It's deep enough to stop most spawn but too slow to keep horsemen from swimming it."

Captain Rimor, a blocky Fratalander standing opposite Errol, cleared his throat. "Where are the other captains?"

Errol's guts twisted at the question and the tense silence after it.

Rale shifted his weight from foot to foot. "The rest of the captains have moved north to aid Liam and Merodach."

He couldn't help himself; the question came tumbling out of Errol's mouth before he could clench his teeth to keep it in. "He's alive, isn't he?"

Rale's shadowed gaze offered no comfort. "He's north of us. That we haven't had reports of the enemy coming from that direction is testament to his skill." He sighed and shook his head in defeat. "But they will have to pull back and retreat with the rest of our forces. Once we've crossed the river, we'll take down the bridges and defend the ford. It's narrow. As long as the spring melt lasts we can keep them at bay."

Rale didn't bother to explain what would happen when the waters subsided.

It took them two days to reach Cruin's Gap, which held a broad road that led into the Arryth through a saddle in the hills. Liam's and Merodach's command fought a scant five leagues south of the river. A single day's march would put them back in sight of Duke Escarion's fortress. Rale and Cruk placed their men under temporary command of Indurain and Merkx and sought Errol early in the morning.

"You should come with us, lad," Rale said. Cruk's lumpy face twisted into an approximation of discomfort, a witness to some prior conversation between the two men.

"Why?"

Rale's face hardened, the first time Errol had ever seen that expression directed toward him. "Because we do not know the time or the hour."

"Or the man," Cruk added.

He understood. Errol inhaled a deep breath, held it as he wondered just how many remained to him. He reached into the pocket of his cloak and pulled the lots he'd carved last night, the cast that had told him Liam still lived. With a flick of his wrist he tossed them aside. The time for lots was past. The entire conclave couldn't tell him his fate; why should he try?

His foot slid into the stirrup as he mounted Midnight. Rale had never asked for the return of the horse, and Errol hadn't offered. Midnight's presence had become a fixture for him.

They ascended the road to Cruin's Gap in eerie silence. Ahead, men stood in formation—still, as though some sorcery had spelled them. Yet when the three of them approached, men stepped back, making way for their horses. Somewhere ahead a deep-throated challenge split the air.

Cruk spewed a string of curses as he dug his heels into his mount. "That's Liam."

Rale followed. Errol felt for the reassurance of his staff as he swung Midnight into line behind. After a hundred paces the columns of archers, pikes, and swords ended, leaving a broad flat space between Illustra's forces and those of the enemy.

Liam stood another fifty paces beyond, alone. He brandished his sword and mocked the Merakhi army some hundred and fifty paces away. "Craven! Dogs possessed by dogs. Do you think I fear you?" He drew back his foot and kicked an object toward their line. It fell hopelessly short, but the army drew back as if it might reach them.

Errol squinted. It was a head, but too big to be human.

Cruk grabbed Merodach by the arm. Errol hadn't noticed him before. "What in the name of Deas and all that's holy does he think he's doing? Challenging one of the malus? And you let him do it?"

Merodach turned to face Cruk, his face placid. "This is his

command, Captain, not the other way around." He shrugged. "Besides, it would seem he is up to the task. That head he just kicked belonged to the Merakhi troops' leader, a malus Captain Liam defeated."

Cruk's mouth worked. "Impossible."

Merodach shrugged. "Evidently not."

"Which one?" Errol asked.

The three captains of the watch stared at him, uncomprehending.

"Which of the malus did Liam kill? Was it Belaaz?"

Merodach shook his head. "No. He called himself Azak. I recognized him as one of the ilhotep's council of nine, but it wasn't their leader."

Cruk grunted. "That's a shame."

Rale pointed. "It would seem Captain Merodach is correct. The other malus don't seem interested in answering Liam's challenge."

A stir at the back of the Merakhi line warned him. "Bowmen!" Errol grabbed the shield of the closest pikeman and raced toward Liam.

Cruk bellowed behind him. "Curse your wormy guts, Liam! Get back here!"

A hail of arrows soared into the sky as Errol pushed his legs to go faster. He cursed himself for looking up and sacrificing the speed it took to do so. Liam raced to meet him, his face angry.

They crashed together and huddled under the pitifully small shield as broadheads thunked into the dirt or struck sparks from stone. The sound of tearing cloth reached Errol's hearing, and Liam hissed.

"This is the first time I've ever seen you do anything stupid," Errol said as he and Liam backed toward their lines under cover of the shield. The hail of arrows diminished, died to a trickle as they retreated.

Liam nodded. "I didn't think the malus's caution would outweigh their pride." He darted a glance at Merodach, Cruk, and Rale. "The other gaps have fallen?"

"The south is lost. We have to fall back to the river."

When they reached the safety of their lines, Cruk's face seemed unable to settle on a single shade of red. He spluttered unintelligibly—the captain's extensive vocabulary had failed him at last.

"Give over, Cruk," Rale said. "Captain Liam seems mostly unharmed."

"More than I can say for myself once Archbenefice Arwitten hears of this."

"I can answer for myself, Captain Cruk," Liam said.

"Splendid," Cruk snorted. "You do that."

Liam nodded, but Errol thought he saw a hint of doubt in his eye. That would be another first.

Rale outlined their strategy.

Two days later, Errol crossed the Clearwash River with the last of Illustra's forces. Duke Escarion's fortress loomed in the distance.

There was nowhere left to run.

39

REVELATION

AS HE PACED THE HALLS of Escarion's fortress, Martin's mind ran in tracks that trapped his thoughts the way rutted paths captured a cart's wheels. By Deas and everything holy, he had no desire to shoulder the last decision of the war, perhaps the last decision of any archbenefice of Illustra.

"How did we come to this?"

"Your pardon, Excellency, what did you say?" Breun padded at his side like a faithful puppy, cheerful and attentive to his commands.

Martin shook his head. Had he spoken? "I'm not sure, lad."

Luis and Willem met him at the door. Strange that Enoch Sten, the true primus of the conclave, was not there. He sighed. Everyone fought the war in their own way. For Sten, it seemed, the best thing to do was to let younger, stronger readers take the lead. Martin's gut knotted as he thought again of the decision required of him.

"Breun," Martin said. "Why don't you visit the kitchen? If I remember correctly, boys your age are always hungry." He met the solemn faces of the conclave's leaders as his page loped away. "Do the questions have an answer?"

They nodded.

"Where and when?" His voice rasped like a saw struggling through wood.

Willem and Luis bowed. "Three hours after sunrise tomorrow morning, Archbenefice, at the ford just south of the fortress."

The air turned thick in his lungs. "So soon?" They didn't reply. He hadn't expected them to. "Humph. It is like Deas to set the time and place so we could watch from the ramparts. He has a flair for the dramatic, I think." He caught Luis's gaze. "Are we still without an answer to the question of who?"

Luis nodded. "I cast for it less than an hour ago."

Willem lent the secondus his support. "As did I. There is still no answer. Perhaps Deas has yet to decide who will be the soteregia."

Martin could almost believe it. "I will have to crown the pair and send them both."

"That may leave Illustra without a king," Luis said. "What kind of war would we have then?"

Martin pulled at the muscles along his jaw. His teeth hurt. "Illustra can survive a civil war, but we must have the barrier. Errol and Liam understand this." He sighed, his hope as thin as his breath. "I will serve them the sacraments at sunrise. If they wish."

Rain soaked Adora's cloak. The fabric surrendered to the water and grew sodden, heavy. She considered stopping to wring out the excess weight. How long could they push their mounts before the noble animals' hearts gave out? Escarion lay another ten leagues to the east. She didn't know if the horses would make it at any pace.

Thunder rolled to her right, but it continued to peal long after the lightning ceased. *Horses.* Rokha and Waterson drew as they steered their mounts to face the threat.

Rokha eyed the hills and shook her head, her hair shedding water.

"How many?" Adora yelled over the growing rumble.

Rokha threw her answer back over her shoulder. "Too many to guess."

A line of shaggy ponies, tails and manes flying, crested the ridge, came pouring toward them, their hooves throwing gouts of mud.

"Morgols," Waterson said. He looked toward Adora and Rokha. "I've heard stories from the war"—his eyes darted to the edge of his sword—"about what they do with women."

Rokha slashed her sword through the air, making it whine. "I doubt they'll want me alive."

Adora left her sword in the scabbard. Another blade would make no difference, but more than hopelessness kept it in its sheath. "They can't have come so far west from the passes in so short a time."

Horses streamed around them, circling until she became dizzy with trying to see them all at once. At last they reined in, thousands of hooves skipping and prancing to a stop as their riders called to each other in ululating cries.

Their leader, mustache swirling in the air of their commotion, sought them, his dark brown eyes serious in a nest of sun-wrought wrinkles. He nudged his horse closer, his short saber by his hand but still sheathed. Next to him, riding one of the long-haired ponies as though born to it, sat a kingdom man, Karele. Adora released the breath she hadn't realized she'd been holding.

The leader reined in, paused just long enough to cast an inquiring glance at his companion, who spoke briefly in the Morgol tongue. He pointed to the three of them by turns. "You are far from the rest of your people." He gave a pointed glance at their swords. "If you carry weapons, then should you not be where they are the most useful?"

Adora knew him. "We are headed for Escarion now, but there are weapons stronger than steel."

Their leader nodded. "Truth."

"How did you come to be here?" Waterson asked.

Ablajin nodded. "My son guided us along the paths of wind, bringing us to you. He tells me we must get to this place—Escarion—tomorrow, else your kingdom will fall."

A fist closed around her heart. Tomorrow? Their horses would never make another ten leagues in that time.

"Can it be done?" Her voice cracked and broke.

Ablajin laughed. "The horses of the steppes do not have the stride of kingdom mounts, but they have been hardened by cold. They can take many more of them. We will make it."

"You have to take us with you." She didn't pose it as a question.

To his credit, he didn't take offense, but his eyebrows rose at the demand. "And what token can you give me of why this must be?"

She could not afford dissembling or intrigue. With trembling hands she jerked the cloth from the sculpted face of her father and held it so Ablajin and Karele could see. "I know who must be soteregia."

Karele's eyes widened, as if someone had given him the answer to a puzzle long attempted. He nodded. "They have to be there, Father, by sunrise."

Ablajin stroked each side of the long, thin mustache that framed his mouth. "By sunrise? The issue is in doubt, especially with the rain. Come, Highness, choose ponies for yourself and your friends. Words are a waste of time."

Martin's messenger left Errol's doorway to be replaced by one from Captain Rale a moment later. The watchman looked familiar, but Errol couldn't place him.

"Do I know you?"

The proverbial stoicism of the watch slipped a notch as the craggy face drew to a lopsided grin. "Not so you'd remember. I was the second man you faced in your challenge to the watch,

Captain Stone. I think you might have seen me for all of a minute before I was unconscious."

Errol nodded, but the memory refused to come into focus. Too much had happened since. "I'm sorry for that."

The man before him shrugged. "No need to be. Taught me a thing or two, it did." He coughed and stepped aside with a beckoning gesture. "I was told to escort you to the captains' meeting."

Duke Escarion's audience hall seemed much like the man himself: practical but with an understated elegance designed to invite candid conversation. A fire burned in a pair of large arched fireplaces on opposite sides of the hall, flanking a table that had been set up in front of the low dais at one end. Most of Illustra's captains, those not guarding the north against the coming of the Morgols, surrounded the table as though a body, not a map, lay upon it.

Liam, his blue eyes somber, nodded to him in greeting. Escarion did as well, though his head dipped a fraction of an inch lower and he closed his eyes as he did so. Perhaps he thought the allegorical body on the table was Errol's.

Cruk opened the meeting. "We're all here. Everybody that's going to show up, at any rate."

Rale pointed to the area on the map that showed the region just south of Duke Escarion's fortress. A section of the river had been rendered in pale blue, distinguishing the shallow depth of the ford from the rest of the river, affected in darker shades. "They'll try to cross here. The malus have always commanded close to the front. From everything we've seen, they believe themselves immune to our attacks."

"They did, at any rate," Cruk growled, "until Captain Liam managed to relieve one of them of some excess head."

Rale bit his lower lip. "It would have been better had he not. They might be more cautious now."

Errol shook his head. "I don't think one death will teach them humility, and our men have taken courage from the stroke."

He caught Liam's gaze across the table. "They call you Demon Slayer now."

"I hope you're right," Rale said. "If not, our challenge becomes difficult."

Cruk snorted. "That's not the half of it, Elar. It becomes impossible. There are more Merakhi arrayed against us than maggots on a thousand dead horses. Even if all of us could fight as well as Captain Liam, we would be hard-pressed to counter their numbers."

Rale answered by using a thin piece of wood to point toward the map. "All we ever had, Captain Cruk, was hope. By the order of the archbenefice, the Judica, and the conclave, we are commanded to attack the enemy here tomorrow. Captains Liam and Stone will lead. They . . . they . . ." Rale exhaled, searching for words.

"We will fight until we have defeated the enemy or restored the barrier," Errol said.

As if his words had somehow strengthened Rale's resolve, his mentor continued. "We will form a wedge, captains and lieutenants of the watch close to the vanguard. Archers will be positioned behind us to clear Merakhi forces from the field until we engage. After that they'll continue to fire at the back ranks of the enemy." He paused to gaze at every man in the room. "They will do this regardless of any flanking tactics the enemy will use."

Errol stared in horror. "You can't be serious. Our forces will be slaughtered. They'll pincer us from the sides."

"We know that, Errol," Cruk said. "I think we talked once or twice before about what needed to be done. If we don't reestablish the barrier, every victory will be short-lived."

Rale smiled at him as if he'd coaxed the expression from unwilling muscles. "If we win quickly, they won't have to time to flank us." He glanced down at the map, then up again. "That's all, gentlemen."

The captains didn't waste time. Each turned and made his way to doors and hallways leading to whatever friends and family or solitude they needed.

Errol followed Liam from the room, pushed by instinct and a desperate need for some measure of hope. "Can I have a moment of your time, Captain Liam?"

The blue eyes twinkled at the use of the title. "You've learned formality in the last year."

A surprised laugh exploded from Errol's lips. "Along with a lot of other things."

"Come. I have food in my quarters. I don't think I'll feel like eating tomorrow morning."

Once there, they sat, but Errol couldn't muster an appetite. He watched Liam dispatch the remains of a roasted chicken and a wedge of cheese with aplomb.

"Can I beat him?" Errol asked.

"Who?" Liam asked. He swallowed and moved the plate to one side.

"Belaaz."

Liam took a handful of breaths to reply. "I don't think so. I'm not bragging when I say I'm far more skilled than when we first came to Erinon, yet Belaaz's inferior came within a hair's breadth of taking me." His gaze softened. "I've done nothing in any spare moment except work the sword. You must let me fight them."

Errol forced his face to neutrality. "Gladly, but there will be more than one. If they come at us in a group, I will do what I can to keep them off of you as long as possible."

Liam shook his head. "We don't know which of us will die."

His lungs needed prompting. "I know. I've always known."

"Has Aurae told you?" Liam asked softly. "Have you succeeded in casting where the entire conclave has failed?"

Honesty forced him to shake his head. "No."

"Then do not esteem yourself more lightly than you should." Liam pulled the plate back in front of him, and Errol departed.

He set his path back toward his own chambers, but a sudden indifference overcame him, and he turned left to make his way to the archbenefice's quarters. Only the occasional servant walked the halls of Escarion at this hour, and loneliness filled him. At the door reluctance stole over him, diminishing his knock to the barest tap. Instead of trying again, he turned away, but the door opened to reveal Martin Arwitten's bluff features.

"Errol." He smiled. "I thought I heard someone." He stepped aside and motioned Errol into his apartments. When Errol entered his sitting room, he saw a chair perched in the glow of candles with a copy of the book of Magis on a reading stand in front of it.

Errol gestured toward the book. "How much have you read?"

Martin gave him a self-deprecating smile. "Not as much as I'd like. I've been skimming mostly, looking for some weakness in our enemy you and Liam might be able to exploit."

Hope kindled in his chest, pounding in time to the racing of his heart. "Have you found anything?"

Martin lifted his shoulders. "Much of the language of the book is difficult to understand, written as it was untold centuries ago, but it is clear the malus are not omniscient, despite what they would have us believe. That is reserved for Deas alone." Martin eyed him, his gaze intense. "Our own history tells us as much. If the malus had known of the covenant Magis made with Deas, they would never have killed him. It may be possible to use their incomplete knowledge of Deas's intent against them."

Errol leaned forward, eager. Perhaps, despite the answer of his lots, there remained some way to achieve victory. "How?"

Martin shook his head. "To answer that question, we would have to know Deas's intent ourselves." He sighed "We're not even sure which of you is supposed to be king and savior."

Martin didn't say it, but within the vaults of Errol's mind, he finished the archbenefice's thought. *And which of you therefore must die.*

He wanted to leave, but fear and curiosity rooted him to the floor. "What does it say about . . . about dying?"

Martin's eyes welled, but his voice remained steady enough.

"Our knowledge is imperfect, lad, but Deas has made us eternal, hard as that may be to understand. Death is only a passage."

Errol tried to grasp the truth within those words as he walked the halls of Escarion, but the fear remained—a bulwark within his mind impervious to hope. Back in his chamber he fashioned lots, as he did every evening to reassure himself Adora still lived. An ache to see her hollowed him out inside. "I hope she marries someday." In the emptiness of his room, no one replied.

40

SOTER REGIA

"MAY DEAS BE WITH YOU." Martin's voice, quiet and subdued, still filled the expanse of the audience chamber where Errol and Liam knelt on opposite sides of the dais.

"And with all who gather in his name." Luis intoned the traditional reply on Martin's left.

Errol's head filled with memories of a distant cabin so many months before. The crude vessels had been replaced with the finest implements the most skilled goldsmiths in the kingdom could create, but the voices were the same.

"Lift up your praises," Martin exhorted.

Fear, not sickness, clenched Errol's stomach now. He hoped he wouldn't throw up or soil himself. A tremble started in his hands.

"Do not be afraid; lift them up to Deas, and Eleison, and Aurae," Luis responded.

"Let us give thanks to the Father Deas," Martin said. His voice sounded different, as though he could hardly force the words through his teeth.

"It is right for us so to do," Luis said, but the clear tenor almost failed to reach Errol's ear.

"It is right and our bounden duty, in all times, in all places, to give thanks unto thee, O Deas, Father, ever-everlasting."

The smell of fear, a sour stench of panic sweat, drifted from the archbenefice and the secondus, mixing in Errol's nose. Bile, metallic and salty, sat on the back of his tongue, and he gagged with the realization this might be Illustra's last sacrament.

"For by Deas, through Eleison, and with the unity of Aurae, the heavens were cast and the world found purchase in the firmament. All glory be unto thee, Deas, Eleison, Aurae, world without end."

A picture of their world, nothing more than a casting stone set in the heavens, intruded on Errol's dismay. World without end. Was Illustra, their entire world, nothing more than a lot for the ultimate reader, too small and insignificant a thing to care about?

"Lift your voices," Martin said, his voice firming. "Eleison our champion has triumphed." The last words rebounded from the walls.

Whatever fear had gripped the archbenefice, he had somehow worked through it.

"The body of Eleison, interposed to keep us safe so long as the world lasts."

Martin slipped a wafer into Errol's waiting hands. The bread, unadorned but made with the finest flour, melted on his tongue.

Luis leaned forward, the light glittering off the wine and polished gold like jeweled blood. "Errol, this is the offering of Eleison, the champion of our world."

He took a sip, the first drink of ale or wine since the tavern in Windridge. The red liquid wet his lips, filled his mouth with warmth and hints of oak before sliding down his throat to his belly, where it spread its heat outward. The room canted, swung, before righting itself.

"Are you well?" Luis asked. His dark Talian face rippled before coming into focus.

Errol forced his head into motion. "Yes."

Luis moved to Liam, who held the chalice to his lips before

rising. His face, framed by his lamp-lit hair like a halo, looked utterly calm and assured.

Errol pushed on the rail, forced his unwilling feet to take his weight, and walked the few steps to meet Liam at the center aisle, where they bowed. The archbenefice and the secondus bowed in return.

Commotion erupted in the hallway and shouts seeped through the closed doors. Errol raised his head, saw Luis looking at him, his eyes staring, showing the whites all around.

Adora urged the shaggy-haired pony over the heavy-timbered bridge that served as Escarion's last defense. At the broad stone archway leading into the fortress, she threw herself from the back of her mount and paused long enough to throw her arms around its neck, burrowing her fingers in the warmth of its shaggy coat.

"Now, Your Highness," Ablajin said in his lilting voice, "you know why we prize our horses so."

She pulled her face away, her cheeks wet with hope and relief. She'd made it in time. "You are right to love them, honored Ablajin. They are magnificent."

"They are not so handsome as some," the chieftain said, "but their worth is there for those who have the eyes to see."

Errol. "Yes." She turned and ran with her bundle into the fortress, Rokha and Waterson at her side.

Doors and lamps flashed by as they ran for the archbenefice's hall. When she saw the entrance, she yelled over and over again, crying his name.

An attendant who managed to recognize her despite the sweat and grime of her travels opened the door. She entered holding the cloth-wrapped sculpture of her father in her hands, as if Martin and the rest had the power to see through the fabric to the truth.

The look on Luis's face, staring back and forth at Errol and Liam as though he'd seen a horror within himself, stopped her, but she hugged the sculpture close and forced her feet into motion once more to stand before Martin.

"Liam is the king," she said as she handed him the package. "He will save us." A corner of her mind accused her, saying what she hadn't: *He will die and rebuild the barrier.*

Luis shook his head as Martin unveiled the bas-relief of Adora's father, his face lit with disbelief.

"Soteregia," Luis said. "Oh, Deas, I am a fool!"

Martin lifted the carving as if he held something holy, the likeness of Jaclin—Liam's likeness—plain to see.

"The herbwomen," Martin breathed. "They guarded him. For twenty years they safeguarded Prince Jaclin's child from the ghostwalkers and the conclave."

Liam stepped forward. He studied the sculpture Martin held in his hands, ran his fingers across the features beginning with the nose, as if familiarizing himself with some forgotten memory, as if comparing each to his own.

He leaned over her then, bending down to brush his lips against her brow. "Thank you, *sister*, for giving me my birthright."

Inside, her conscience railed at her for sending her brother to fight the malus.

Liam clasped Errol by the arm. "This is my battle, Errol. I was born for this." His eyes included Adora in his blessing. "Stay here in Escarion. You've done enough."

Luis's anguished wail cut across Adora's jubilation.

"No, oh, Deas, no. *They* are soteregia."

Martin turned at the sound of Luis's cry.

The secondus pointed, his arm shaking, at the two men, one dark and one fair, at the foot of the altar. Errol and Liam. He struck himself with his free hand, beating his fist against his skull as imprecations coursed from him. "Fool. Stupid, stupid, fool. Of course they both came out of the drawing. I asked the wrong question."

Adora stood before him, basking in her revelation, her eyes glowing as she looked upon Errol. Liam held the sculpture of his father's face. Already he appeared taller, as if the revelation had uncovered the identity anyone could have seen if only they had looked.

But Errol looked at Luis with comprehension beginning to dawn in his eyes. Martin's chest hurt. Oh, Deas, they could not afford the chances of intuition now. "Luis," he commanded. "Be plain."

The reader's face looked as if it would crumple any moment. "Don't you see? Soteregia means savior and king. Magis was both. We assumed Deas would send a Magis to us again." He stumbled as he took a step toward Errol and Liam. "But they're different this time. Errol is *soter*. Liam is *regia*."

Adora nodded. "Errol has saved the kingdom twice over. Liam is Illustra's king, and her king will save her now."

One look at Luis told Martin that Adora was wrong. "My friend, you know we cannot leave this to chance. We must cast."

Yet even as he said it, a voice in his mind, as if the wind spoke to him, told him a draw of kings was unnecessary.

Adora shook her head. "To what end? You know Liam is to be king. He's the greatest fighter Illustra's ever seen. Who else can defeat the malus?"

Martin stepped from the dais, bringing his eyes on a level with hers. By the three, why did he have to be the one to do this? Someone else needed to be archbenefice, someone who could do what needed doing regardless of the cost.

He bowed low. "Your Highness, we do not *know* what to do. We must ask the conclave."

Her head jerked back and forth with denials.

Errol stepped beside her, took her hands in his. "There's no need to call the conclave, Your Excellency. Luis is here, and so am I. I'm sure he has wood with him, and I have my carving knife."

Martin wanted to weep at the resignation in Errol's face. He knew. By the gift of the three, he knew. The cast would be a mere formality. He pulled his knife from somewhere within his cloak and approached Luis, the secondus refusing to meet his gaze.

Errol put a hand on his shoulder. "It will be quicker if both of us cast at the same time, but I need blanks."

The wood, the familiar pine he'd worked so often, rested against the ridges of his skin. He savored the touch of it, the feel of the open grain against the ridges of his fingertips, the smell of the resin embedded within the fibers.

"What question would you have me cast, Omne?" Luis asked him.

Errol accepted the secondus's deference with a nod, then considered and rejected half a dozen queries, each which seemed inconclusive, before settling on one. "Which one of us, Liam or I, should go to battle?"

Luis smiled his approval. "Clever. By assuming it should be only one of you, you've saved us the effort of a second cast."

"Please explain, Secondus," Liam said.

Luis turned. "If Errol's assumption is incorrect and both of you should go, the outcome of the cast will be gibberish. He'll pull both lots in equal amounts. But if his assumption is correct, then I'll cast a preponderance of one lot or the other. In effect, we're answering two questions with a single cast." Errol felt Luis's gaze upon him. "Master Quinn would have been proud."

The secondus pulled a pair of blocks from within his ceremonial blue robe. "And what question will you cast, Omne?"

Fear threatened to burst from the bonds of Errol's control, and he stifled it, but tremors, like the onset of ague, shook his hands, defying his efforts. As the question came to him, he ignored the palsied spasms of his fingers to give Luis the best smile he could summon. "I will keep my cast simple. It's difficult to concentrate just now."

Adora's eyes begged him to find the answer that would let him live. His fingers slipped, and the knife marred the edge, forcing him to turn the block to remove the imperfection he'd put upon it. He bent over the cube, striving to lose himself in the question and the answer.

Over and over in his mind he repeated the answer *Yes* in time with his laboring heartbeat. Even before a rounded piece of wood lay within his palm, he knew it to be true. He put the lot aside. Only he could see the word upon it, but even had the kingdom possessed another omne, they would still be unable to decipher the question he'd locked within his heart.

For a moment temptation gripped him. Whatever else he might be, he was his own man. The power to choose was as much his birthright as it was anyone's. Deas might want him for this, but not even the three could force him to the path if he refused.

A breath of laughter ghosted from him. Powerless. Even Deas was powerless in this. He could not force Errol to battle. The creator of the universe required men to be the instrument of his will. What would happen if he refused to go? The ludicrousness of it struck him. He laughed again, felt the bitterness as the burst of air scraped his throat. If he said no, he would die, and everyone else with him—or worse, the malus would take them as slaves.

He bent to his task, pointless as it seemed. As he carved, *No* echoed repeatedly in his thoughts, but even as he thought it, he knew this lot would not be chosen. When the second sphere lay in his hand, smooth and complete, he looked up to see Luis waiting for him.

The secondus shot Adora the briefest of glances. "I don't think I should be the one to draw this question," he murmured.

Errol understood. He accepted the drawing bag Luis offered and held it open for the secondus, who dropped his lots in. With a trio of brisk shakes he mixed them, then drew, catching Luis's look of surprise. "We should probably do this as quickly as possible."

His name.

He put the lot back in the bag without speaking.

His name again.

Ten times in a row he drew his own name. He'd never seen pine behave with such consistency.

He returned the lots to Luis, then dropped his own lots in before fear could unman him. Without explanation or pause he drew, his motions stiff as a marionette's. When the first lot gave him the expected answer, he almost wept, but he shoved the emotion aside and continued. After the tenth draw yielded the same answer, he left the lots in the bag and returned it to Luis. "I don't think there's supposed to be any doubt."

Luis nodded, staring at his own lots as if they'd become strange to him. "They might as well have been durastone."

Errol faced the archbenefice. It would be easier if he didn't have to look at her. He needed to pretend that he could somehow put aside his feelings and do this thing. Perhaps if he pretended hard enough, he could. "I have to go."

"Liam has to stay," Luis said.

Martin tried to ignore the broken sobs that tore themselves loose from Adora's throat. Liam filled his vision.

"I have to fight. This is what I was made for."

"Do you?" Martin asked. "Are you the one who must die?" He threw his questions at Liam as if they were physical weapons he could use. "Didn't the herbwomen raise you to be solis? What does Aurae say?"

He overtopped Martin by half a hand, his shoulders stretching the fabric of his shirt, his blue eyes showing the struggle within his mind. After a moment, Liam exhaled. "Not yet."

Martin nodded. "Come, Liam, we must convene the Judica and the conclave. Illustra has been without a king for too long."

They turned together, but everyone else in the room stood watching the spot where Adora had buried herself in Errol's arms, her limbs slack, deprived of strength. Errol held her as though the princess had become as brittle as glass. Soft cries came from her, muffled where she'd buried her face into his shoulder.

Rokha and Waterson looked on, their cheeks wet, but Luis gaped, stricken, as if he'd been forced to kill Errol himself.

One by one, each of them turned away as the moment stretched and Adora and Errol showed no signs of parting. Waterson left first, followed by Liam, then Rokha. Martin stepped to the entrance, determined to bear witness, unwilling to spare himself. He stood at the doorway, his heart laboring.

His resolve failed him at last, and he turned his back. "Oh, Deas, how can you bear it?"

41

SAVIOR AND KING

THE CAPTAINS WAITED for him across the draw-bridge, questions written in the surprised pain of their expressions and darting glances. Storm clouds seethed overhead, dimming the light until the midmorning resembled dusk. Errol forced his unwilling legs to obey him and swung into Midnight's saddle, the horse calm beneath him while the other mounts shied, hooves shifting in response to their mood. "Captain Liam . . ." He caught himself. "His Majesty, Liam, won't be coming with us."

He raised a hand, asking for quiet, trying to keep the waver from his voice. "All your questions will be answered if we live." He swallowed, but the lump in his throat refused to move. "You must get me to Belaaz," he told the captains. "He will be lead-ing them."

Errol hoped they would simply accept his command. Despite the answer from the lots, he didn't know what would happen or what he needed to do.

Cruk nodded. "That sounds about right." He directed the captains into a wedge around Errol with Merodach in the front and Cruk and Rale on the left and right. Indurain and Merkx, along with the rest, settled in behind.

They rode across the drawbridge, the rest of the watch following close behind. Over five hundred of the black rode with Errol down into the meadow, where rank upon rank of bowmen, pikemen, and swordsmen waited.

"I've never seen the like," Errol said. The enormity of it stunned him. How many tens of thousands of men were there?

Cruk grunted. "It always looks nice before the fighting starts. After that, it's just a mess of men and weapons."

They crested the small rise that led down to the river. Approaching it in the dusky light that filtered through the storm clouds overhead, Errol could see a mass of men and spawn stretching into the distance, dwarfing their forces.

Errol fought to keep his voice calm. "How are we going to find Belaaz and the rest of the malus?"

Rale pointed to a forward section of the seething mass. Even at that distance, Errol could see a group of riders surrounded by a sparser grouping of men and spawn.

"They will be there."

"So few?"

"No. There are more, but it takes time for a malus to corrupt its host. Those are what remain of the nine from the ilhotep's council."

Errol's heart labored through the fear that squeezed it like a vise. Thousands of men and spawn stood in their way. If the Merakhi came across the ford, their line would thin and stretch for miles. "We'll never be able to get to them on the far side of the river. Our forces will be too stretched out."

Merodach, Rale, and Cruk all gave him a curt nod. "That's right. We'll have to let them cross the river," Rale said.

Cruk grunted. "Lousy tactics. That's the kind of thing you're supposed to avoid."

"We're not trying to win the war," Rale said. "Just a portion of it."

The need for haste pounded through Errol's veins. "What are they waiting for?"

A long rumble of distant thunder rolled across the mountains, and flashes of lightning within the clouds turned patches of sky a sickly green over the dark umber of the hills.

Merodach turned to him, his eyes flat, emotionless, the way Errol had seen them before, when he was about to kill. "They wait for a sign, Captain Stone. Despite their advantages, all battles are unsure and the outcome less than certain."

Errol stared at the throng across the river that made his own forces appear small. "Even the malus?"

Merodach nodded, his face grim but unafraid. "In spite of their bluster, they are acquainted with defeat."

Errol nodded. Who wasn't? "Is everyone in position?"

Rale and Cruk nodded.

Errol drew a shuddering breath. "Tell the trumpets to sound the charge, but have the men stop short of the water. Let us see if we can lure their vanguard into battle."

Runners carried word to the companies of men. A moment later a peal of thunder preceded the brassy-throated fanfare that threw their defiance into the enemy's teeth. Errol stood in the stirrups with his hand raised, waiting until the small movements of ten thousand upon ten thousand men stilled, looking at him.

He thrust his arm forward.

In the end, Martin submitted to the rules of the church. The king would be crowned by a vote of the Judica after confirmation by the conclave. Liam walked before Martin toward the meeting, frustration evident in the corded muscles of his forearms and the clench of his fists. Martin hurried to keep pace with the presumptive king. There would be no fanfares, no stately walks on carpets of crimson and purple. Liam would be crowned in haste.

Word raced ahead of them like fire through driest tinder, and priests and benefices in crimson came running toward them like embodied flames. "Breun," Martin called. The boy appeared at his side as if by magic. Martin pulled a thick, heavy key from his pocket, placed it in the boy's hand. "Go to my quarters. There's a heavy chest at the foot of my bed. Inside you'll find a wooden box covered with gold inlay. Bring it to me please. I will be in the Judica's hall." The boy nodded with the wide-eyed earnestness of the young and darted away, his skinny legs flying.

Martin resumed the task of trying to keep up with Liam. Another page, a girl somewhat less than twenty, shot past him. He reached out and snagged her arm as she raced by. They spun around each other for a moment, off-balance and trying to avoid a fall onto the heavy stone floor. Her eyes flashed at Martin's presumption before she caught sight of the clothes of his office. One foot went behind the other as she prepared to curtsy.

Martin held her upright. "Thank you, lass, but there's no time for courtliness just now. What's your name?"

Lips parted beneath earnest brown eyes. "Emma."

A memory tugged at Martin. There were few females on the staff of Escarion's castle who weren't related to its master. "You're the duke's daughter, the one he calls Rose."

She nodded. "Yes, Your Excellency. He gave me the nickname when I was just a little girl because he said I was a fair blossom and . . ."

Martin placed two fingers over the girl's mouth, cutting off the rapid torrent of words. "Emma, I need you to gather all the members of the conclave to the hall of the Judica. Use every page in the castle if need be, but I want every reader there with the tools of their craft before the sun moves."

She nodded and spun, her thick brown hair flying, running toward the conclave's meeting room.

Martin took a deep breath and resumed his trek. Liam was lost to sight, but already portly middle-aged men in crimson and blue came running from every direction in response to the small army of pages who ran through Escarion's keep, yelling their summons.

Martin entered the hall of the Judica unnoticed as benefices scrambled for seats. Readers crowded to one side, holding knives and blocks at the ready, and everywhere voices assaulted him with a thousand variations of the same question: Who would be king?

Luis and Willem entered through a side door and came forward, supporting Enoch Sten's weight between them. Martin shifted in surprise. The primus walked with his face wreathed in the pinched lines peculiar to men in thought.

"Fools," the primus said. "Fools to disobey the first stricture of casting. We never questioned ourselves, never suspected the savior and king might be two different people." He raised his head to stare Martin in the face. "We dare not make the same mistake again."

Tremors of cold spilled down Martin's back like a premonition. Too much could go wrong. "Primus, we cannot do more than what we have. The lots have been cast and confirmed: Errol must fight for us, and Liam must be crowned. The rest is in the hands of Deas."

Sten nodded, his patient forbearance rasping against Martin's nerves like sanding cloth against his skin. His old man's eyes sharpened. "But what will secure our survival; what will kill the malus and raise the barrier—Errol's death or Liam's coronation?"

Spots swam in Martin's vision as shock coursed through him. He swayed on his feet. "No, did we send him to die for nothing?"

Adora threaded her way through the press of people hurrying the other way, desperate to see if hope had been granted at the last minute. People brushed against her without malice or apology or recognition, as if she'd already passed from their knowledge. Their passage lifted tendrils of hair from her face, left them fluttering aimlessly behind her. The crush thinned as she passed through the gates and gazed down the long slope toward the river.

Somewhere behind her Rokha followed, waiting, possibly, for the moment her consolation would be required. A ring of people—those who hadn't heard of Liam's elevation or couldn't tear themselves from the sight of battle—stood watching with her.

Errol gripped his staff with one hand and the reins with the other and tried to settle into Midnight's trot. On a large knoll overlooking the field, ranks of archers waited, equipped with longbows or crossbows.

Rale and Cruk rode beside him, the two men attempting to look everywhere at once. Errol's throat tightened as the Merakhi forces surged across the river to meet them. Ferrals and other misshapen spawn raced toward their forces, howling for blood.

The Merakhi hit the pikes with the deafening impact of a thousand collisions, screams of men and animals mixing with the clang of weapons as thunder rolled in the distance. Errol looked toward the sky. Crows flew across the space, looking for refuge in the few trees on the rolling hills.

"Where are the arrows?" Errol yelled across the few feet separating him from Rale. He could hear the grind and groan of steel-headed pikes driving through enemy chain mail, but the snap of wood, the sharp retort of shafts being broken, came to him as well. They needed those archers.

Rale leaned across his saddle, pointing left and behind. "We must lure the malus closer to us. The bowmen have been ordered to shoot behind them to force the enemy forward. Once the malus are across the river, they'll change targets."

Rale's strategy left Errol gaping. "We'll lose most of the pikes if we don't bring the archers to bear." Stress cracked his voice until he screeched.

Rale's face was somber. "We know, but there's no other way."

The line of pikes bowed under the onslaught of ferrals, forcing them back. Errol watched in horror as thick-limbed spawn surged against the line, their dense hides turning the points aside and trampling the soldiers in the van. The point of the Illustra's wedge stood perilously close to collapse.

He pointed, trying to pitch his voice above the riot of battle. "We're losing them."

Rale nodded. "A moment more."

Errol swallowed, forcing panic back down his throat. In an instant the spawn would break a gap through the pikes and be among the swords. Blades would be useless against them.

With a sharp whistle, Rale signaled a pair of lieutenants who surged through the riot of battle toward the flanks. A moment later, the pikes there swung in toward the middle. The bulge in their line steadied, and held.

A steel-tipped lance found the eye of one of the striped spawn. A howl, eerily human in sound, erupted from the mouth of the beast, and it reared, the pike still lodged in its skull.

Soldiers from Illustra and Merakh threw themselves back from the creature's death throes, pushing against their own lines in their efforts to escape. The spawn rolled, crushing Merakhi soldiers beneath it. Men and ferrals surged into the empty space.

"There." Cruk pointed. A group of Merakhi, huge and distorted, forded their way across the river on draft horses that looked like ponies beneath them. In their center rode Belaaz, the oversized shirra in his grip appearing as a child's plaything. Behind them, stretching across the river and disappearing into the distance, came an endless tide.

"Now," Rale ordered the lieutenant beside him, who hoisted a patch of red cloth on a long pole.

From the rise on Errol's left, hundreds of bowmen rose from the long grass. A swarm of arrows ascended toward the boiling clouds of the sky, then plunged to earth in a black ribbon that raked death upon the Merakhi still crossing the river. From behind Errol came another hail of arrows that poured into the same spot. The river churned with the dying struggles of thousands of men.

A tug on Errol's sleeve broke his horrified fascination with the tableau.

Rale bit his lips, nodded toward the malus. "This is our chance, my lord. Today the men of the watch will redeem themselves."

Errol tightened his grip on the metal staff Martin had brought from the ancient city of the malus. He hoped Deas would help him to be brave. He tried to speak and failed, nodding his assent instead.

Lightning arced across the sky as Errol urged Midnight into a canter. The black-garbed watchmen moved with him in a tight wedge.

42

THE COMING OF THE KING

MARTIN STARED AT THE PRIMUS, his mind struggling to think past his abhorrence of Enoch Sten's observation. "What question are we supposed to ask?"

The primus shook his head. Martin turned to Luis and Willem, found himself clutching their robes in shaking hands though he couldn't recall moving to close the space between them. "You've trained your whole lives for this! What is the question?"

Luis drew a breath. Beads of sweat appeared on his head. "We know Errol is supposed to be in battle and Liam is supposed to be here. We only require the next query."

"Can you cast for that?" Martin asked.

The three men shook their heads at him. "Too complicated," Sten said.

"And too time consuming," Willem echoed.

Luis nodded. "We must choose the best question we are able and hope."

Martin stared at his friend as if he'd become unrecognizable. "We stand on the edge of destruction and you're telling me we must guess?"

"No, Your Excellency." Luis bowed. "You must choose."

Martin's lips had already closed from their openmouthed indignation to frame the question "Me?" when he caught himself.

"You are the archbenefice and one of the solis," Luis continued. "If you cannot discern the question, it cannot be determined."

Martin stilled. Could it be possible? Until now, he'd waited for those times when he felt the presence of Aurae, waiting for what he'd once considered unknowable to stir the air and tell him the will of Deas. Could he inquire? Who was he to demand an answer from Deas?

But there was more to his hesitation. Honesty compelled him to admit as much. He didn't want to inquire of Deas or listen for Aurae. Lots didn't require the personal interaction with something incomprehensible, something whose vastness frightened him. And casting was resolute, the answer absolute, honed to surety by hundreds of years of research by the conclave.

So long as they knew which question to ask.

Benefices and readers filled the hall, no longer milling about, but watching. With a flush of embarrassment, he realized many of them had witnessed their exchange. Liam stood in front of the dais, his hand upon his sword, as if he expected to draw it any moment.

Luis and Willem and Sten waited.

Emma reappeared at his side, sliding through the door at a run, her thick brown hair streaming behind her. She skidded to a stop three feet from him, incorporating a bow into the motion. "That's all of them, Your Excellency. They're all here."

The girl's interruption served to focus his thoughts. Perhaps it couldn't be done, but he would not leave it unattempted. In the end, the world was Deas's, to save or sacrifice as he chose. He mounted the dais and sat in the chair reserved for the archbenefice, his chair, and inquired of the three.

The air in the room stilled.

He looked upon Liam and felt a stir on the back of his neck as if the castle had sighed. At the least, Illustra needed a king and there were formalities to be observed. Yes, he knew what must be done next. "Honored benefices and readers, I will be brief. Battle rages and we must make haste. Illustra needs a king. In the person of Captain Liam of the watch, I believe we have one, but he must be confirmed. I request the conclave to cast the question confirming him. Is Liam to be king?"

He turned to address the Judica. The benefices had found their chairs at last. "Members of the Judica, please stand if you so agree."

Dozens of red-robed men rose from their seats. The conclave didn't wait for the order—two hundred readers began their cast.

Their wedge surged forward as the pikes melted into the flanks. Out of the corner of his eye, Errol saw Merakhi soldiers split left and right to attack them from the sides. His forces, concentrating on their forward attack, took grievous losses. The unending rain of arrows exacted horrendous damage on the enemy crossing the river, turning the water a dark russet colored by mud and the blood of all who fell there. Yet scores upon scores of Merakhi soldiers and spawn made their way to Escarion's side of the river to join the attack.

Only a hundred paces separated Errol from Belaaz, but the sheer number of soldiers separating them seemed insurmountable. As quickly as a soldier from either side died, they were replaced by two or three more. The wedge slowed, its pace crawling. Time crept as the two sides sought advantage.

Without warning, the Merakhi on Illustra's left flank peeled off to attack the archers, rushing the knoll. Possessed Merakhi drove the soldiers before them in a headlong charge toward the bowmen. Errol watched, the pounding of his heart rocking him back and forth in the saddle, as if the ground moved beneath him.

The bowmen refused to be deterred from their assigned targets. He could see them, each man equipped with a longbow and uncountable arrows placed point down in the turf before them, drawing and shooting without slowing, seconds from being butchered.

A long peal of thunder filled the air.

Despair tore at Errol's throat. "No."

Rale caught his look, darted a glance toward the archers, and shook his head. "If they change targets, lad, we'll be washed under. If we don't reach the malus soon, we won't reach them at all."

Errol looked ahead. Their wedge had managed to shrug off the attacks on the flanks so far, but they would never make it to the center of the Merakhi position before the archers were swarmed under.

Rale reached across his horse to grip his shoulder. "Watch, lad, and you'll see why Cruk is accounted the best tactician in the kingdom."

A stream of horses, hardly more than ponies, snaked out from behind the rise to fall upon the Merakhi foot soldiers. Sabers rose and fell as Morgols ripped through their ranks. The Merakhi attack ceased to exist. Men tried to flee to the safety of the enemy lines only to be ridden down from behind. The mounted Merakhi wheeled and retreated.

Arrows continued to fill the sky.

Errol's forces pushed forward on the right, drawing within two dozen paces of the core of the enemy—Belaaz and his council.

Adora stood, watching in disbelief. Impossible. No force so greatly outnumbered could hope to win, yet from her viewpoint, she could see Illustra's forces exacting a staggering toll on the enemy. Hope, wild and unexpected, raged like a fire within her chest, and she screamed until her face heated and her throat rasped.

She grabbed Rokha by the arm, pointing. "They advance. The malus committed themselves too early."

Rokha nodded, her full lips pursed, but she refrained from adding her voice to Adora's. Her shoulder, where Adora's hand gripped it, tensed as she watched the battle. Adora's heart switched rhythm. Rokha saw something she did not.

"There." Rokha pointed. "They've lost over half the pikes, and they've yet to meet the worst of the Merakhi forces." Adora followed the gesture, looking past the large flatbed carts shuttling back and forth, carrying supplies and wounded to and from the battle.

Panic made her voice harsh. "What do you mean? They're over halfway there."

Rokha shook her head. "There are more malus-possessed than just the council. I can feel them, swarming like hornets around Belaaz, waiting. Look how the circle of soldiers around the nine move and flow. Those aren't men. They're not concerned about Errol's charge because they filled the ranks next to Belaaz with their own kind."

Adora peered into the depth of the battle, searching the faces of those surrounding the council. Laughter. They didn't wear the dour expressions of men in battle. Pain and death surrounded them on every side, and they greeted it with grotesque expressions of elation.

Adora struggled to clear the sudden spots in her vision.

Pages shuttled back and forth, bringing Martin news from the battle that twisted his guts with apprehension. Errol and the watch approached the center of the Merakhi vanguard where the malus waited.

In Escarion's hall, a sea of blue-robed arms thrust skyward, the record of each reader who'd completed his cast in favor of Liam's crowning. The remainder would finish in the space of heartbeats.

But then what? *What is the next question, Deas?*

Liam paced the floor like a caged animal, a picture of restrained violence. Martin paused. *"Made for this,"* Liam had said. Illustra's next king had been trained by the solis.

A knot of tension, one of many, eased in his gut. He knew

the question. Martin beckoned the primus, Luis, and Willem forward. They'd been among the first to finish their cast. "I want to know if Liam is supposed to go to battle once he's crowned."

Primus Sten nodded approval. "The next right question."

Luis demurred. "Perhaps." His gaze lost focus. "From the beginning, Martin, we've been behind the course of events. Liam is supposed to be king, but exactly when are we supposed to crown him?"

His breath left him. "My friend, am I hearing you? If we crown him quickly enough, his coronation may restore the barrier and save Errol."

Luis nodded, but lines of sorrow etched the corners of his eyes and mouth. "It's a possibility."

Grief, sharp and cold, pierced Martin as Sten and Willem signaled their agreement. "But that question—when to crown Liam—is too involved to answer quickly. Yes?" He prayed they would disagree with him as he stood panting with desperation, waiting for their answer.

In the end, they didn't have to. Emma came running, breathing hard from her trips back and forth from their meeting hall to the outside. "Your Excellency—" she gasped a pair of breaths—"the captains are almost to the giants."

Martin surveyed the hall filled with blue-robed readers standing against the backdrop of red-robed benefices, his to command. The air in the room felt thin. The conclave had failed. No cast could be done in time. He would have to crown Liam and hope.

He lifted his arms for quiet. "Members of the Judica, you have witnessed the cast of the conclave in its unanimity. Three-fourths of sitting benefices must confirm him as king. Please rise if you consent to Liam's kingship and authority." He swallowed. "You are adjured by Deas, Eleison, and Aurae."

As one, the entire Judica rose, a surge of red that swelled upward. Martin met Liam's eyes and gestured toward the chair he had held moments before. Rodran's throne had been left in Erinon, but protocol only required the crown, not the seat.

He beckoned Breun forward with the burnished wooden box that held Rodran's crown, a simple affair, passed down from Magnus. Martin held the thick gold circle with three points in his hand, noting the nicks and scratches in the metal, a diadem of strife, a war crown.

Haste impelled him up the steps of the dais to stand next to Liam where he sat in the high-backed chair, his shoulders and head erect, waiting, the hand still on the sword hilt. Martin lowered the crown toward the blond mane of hair.

"By the manifest will of Deas, Eleison, and Aurae, confirmed by their servants, benefices of the Judica, and readers of the conclave, I, Archbenefice Martin Arwitten of the kingdom of Illustra, crown you, Liam the first, rightful king."

He moved to lower the crown onto Liam's head.

And stopped.

43

AVENGED

Swords!" Cruk's scream cut across the din of battle, and five hundred soldiers in black drew weapons with a long hiss of steel. The heavy concentration of pikes had vanished, leaving holes in the attack. Ablajin's men thundered past on the flanks but could do little against the concentrated fire of the Merakhi short bows.

But they were within reach of Belaaz.

A pair of watchmen engaged one of the soldiers of the enemy's cordon. The Merakhi laughed as they advanced, his eyes dancing, unfocused.

No. "Wait," Errol cried. "That's a . . ."

The rest of his sentence faltered as the Merakhi parried their strokes before cutting the horses at the legs. Before either of the watchmen could recover, the Merakhi was upon them. Errol looked on in horror at the soldiers surrounding Belaaz and the rest of the nine. Each wore the savage look of glee and the vibrating eyes of the malus-possessed.

"They're all malus."

Cruk nodded, but instead of answering, he shouted another

order to the lieutenant at his side, who hoisted a flag of yellow. The swords and pikes wheeled to hold the left and right flanks, pinning the enemy lines in place. It wouldn't last long. Already the ranks of Illustra thinned as men went down beneath greater numbers.

Cruk stood in his saddle. "Watch, dismount! Capture and hold!"

Rale and all the watch slipped from their saddles, pushing their horses to the rear. Errol copied the motion without understanding, moving forward with his staff. Rale caught his arm, forced him behind. "Wait for your chance, Errol. It may not last long, but we have the numbers to get you to Belaaz. After that"—his shoulders curled—"you'll need to trust in Deas."

He shook his head in incomprehension. Two of the watch had been taken as if they were the weakest swordsmen in the kingdom. How could they hope to get him to Belaaz?

The wedge of black split as pairs of watchmen moved forward to engage each of the Merakhi. Errol watched as the first pair stepped forward. Faster than thought, the Merakhi sent a sword stroke toward the soldier on the left.

Instead of parrying, he lifted his arm to take the blow, the stroke biting deep into the mail with a crunch of metal and bone. The watchman screamed but clamped his arm over the sword. The Merakhi tried to withdraw, but in that moment the other watchman took the Merakhi's head. A pair of bodies slumped to the ground. Another soldier in black rushed forward to take the place of the one who had fallen.

All around, the same scene repeated itself as over and over again watchmen accepted killing strokes in exchange for a chance to strike back.

"This is your plan?" Errol cried.

Rale and Cruk, their faces hard and unyielding, nodded.

"Magis is avenged."

The Merakhi cordon evaporated. No longer laughing, the

malus-filled soldiers sought to escape the pairs of watchmen who pursued them, always sacrificing one of their own in exchange. And then there was only the council.

A hush settled into Adora's chest, not peace, but acceptance, as she watched the desperate strategy unfold. The watchmen, those few that remained, moved to attack Belaaz and his monstrous council. She wanted to ask why, but she knew the answer already. Illustra's mistakes required blood and sacrifice to correct. Somewhere in the mass of people stood the one she loved, but distance obscured faces, and she couldn't find him.

Rokha moved to stand at her side. When Adora turned and met her gaze, Rokha stared back, her eyes flashing as she drew and brandished her sword. "My love fights down there as well. Do you want to live without him?"

Adora's lips moved in response, as though the answer resided in the beat of her heart, the rise and fall of her chest, the thrum of blood through her veins, instead of in her mind. "No."

Rokha's eyes flared with sudden heat, and she bared her teeth in a savage smile.

Drawing her sword, Adora followed Rokha down the hill, her strides steady. Chaos reached for her as she passed through the rearmost portion of Illustra's lines. Men and horses and carts dashed everywhere, testimony of their struggle to keep from being surrounded. Next to her Rokha stiffened, her eyes wide with shock, and she clutched at Adora's arm.

"They're behind us!"

Fifty paces away, shapes boiled out of the back of one of the wagons, figures too tall to be men. They raced away from her toward the castle, except one.

Sevra.

The call from Duke Weir's misshapen daughter ravaged her hearing, tearing through her courage like a dagger ripping cloth. "Well met, strumpet." The giant drew her long blade and advanced.

Martin's hands moved to lower the heavy gold circlet onto Liam's head, but reticence filled him. Almost he gave the order for a final cast, for some question that could tell him what to do. Liam waited before him, still, like the sky before lightning, like the air before thunder.

"Archbenefice," one of the benefices called, "why do you wait?"

Why did he? He faced four hundred men. "Perhaps I am weak or old, but I desire a sign. The cast of stones failed us because we did not know the question to ask. Do we ever? If Aurae is knowable, how do we begin knowing Him?"

He turned to regard Liam, who faced him now. "I hold this crown, and some misgiving tells me that the time is not yet. Something restrains me. Is this Aurae?" He shifted, uncomfortable in robes that suddenly felt too tight. No one answered. Martin waited.

A distant clash of steel sounded.

Lightning arced across the sky and the crack of scorched air drowned the sounds of battle. Merodach, Cruk, and Rale stepped forward, leaving him. Five of the council were down, their bodies stretched upon the grass and rock, their faces hideous and surprised in death. A dozen of the watch were all that remained. To the right and left, the ranks of their soldiers thinned, their cries becoming frantic as spawn and Merakhi struggled to break through.

With each death of the malus-possessed, Belaaz shuddered and laughed. Distortions grew on his face and skin. The Merakhi, grown monstrous under the influence of uncounted malus within him, screamed orders in his strange tongue, directing his forces away from Errol. Spawn scented the air and withdrew, leaving him to face the giant alone.

Belaaz saw him and laughed with the sound of a dozen voices. "You think to try me, little one?" He peered down at Errol from his height, his face twisted with derision, but he made no move to attack. Instead he planted his shirra point down into the ground and rested one arm upon it. As one, the remaining malus raised their arms, and the wind stilled.

Errol's shock robbed him of breath.

"Do you think I've come to kill you?" Belaaz laughed, lifting his head to the sky. "How like him, to take someone defenseless and demand his blood." His gaze lanced through Errol, his eyes boring through his pretense of bravery, laying him bare. "I have not come to kill you, Errol, but to offer you life."

He clenched his fists around the staff, unwilling to credit the malus's promise. He gestured at the misshapen face, the knots moving like living things beneath the skin. "Sarin Valon already made the same offer. Do you think I would ever consent to live as a prisoner in my own skin, forced to watch while your corruption twisted my body from the inside?"

Belaaz's mirth washed over him. "This? You misunderstand, little one. Flesh serves us. We have made ourselves hideous to hinder you in battle." He waved his hand. "If you do not wish to appear so, do not." A shimmer washed over Belaaz, cleansing the malus of his disfigurement, and when it faded, Errol found himself looking upon a figure such as he'd never seen before, had never imagined.

The Merakhi's beauty stunned him, the flawless perfection of his skin and limbs triumphed only by the stunning glow of his visage. He had thought Adora beautiful beyond compare, but human beauty only hinted at what stood before him.

Sevra was still thirty paces distant when Rokha pointed toward a cluster of wounded soldiers limping their way up the hill. "We could run."

Rage at the colossal injustice and her own helplessness poured through Adora. Her skin burned at the sight of Sevra, and the outraged beat of her heart roared in her ears. "No! I will not show my back to her again."

Rokha laughed, throwing her head back to crow at the sky. "Well spoken, sister."

They drew, spreading to come at the malus from opposite sides. Adora looked for hope in her friend's face but found only resolve. They were going to die. Sevra closed the distance and darted toward Rokha. Adora stood rooted to the ground in surprise before forcing her legs into motion. Stupid fool. Of course the malus would attack Ru's daughter first. Adora was no real threat.

Rokha fell back beneath vicious sweeps of Sevra's blade, throwing frantic parries at the onslaught. Adora leapt, swinging for Sevra's unprotected back.

Sevra pivoted to knock her attack aside. Adora rolled across the wet grass, fighting to keep a grip on her sword. She gained her feet a few paces from Rokha to face the twisted form of Weir's daughter again.

The two of them parted once more, staying closer this time, but Sevra only watched them. Though every line of Weir's daughter strained, and froth gathered at her lips, Adora's tormentor made no move to attack.

Belaaz's voice came to Errol, no longer harsh or belittling, but warm, encouraging, the voice of a friend of long acquaintance. "What kind of god demands blood, Errol? Give up this hopeless fight. There is no need to die, not for you or your friends." With a casual gesture, Belaaz signaled his forces, who promptly withdrew a dozen paces and stilled. Illustra's forces looked upon the Merakhi army as if suspicious of sorcery, holding their ground, their lungs heaving in the silence.

The panting of men and beasts filled the silence of Belaaz's impromptu truce. "Oh, Errol, there is so much I can give you."

The malus stepped forward, pushed Errol's staff aside, and placed a hand on Errol's shoulder. A chill went through him. "Are you hurt?" Belaaz asked. "Your pains can be washed away as easily as the dust of the road."

Errol gasped as if he'd plunged into the iciest pool in the Sprata. Each of the nagging pains and injuries he'd collected in the last year left him. The scar in his side no longer burned. He rolled his shoulders in shock, then reached behind with one hand to feel for the scars that laced his back. "They're all gone."

Belaaz nodded, his eyes glinting. "Didn't I say flesh serves us? There is no suffering among the exalted ones, Errol. It's only your god who requires it."

Errol turned, his muscles responding in a way they had not since he'd first come to himself on Rale's farm, but thousands of dead lay before him on the fields of Escarion, images of death and suffering wrought by Belaaz, giving the lie to his words.

The malus must have sensed his mood, though Errol tried to keep revulsion from showing on his face. "If healing is not enough for you, then content yourself with other gifts I have to offer. The crown could be yours." Encouragement filled Belaaz's face. "No longer would you be subservient to the whims of churchmen who would use you for their own ends."

Almost, the offer tempted him, reviving bitterness he'd harbored at being a tool the church used in its struggle. Could he deny they had used him? No, but neither could he deny the reasons behind their desperation. Caught in their circumstances, the benefices had grasped for any chance they could. Was it their fault Errol had been a weapon, one of many Deas offered?

He met Belaaz's gaze, but the mask of unearthly beauty no longer awed him. If it had not been for the malus and their evil, no sacrifice would have been required. If Deas had not chosen Errol, he would have chosen someone else. Errol's resentment and cries of "Why me?" would only be answered by Deas with "Why not you?"

Belaaz's temptation slipped from him like ice slipping from

the walls of a cliff beneath a spring sun. Errol clung to the truth of Magis's book: Deas hadn't even exempted himself from the necessity of sacrifice.

Errol stepped back, breaking contact, shaking Belaaz's offer from his mind.

The malus peered down at him, the chiseled perfection of his face filled with regret. "I can see I have failed to persuade you, but I have one thing more to offer, Errol." The malus smiled, closed his eyes, and shrank, diminishing until he matched Errol's size. His shirra, now woefully oversized, fell from his open hand, and he stepped forward, his face still handsome but without the unearthly beauty it had possessed before.

"I know what you truly want, Errol, what you've desired for months. Deas cannot give it to you. He requires your death. But if I refuse to kill you . . . what then? Will you consent to live the rest of your life as my prisoner?

"Look at your men. They are outmatched and overwhelmed, and my allies to the north have yet to take the field. Stop this senseless bloodshed. If you choose, I will allow you to serve me, Errol, without becoming one with us. You may take Adora to some remote part of the kingdom and live your life undisturbed." Belaaz extended his hand. "Choose peace, Errol."

Deep in his mind, Errol's thoughts labored beneath the assault. The fear of dying he'd managed to keep submerged surfaced, rampaged through him, and he panted with the effort of keeping it at bay.

The kernel of his identity struggled to shake the terror of death, but the wind had died, and in the unnatural silence, he couldn't summon the will to defy the malus.

A weight crashed into him from behind, sent him sprawling. He tumbled, caught a glimpse of Cruk attacking Belaaz with a storm of sword strokes. The watchman conjured blows, striking with his blade, his legs, his fists, blows that never landed.

Belaaz's laughter sent shards into Errol as the malus slipped each blow with contempt. "Human. You've hardly crawled from the mud and you think to challenge me? Come then, see what your folly has brought you."

Belaaz twisted, wrenching himself from one spot to the next, seemingly without transition, snatching up his sword and sending Cruk's attacks into empty air. The shirra whistled as the malus whirled it behind his head and sent it screeching in a horizontal arc toward Cruk's unprotected side. The blade crunched through the chain mail like a knife parting cloth, and blood fountained from the wound. The malus wrenched the sword away, twisting, leaving Cruk to fall backward.

The watchman's head bounced as he hit the ground, his eyes dimming. Errol knelt, looking into Cruk's plain face, waiting for some word. The watchman's arms hung useless as blood soaked the ground, but the captain's eyes beckoned him.

Errol's nose came within inches of Cruk's and he strove to hear, but the captain didn't speak. As life faded from his eyes he inhaled a wet sucking breath into his lungs, thrust his face forward, and breathed, "It's just a door, boy."

The captain's dying breath, warm and smelling of blood, held nothing in common with the wind, but though it lacked the power to stir his hair, it tore through the temptations of the malus's spell, rendering it useless. Errol struggled to his feet.

"No."

Belaaz flung his mirth at the sky. "Do you think your denial will avail you? I will deny Deas your death and break his power over me." He pointed toward the coruscating flashes in the sky above. "Do you think he will save you? Look around, manling. Your forces are dying. Your watch is gone. I am many, and your kingdom has no king."

Errol pulled breath into his lungs, willing himself to play his last desperate gamble. Wind swept across the field to accompany his cry of triumph. "But we do. You arrived too late. Liam is king."

He turned to point to Escarion's fortress behind him. "You've failed. For all your age and knowledge, you have erred, Belaaz. The son of Prince Jaclin is being crowned even now. Do you really believe I came to die? Did you never question why the man who killed one of your council was absent from this fight? It is because he is being crowned king! You and your army will never get there in time to stop it."

The malus screamed, his mouth stretching, showing twin rows of pointed teeth as he sent his gaze toward the castle. He spun back to face Errol, growing and distorting until he towered over him once more. "You think to surprise me, worm? My brothers are within the castle, on their way to kill that childless heir." His face stretched into a parody of a smile. "If Deas does not require your sacrifice, I will."

Errol reeled as if the earth canted under his feet. If the malus managed to kill Liam, Illustra was lost. Rale's voice crackled in his ears.

"Strike! Belaaz controls them."

Errol spun his staff, readying himself to attack, leaping for the malus. Sparks danced as the weapons collided.

Scorn filled Belaaz's twisted face. "You think to touch me, insect? I will take you piece by piece until your ability to fight is gone. Then I will eat your heart."

Sevra sprang into motion as if released from some compulsion, her sword coming for Adora in a vast cut. A shower of sparks glittered in her vision as Weir's daughter snapped her smaller blade in half. Rokha dove, slicing into Sevra's calf and rolling away. Sevra spun, her shirra whistling in the air in a wild swing that plowed a furrow across Rokha's shoulder. Ru's daughter stumbled back, too far away now to engage. Sevra spun, looming over Adora, her mouth stretched in a rictus of hate and glee.

"Now, strumpet, you will die."

Half a dozen paces away, Rokha fought to her feet, blood soaking her left arm, her lips stark against her pale face. She stabbed her sword into the ground, using it as a crutch to force herself to her feet, fighting to reach Adora in time. She was only half a dozen paces away, but it might as well have been a hundred.

Adora struggled to get her feet beneath her as Sevra lifted the long blade with the finality of an executioner. Adora's feet scrabbled against the wet ground, refusing to find purchase. Thrusting against the turf with her hands, she came to her knees.

Rokha slipped to one knee, her eyes searching Adora's, eyes filled with apology and sorrow. With a cry of rage, Ru's daughter pulled her sword from the ground to grip the blade with one hand just in front of the pommel and threw.

The sword came for Sevra's unprotected back like a spear. In the space between heartbeats Adora watched its flight, finding impossible hope. Sevra, seeing her eyes, ducked and wheeled, swinging her sword blindly against the threat she sensed behind her.

Three inches of steel buried itself in her chest before her riposte found its mark, and Rokha's sword fell to the grass, out of reach, useless.

Sevra brought her free hand up to touch the wound, smiling at the blood on her hands as she raised her sword once more. Her eyes vibrated with insane delight. "So close, strumpet, but not enough."

She watched Sevra slowly raise her sword, savoring her victim's helplessness. When it began its descent, Adora refused to close her eyes. She looked through the malus, willing her last memory to be of Errol.

Belaaz leapt toward Errol, his shirra blurring and then disappearing. Errol leapt, throwing himself from its path. He should have died in that moment, but the massive sword found only air. The stroke missed, impossibly anticipated. Wind swirled around them and Errol found himself moving before each attack, laboring to get close enough to the giant to strike.

Again and again he twisted, jumped, and rolled, flowing with each strike, the deadly shirra missing him by the barest margin. The sounds of battle faded to stillness until only the roll of thunder sounded. Errol's mind split, and he watched himself moving with the attacks. He gathered his legs as Belaaz attacked his mind once more. The two-pronged assault threw him off balance, and the shirra sliced through the meat of his shoulder. Again the weapon whistled toward him, changed direction at the last instant to furrow a gouge through his thigh. Errol faltered, slowing despite the urging of the wind. Blood oozed down his arm, betraying his grip. More flowed down his leg to wet the ground beneath his feet.

Belaaz struck again, and Errol threw himself to one side, his feet slipping. He rolled by instinct, bringing his staff up in a desperate parry as he struggled once more to stand. Blows from Belaaz's shirra came like a storm of strokes. Spots danced in his vision, and his sight narrowed to a tunnel filled by the malus's laughter as he sent his blade in a whistling stroke toward Errol's neck.

A breeze, so soft he couldn't be sure of it, caressed his face, and in the whisper of its passing Errol heard a single word.

"Now."

The wind stopped, halted as if hitting a wall. Belaaz screamed, swinging as Errol gathered himself, leaping as his hair lifted, standing on end. He swung his staff as he passed over the sword, striking the malus.

The sounds of fighting erupted in the hallway.

"Martin," Luis screamed. "Now."

He pushed, striving to place the crown on Liam's head, but his arms refused to move. The door to the makeshift throne room burst, throwing splinters and chunks of wood into the hall. Men, hideously large and swollen, spilled into the hall, pushing Waterson and the last of Escarion's defenders before them.

Lightning, white hot and savage, flashed beyond the window, the sharp sound of thunder deafening. Martin gasped as the pressure on his arms changed. He thrust the crown onto Liam's head. The malus dropped, twitching, to the floor, lifeless before the echoes of thunder faded.

Liam ran from the room, the crown falling from him as he drew his sword, gathering men as he went. Martin moved to follow, not hurrying, his heart strangely empty.

Sevra's sword began its descent as light and sound filled the sky. Incandescence flashed into the middle of battle accompanied by deafening cracks of sound that rolled over them, booming over and over again as lightning flickered back and forth between the ground and the cloud bank.

Weir's daughter collapsed, the cords of her unnatural life severed at last. Deprived of strength, her sword fell against Adora's side, but without the force to wound.

Adora forced her feet to serve her at last, racing toward the blackened circle of earth, fighting to see past the afterimages of the strike. When her vision cleared, a circle of dead surrounded the charred, smoking remains of Belaaz. Men in black raced toward the castle, marshaling forces to pursue a fleeing enemy.

She didn't see him. Sobs choked her as she hopped over Belaaz's twisted and blackened form, the metal staff lodged in his chest. A few paces away she found him, lying in the grass as if he'd been discarded. Kneeling, she pulled Errol's head into her lap, his skin so very pale, hardly more than the face of a boy. Men and horses thundered past her, heading south.

Martin walked—there would be no point to running now—down the hill toward the river. Luis followed, the rest of the Judica and the conclave coming with him. The dead lay everywhere. They would say the panikhida later, after they found him. Liam and the remnant of their forces disappeared into the distance as they chased down the Merakhi army. Only men fled. Every malus and spawn lay dead on the field, with or without wounds, lifeless. The barrier was restored.

"He might have survived," Luis said. "Perhaps you crowned Liam in time."

Oh, how he wanted to believe that was true. "No. He died. Deas took the last measure of sacrifice from him."

"He will be a legend, Martin. Before a year has gone by, he will be seven feet tall and the mightiest man who ever lived."

Martin stopped, his feet skidding a little on grass slickened by water and blood as he grabbed Luis's sleeve. "We must ensure that doesn't happen. I will not permit his sacrifice to be diminished in such a way."

He saw Rokha first, then Adora a few paces away with Errol's head on her lap. He held out a hand to pull Luis to a stop. They stood for a moment, silent, and then he turned to Luis. "Come, friend, let us return. She will see to him."

Rokha sat cross-legged on the ground holding vigil with her, but removed enough to provide some impression of privacy. Adora bent over him, hovering as grief emptied her of the ability to speak, weep, or breathe. She searched him for injuries, her fingers brushing first the skin of his face, now his hair, and then the lips that had kissed hers. She found the cuts, serious but hardly fatal, before noting the burns on the palms of his hands.

Bending low, she held him close, the skin of his face already cold against hers. A wordless cry of loss and longing built somewhere within her, a prayer of pleading sorrow. She stayed, her tears bathing his face, unwilling to move, the passage of time noted only by the growing quiet as the fields of Escarion emptied of the living. The sun touched the horizon to the west, casting ruddy light across Errol's pale face.

She pressed her head to his, fresh anguish tearing through her at the touch of his face against hers. "Deas, is this all there is for him, to have everything taken? Where are you?"

A breeze from the west broke the stillness, swirled around her to lift a strand of hair and send it fluttering behind her before it gathered, growing. A gust from the south joined it moments later, ruffling the grass where she sat as it combined with the west wind. When a push of air from the north, the direction of Escarion's fortress, came to merge with its brothers, the winds became visible, lifting water and blood from the blanket of grass to sparkle in the dying light.

Adora gasped, her lungs struggling for air, as if the winds had stolen her breath. The glittering swirl of air covered Errol, but no color or animation showed in his flesh. Some instinct or intuition drew her gaze east. In the last light of day, the grass flattened before the racing approach of a column of air. It swept the others into its embrace, and her vision of the world shrank to the swirling column of luminous dew that enveloped the two of them.

The whorl of light, wind, and water tightened, growing in intensity even as it shrank, until it covered Adora and Errol like a shroud. It remained so while the last of the sun drifted below the horizon to the west. But as the final crimson rays fled the fields of Escarion, the whirlwind shrank to cover only Errol, leaving Adora gasping, watching in wonder as the coruscation melded with his flesh, disappearing.

44

THE WEDDING AND THE FEAST

ADORA MOVED THROUGH THE CASTLE, drifting on the tide of humanity that had come to witness the wedding of their king. It seemed as though Erinon had recovered its populace overnight. The streets close to the royal compound were filled with bustling merchants and churchmen, but she knew better. Much of the outlying city waited for shopkeepers or tradesmen or guards who would never return.

And the provinces were no different.

Adora slipped from room to room, avoiding contact when she could, acknowledging the endless offers of commiseration when circumstance required.

A touch on her arm surprised her, and she turned to find light-blue eyes—no longer stoic—regarding her. On his right, one arm looped through his, stood Rokha. Merodach's left hand gripped a cane. The harsh clench of the fingers holding it testified to its necessity.

He bowed to her, held it longer than her position or bereavement required. "Your Highness, how may I serve you?"

His regard threatened her resolve. With a sharp intake of breath she steeled herself. "You are too kind, Captain." She reached out to finger the rich blue of his robe. "Or should I say, Tremus?"

Rokha didn't laugh, but her face glowed and the look she gave her husband held all the fierce pride Adora remembered. "Luis claimed him for the conclave, despite his marital status. He is a man of many talents." Now the laughter came, and the former watchman's face heated, making him appear boyish.

Adora nodded, her heart filled with longing at the acute emptiness of her arms. "New things come. Would you accompany me to the throne room?" she asked. "I'm hoping your presence will keep others from offering condolences."

"Is it bad?" Rokha asked.

She nodded once, pausing to consider her words in case they were overheard. "Yes, but I think time and distance may help somewhat. Avenia is remote. Few there have ever been to Erinon, and fewer know what I look like. With care, I can move about at need, unknown and unremarked."

Merodach's slow pace served to provide a measure of privacy as they traversed the royal palace to Liam's throne room. The three of them slipped in through a side entrance and took their place at the front as befitted the last princess and the tremus of the conclave.

Moments passed as the hall filled, nobles, churchmen, and functionaries jockeying for seats on either side of the promenade beneath banners of purple, red, or royal blue.

The immense chamber hushed, and a fanfare announced Liam's presence. He approached the dais from the right, resplendent in white, Magnus's crown catching the wealth of his hair.

"He looks as perfect and untouchable as ever," Rokha said.

Adora couldn't deny it, but her mind drifted home, aching for something less divine, and a stab of longing threatened her.

Rale, Waterson, and Reynald came to stand by him, austere in the black of the watch, standing as his seconds if anyone dared challenge. The trumpets voiced a different call, and Martin approached down the center aisle, the crimson train of his archbenefice's cloak trailing behind like a victory banner. Luis followed in the cerulean robes of the primus, only slightly less grand.

They took their place on top of the dais, above Liam and the captains, and the hall quieted as everyone held their collective breath.

"The conclave chose his wife," Rokha said. "Martin ordered the cast in stone, but I've heard rumors that it only confirmed the girl he said Aurae had already named for our king."

Merodach nodded. "It's true. Some in the conclave think the archbenefice is a sorcerer." One side of his mouth pulled up in a smirk. "The knowledge of Aurae will take some getting used to."

Adora digested this last remark, but it did not lessen her discomfort. She wanted nothing more than to escape the gaze of people who looked upon her as the embodiment of Illustra's loss. "Who did they choose?"

Rokha smiled and pointed. "Here she comes now."

The trumpets blew a slow march, and a woman of an age with Adora appeared, tall and raven-haired, draped in shimmering folds of blue silk. Her breath exploded from her, and she clamped her teeth against the noise. "Liselle?" she asked. "She's going to be queen?"

Rokha nodded, her raven hair bouncing with mirth. "You should have seen it, Your Highness. Every time she came into Liam's presence, she looked at him with a gaze that could have set rocks afire, and he stuttered and stumbled over his words like a schoolboy." Her laugh made it plain she supported Liselle's approach. "I think she'll be good for him. Every man should know a little doubt and uncertainty."

Something in Adora's mind clicked, and she turned to search Merodach's face. "Was the cast true?" she asked. At Merodach's nod, she forgot herself enough to smile. "Of course."

"What?" Rokha asked.

Adora bent close as the bride approached the altar and her betrothed. "Liselle is the great-granddaughter of Lorelle." She shook her head, amazed still. "The conclave chose Lorelle to marry my grandfather, King Rodrick, but he refused. The church said Rodran's sterility was Deas's judgment for Rodrick's pride." A tear found its way down her cheek and she smiled. "I suppose Deas does give second chances." She paused. "Sometimes."

Merodach and Rokha nodded.

Adora left the Green Isle soon after the ceremony. She tried to ignore the way people she'd known her whole life relaxed at her departure, as if a burden had been removed.

Four weeks later she passed through the arched gate of the earldom far to the east. She was almost home.

The farmwoman stood in the doorway, bathed in the last light of a spring day. The chopping sounds of food being prepared by the couple behind her made a counterpoint to the movements of the man who floated across the hard-packed dirt of the yard between the cottage and the barn. She heard music as he moved, the wooden staff in his hands spinning as though he sought to weave a tapestry in the air.

"Don't you ever get tired of watching him?" the sultry voice behind her asked.

She turned with reluctance to regard the dark-haired woman who'd spoken and nodded toward the silver-haired man who supported himself with a cane next to her. "Do you?"

The throaty laugh filled the cottage, and the man blushed, his blue eyes bold against the flush of his skin. The woman patted the swell of her belly. "No. Your priest, Pater Conger, came by to bless the child. I think I liked it."

She moved to stand next to Adora in the doorway. "He's a strange man. I can't think of any other captain or noble who would willingly pose as their own servant." She could feel the dark eyes of the woman on her as if there were questions she wanted to pose. "Lorre seems a bit obvious, don't you think?"

She shrugged. "People see what they expect to see. Errol Stone is dead and already a myth. Heroes are seven feet tall, aren't they?"

The silver-haired man stumped over to join them, the rhythm of his good leg and the cane loud against the rough boards of the floor. "No," he said, his voice quiet. "They are not."

The sound of a carriage broke Adora's contemplation, and she stared as she saw four men of various ages in plain clothing departing the conveyance, one rubbing his backside in obvious dissatisfaction.

"Beastly things," he muttered, his lips twisting beneath the thick gray hair. "Given my experiences of the last few months, I think I prefer walking." He sighed. "Ah well, it couldn't be helped." The four turned to the man in the yard but waited for him to approach.

Lorre put away his staff as the light dimmed to crimson, reflecting off the keep in the distance. He flexed his hands, working to extend the fingers, stretching to open them.

Martin Arwitten and Liam bowed as Lorre approached. Rale and Luis echoed their move a heartbeat later. Lorre waited for them to straighten and speak, questions plain on his face.

The archbenefice spoke first. "We've come to ask you to reconsider."

Melting sensations ran the length of Adora's body as she saw him smile in return. Despite his experiences, his face still carried a trace of the open boyishness he'd owned when they'd first met.

"Why?" Lorre asked.

Liam stepped forward, put a hand on his shoulder, the gesture friendly, not commanding. "Illustra . . . " He paused to laugh. "The world owes you recompense, and I think it would cheer many in the kingdom to know you survived."

Lorre shook his head. "I don't want payment or recognition." He paused to send a glance Adora's way that brought a blush to her cheek. "What can you offer a man who has everything?" He shook his head. "I am Lorre. Errol Stone died along with Cruk and countless others who were the true heroes of the kingdom. Don't worsen the grief of those who lost their beloved by telling them otherwise."

Rale nodded as if the man before him had passed one final test. "You'll teach the lads hereabout, I hope. You have much to offer."

Luis smiled at Martin. "I told you he would feel this way."

Liam and Martin sighed. "We suspected as much," Liam said.

Luis stepped closer to him, the ghost of a smile pulling his mouth to one side. "May I ask you a question, Lorre?"

He nodded. "If I may ask you one in return." His gaze took in all of them.

"What was the last question you cast before you left Escarion's castle?"

Lorre's mouth pulled to one side, but his eyes clouded. "I asked if it was possible to deceive the malus."

Luis straightened in shock, a motion echoed by the other men.

Lorre nodded. "Adele and Radere had never been wrong. Not once. I knew I had to die, but Belaaz had no intention of killing me. So I led him to believe that Liam's crowning would be his undoing." He smiled. "Once he believed that, I was just another man to be killed."

The men around him smiled. Then joy burst from them in gales.

"Well done, lad," Martin said. "So very well done."

Lorre shrugged, but his face glowed beneath their praise. "Why have you come?" he asked. "Avenia is a long journey from the Green Isle. You could have sent a nuntius."

Martin came forward to gather him in a rough embrace. "Because we missed you, lad."

The other three men stepped forward to place their hands on Martin's and Lorre's shoulders, enfolding the pair. When they parted, Lorre stepped toward the cabin, beckoning them in to dinner, and the group approached, their faces radiant.

At the doorway he took her in his arms as he always did, no matter who was present, kissing her without hesitancy or restraint.

Laughter filled the cabin.

ACKNOWLEDGMENTS

To say this last volume of THE STAFF AND THE SWORD was the most difficult of the three books is a huge understatement, and I would like to thank the people in my life who provided the margin required to bring it to fruition.

So many people have helped make this a work of which I could be proud. Chief among them are Deede Melder, Debbie Smotherman, and Sharon Smith, three fine math teachers at MLK High School who helped me through a year of working and writing under a deadline. I would also like to thank Mickala Murphy, who allowed me to use her name and likeness for one of the characters in my book.

Most recently, I have been aided by Emma Fischer and Joel Sinha, my teaching assistants at MLK, who have been more helpful than I can say and helped provide the time I needed to edit this final volume of the trilogy. I also want to thank Doug Dabbs, who loaned his incredible artistic ability for the first book cover.

Finally, thank you, dear reader. The desire to bring you a tale that you come to regard as a friend is my greatest hope and ambition.

After graduating from Georgia Tech, **Patrick W. Carr** worked at a nuclear plant, did design work for the air force, worked for a printing company, and was an engineering consultant. Patrick's day gig for the last six years has been teaching high school math in Nashville, Tennessee. Patrick is a member of ACFW and MTCW and makes his home in Nashville with his incredible wife, Mary; their four awesome sons, Patrick, Connor, Daniel, and Ethan; and their dog, Mel.

More Fantasy From Bethany House

Don't Miss the Beginning of Errol's Journey!
As a dynasty nears its end, an unlikely hero embarks upon a perilous quest to save his kingdom. Thrust into a world of dangerous political intrigue and church machinations, Errol Stone must leave behind his idle life, learn to fight, come to know his God—and discover his destiny.

THE STAFF AND THE SWORD: *A Cast of Stones, The Hero's Lot, A Draw of Kings*
by Patrick W. Carr
patrickwcarr.com

Journey to an Old Testament–style world full of action and intrigue! An unlikely prophet, a headstrong judge, and a reluctant king are called by their Creator to fulfill divine destinies akin to those of their biblical counterparts. All three face unforeseen challenges as they attempt to follow the Infinite's leading.

BOOKS OF THE INFINITE: *Prophet, Judge, King*
by R. J. Larson
rjlarsonbooks.com